Seal's Resolve

REBECCA DEEL

Copyright © 2020 Rebecca Deel

All rights reserved.

ISBN-13: 9798670944403

DEDICATION

To my amazing husband, my safe harbor in the storms of life. I love you.

ACKNOWLEDGMENTS

Cover by Melody Simmons.

CHAPTER ONE

Kristi Stewart breathed in the cool, damp Tennessee mountain air as she exited her silver SUV and looped her small cross-body bag across her torso. Although she'd visited the Great Smoky Mountains in the past, she looked forward to exploring Gatlinburg before her return trip to Bakerhill, a town an hour outside of Nashville. First, though, she planned to attend the wedding of a friend.

Opening the back door of her vehicle to retrieve the wedding dress Kristi had designed and made for Abigail Lawrence, a smile curved her lips. Ironic that a wedding dress designer dreaded attending her friend's ceremony. Her reluctance was tied to Kristi's father pressuring her to marry Hugh Ward. Abigail's wedding was an excuse for her father to crank up the heat.

The fault was hers, though. She shouldn't have agreed to consider Hugh's proposal. They were friends, but that was all. No sparks. Alan Stewart was persistent and had offered Hugh a coveted position as vice president of Stewart Group once Kristi and Hugh married. For the past month, Hugh had added his voice to her father's, pressuring Kristi to say yes to marriage.

Fed up with both men, Kristi used the delivery of Abigail's wedding dress as an excuse to escape the constant pressure and think about what she wanted and needed.

Kristi freed the hanger from the garment hook, draped the heavy, plastic-shrouded wedding dress over her arm, and walked toward the hotel. The tug-of-war with her in the middle couldn't continue. If she rejected Hugh, she would disappoint him and her father. Of the two men, her father's opinion mattered more. That truth spoke volumes about her feelings for Hugh.

Hugh deserved a wife who adored him and couldn't wait to spend time with him. That woman wasn't Kristi. She often found excuses to avoid Hugh. He deserved better, and so did she.

Resolve hardened inside her. When she returned home, she'd end the suspense with Hugh. Although she and Hugh looked perfect together on the surface, they lacked chemistry and love, a fact both Hugh and her father ignored.

"Ms. Stewart, welcome back. May I assist you with your vehicle and luggage?"

She smiled at her favorite Sandoval bellhop. "Thanks, Harry. I appreciate the help." Kristi handed him her key fob and a generous tip.

"My pleasure, ma'am."

Shoving the turmoil to the back of her mind, Kristi turned her focus toward finding Abby. Her friend's rehearsal dinner was in full swing somewhere in the hotel. Knowing Abby, she had commandeered the same ballroom where her wedding was to take place. The fact that the hotel staff would scramble to clear the remnants of the rehearsal dinner and set up for the scheduled wedding at noon tomorrow wouldn't have registered as a problem. She loved her friend, but Abby didn't consider logistics when she wanted something done a certain way.

Kristi's lips curved. No doubt Abby had reasoned that if she wasn't happy with the arrangements, Kristi would convince hotel management to fix the problem, a reasonable assumption since Stewart Group owned the Sandoval.

She approached the Sandoval's front entrance and the glass doors slid open, inviting her into the marble-tiled lobby. Hidden speakers played soft music. A large chandelier lit the reception area. Glass glittered and chrome gleamed. Over-sized flower arrangements lent a delicate scent and cheer to the elegant entrance.

The woman behind the front desk smiled. "Welcome back to Sandoval Hotel, Ms. Stewart. Your suite is ready. Would you like dinner sent to your room?"

"That's perfect. Thank you, Lana." Abby would be disappointed, but Kristi wasn't part of the wedding party, and the prospect of making small talk with 50 people caused Kristi's stomach to knot.

She'd worked 18-hour days for the past month, juggling her designing and dressmaking responsibilities. She needed more help on the dressmaking side of Kristi's Bridal even though Kristi planned to keep working in that part of the business as well. The feel of fabric sliding along her fingers and the whir of her sewing machine called to her as nothing else did aside from her design work.

"Do you need help?" Lana's gaze locked on the garment bag.

"No, but thanks for the offer. Where is the Lawrence-Thomas rehearsal dinner being served?"

"The Swan Ballroom."

Of course. That was the same room where Abby's wedding would be held tomorrow. The Swan Ballroom was on the other side of the large hotel, too. Good thing she had changed into comfortable clothes and running shoes before leaving Bakerhill. "Thanks."

She headed for the ballroom, walking familiar halls and greeting workers she recognized from previous visits to the five-star hotel. The journey took fifteen minutes longer than she anticipated. More than one of the hotel's employees stopped to speak to her.

As Kristi walked toward the ballroom's open double doors, her nape prickled, a familiar sensation over the past few weeks. Frowning, she glanced over her shoulder and saw what she expected. Nothing. The hallway was empty.

Kristi growled, frustrated with herself and her overactive imagination. When she spoke to her father's chief of security about feeling as though someone was watching her, he assigned a bodyguard to follow her around for two days. Hale hadn't spotted anyone. Worse, the bodyguard gave her the creeps.

Her stomach growled, reminding Kristi that she had neglected to eat since breakfast. She continued toward the ballroom. The sooner she delivered the wedding dress to Abby, the quicker she could eat and fall into bed.

Approaching the ballroom, she spotted a waiter. "Doug," she called.

The waiter stopped, turned, and grinned. "Ms. Stewart. What can I do for you?"

"Tell Abby Lawrence that I'm here with her wedding dress. I'd rather not crash the party." Especially since she was dressed in casual clothes, and the rehearsal dinner was a formal affair.

"Yes, ma'am." He continued into the ballroom.

A minute later, a blond bombshell rushed into the hall. As usual, Abby wore sky-high heels and a designer dress, with perfect hair and makeup. Her friend could easily strut down a runway as a model.

"Kristi, thank goodness you're here. I was afraid you wouldn't make it in time to eat."

She laughed. "You're not fooling me. You were afraid your wedding dress wouldn't make it."

Her friend blushed. "Well, do you blame me? Everything that could go wrong has blown up in my face. My maid of honor had a huge fight with her boyfriend who is Adrian's best man. Now, Candy and Jared won't talk to each other and refuse to walk together tomorrow. My divorced parents can't be in the same room together without throwing verbal jabs at each other, and the florist couldn't locate the flowers I wanted for the tables tomorrow. It's been one disaster after another."

Kristi hugged her friend. "Don't be such a drama queen. Everything will work out. That's why you hired a wedding planner. She can deal with the problems. Your job is to be a beautiful bride. Let your wedding planner deal with the rest."

"I should have chosen you as my maid of honor."

"Candy is your sister. She'd never forgive you for leaving her out of the big day."

Abby sighed. "You could have at least agreed to be one of the wedding party."

"Being a bridesmaid in ten weddings is more than enough for me." She'd put in her time wearing hideous bridesmaid dresses. Kristi would happily stay in the audience from now on until she wore her own wedding dress. "Besides, you already have nine bridesmaids. You don't need another one. Don't worry. I'll be in the audience, admiring my handiwork."

Her friend smiled. "You should. My dress is a work of art."

"Honey, is everything all right?" Darlene Lawrence walked toward her daughter and Kristi. "Oh, Kristi, you made it. Thank goodness. Abigail was so worried about you."

"I have the dress right here."

"Perfect. Abigail, go back to your rehearsal dinner, dear. I'll take your dress to the suite. We don't want anyone to see it until tomorrow."

"All right. Thanks, Mom." Abby took the dress and handed it to her mother, then hugged Kristi. "Thank you, Kristi. You're the best. How can I ever thank you?"

"Tell people who designed your breath-taking dress."

"Count on it. I'll plaster your name all over my social media pages with pictures." Abby released her. "I'll see you tomorrow."

"Thank you, Kristi." Darlene smiled. "Please, join us for dinner. We have extra place settings."

"Thanks for the offer, but I'm not dressed for it and dinner is waiting for me in my suite. Enjoy the rehearsal dinner. I'll see you tomorrow."

Minutes later, Kristi stepped into the owner's suite and closed the door with a sigh. Thank goodness. Maybe now the invisible spiders crawling along her nape would go away.

Her suitcase and overnight bag stood near the serving cart with her meal. Perfect. Kristi made a beeline for the serving cart.

She lifted the dome from the plate. A spinach quiche and a salad. Besides her plate, the kitchen staff had included two bottles of water. They knew her preferences and catered to them every time she stayed here. You couldn't beat the Sandoval for service.

She carried the food and water to the living area, and set them on the glass-topped coffee table. Kristi watched a news program while she ate and polished off one bottle of water.

After placing the dishes on the cart, Kristi wheeled it to the hallway. As she turned to go back inside the suite, a whisper of movement sounded behind her. Kristi heard a snap, and a second later, horrible pain traveled along her nerve endings, locking her muscles and preventing her from screaming for help.

She fell to the floor and into darkness.

CHAPTER TWO

Rafe Torres scowled when his satellite phone rang. His boss at Fortress Security and his Wolf Pack teammates had promised him space, something he desperately needed to heal. Although tempted to ignore the strident summons, he couldn't. Blowing off a plea for help wasn't in his nature. Plus, Maddox or Wolf Pack wouldn't call except for an emergency. Something was wrong.

Stopping to take a breather on the trail, he dug his phone from his cargo pocket and glanced at his screen. "Torres," he snapped, his voice just over a growl. "This better be important, boss."

Brent Maddox, CEO of Fortress Security, said, "You're back on active duty as of now."

Rafe stepped off the trail and further into the darkness of the trees, cheeks burning. "Sir, you gave me two weeks off. You owe me twelve days of leave time. Whatever the mission is, send someone else."

"Can't. This op is time sensitive."

"Aren't they always?"

"Shut up and listen, Torres."

He straightened at the sharp edge in his boss's voice.

"A woman was kidnapped at the Sandoval Hotel in Gatlinburg. She's being held on Hart Mountain. Zane sent you her coordinates. Since you're currently hiking the trails on Hart Mountain instead of sleeping like a normal person and you're the closest operative, you drew the short straw."

A frown. Zane had her coordinates? "How do you know where she is?"

"A GPS tracker is embedded under the skin at her lower back."

Uneasiness curled in Rafe's gut. Why did this woman have a GPS tracker? "Since you know her location, why not send in law enforcement?"

"The kidnappers warned her father not to involve the police or his daughter would pay the price."

He rolled his eyes. Kidnappers always made that stipulation. "Details?"

"Zane sent the relevant security cam footage."

While Maddox spoke, Rafe brought up the video clip. Although unable to see the vic's face, he watched the kidnapper pull a stun gun from his pocket, slip up on the vic, and jam the device against her neck. She stiffened and dropped to the floor. The kidnapper hoisted her over his shoulder in a fireman's carry, and walked quickly to the stairs.

"At least two kidnappers were involved in the grab-and-go," Maddox said. "Not sure yet if there are more people involved. The ransom demand is for $5 million, and the payment deadline is in six hours."

Rafe frowned, his stomach twisting into a knot. Something about the victim was familiar. "When did they take her?"

"Ten o'clock last night. Hotel security saw the abduction on camera, but by the time they mobilized, the kidnappers were gone with the woman."

A ten-hour deadline of $5 million? Who had that much money sitting around in an account? "Do I have backup?"

"On the way, but Durango is two hours out. Coordinate with Cahill."

"Instructions after I have the package?"

"Take her to Otter Creek."

Rafe's brows knitted. Wouldn't she prefer to go home to her father, boyfriend, or husband? "Who's the vic?"

"Kristi Stewart, owner of Kristi's Bridal."

He stiffened. No way. "Send in Durango. Two hours won't make a difference. I can't do this, Brent."

"Explain."

"No."

"Can't or won't?"

"Both."

A growl. "I know she ran in the same social circles as Callie. Suck it up and deal, Torres. Callie is dead, and Kristi will be, too, if you don't man up and take the mission."

"The kidnappers want money. Her father has that much in petty cash. End of story."

"They threatened to cut Kristi into pieces and mail her body back to her father if he missed the deadline. While he might agree to pay the money, you and I know they won't release her. Move, Torres. That's an order." Maddox ended the call, effectively forcing Rafe's hand.

He stuffed the raw pain ripping at his insides behind a mental wall, checked the tracking program for Kristi's location, and grimaced. Great. Kristi was on the other side of the mountain, a hard hour of fast hiking off the trail to reach her. Based on the coordinates, she was likely being held in one of the rental cabins popular with tourists during the summer.

Rafe adjusted his pack for a more comfortable fit and set off at a fast pace. At least he was armed, although not as heavily as he would have liked. No bullet-resistant vest. Guess he'd have to dodge bullets if the kidnappers discovered him.

He skirted fallen trees and boulders, all the while moving toward Kristi Stewart. He dreaded the coming encounter with the society princess. Maddox was right. Callie, the woman he'd loved and lost to a crew of killers three years earlier, had been friends with Kristi. Although Rafe hadn't spent much time with her, he'd been aware of Kristi and her father, Alan Stewart, owner of Stewart Group.

Now that he knew the identity of the kidnapping victim, Rafe understood why the kidnappers believed they could score so much money in a short period of time. Callie had told Rafe that Stewart was worth at least $100 million, easy. Kristi's father could pony up $5 million without blinking an eye.

Even if Stewart paid, the kidnappers might kill Kristi rather than risk her divulging too much information about them. Based on conversations with Stewart in the past, the powerful millionaire wouldn't cave to the kidnappers' demands.

Rafe frowned. Callie had mentioned another kidnapping incident when Kristi was in elementary school, at least twenty years ago. Was it possible this kidnapping was related to the other one? Unlikely, he decided.

He crested the mountain and started down the other side, working his way closer to the coordinates indicated by the tracker. Now that Rafe knew who the vic was, the GPS tracker made sense. Ransoming Kristi Stewart would net the kidnappers a fortune if the point of the kidnapping was to score a boatload of money.

He couldn't discount the possibility that this was more about Kristi than her father's fortune. Sure, the kidnappers stood to gain wealth. However, their main goal might be connected to the woman herself rather than her father.

Since Callie's death, Rafe had stayed away from her social circles. The corners of his mouth curled. Not like that had been a difficult task. He didn't belong in that world and never would. After Callie died, none of her friends had sought him out to offer condolences. None, that is, except for Kristi.

She had sent him a letter, sharing two funny incidents involving Callie that made him laugh on a day when grief consumed him from the inside out. Even though they were from different worlds, Kristi Stewart was a class act. She didn't deserve this.

Rafe would do as his boss ordered, suck it up and do the job. Once Kristi was back in her ivory palace, Rafe would return to the world's underbelly to fight terrorists who loved to destroy innocents like her.

As Rafe hiked closer to Kristi's location, he called Durango's leader, Josh Cahill.

The Delta warrior answered immediately. "Sit rep."

"Heading to the vic's location." Rafe relayed his location and the best extraction point. "My SUV is on the wrong side of Hart Mountain."

"We'll collect your ride and drive it to PSI. We're tracking your phone and the vic's tracker. Don't lose your phone, frog boy."

Rafe's lips curved at the teasing moniker from the seasoned soldier. "I hear you, grunt."

He switched his phone to silent and hugged the shadows. Although he doubted the kidnappers had posted guards this far out, he wouldn't chance being wrong. Kristi's life depended on him.

Rafe checked the tracking program again. No movement. That meant the kidnappers believed they were safe or they had removed the tracker and left it behind to throw off a possible rescuer.

Praying it was the former, Rafe stepped up his pace. He had much to accomplish in a short window of time. Minutes later, he crouched in the deep shadows of the tree line, gaze locked on a lone rental cabin. The kidnappers had chosen their location well. The closest neighbor was two miles away.

Lights were on in one half of the target cabin. The other half remained in darkness. He suspected that area contained bedrooms.

Rafe stayed in place, watching for a guard outside the cabin. Two minutes later, a man dressed in black walked around the corner of the structure, gaze scanning the area as he headed toward the front door. When the man appeared satisfied that he was alone, he climbed the porch stairs and went inside.

Within less than a minute, a dim light illuminated a previously dark room. Seconds later, the room was dark again and stayed that way.

Wondering if Kristi was in that room, Rafe remained in place for ten minutes longer. How often did the kidnappers search the perimeter? The mission clock in his head reminded him that Kristi's safety margin was running out. If Stewart had hired Fortress Security to rescue his daughter, he wasn't planning to pay the ransom. That left only five hours to come up with a series of plans and free Kristi.

Still no movement. Time to move. Rafe needed to get Kristi off Hart Mountain.

He remained in the safety of the tree line as he circled the clearing to reach the dark end of the cabin. With no sign of the guard returning for another perimeter check, Rafe slid off his pack and set it behind a tree to retrieve after he freed Kristi. He checked his weapon and slid a Ka-Bar into the scabbard he strapped to his thigh.

Rafe searched for the best approach and, after choosing his route, crossed the clearing to the cabin, utilizing the meager cover available. When he reached the cabin's wall, Rafe peered around each corner to confirm no guards were in sight.

Male laughter came from the other end of the cabin. A door closed. More male laughter, this time louder.

Rafe glanced around for cover. The only hiding place was the bush ten feet away. With silent steps, he hurried to the bush and slid between the plant and the wall, careful not to let the shrub brush against his clothes and give away his presence.

Male voices drew near. "Think the old man will pay up?" Guard One asked.

"He knows what will happen if he doesn't," Guard Two answered. "Stewart has the money. Five million bucks is pocket change to him, and he adores his daughter. He'd be stupid not to pay to get her back." Contempt filled his voice.

"What if he calls the cops?"

"He won't. Have you seen anything out here?"

"Nope. This place gives me the creeps. There ain't nothing out here but trees and more trees. I heard black bears and wolves roam the woods, too."

"That's the point, man. If the woman gets loose, she won't have anywhere to run. The pampered society princess won't survive out here."

A snort. "She's trussed up like a turkey. I don't think we got anything to worry about. She's not going anywhere."

"She's smart. Don't underestimate her." The two guards passed Rafe and kept going.

At least Kristi was still alive. If she was unhurt and able to maneuver under her own steam, so much the better.

Once the men went back inside the cabin, Rafe eased from his hiding place and returned to his target window. He waited. Sure enough, seconds later, a dim light shone in the room, then went out again. He heard the muffled sound of a door closing.

He stayed in place another two minutes, waiting. At the two-minute mark, Rafe tried lifting the window.

Locked. He grabbed his Ka-Bar, pried open the lock, and raised the window. He waited, but no sound came from inside the room or the rest of the cabin occupants.

Grasping the ledge, Rafe pulled himself up enough to peer inside the room. A woman sprawled on her back was tied hand and foot to the bed frame. Moonlight illuminated Kristi's face. She appeared to be sleeping and was alone.

He frowned. Had the kidnappers drugged her? If so, rescuing Kristi would be more complicated, especially since he was working alone for the moment.

Rafe hoisted himself over the ledge, landing in a crouch, alert and ready for trouble. Now came the tricky part.

He approached Kristi's bedside. Rafe didn't have time to rouse her gently. The guards could return at any time. While he could take on several men at one time, the odds of Kristi being injured by accident were too high for his comfort.

Rafe clamped his hand over Kristi's mouth.

CHAPTER THREE

Rafe easily controlled Kristi's struggle to get away from him. He bent until his mouth was close to her ear. "It's Rafe Torres. Your father sent me."

Kristi's eyes widened. Her muscles relaxed as she focused on his face.

"You with me?" he whispered.

A slight nod.

"I'm lifting my hand. If you scream, the kidnappers will come."

Another nod.

Hoping she was awake enough to cooperate, Rafe eased the pressure from her mouth, then removed his hand entirely.

"How did you find me?" she whispered.

"Escape first. Explanations later." He straightened and unsheathed his Ka-Bar. Ignoring her soft gasp, Rafe sliced through the rope binding her hands and feet to the bed frame. Kristi wore jeans and running shoes. Excellent. Her clothing would help protect her while they navigated through the woods.

After sheathing his Ka-Bar, he massaged her shoulder joints before lowering her arms to her sides. "Okay?"

She nodded despite the tears on her face.

He admired Kristi's fortitude. Although her shoulder joints must ache and burn from the position she'd been in for hours, she didn't complain. "How many kidnappers?"

"I counted eight."

Holy cow. Were all eight of them on site? "You injured?"

"Nothing that can't wait."

Fury rocked through him at the knowledge that the kidnappers hurt Kristi. Not his priority at the moment, he reminded himself. He'd take her word and assess the injuries after they were safe. "Can you run?"

"Watch me." Grim determination gleamed in her eyes.

He helped her stand and kept his hands on Kristi's shoulders to steady her while her equilibrium adjusted to the change in position. When she nodded to let him know she could stand on her own, Rafe nudged her toward the window. He climbed through first and lowered himself to the ground, then turned back for Kristi. When she stood beside him, Rafe lowered the window, clasped Kristi's hand, and led her toward the tree line and his pack.

Breathing easier when they reached the safety of the forest without incident, Rafe released Kristi long enough to shrug into his pack, then reclaimed her hand. "Do exactly what I tell you without questions. We don't have much time before the kidnappers discover you escaped. They'll search for you."

"Go."

Taking that for a promise to obey his orders, Rafe set a brutal pace, frequently checking on Kristi. They needed as much distance as possible between them and the kidnappers. Considering the trauma she'd been through in the last few hours, she was doing remarkably well. Kristi's kidnappers had underestimated her.

Five minutes later, an angry shout disturbed the peaceful night.

"Was that…?"

"Yeah." He quickened his pace.

Rafe skirted obstacles Kristi would have difficulty scaling in the dark, especially with running shoes instead of tactical boots like his. As they hurried through the rugged terrain, she began to stumble. Although she hadn't complained, Kristi was tired. He slowed the pace even though his gut warned him that the kidnappers were closing in on them.

Kristi's hand pressed against his back. "Go. I'll keep up."

"Won't help us if you sprain an ankle." He glanced back. Despite her words, one look at Kristi's face confirmed that her stamina was failing. Unfortunately, the sounds of men pursuing them were increasing by the minute.

Making a split-second decision, Rafe tugged Kristi in a different direction. For her sake, they needed to take a different route to the extraction point. "Are you claustrophobic?"

"Why?"

"The kidnappers are closing in on us. We need to get out of sight while still moving toward our extraction point."

"Lead on."

He flashed her a quick grin over his shoulder, then focused on the terrain in front of him, looking for signs that they were near his best option to safeguard Kristi and elude the kidnappers.

To her credit, Kristi didn't ask questions as she hurried through the forest with Rafe. Callie's friend had serious grit.

Finally, he spotted the rock formation he'd been looking for. He guided Kristi around the rocks, relieved that they were out of the direct line of sight of their pursuers.

Breaking into a jog, he led her toward the cave that would provide safety and escape from their pursuers. Rafe urged her into the dank and dark interior.

"I hope you have a flashlight," Kristi murmured. "I'm not a fan of the dark."

He stopped. "If you can't handle it, I'll figure out something else."

"I'll deal." She nudged him. "The faster we're out of here, the better."

"Just a little farther before I can safely turn on a flashlight."

A soft sigh. "I understand."

She lapsed into silence as Rafe walked deeper into the cave's interior by feel and memory. Thank God he'd spent several hours exploring this cave system and could navigate the interior with a source of light. Made escaping the kidnappers that much easier. Unfortunately, being underground meant he couldn't contact Cahill and his team for help if things went south inside the cave.

A muscle in Rafe's jaw twitched. If anything happened to him, he doubted Kristi would find her way out of the cave. If she did, she still had to elude her kidnappers and trudge two miles to get help. He'd have to stay injury free.

A short time later, he stopped and caught Kristi when she stumbled into him. "I think it's safe to turn on my flashlight now." He guided one of her hands to his belt, knowing she was disoriented by the total darkness. "Hold on to me for a minute."

Rafe shrugged off his pack and unzipped the pouch that held his flashlight. Within seconds, light illuminated the immediate area.

Kristi breathed deep. "Is it safe to talk while we walk?"

"Sure." He settled the pack on his back again and threaded his fingers through Kristi's before starting them forward. "How are you holding up?"

"You want the truth?"

He glanced at her. "Always."

"I'm tired and weak, and my legs feel like limp spaghetti at the moment. I have a massive headache, and I'm sore everywhere."

Rafe frowned. "Did the kidnappers drug you?"

"They gave me a shot when they tied me to the bed. I woke up a short time before you arrived."

His stomach knotted. Not good. "You said you had injuries that could wait. What happened?"

"I wasn't cooperative enough to suit the men who grabbed me."

Rafe analyzed what she said and what she didn't. "They hit you?" Had they done something worse? She needed to see a doctor as soon as possible. Those men could have assaulted her while she was unconscious, and Kristi wouldn't have been able to stop them.

"Several times. I have bruises on top of bruises. I don't know what they wanted although I can guess." Disgust filled her voice.

"Money. A lot of it."

"How much?"

"Five million dollars."

She groaned. "I hope Dad didn't pay."

"He didn't. That's why I came for you."

"You said Dad sent you. Why you specifically?"

He hesitated. How much should he tell her? No point in hiding the information. She'd find out soon enough. "He didn't ask for me. He contacted Fortress Security and asked for a team to extract you. I work for Fortress."

"Fortress has teams of one?"

Rafe chuckled. "In this case, yes. I was hiking an hour from the cabin. My boss called me back to active duty."

"You were on vacation?"

"You could say that."

"No matter why you were nearby, I'm grateful to you. Thanks for rescuing me, Rafe."

"Thank me after we're off this mountain, and you're safe." They weren't at the extraction point yet, and men scoured the mountain, looking for their golden goose.

"I wouldn't have made it this far without you."

"Do you remember what happened when you were taken?"

"I remember eating dinner in the suite, then pushing the food cart with my dishes to the hallway. I heard something behind me. Pain shot through my body, and I hit the floor. I woke up in the dark in a van, but my muscles wouldn't cooperate. By the time we reached the cabin, I had enough muscle control to attempt an escape." She gave a wry laugh. "Obviously, I didn't get far. After they hit me several times, one of the men carried me into the cabin and tied me to the bed. That's when he drugged me."

Rafe couldn't speak for a moment, enraged at her mistreatment. When he'd tamped down his temper, he said, "One of the kidnappers zapped you with a stun gun."

"How do you know?"

"I watched the security cam footage of your abduction on the way to the cabin."

"You can identify the men who took me?"

He shook his head. "The man who knocked you out knew the location of the security cameras. The cameras never caught his face."

"Of course not. Nothing is ever that easy." She sighed. "How long ago was I abducted?"

"Five hours."

"You said your boss called because you were the closest person. How did you find me so fast?"

Interesting question. Didn't she know about the tracker? "You have a tracker."

"A what?"

"A GPS tracker. Your father had the tracker embedded under the skin near your lower back."

"I can't believe he did that. It's a violation of my privacy."

"In all fairness, I don't think your father tracks your movements every day. You've already been kidnapped once and because of your father's wealth, you're a prime target. He wanted to protect you. You might feel violated, but his actions probably saved your life." Rafe squeezed her hand gently. "Why don't you have a bodyguard, Kristi?"

"Been there. Done that. No, thanks. Besides, no one has threatened me since I was a kid. I'm not interesting enough to need a bodyguard."

"You're a wealthy woman in your own right."

She snorted. "My father is wealthy. I'm not."

He doubted that. From the rumors in her and Callie's social circle, Kristi was a trust fund baby. "You're worth at least $5 million to the kidnappers." He glanced over his shoulder. "Unless you know of another reason someone wants to kidnap you. Would someone target you and opt to score more money from your father as a side benefit?"

"Oh, come on. I'm not a nuclear scientist or a chemist. I design and make wedding dresses. I deal with bridezillas on a daily basis, not home-grown terrorists. Someone wants to make a quick buck off Dad. Maybe a business rival wants to hurt him. You know my father, Rafe. He's ruthless in the business world and has a string of people who would love to see his business empire topple."

A kidnap-for-ransom plot wouldn't stop the empire. Another hand squeeze. "We'll talk about it more once you're safe and see a doctor."

"I won't be your problem."

"What do you mean?"

"Your job was to rescue me. Once you deliver me to my father, your job is done."

"That's not how this works."

"I don't understand."

"We don't walk away from an unfinished job."

"What does that mean?"

The cavern chamber ended with tunnels branching off in different directions. Rafe tugged Kristi toward the right tunnel. "Fortress won't consider the job finished until we know who's behind the kidnapping and why. Otherwise, you won't be safe."

"You're scaring me."

"The world's not safe. Never forget that." Rafe led her deeper and deeper through the mountain, taking winding passages with unerring accuracy. Yeah, he'd spent a lot of time in this cave, unsuccessfully running from his colossal failure to protect the one woman who meant everything to him. Instead of being by Callie's side when she most needed him, he'd been fighting terrorists overseas as a Navy SEAL.

A lot of good that did him. He'd lost the woman he loved, and the terrorists kept coming even as he worked alongside his teammates in Wolf Pack to stop them. But someone had to take out the world's garbage. Otherwise, more innocents would be victimized.

When they were within a few hundred feet of the exit, Rafe stopped and turned to Kristi. "In another hundred feet, the passage will turn toward the exit. I have to turn off the flashlight."

She flinched. "How could they know where we are?"

"You saw eight men. There might be more. If they're as desperate to get their hands on you as I think, they'll fan out over Hart Mountain to find you."

"That doesn't make me feel better."

His eyebrow rose. "You want me to feed you a pretty lie?"

Kristi shook her head. She motioned toward the flashlight. "Go ahead. I'm ready to breathe fresh air again."

"Ten minutes, tops," he promised, and doused the light.

She jerked, sucking in a ragged breath.

Oh, man. Not good. "You okay?"

"Spooked. You must have incredible eyesight to navigate through this pitch-black maze. I can't see my hand in front of my face."

Rafe chuckled. "My eyesight is 20/20, but I have the advantage of spending a lot of time in this cave."

"Can't imagine why," she muttered. "It's cold, musty, and smells like ammonia."

He decided not to mention the bats inhabiting another part of the cave. No need to push Kristi harder toward a panic attack. From the sound of her voice, she was skating close to a meltdown.

The best thing he could do for her was leave the cave and head for the extraction point. Once she was safe, he could hand her over to one of the other operatives and return to his solitude.

Rafe ignored the guilt spearing his conscience. Solitude was best for his peace of mind. Why didn't he believe his own argument?

He slowed at the bend in the tunnel. "Turning right," he murmured. "Two hundred feet to go."

"Thank God."

Frowning at her shaky voice, Rafe drew her to his side and wrapped his arm around her shoulders. "Better?"

She sighed. "Yes. Thanks."

"You're doing great. Just a little bit longer."

"Easy for you to say. You're not having a screaming meltdown inside your head."

Rafe tucked her tighter against him. "I understand."

"Not buying it. You're a Navy SEAL, a legitimate American hero. I can't see you screaming even on your worst day."

Memories threatened to resurface. He shoved them back down. Now wasn't the time to deal with his personal baggage. "You'd be wrong."

"Want to talk about it?"

"Nope. Might tarnish my macho image." And send him down a rabbit hole of nightmares when Kristi's safety depended on his vigilance.

When Rafe estimated they were about one hundred yards from the exit, he stopped and nudged her until her back was pressed against the cave wall. "Stay right here. I won't be long."

"Wait." A small hand clamped around his forearm. "Where are you going?"

"To make sure the coast is clear before we leave the cave. I don't want to lead you into an ambush." He pressed his hand on top of hers. "I won't be long," he repeated, and waited for her to make the next move. If he had to, he'd knock her out, but Rafe didn't want to do that. She'd been through enough trauma tonight.

A long minute later, Kristi let go of his arm. "Please, be careful." Her breathing was quick and shallow.

"Kristi." Rafe laid his hand on her shoulder. "You can handle this."

"Sure. Go."

He hated to leave her in the darkness, especially knowing she wasn't comfortable, but he didn't have a choice. "Close your eyes."

"What good will that do? It's dark with my eyes closed, too."

He smiled at the snark in her voice. She was still with him. "Trust me."

A moment later, she said, "This is much better. I'm not so disoriented."

"Your brain associates closed eyes with darkness. When your eyes are open and you still see nothing but darkness, your equilibrium can go haywire." He squeezed her shoulder lightly. "Can you handle the darkness for two minutes?"

"I'm fine."

"I'll be back." He made himself go toward the entrance despite his puzzling reluctance to leave her side. He had to do reconnaissance. Protecting her was his mission.

Rafe didn't want to look too deeply into his rioting emotions. He needed to get his mind on the job and off the disturbingly attractive woman. He wasn't interested in any woman. The sooner he got her off Hart Mountain and accompanied her to the safety of Otter Creek, the quicker he could hand her off to someone else. That course of action was safer for both of them.

CHAPTER FOUR

Kristi stood with her back pressed against a cold stone wall, listening for every sound. Tough to hear anything over the drumming of her heartbeat, the rhythm much too fast.

Scowling, she used the breathing exercises her childhood therapist taught her as a way to calm herself, the only thing he'd done right in her opinion. She was a grown woman, not a child. Handling total darkness for two freaking minutes ought to be easy. Right. Maybe that was true for someone without her background.

Many people had hang-ups. Kristi just happened to be afraid of the dark. She handled it without a problem at home. Night lights all over the house did wonders for her phobia. When she left this cave and went with Rafe to a safe haven, she would turn on every light in the place.

She shivered, fingers aching from the cold. Asking for a blanket had moved up on her priority list. Maybe hot tea to chase the chill from her bones, too. Who knew being stuck underground for what seemed like years could sap the heat from your body?

Although she longed to open her eyes, Kristi kept them shut. With her luck, she'd become disoriented again, and do a face plant on the nasty cave floor. She didn't want to know what kind of muck littered the ground.

A displacement of air on her right side had her shifting to face the potential threat. Please, she prayed silently, let this be Rafe and not a bear coming back to his den to sleep for the remainder of the night.

"Kristi, I'm coming up on your right side."

"Find anything?"

"We're clear for the moment."

More cold chills surged up her spine. Not the answer she'd hoped to hear. "The kidnappers are still searching for me."

"Oh, yeah."

"What if they spot us?"

"I'll handle it. Do what I tell you, and we'll be fine."

"Are you armed?"

A snort. "Of course. I never go anywhere without weapons."

The invisible band around her chest loosened. Weapons. Plural. Good to know. What else was he carrying besides that scary-looking knife he'd cut her bonds with?

"You have more questions before we head out?"

"They can wait. I'm ready for a blanket and hot tea. A hot bath or shower, too." She shuddered, still feeling the hands of kidnappers on her body as they manhandled her.

"I hear you. I'm going to hold your hand and lead you out of here." A second later, his strong, roughened hand clasped hers.

Heat seeped from Rafe's palm into hers. Kristi almost groaned as the warmth penetrated her cold fingers and radiated up her arm.

"Once we're outside, we have to move fast. I have friends closing in on our location, but the kidnappers may slow them down."

"More men from Fortress Security?"

"That's right."

They walked in silence for a short time, then Kristi felt fresh, cool air on her face.

"Ready?" Rafe whispered.

"Yes." If she never had to take shelter in a cave for the rest of her life, she'd be happy. The bears could have this habitat. She'd stick to her cozy, warm house with her blankets and night lights.

Her rescuer tugged her from the mouth of the cave and down the mountainside at a decent speed. Thankfully, after being in total darkness, the moonlight dispelled her fear of the dark.

Somewhere nearby, a heavy thud sounded, and a man uttered vicious curses.

Kristi tightened her grip around Rafe's hand. She recognized that voice. The man cursing had punched her outside the cabin. He'd sounded as if he hated her when he railed at her for resisting his orders. She scowled. The guy was a creep and enjoyed hurting her.

Rafe changed direction and headed for a large tree with several thick bushes in front of the trunk. He led her around the bushes and behind the tree, then motioned for her to crouch at the base.

When she complied, he shrugged off his pack and set it beside her. With a hand signal to stay put, he went in the direction of the cursing kidnapper. Within seconds, the darkness seemed to swallow him. One minute he was there. The next, he disappeared.

How could anyone walk in total silence? If Kristi hadn't watched Rafe walk away, she wouldn't have known he left. The man moved like a ghost. Less than a minute later, the cursing kidnapper went silent. She hoped that meant Rafe had knocked the man out, and not the other way around.

A noise came from her right. Kristi turned her head, straining to see the potential threat. Was that a four-legged or two-legged problem? Maybe the wind was to blame.

She heard the noise again, this time closer. Her eyes widened. That sounded like fabric brushing against a bush. Definitely not a four-legged predator. Was it Rafe or one of her kidnappers?

A ball of ice formed in her stomach. Rafe hadn't made noise when he left. She doubted a SEAL would be careless enough to give away his location. The noisemaker was one of the kidnappers. Praying he would pass by her, Kristi watched and waited. Thank goodness she was wearing a black shirt with her jeans.

More fabric scraped against a bush near her tree. Kristi stiffened as one of the more vicious kidnappers shoved his way through the foliage like a bull on a rampage.

Bull turned his head and pointed a gun at her. "You've led us on a merry chase, Ms. Stewart. You're going to pay for that." He motioned with the muzzle. "Stand up and come here."

She slowly stood. Where was Rafe? If he didn't find her here, would he return to the cabin? Kristi took one step toward him when Rafe appeared behind Bull and wrapped his arm around the kidnapper's throat.

Although Bull struggled to free himself, Rafe continued to hold on. Seconds later, the kidnapper sagged. Rafe lowered him to the ground, rolled Bull to his stomach, and tied his hands with a zip tie.

She blinked. Who carried zip ties around on a hike in the woods?

After Rafe stripped Bull's belt and used it as a gag, he shrugged into his pack again and wrapped his hand around Kristi's. "You okay?" he whispered.

"That's my question for you. Are you hurt?"

"Nope. If you're uninjured, let's go. There are at least five more kidnappers out here looking for you."

Five? He'd taken down three of the kidnappers on his own without making a sound. Good grief. Rafe Torres was amazing.

He started them down the mountain again, helping Kristi over fallen logs and loose rocks. Occasionally, he tapped his watch face as they continued walking and adjusted their direction. He must have a compass or GPS app on his watch.

They walked so long that Kristi lost track of time. She thought she would have to own up to being a wuss and beg Rafe for a two-minute break when two men dressed in black emerged from the shadows ahead of Rafe.

He stepped in front of her, a gun pointed at the two newcomers. When they moved into a shaft of moonlight, Rafe holstered his gun. "Took you long enough." He reached back for Kristi's hand and drew her up beside him.

One of the men raised an eyebrow. "We're not the ones who took a detour to the wrong side of the mountain." He nodded at Kristi. "I'm Josh. This is Rio, our team medic. Do you need medical attention?"

He had to be kidding. No way was she letting anyone treat her on this mountainside with kidnappers roaming around the area. "I'm fine."

"Kristi's injured but mobile," Rafe said. "She can wait until we're in a more secure location."

A slight nod. "Good enough. Let's go."

Although Rafe knew the two men, Kristi edged closer to him anyway. Josh and Rio looked strong enough to bench press the bear she'd been worried about in the cave.

Josh led the way down the mountain followed by Kristi and Rafe. Rio brought up the rear. Minutes later, they were joined by three other men, each of them as intimidating as the first two. They walked at a fast clip, guns in their hands, constantly scanning the area for the kidnappers.

When Kristi stumbled over an exposed tree root, Rafe caught her on one side, Rio on the other. "Sorry," she whispered.

"I can carry you," Rafe said. "You've been through a lot."

She shook her head. She'd make it on her own two feet as long as she could. Otherwise, she might slow them down unnecessarily.

The trek down the mountain continued with the group of men surrounding her and Rafe. Minutes later, the noises from the kidnappers searching the mountain faded away to nothing.

She watched the other five men as they walked. Their movements reminded her of Rafe's. Had they also been in the military, possibly SEALs like him?

That thought alleviated some of her uneasiness. Military backgrounds were common among the security team her father employed. The Fortress Security men were nothing like her father's security guards, though. All of them seemed to be a cut above a regular soldier. Perhaps several cuts above. Special Forces of some type, she decided. No other explanation seemed to fit their skill level.

Callie had talked about Rafe, but never about his military career. She didn't seem to know much about what he did aside from the fact that he was a SEAL and was gone more than she wanted. Man, if Callie could see him in action, she would be impressed. Kristi was. She pushed her guilt aside at admiring Callie's boyfriend. Callie had been gone for three years.

Minutes later, Josh held up his fist and Rafe stopped Kristi, a finger to his lips to indicate a need for silence.

Kristi saw nothing but trees and heard only the rapid beating of her own heart. Josh glanced at Rafe and held up two fingers, then gave him another hand signal. As Rafe started them moving again, he angled toward the left. Rio kept pace with them while Josh and the rest of his group disappeared into the woods.

Less than a minute later, a man's shout cut off abruptly. Oh, man. She prayed none of Rafe friends had been injured.

Rafe and Rio glanced at each other, then picked up the pace so much that Kristi was practically running to keep up with their longer strides. Although she understood the reason they wanted her out of the area as fast as possible, Kristi didn't have the stamina of soldiers who obviously trained their bodies to endure long runs in rough terrain. She was totally out of her element. She rocked at making a surgical strike through a fabric shop, not running for her life down a mountainside in the dark.

When she started to lag behind, Rafe scooped her into his arms without breaking stride and ran faster. Although Kristi wanted to protest that she could keep going under her own steam, she would have been lying. Her energy reserves were tapped out. The best thing she could do was hold on to Rafe, stay quiet, and help Rio watch for the kidnappers.

One minute they were hurrying down the mountain alone. The next, Rio's teammates had rejoined them. She stared at the group of men dressed in black. How did they move so quietly?

"Two down," Josh said. "How many are left?"

"At least three. Hopefully, they're searching on the other side."

"Need one of us to carry her?"

"I've got her. Just keep the bogeys off of us."

They continued in silence. As the sky began to lighten with the coming sunrise, the terrain leveled off. Josh pointed to the left. Rafe angled that direction along with the other Fortress men. Within minutes, Kristi saw three black SUVs parked in the shadows of the woods near an asphalt road.

"Rafe, you and Kristi ride with me and Rio," Josh murmured. "The rest will follow us in Nate's vehicle. Toss Quinn your key fob. He'll drive your SUV."

Rafe carried her to the first vehicle and set her on the backseat before grabbing his fob and tossing it to one of the three men she had yet to meet. "Thanks, Quinn."

"Yep. See you at the compound."

Compound? Kristi frowned. She thought Rafe would take her back to the hotel, or maybe drive her to Nashville to her father's fortified estate with the army of guards he employed.

No matter what their plan was, Kristi couldn't be gone from Bakerhill for long. She had a design consultation with a client on Monday. The time line for choosing a dress design and making the wedding gown was tight as it was. She couldn't afford to miss the consultation.

Shivering, she wrapped her arms around her middle. Her teeth chattered. Hopefully, the vehicle would warm up quickly. She glanced at the men who had run down the mountain with her. The cold didn't appear to faze any of them.

Rio climbed in beside her with his bag. After a glance at her, he twisted and grabbed a blanket from the cargo area. He draped the cover over her, then rooted in his bag for a bottle of water and a small packet. He ripped open the packet, dumped the powder into the water bottle, and shook it up. When Rafe got into the vehicle on Kristi's other side, Rio tossed the bottle to him.

"Thanks."

"Yep." Rio prepared another bottle with the powder and handed it to Kristi. "Drink this. It's an electrolyte mix."

Kristi unscrewed the top and drank the treated water. So good. She hadn't had anything to drink in hours.

Josh climbed behind the wheel and cranked the engine. "Is this the only road out of the area, Rafe?"

"Yes, sir."

He touched his ear. "Alex, get ahead of us. Quinn, on our tail. Chance of ambush."

Kristi's breath caught. Ambush? Oh, no. Wasn't the race down the mountain on foot enough? Surely those men would give up now. After all, she'd escaped.

Rio turned to Kristi. "Where are you injured?"

Uneasy, she glanced at Rafe.

"Rio is one of the best paramedics in the business," Rafe assured her. "He's as well trained as a doctor. You can trust him."

"Rafe's right," Josh said. "Let Rio assess your injuries so we know what medical care you need and how fast."

"She'll need a doctor," Rafe said. "The kidnappers zapped her with a stun gun and drugged her."

Josh's expression grew grim as he glanced at Rio in the rearview mirror. "Hospital?"

"As soon as possible. We need to know what they gave her. The doc will also want to run a battery of tests."

"Memorial Hospital, Alex," Josh said.

Kristi frowned. "How is he talking to the others?"

"He has a communication device in his ear," Rafe said. "He and his teammates stay in contact with each other that way." He laid his hand over Kristi's and squeezed. "I trust Rio. He can help you."

She looked at the medic who waited in silence for her to decide if she would allow him to treat her. "What do you want to know?"

"Where do you hurt?"

That made her smile and wished she hadn't. One of the men had slapped her face. "You should have asked me what doesn't hurt. I'm sore all over, Rio. The kidnappers punched me in the stomach and face, kicked me in the ribs, and shoved me against the side of the van hard enough that I almost passed out at their feet."

Rafe growled.

"Shut up and drink, Rafe," Rio said, his tone mild. "I need to check you for internal injuries and cracked ribs, Kristi."

She nodded.

"Before I do, what part of your head connected with the van?"

"The back."

"I'll check that first, then your face and ribs." Rio ran his fingers along the back of her head. He paused when Kristi sucked in a breath at a tender spot. "You have a nice bump there." The medic grabbed a small flashlight. "Turn your head for me. I want to check for a cut."

Rio's light clicked on. He parted her hair at the back and examined her injury. "Lucky lady. No cut, but your head will be sore for a few days. Your face is next." Seconds later, he whistled. "Somebody clocked you good, sugar. How does your jaw feel?"

"Like a gorilla slugged me."

"I bet. May I touch your face?"

"Knock yourself out."

A minute later, Rafe said, "Well? How bad is it?"

The light turned off again. "A deep bruise is forming."

Kristi sighed. "Great. My head and face should heal at the same pace as the rest of my body."

While the men chuckled, Rio reached into his bag again and brought out two small packets that he shook. He laid one of the packets against the back of her head and glanced at Rafe.

Her rescuer polished off his drink and took over holding the cold pack against Kristi's scalp.

She shivered. The cold increased her trembling, but lessened the headache that had plagued her since the abduction.

The medic handed her the other cold pack. "Press that against your jaw to reduce the swelling and pain. Ribs next." Rio traced each rib, pausing when she gasped. "Here?"

"Can't you tell?"

He smiled. "Any other sore places on this rib?" he clarified.

"Yes. Sorry for snapping at you."

"You're allowed to be cranky."

Josh snorted. "You don't tell the rest of us that."

"She's beautiful."

Rafe scowled. "You're married, Kincaid. You aren't supposed to notice other women."

"I'm married to the most beautiful woman on the planet, but I still appreciate the beauty of other women."

"Yeah? Keep your compliments to yourself."

Rio chuckled. "Kristi isn't the only cranky person in this vehicle. What rubbed your fur the wrong way?"

"Keep it up, Kincaid, and you'll find my fist in your face."

"Dial it down, Torres," Josh ordered.

"Yes, sir."

Rio continued his examination of Kristi's ribs, asking questions in a low voice as he finished the left side and shifted to the right before moving on to check her stomach.

As the medic completed his exam and sat back, Josh stiffened. "Copy that," he murmured. He glanced into the rearview mirror. "We have company, boys."

CHAPTER FIVE

Adrenaline poured into Rafe's veins by the bucket. He'd hoped the kidnappers would still be searching the mountain for Kristi. "Where's your gear, Josh?" Rafe's Go bag was in his SUV.

"Cargo area."

Rafe pressed Kristi's hand to the cold pack on her head. "Hold this in place." When she took over, he twisted in the seat and reached into the cargo area for Josh's gear bag. Inside, he found the Delta soldier's AR-10 and two magazines. He hoped he didn't need that much ammunition.

Although Kristi noticed eight kidnappers, Rafe wasn't convinced there were only eight. She had been unconscious for hours. He didn't know how many men were involved in this scheme, and that worried him. The kidnappers should have cut their losses and disappeared. Instead, they were pursuing her. Any advantage Fortress had was gone. The kidnappers knew a team had rescued Kristi.

He checked Josh's AR-10, unsurprised to find everything in perfect working order. The Delta Force soldier never took chances with his equipment.

Rafe scrambled over the seat into the cargo area and pressed a button to lower the back window. "Rio."

"I've got her. Kristi, get on the floor."

"Why?"

"Safety. Come on," the medic said. "I'll help you. The floor won't be comfortable for your ribs. I'll fix you up once we're clear."

"Rafe?"

His stomach clenched at the uncertainty in her voice. "The floor is the safest place inside the vehicle."

"What about you?"

"The SUV is reinforced. I'll be fine." A reinforced vehicle wouldn't help if the kidnappers shot him. He wasn't wearing his bullet-resistant vest, and nothing would protect him from a head shot.

A soft groan had him glancing over his shoulder and glaring at Rio. The medic ignored him.

"Focus, Torres," Josh snapped.

Rafe shifted his attention from Kristi to the job at hand. "Tell Quinn to get in front of us. I don't want to explain to Bear why my ride needs repairs." Quinn was also driving alone. He couldn't fire a weapon at the pursuers unless they pulled up beside him.

After a pause, Durango's leader laughed. "Quinn heard you. He's coming around us."

"Who's Bear?" Kristi asked, her voice muffled.

"The mechanical wizard who upgrades all of our vehicles and keeps the fleet running in top form," Rio answered. "He takes repairs personally and lets us know about it."

"You're afraid of him?"

"Anybody with common sense is afraid of Bear."

"The only people he's not gruff with are our wives or girlfriends," Josh added. "They think he's a teddy bear." He shuddered. "The rest of us know better."

"Will I meet him?"

"He's not based in Otter Creek, so probably not." Another pause. "Rafe."

"I see him." The vehicle behind them was closing in fast.

"Got one in front of Alex, too."

He frowned. How did that happen? Only one road led in or out of the area where Kristi had been held captive. His jaw clenched. As he'd feared, more than eight men were involved in Kristi's kidnapping. Fortress needed to get to the bottom of this mess soon.

Rafe raised the AR-10, waiting until the vehicle moved closer before he pulled the trigger. "Hold it steady, Josh."

"Do it. I want Quinn behind us as soon as possible."

Rafe's SUV would offer another layer of protection for Kristi. "Copy that."

"Cover your ears, Kristi," Rio said. "Ready, Rafe."

He blocked everything from his mind except the target vehicle. Rafe aimed and squeezed the trigger.

The center of the kidnapper's windshield cracked. The driver swerved, but kept coming. Growling, Rafe fired again, this time aiming for the driver. When the bullet hit his target, the kidnapper's vehicle veered off the road, broke through the railing, and plunged into a ravine. Seconds later, a ball of fire lit the night.

"Nice shot," Josh said. "Quinn, fall back."

"What about the other vehicle?" Rafe asked.

"Nate took care of it. We're clear for now."

Excellent. Rafe secured the AR-10, pressed the button to raise the window, and crawled over the seat to help Kristi. He frowned when he noticed her fast breathing and beads of sweat on her forehead. "Kristi?"

"I'm okay."

"Liar," he murmured and frowned at Rio.

"Back off, frog boy," the medic said. "I'll do what I can to alleviate the pain."

"Cracked ribs?"

"Bruised. Still painful." He inclined his head to the cold packs Kristi held in her hand. "Reposition those while I grab another one for her ribs."

Rafe plucked one of the chemically-activated cold packs from her hand and laid it against the back of her head. Kristi held the second cold pack against her jaw while Rio activated a third pack and placed it against her ribs. "Can't you give her a pain killer?"

"I don't know what the kidnappers used on her. I don't want to risk a drug interaction." He looked at Rafe. "Chill. Another hour, and she'll be at Memorial Hospital. Kristi's tough. She can handle this for another hour."

She was tough, but that didn't mean he wanted the dressmaker to suffer. Since he couldn't prevent it, Rafe closed his mouth and seethed in silence.

Once off Hart Mountain, the caravan headed for Interstate 40. Minutes later, they exited onto Highway 18. At that point, Josh took the lead and zoomed past the speed limit. As an officer with the Otter Creek police, Josh would be able to flash his badge if they were pulled over for speeding before they hit the Otter Creek town limits.

At the one-hour mark, Josh drove up to the emergency entrance of Memorial Hospital. "Stay with her while we check the area, Torres." He and Rio joined the rest of Durango.

Rafe scanned the area as well. While he trusted Durango, he trusted his own judgment more. Although he hadn't seen a tail, Kristi wasn't secure. She had a GPS tracker embedded under her skin. Anyone with the right information could track her to their current location.

Within two minutes, Josh was back. "We're clear. Need help?"

Rafe shook his head. He climbed out, then lifted Kristi into his arms.

"I can walk," she protested.

"You pushed yourself as far as you need to for tonight." He winked at her. "Besides, carrying you makes me look good in front of the nurses."

She smiled. "From the looks you're receiving from the women in the waiting room and behind the desk, your plan is working."

When one of the nurses pointed him to an exam room, Rafe carried her inside, anxious to have her out of sight of others. He set Kristi on the exam table. Within two minutes, someone knocked on the door.

Rafe stepped in front of Kristi, his hand on his weapon. Rio peered into the room. "Dr. Anderson is here."

Relaxing, Rafe motioned for Rio to send him in. He turned to Kristi. "He's the best doctor in town. All the ladies, from babies to gray-haired grannies, love Doc Anderson."

The doctor walked into the exam room, his eyes twinkling. "Nice to see you again, Mr. Torres. Glad you're not in need of my services this time. Who's your friend?"

"This is Kristi Stewart. Fortress rescued her from kidnappers who used a stun gun on Kristi and drugged her."

Anderson sobered. "I see. Let me take a look at you, my dear. Mr. Torres, please wait outside."

He frowned. "She's still in danger, Doc." Although the town's favorite doctor was old enough to be Kristi's grandfather, she would feel vulnerable with any unknown male. He didn't want to leave her if she was uncomfortable.

The doctor raised an eyebrow. "I assumed you would stand watch. Grace St. Claire will be joining us in a moment."

Immediately feeling better about leaving Kristi, he laid his hand on her shoulder. "I'll be right outside the door. If you need me, call out. I'll hear you."

The door to the exam room opened again, and Grace walked inside. Her face brightened. "Rafe, it's good to see you again. How are you?"

He gave the nurse a one-armed hug. "Better now that your husband can't torture me in PT every day."

She grinned. "He'll be pleased to know that you appreciate his efforts. Who's this?"

Rafe introduced Kristi. "Take good care of her, Grace. Kristi is a friend." That might be stretching their acquaintance a bit, but Kristi didn't dispute his claim of friendship. Then again, that might have more to do with her physical state than anything. She was exhausted and fighting adrenaline dump.

Grace's expression softened. "Don't worry. I'll stay with her."

As Rafe left the room, Dr. Anderson said to Kristi, "Now, my dear, let's talk while I check you for injuries, all right?"

Even though Rafe knew he couldn't stay in the room, he still felt as though he was abandoning her. Closing the door behind him, he took up a watch position in front of the door. Anyone who meant to harm Kristi would have to go through him first, and he was hard to take down.

Rio came to stand beside him. "How is she?"

"In a great deal of pain, but she's not complaining. Do you think Anderson will keep her overnight?"

A nod. "You have a problem with that?"

"I want her in a more secure location."

"If she's admitted, Durango will help with security until Wolf Pack arrives. They should be here in two hours."

Rafe stilled. "Maddox is sending my team?"

"The mission isn't finished. Your principal is in danger, and the man or woman calling the shots is still out there. Based on what we saw tonight, someone is determined to get his hands on your girl."

He scowled. "She's not my girl." Although his traitorous heart skipped a beat at Rio's words. What was up with that? Maybe he needed to have his heart checked by a doctor.

"A figure of speech, not a statement of fact."

Cheeks burning, Rafe asked the question foremost on his mind. "What tests will Anderson run?"

"You used to be an FBI agent. You know what tests he'll order. Physical exam, including a blood test and a rape kit. Kristi was drugged. For the sake of her health, she needs to know if she was assaulted while she was unconscious."

The possibility that she might have been raped twisted Rafe's stomach into a knot.

Rio laid his hand on Rafe's shoulder and squeezed. "Whatever the outcome of the tests, she'll recover. That's the most important thing."

"She didn't know about the tracker."

The operative stared at him. "How is that possible?"

"She was kidnapped when she was kid. Her father had the tracker implanted after he got her back, but she doesn't remember him having it done."

"How did she react?"

"She feels the tracker is a violation of her privacy."

"He saved her life."

Rafe hated that he had two trackers embedded under his skin, but the nature of his work made them a necessity. The trackers were a safety measure Maddox insisted on for every operative in the field.

Josh walked toward him and Rio. "Any word?" he asked.

"Not yet. Anderson and Grace are with her," Rio said.

"Nate, Quinn, and Alex are checking the perimeter. Once they're finished, Alex will join us in the hall while the other two watch the entrances. We have her covered, Rafe."

Why didn't that make him feel better?

CHAPTER SIX

Rafe turned when the door to the exam room opened and Dr. Anderson walked into the hallway. "How is she, Doc?"

"In remarkable shape considering her experience." He glanced at Rio. "Your assessment was correct, Mr. Kincaid. She'll have a colorful jaw by morning, I'm afraid."

"Any signs of sexual assault?" Josh asked softly.

Rafe's hands fisted at his sides. When the doctor hesitated, Rafe said, "We need to know how best to help her while keeping her safe. We're her protection detail." For now. He expected Stewart to assign a personal security force to safeguard Kristi, an idea that made him uneasy although he refused to dwell on the reason why.

Anderson sighed. "I didn't see signs of assault. However, I recommended that she see a counselor because this experience may trigger memories from her childhood kidnapping."

"Fortress has several counselors on staff. We'll make sure she consults one." The Fortress counselor Rafe wanted Kristi to talk to lived in Otter Creek. Perhaps Marcus Lang would talk to Kristi tomorrow. "Are you releasing her?" The sooner Kristi was in a secure location, the better.

"I'm admitting her for observation."

"She's still in danger, Doc. We don't know who's behind the kidnapping, and Memorial Hospital has too many entrances and exits."

"Keeping her safe is your job, Mr. Torres. My job is to monitor her health. Her blood test results will be back in a few hours. If I'm satisfied with her progress, I'll release her then."

"Rafe," Rio murmured. "We'll handle it. No one will get to her on our watch."

Outnumbered, Rafe gave a slight nod. "She needs to stay in her street clothes in case we have to leave in a hurry."

"I'll inform the medical staff." Anderson glanced at Rio. "You'll stay with her and Mr. Torres?"

"Yes, sir."

"Excellent. Make sure she drinks plenty of fluids. I've given her a mild pain killer." He told Rio the name of the drug. "She should sleep a few hours. Stan will transport her to her room. If you need me, I'll be on duty for several more hours."

"Thanks, Doc."

Rafe breathed easier knowing that Kristi would recover soon. His gut still said trouble was closing in on them. "May I go in now?" he asked the doctor.

"Of course."

Leaving Dr. Anderson and the others standing in the corridor, Rafe tapped on the door and slipped inside the room. Kristi sat on the examination table watching Grace store unused medical supplies in one of the many cabinets in the room. When she saw Rafe, Kristi's tense expression eased.

"I'll check on you while I'm on shift, Kristi," Grace said. "If you need me, have Rafe call me. I'm on duty until noon."

"Thanks, Grace."

The nurse patted Rafe's arm on her way out of the room.

"Well?" he asked Kristi, eyebrow raised.

She frowned. "What?"

"Are you crazy about Dr. Anderson like the rest of the women in town?" His lips curved when she laughed, glad he got the response he wanted.

"I'm afraid so. He's a sweetheart."

He sent her a look of mock disgust. "That's what I figured. None of the single guys in town have a chance until the good doctor lets the women down easy."

"I can see why." She tilted her head and winced. "Ouch. Remind me not to do that again."

Rafe sobered. "Head still hurts?"

"I swear there's a bear pounding on it with a hammer."

That surprised a laugh out of him. "A bear?"

"Probably the one I was worried about eating me in the cave," she muttered.

A tap sounded on the door.

Rafe stepped in front of Kristi as Rio stuck his head inside the room.

"Stan's here."

The orderly entered the room, pushing a wheelchair. "Ready to go to your room, Ms. Stewart?" the cheerful older man asked.

She sighed. "I guess." Kristi glanced at Rafe. "You sure you can't spring me from here?"

He wanted to do exactly that. "As soon as we can," he promised.

Her eyes widened. "You're staying?"

"We'll talk about the arrangements later." Rafe didn't want to talk with Stan in the room. He was a nice man who also fed Otter Creek's gossip mill.

Rafe scooped Kristi into his arms and set her in the wheelchair, ignoring how good she felt in his arms. He didn't want the orderly touching her. He told himself that his protectiveness was for safety reasons.

Minutes later, Kristi was in her temporary bed, huddled under two blankets. After Stan left, she said, "At least I'm not wearing a hospital gown."

"I asked Anderson to let you remain in your street clothes."

"In case we have to run."

"I hope the precaution is unnecessary."

"What if it's not?"

"I'll take care of you."

"Who takes care of you?"

A spear of pain shot through Rafe's heart. He breathed past the hurt. "My teammates." He squeezed Kristi's hand. "Rest while you can."

"Who will stay with me?"

Rafe moved a chair to her bedside. "I'll be in here with you. Rio and Josh are outside the door for the moment. My teammates will arrive soon, and they'll take over the watch in the hall."

Shivering, Kristi tugged the blankets higher. "Is that necessary?"

He stilled. "If you don't want me in here, I'll have Rio sit with you."

"I'm glad you're with me, Rafe. I wanted to know if having Josh and Rio in the hall was necessary."

The ball of ice in his stomach melted. "Another safety precaution. Someone else may know about your GPS tracker."

"Dad and I will talk about that."

"Cut him some slack."

"I still don't like knowing he can track my movements. How would you like it if you had a tracker embedded under your skin?"

Rafe's lips curved. "I do."

Her breath caught. "Why?"

"Safety precaution for a dangerous job." He frowned as she continued to shiver. "Are you all right?"

"Freezing."

"I'll be back in a minute." Rafe strode to the door. "Rio, Kristi is still cold. She needs another blanket."

"Adrenaline dump." The medic straightened from the wall. "Let me talk to her for a minute, then I'll find her a blanket." Rio followed Rafe inside. "Rafe says you're still cold," he said to Kristi. "I'll find you another blanket. You also need to drink fluids. What soft drinks do you like?"

She wrinkled her nose. "I usually drink water or herbal tea."

A nod. "I can work with that. Does your head still hurt?"

"Oh, yeah."

Rio turned on the dim light near her bed, then turned off the overhead light. "Better?"

"Much. Thanks, Rio."

"No problem. I'll be back with the blanket and a drink."

As Kristi snuggled deeper into the pillow and tugged the blankets up to her chin, Rafe sat on the chair. Kristi struggled to stay awake as her pain medication kicked in.

Ten minutes later, Rio returned with a blanket in one hand and a to-go cup in the other. "Chamomile tea with a little sugar." He set the cup on a rolling table and draped the third blanket over Kristi. After raising the head of the bed so she could drink the tea, he pulled a bottle of water from his cargo pocket. "Drink the water after you finish your tea."

"Thanks, Rio." She reached for the tea with a trembling hand as the medic left the room.

Afraid she might drop the cup and burn herself, Rafe wrapped his hand around hers to hold the cup steady. Kristi flicked him a glance, but didn't comment.

After sipping a quarter of the drink, her hands stopped trembling. "I can hold the cup now. Thank you."

When Kristi finished the tea, Rafe encouraged her to drink part of the water. Afterward, he murmured, "Rest now, Kristi."

"What if the kidnappers find me again? I don't want to be caught sleeping."

"I'll handle it. Trust me."

She sighed, her eyes closing. "Thanks, Rafe. I feel safe with you here." Kristi fell silent, and soon, her breathing settled into a regular rhythm.

Rafe kept watch over Kristi while she slept, listening as the noise level in the corridor slowly increased as the day's activity at the hospital cranked up.

A light tap sounded on the door. Jackson Conner, his team's medic, walked inside the room. He nodded at Rafe and glanced at Kristi. "How is she?" he murmured.

"Been asleep for two hours. Bruises, headache, and a good case of adrenaline dump."

"Concussion?"

"Nope, just a goose egg."

"Good." Jackson studied the bed. "She's buried under a ton of blankets."

"I was freezing," Kristi said sleepily and opened her eyes to stare at the medic. "You must be a friend of Rafe's. I'm Kristi."

"Jackson. I'm Wolf Pack's medic."

She blinked. "Wolf Pack?"

"That's the name of my team." Rafe rose. "How do you feel?"

"Hurts to move."

"When will the doctor release her?" Jackson asked Rafe.

"After her test results come back. Should be soon."

Another knock at the door. This time, Jon Smith, another teammate, poked his head in. "Orderly says he's supposed to take the lady for a CT scan."

Rafe frowned. Anderson hadn't mentioned a CT scan.

"Come on, man," the orderly snapped. "I need to get moving. If I hold up the med tech, I'll be hearing about it the rest of my shift."

His frown deepened. Not Stan. This orderly raised a red flag in his mind.

"I don't understand," Kristi said. "Dr. Anderson said I didn't have a concussion. Why do I need a CT scan?"

Rafe looked at Jackson, eyebrow raised.

"Shouldn't need one. Call Anderson to confirm the order."

He tipped his head to the door. "Hold this guy off. I don't want him in the room until I clear this with Dr. Anderson."

Jackson walked into the corridor, closing the door behind him as Rafe pulled up the doctor's cell number on his contact list. Yeah, he'd been a guest at Memorial Hospital a few times during his training at PSI. Josh Cahill and his teammates were sadists.

When the doctor answered his phone, Rafe said, "An orderly is outside of Kristi Stewart's door, saying he has orders to take her for a CT scan. Did you authorize this test?"

"Absolutely not. I'm on my way to her room now."

Rafe ended the call. "Let's get you into the bathroom, Kristi." He tugged off the blankets and lifted Kristi into his arms.

She gasped and bit off a soft moan, her face draining of color.

"Sorry," he murmured as he carried her into the bathroom. Inside, he set her on her feet and kept his hands on her shoulders until she was steady. "You good?"

A nod, but she was too pale for his liking.

"Stay here until I tell you to come out."

She caught his hand. "Be careful."

His heart turned over in his chest. He seriously needed to have that checked. "Always." With that, he left the bathroom, closing the door behind him. He took a minute to call Josh.

"Cahill."

"It's Rafe. We might need a man with a badge."

"I'm in the hospital lobby. Two minutes." Josh ended the call.

Rafe walked out to the corridor and stood in the doorway, blocking the orderly's access to the room.

The dark-haired man glanced uneasily at the three men barring his path. "Look, the scan won't take long, but if I don't take Ms. Stewart now, her test could be delayed for hours."

Rafe used a hand signal to warn Jon and Jackson of trouble. "Dr. Anderson didn't authorize the scan."

Sweat beaded on the man's forehead. "I'll sort this out."

"Dr. Anderson will be here soon. You can sort it out with him."

A frown. "Dr. Henderson authorized the test, not Anderson. I have to speak to Henderson." The orderly started to back away when Jon moved, blocking the man's retreat.

"You wouldn't want to disappoint Doc Anderson," Jon murmured, his voice soft and his gaze glacial.

"You can't keep me here against my will."

Rafe pointed to Josh. "He wants to talk to you."

"Sorry, man." The orderly shook his head. "I have a schedule to keep."

Josh flashed his badge. "I have questions for you first."

Dr. Anderson hurried up the corridor, frowning. "Who are you?" he demanded of the orderly. "Where's your hospital badge?"

The guy swallowed hard and glanced down at the front of his shirt. "I must have lost it somewhere."

"I haven't seen you before."

"I'm a new hire."

A frown. "Who sent you to get my patient?"

The orderly clammed up.

"He claims Dr. Henderson sent him," Rafe said.

"We don't have a physician named Henderson on staff."

The orderly tried to dodge around Jon and escape. Rafe's teammate slammed him against the wall face first. "Running is not wise or good for your health."

"Are you threatening me?"

"Am I threatening this man, Officer Cahill?"

Josh rolled his eyes. "Sounds like he's offering smart advice to me. You should listen to him. What's your name?"

No response.

"Want to tell me what you're really doing here?"

Again, nothing.

Josh sighed. "I was looking forward to having breakfast with my wife. Looks like I'll miss that." He cinched the man's wrists with a pair of handcuffs he'd pulled from his pocket. Durango's leader easily controlled the man's struggles. "Let's talk at the station."

"Need a hand?" Jon asked.

"I've got him." He glanced at Rafe. "I'll talk to you later."

Rafe gave him a chin lift in acknowledgment. Once Josh and the stranger left the floor, Rafe turned to Dr. Anderson. "I'll find out if Kristi's ready to see you. You're releasing her now?"

A troubled expression settled on the doctor's face. "Under the circumstances, I think that would be wise."

"Wait here." Rafe returned to the room and closed the door before knocking on the bathroom door. "It's Rafe. Are you ready to see Dr. Anderson now?"

Kristi flung open the door. "If that means I can leave the hospital, you bet I'm ready."

He scanned her, pleased that she looked steadier now than she did when he carried her into the hospital. "Anderson is waiting in the hall." He cupped her elbow as she walked to the bed.

She studied his face. "Is everything all right?"

"The orderly is a fake. He doesn't have hospital ID and claimed to have orders from a doctor who doesn't exist."

"They found me," she whispered.

"Yes."

"How? Did someone follow us from Gatlinburg?"

He shook his head. "We would have noticed a tail. My guess is someone else accessed the information on your tracker and followed the signal here."

"I'm not safe, am I?"

"You're as safe as we can make you."

"I want the tracker out."

"When we're in a secure location, we'll talk about the tracker." He opened the corridor door and motioned for Anderson to come inside.

"Wait outside, Mr. Torres. I won't be long."

He looked at Kristi, eyebrow raised in a silent question. If she wanted him to stay, he wouldn't budge no matter what Anderson wanted.

"I'll be fine."

Anderson frowned. "We won't be long, Mr. Torres. The sooner you step into the hall, the quicker your friend will be ready to leave."

"I'll be outside the door, Kristi."

Five minutes later, Dr. Anderson walked into the corridor. "The nurse will bring her discharge papers. If her headaches persist more than a few days, take her to a doctor."

Rafe held out his hand. "Thanks, Doc. I appreciate you taking such good care of her."

"Who is she to you, Mr. Torres?"

"I'm on her protection detail."

"Is that all?"

His face burned. "She's a friend," he said.

"Take good care of her. She's a nice woman who's been through a great deal in her life. If you need me, call."

Rafe ignored the curious glances of his teammates, and returned to the room. "As soon as the nurse arrives with your discharge papers, we're out of here."

"Where are we going?"

Good question. He preferred to take her somewhere besides PSI, Fortress Security's bodyguard training school, but PSI was the safest place for her. "A safe place."

"I'm beginning to think there is no such place."

"Hey." Rafe waited until her gaze connected with his. "Everything will be fine. I'll find out who's after you."

"What if you can't?"

"I won't stop until you're safe."

From the hall, Jackson said, "Rafe, the nurse is here."

Excellent. He turned, keeping his body in front of Kristi. "Send her in."

Within minutes, Kristi was free to leave. When another orderly appeared with a wheelchair, Rafe shook his head. "She won't be needing that."

"It's hospital policy, buddy."

"Not this time." He grabbed his phone and called Dr. Anderson again. When the physician answered, Rafe explained what he wanted, then handed the phone to the orderly. "Talk to Dr. Anderson."

After a short conversation, the orderly handed the phone back to Rafe. "The doctor cleared it. You're free to go, Ms. Stewart."

Once the orderly left, Rafe glanced at Jon. "My SUV is in the parking lot." He tossed his key fob to the sniper. "We'll use the rear exit instead of the ER entrance."

"I'll have Eli come up, then I'll drive your SUV to the back of the hospital."

Minutes later, Rafe tucked Kristi close to his side and escorted her to his SUV. Once they arrived at PSI, he'd contact Maddox. Decisions had to be made for the good of Kristi's safety, decisions that would anger the man paying the tab for this operation.

CHAPTER SEVEN

Kristi stared at the iron gates looming in front of Rafe's SUV, blocking entry into a military compound. She couldn't think of another way to describe the utilitarian buildings. The grounds had no landscaping to speak of, either.

Glancing to the right, her eyes widened at the sight of the small town inside the compound with a group of men and women dressed in black like Rafe and his teammates. The people were heavily armed and intent on infiltrating one of the buildings. They must be some of the Fortress trainees Rafe had told her about on the drive to Personal Security International.

When they approached a scanner outside the gate, Rafe held up an ID card. A second later, the gates slid open and he drove to the back of the main building. When he parked, Rafe murmured, "Wait here."

She studied her surroundings as he rounded the hood to open her door. After helping her to the asphalt, he wrapped his arm around her shoulders, tucking Kristi close to his side.

The weight of his arm felt good. Kristi reminded herself that Rafe had been Callie's boyfriend, and she shouldn't enjoy his company and touch as much as she did. Although Callie wasn't here anymore, that didn't mean Kristi should be so comfortable with the man her friend had loved.

How much Kristi admired and respected Rafe didn't matter. His job was to keep her safe. Perhaps Kristi felt more comfortable with Rafe than his teammates because she knew him. However, speaking to each other every few months when Rafe was home on leave couldn't be construed as a relationship.

In fact, she didn't have a relationship with a man aside from her father and Hugh. Her social life had been lacking since she started Kristi's Bridal.

When her mind turned toward Hugh, she grimaced. Compared to Rafe Torres, Hugh Ward didn't measure up. Why had she agreed to consider marrying him? She didn't love him and deserved a man who only saw her when they were together. Hugh paid more attention to the people who noticed him than he did Kristi.

Their dinners together were usually tedious and boring. Sure, she and Hugh were friends, but they didn't have much in common. Kristi refused to marry a man she didn't love, even to please her father. That meant a conversation with Hugh was on her agenda as soon as possible.

At the back door to the building, Rafe waved his card in front of another reader and tapped in a code on the key pad. He ushered Kristi inside, then led her down a long, winding hallway to a large cafeteria. He escorted her to a table at the back of the room. "Do you want water or tea?"

"Water, please."

"Are you hungry?"

Her stomach growled on cue. Cheeks burning, she smiled. "Guess that answers your question."

Rafe chuckled. "I'll see what Nate prepared for the trainees."

She blinked. "The same Nate who helped with my rescue?"

"That's the one. He's a professional chef."

Her mouth gaped. "You're kidding."

"Nope. The man can make anything taste good."

As he spoke, the rest of Rafe's teammates entered the cafeteria. Eli Wolfe, Wolf Pack's leader, walked to their table while the others headed for the kitchen.

"Maddox wants an update," he said to Rafe.

"As soon as Kristi eats, we'll call from the conference room."

Eli's eyes twinkled as he turned to Kristi. "You didn't like the food at Memorial Hospital?"

"To be honest, the food didn't smell all that appetizing."

He laughed. "I agree. You won't be sorry you waited."

She glanced at Rafe. "I'm guessing the trainees have already eaten. I don't want to inconvenience Nate, especially since he was up half the night running down a mountain to protect me. A bagel or something simple is fine." The way her stomach felt this morning, simple was better than a five-star gourmet meal.

"I'll see what he has available." He joined his teammates in the kitchen.

"So, you make wedding dresses?" Eli asked.

"That's right. Are you getting married soon?"

He held up his left hand to show his black wedding band. "Already married to the most amazing, gorgeous woman ever born, and we have the most beautiful daughter in the world. How long have you been in business for yourself, Kristi?"

She smiled at his description of his family. Kristi longed for her future husband to describe her as amazing and beautiful. Hugh never said anything like that about her. Definitely not the right man. The sooner she turned down his proposal, the better for both of them. "Almost four years."

"You like it?"

"I love it. Designing and creating the right dress for a bride is a dream job." Her smiled faded. "How long will I have to stay here, Eli?"

His eyebrow rose. "Tired of my company already?"

Kristi's face burned. "I'm sorry. That came out wrong. I need to return to Bakerhill soon. I have responsibilities to fulfill."

"At the expense of your life?"

"My assistant is able to make dresses without me. She can't design them. I have a design consultation on Monday that I can't miss. The wedding is in two weeks."

"I don't know anything about how long it takes to make a dress, but I remember my wife stressing about her own dress six weeks before we married. Why did this bride wait so long to consult with you?"

"She's marrying a Marine who's deploying a week after the wedding. They haven't known each other long, but fell in love instantly. He wants to marry her before he deploys. He's determined that she have the protection of his name before he goes."

Eli's expression softened. "We'll see what we can do to get you back to Bakerhill."

Relief flooded her. She didn't want to let Maggie down. "Thank you."

"Do you only sell your own designs in your shop?"

She nodded.

"How long ago did you decide to design wedding dresses?"

"I was a freshman in high school when I convinced my father to take me to a bridal show." Kristi smiled at the memory of her father's consternation when she requested the outing for her birthday. For her, he'd conceded and accompanied her to the show, then taken her to dinner at her favorite restaurant.

He chuckled. "I bet that went over well."

"You have no idea how many people stared at us during the show. Dad was relieved when the show ended."

Rafe returned to their table with a plate for Kristi along with a to-go cup. On the plate was a toasted bagel a small bowl of cut fruit, and a small container of cream cheese. "Nate said if this isn't what you need, let him know and he'll make an omelet for you." He turned to Eli. "Get your breakfast. I'll sit with Kristi until you or one of the others returns to the table."

Eli's brows furrowed as his gaze shifted to the doorway to the kitchen. "What's taking them so long?"

"Nate is making personalized omelets." He pointed at his team leader. "Mine is the Spanish omelet. No mooching my breakfast, Wolfe."

"That sounds good. I might ask Nate to prepare two Spanish omelets." He clapped Rafe on the shoulder. "I'll bring yours when it's finished."

"Thanks." As the other man strode toward the kitchen to place his order, Rafe turned his attention to Kristi. "You and Eli appeared to be in deep conversation when I walked up."

She swallowed a bite of bagel. "He asked about my business and when I first realized I wanted to design wedding dresses."

"Sounds like an interesting story. When did you decide to focus on that field?"

"I was 15." She laughed. "I convinced Dad to take me to a bridal show for my birthday. He was mortified, but he went anyway. After I graduated from high school, I attended Parsons, one of the top fashion design schools in the country. That day at the bridal show defined my career."

"It's a good memory, then."

"The best."

Soon, his teammates came to the table with their own plates and one for Rafe. Eli handed him a to-go cup of coffee.

Jackson set a bottle of water in front of Kristi. "How is your breakfast?"

"It's perfect. Doesn't get much better than a bagel and mint tea. Although the omelets look fabulous, I don't think I could eat one this morning."

"If you change your mind, Nate will be here through lunch. After that, one of the trainees takes over the cooking duties."

Halfway through their meal, a door to their left opened, and 50 or 60 men and women streamed into the cafeteria. They headed for the metal tubs filled with ice and bottles of water. A few of the trainees glanced Kristi's way, but most ignored her and the men at her table. They soon cleared out, heading to another location in the compound.

When Kristi and Wolf Pack finished their meals, Rafe escorted her to a conference room with a huge screen on the wall while his teammates gathered the breakfast dishes and took them to the kitchen.

Rafe seated her at the large table, then booted up a computer and typed in a few commands. That done, he grabbed his phone and made a call as his teammates filed into the room and took seats at the table. "It's Rafe. Wolf Pack is ready." A pause, then, "Yes, sir. She's here, too." He ended the call.

Seconds later, the screen on the wall came to life. A blond-haired man with a buzz cut appeared on the screen. "Sit rep," he said.

Kristi frowned. What was that? As Rafe relayed the events of her rescue to the man on the screen and the incident with the fake orderly at the hospital, she figured it was some kind of military phrase requesting a report. When Rafe finished, the blond man shifted his attention to her.

"I'm Brent Maddox, CEO of Fortress Security. Your father hired Fortress to rescue you. What did the doctor say about your injuries?"

She shrugged. "I'm a little banged up."

His lips curved. "Your father will be pleased to hear the news although I guarantee he'll want more details. He's waiting outside my office to speak to you."

"Not patiently, I'll bet."

"No, ma'am. What can you tell me about the men who took you?"

"There were a lot of them, and they weren't gentle." She shuddered. "A few of them enjoyed hurting me."

His eyes narrowed as he shifted his attention to Jackson. "Assessment?"

"Bruises to her extremities, ribs, and jaw. When they shoved her against the side of the van, Kristi hit her head which is causing headaches but she doesn't have a concussion. She'll be fine in a few days."

Brent rubbed his jaw. "Torres and Durango took down five men, leaving three of the eight men that Kristi saw. According to Zane, the Gatlinburg police responded to two accidents on Hart Mountain with three fatalities. Now you're telling me that another man tried to get to Kristi in the hospital. Is the fake orderly talking?"

"No, sir," Rafe said. "Josh said he asked for his lawyer."

"No report on his identity?"

"Not so far."

"I'll text Josh. If the man doesn't have a record, I'll ask Josh to send what they have to Zane. He might have better luck. Kristi, do you know what the men wanted?"

"They didn't talk except to threaten me if I didn't cooperate. I assumed they wanted money." She grimaced. "I wasn't coherent long. The drug they used to knock me out did a good job. I woke up about the time Rafe arrived."

Brent turned his attention to Eli. "What's the plan?"

"At this point, I don't know. Josh says they weren't followed to Otter Creek. How did this guy find Kristi at the hospital?"

"Her GPS tracker," Rafe said. "That's the only explanation."

"If I can be tracked by the wrong people, I want the tracker removed," Kristi said.

Brent looked at Rafe. "Opinion?"

"I agree. Unless all six of us missed a tail, which I doubt, the tracker is a liability."

"Her father won't agree. You know her history."

A slight nod. "I think I have a solution to satisfy her father and shut down his tracker. Use ours."

Kristi scowled. "I'm not exchanging one tracker for another one. I'll still be vulnerable."

"The only people with access to the tracker frequency are Brent, Zane Murphy, our tech wizard, and my team. Zane has so many firewalls in place that no one outside our circle can access the information."

"You said the tracker is under the skin at my lower back. Will the Fortress tracker be in the same place?"

"I can do that," Jackson said. "However, we also have jewelry or watches with a tracker embedded in the design."

She breathed easier. "I like that idea much better."

"Rafe?" Brent looked at him. "Preference?"

He glanced at Kristi. "Might be overkill, but I want you to wear the jewelry and the watch."

"I don't have a problem with that. Will I have to return to the hospital to have Dad's tracker removed?"

"I'll take care of it before we leave PSI," Jackson said.

"That's another source of concern," Rafe said. "By now, whoever is behind Kristi's kidnapping knows she's at PSI. If he digs deep enough, he'll connect PSI to Fortress."

Brent folded his arms. "In other words, our anonymity is shot." He scowled. "Not what I wanted to hear, Torres."

"I'm not a fan myself, sir."

"I'll send an operative to Otter Creek with the jewelry and watch. You should have it by this afternoon. In the meantime, Eli, stay at PSI. Since we don't know how many men are involved in this plot, you need to cover your bases before you leave the compound."

"Yes, sir." Eli glanced at Rafe before returning his attention to his boss. "You're assigning Wolf Pack as Kristi's protection detail?"

"That's right. Problem?"

"Nope. You mind checking on Brenna and Dana?"

A slow smile formed on Brent's mouth. "I'll be happy to. Alexa and Rowan would love to spend time with them."

Kristi noticed that Jon seemed to relax at those words. Interesting. What was his connection to the women? The other Wolf Pack member, Cal, looked as though he wanted to say something, but didn't speak up.

Brent looked at Cal and said, "I've already checked on your woman. Rachelle is fine."

Rafe's teammate smiled and saluted Brent.

"Do you need to tell me anything else before I bring in Stewart?"

"I'll contact Marcus and ask him to talk with Kristi," Rafe said.

A slight nod. "Good. Kristi?"

"Yes, sir?"

"If you need anything, tell Rafe or another member of Wolf Pack. If we don't have it, we'll arrange to get it for you."

"The only thing I need is to find out who's behind the kidnapping. I want my life back."

"We won't stop until we've unmasked the culprit." He studied her a moment. "What else?"

Good grief. Brent Maddox was observant. "I need to be in Bakerhill on Monday."

"Unless we have the kidnapper wrapped up, that's not a good idea."

"I have a design consult that can't wait. The bride is marrying a Marine in two weeks, and he's deploying a week after the wedding. I promised to design and make her dress. I can't let her down."

"We'll handle the security arrangements," Eli said. "This is important, Brent."

On the table, Rafe's hand fisted.

Kristi glanced at him, flinching at the anger sparking in his eyes, before turning back to Brent. "I can't hide. I have a business to run with deadlines that can't be moved. I'll fully cooperate with Wolf Pack, but I have to return."

A slow nod from Brent. "We'll work it out. I'll bring in your father now."

A minute later, Alan Stewart appeared on the screen. "Kristi! Sweetheart, I'm so glad you're safe." He stopped speaking abruptly, a scowl forming on his face. "Turn your face to the side. Is that a bruise?"

Kristi turned her face to let him see her jaw. "I'm fine, Dad. The doctor said I'll recover in a few days."

"Where else are you hurt?"

"I'm not showing you my ribs or the back of my head."

"Are you sure you're all right?"

"Positive. Stop worrying. Rafe and his teammates are taking great care of me."

Alan turned his attention to Rafe. "Thank you. I'll never be able to repay you for saving my daughter."

"I didn't do it alone, sir. Several people were involved."

"Still, I owe you. Brent tells me that you risked your life going after Kristi before the others arrived." A grim expression settled on his face. "I shudder to think what might have happened to my daughter if you hadn't reached her in time."

"I'm glad I was close enough to help."

Alan looked at Kristi. "When are you coming home? I want to see you in person."

She glanced at Rafe and received a slight head shake in response to her silent question of how much to reveal. "I'm not sure yet. Rafe and his friends want to give me a chance to recover before we return."

"Good job," Rafe murmured.

Her father scowled. "Are you sure you're okay, sweetheart?"

"Yes. Please, don't worry."

"I can't help it. You and I are a team and have been since we lost your mother in the other kidnapping. I love you, Kristi."

"I love you, too, Dad."

"I'm not the only one who's worried about you. Hugh has been calling me every hour, wanting information."

Rafe turned to stare at Kristi.

Great. Just great. She didn't want to talk about Hugh Ward with her father in front of a room full of security people. "You can tell him I'm fine."

"Call him."

Her cheeks burned. "I don't know when I'll have a chance."

"He wants to release a statement to the press soon, honey. You can't blame him for being worried."

Oh, man. That's not what she wanted to hear. "This isn't the time, Dad. We'll talk later."

"You can't delay the announcement forever."

That's exactly what she intended to do. "I'll talk to Hugh as soon as I can."

"When Fortress brings you home, I want you to stay with me at the estate. I have great security. You'll be safe."

From the corner of her eye, she saw Rafe's hand clench again. Guess he wasn't in favor of her staying with her father. Suited her. She needed to be in her own home with her supplies. Working from home did have some advantages. "I'll see what Fortress recommends," she hedged.

That's as much as she was willing to concede. The truth was, she didn't intend to stay with her father. She needed to work to keep the nightmares at bay. She had plenty from childhood. Now, she had a whole host of new nightmares to add to the toxic brew. Thankfully, Rafe had been close last night. Each time she woke in a cold sweat, he reassured Kristi that she was safe.

Alan Stewart's expression hardened. "I'll talk to Brent," he said, as if that settled the matter. Her father was in for an unpleasant surprise. Brent Maddox didn't seem like the kind of man to cave to demands if a client's life was at stake.

He shifted his gaze to Rafe. "Keep my daughter safe."

"I'll guard her with my life, sir."

A nod, then, "See you soon, Kristi." Her father moved away from the screen, and Brent returned. "Update me in six hours." The screen went black.

The members of Wolf Pack turned to stare at Kristi. "Who is Hugh Ward, and what does he want to announce?" Rafe demanded.

CHAPTER EIGHT

Somewhere in the back of Rafe's mind, he remembered Callie talking about Hugh Ward although he couldn't remember her exact words. Regret welled inside him. Those memory lapses had been happening more frequently of late. A natural occurrence, he supposed. The woman he loved had been gone for more than three years.

Shoving his morbid thoughts aside to deal with later, he focused on what he did remember about Callie's assessment of Ward. She hadn't been impressed with the man which said something about him. Callie had looked for the best in everybody, even a street rat like Rafe. He could never understand what she saw in him, but had been grateful she'd loved him anyway.

Locking the past away for the moment, he focused on Kristi and noticed the color in her cheeks deepening. He frowned. Had he missed something? "Kristi?"

She sighed. "Hugh is a friend who wants to be more."

His suspicions rose. "How much more?"

"He proposed last month."

Shock reverberated through his system. "You're getting married?"

She shook her head. "He proposed, but I haven't accepted, and I won't."

"He seems to think you are. Even your father is anticipating a positive response to the proposal."

"He wants me to be happy and thinks Hugh is the answer. He's not."

"Does Hugh suspect you're going to turn him down?" Cal asked.

"He's an idiot if he doesn't," Eli said. "She hasn't given him an answer to his proposal for a month. My wife took about two seconds to say yes."

"Same for mine," Jon said.

"How will Ward react to the bad news?" Rafe asked. If the woman he'd been dating had turned him down after thinking about his proposal for a month, he wouldn't be happy about it.

"He might be disappointed, but in the long run I don't think he'll care."

Rafe and his teammates exchanged glances. Jackson raised an eyebrow. "Are you sure about that, Kristi? It's a blow to a man's ego for the woman he loves to reject him."

"Hugh isn't in love with me. We're friends. That's all."

"You don't love him."

"No."

"Why have you been dating him?" Jon asked.

"I haven't, at least not in the traditional sense. I told you, we're friends. We've gone to dinner together occasionally, and we attend many of the same fundraisers, but that's all."

Rafe scowled. "Then why does Ward want to tie himself to you in a loveless marriage?"

"Honestly, I think it has more to do with my father offering him a position as vice president of Stewart Group if he marries me."

"You're joking." His words came out flat. This was unbelievable.

"I'm afraid not. Dad likes Hugh and thinks he'd be perfect for me. He's not shy about telling me he wants grandchildren."

"But you don't love Ward."

Her lips curved. "How do you know I don't?"

"If you did, you would have accepted Ward's proposal already." He may not have spent much time in her company, but he remembered that Kristi wasn't afraid to speak the truth. "Why didn't you tell him right off that you wouldn't marry him?"

Her smile slipped. "I didn't want to disappoint my father. He is so sure Hugh is the perfect match for me. On paper, he looks perfect."

"And in person?"

She shrugged. "No chemistry, and I'm not in love with him. I won't ever fall in love with him." Kristi held up a hand. "I know. I should have turned him down and cut him loose. I will at the first opportunity."

He studied her for a moment. "Is he interested enough in the vice presidency to orchestrate your kidnapping?"

"He doesn't care enough to be that invested. Besides, if my father wanted him to join the company bad enough, he could simply offer the job without the marriage strings attached. I think that's what Dad will do when he realizes I won't marry Hugh."

Rafe dragged a hand down his face. No matter what Kristi thought, Ward was at the top of Rafe's suspect list along with any business rivals of Stewart Group. He grimaced. The list was likely to be a long one. Stewart Group was a powerhouse in several industries.

The investigation could wait for a while longer. Rafe wanted Stewart's tracker removed from Kristi's back, then he'd set up a meeting with Marcus Lang. The pastor of Cornerstone Church was the best counselor Fortress employed and frequently made himself available to Rafe as well as his teammates.

Once those two things were finished, he and Wolf Pack would figure out a safe place to take Kristi for the night.

Rafe turned to Jackson. "Can you remove the tracker in the infirmary?"

"No problem. Rio won't mind if we drop in." The medic glanced at Kristi. "You ready to get rid of the tracker?"

"Let's go."

Rafe stood and held out his hand. "I'll walk you to the infirmary."

"Cal, go with them," Eli said. "Jon and I will start digging for information."

Kristi hesitated in the doorway. "What information? We don't know anything yet."

Wolf Pack's leader smiled. "You never know what we can find."

Rafe nudged her into the corridor and started them toward the infirmary. "When they know something to share, you'll hear about it."

"Promise?"

"Your insights will be invaluable. Why would we hold back information?"

"To protect me."

"If that's the way your father treats you, he's doing you a disservice. You're an intelligent woman, and knowledge is empowering."

"Smart answer."

"The right one," he corrected. "You want to return to Bakerhill soon. That means you'll be among people we consider suspects in your kidnapping. If you trust the wrong person, you'll land in the hands of the kidnappers. In my experience, the more information you have, the better."

They arrived at the infirmary a moment later. "I'll wait out here," Cal murmured, and took up watch in the hall.

Rio glanced up when they walked inside and smiled. "How do you feel, Kristi?"

"Not bad, considering."

He studied her. "Still have a headache?"

She grimaced. "It shows?"

"Afraid so." Rio unlocked a cabinet and pulled out a small packet of capsules. "Mild pain medicine," he said as he handed the packet to Kristi along with a bottle of water. "Take two."

"Thanks." She popped two capsules in her mouth and washed them down with water.

"Do you have a privacy screen?" Jackson asked Rio.

"Sure." He opened a storage closet and brought out a folding screen. "Need help?"

"Maybe." Jackson looked at Kristi. "You mind if Rio gives me a hand?"

When she looked uneasy, Rafe asked, "Do you know where the tracker is located, Jackson?"

"Not an exact location, but if it's embedded under her skin I should be able to feel it." He shifted his gaze to Kristi. "May I check your lower back?"

"Just find the tracker, and get rid of it."

Her gaze shifted to Rafe. Despite her words, Kristi's voice conveyed her discomfort. "I can keep my gaze averted and stay with you," he said. "Or I can wait in the hall with Cal. The choice is yours, Kristi." He knew which option he preferred, but his preferences didn't matter.

"Stay."

More gratified than he should be, Rafe turned to Jackson and Rio. "What do you want me to do?"

Rio inclined his head toward the exam table. "Help her up. Kristi, lie on your stomach. Once Rafe closes his eyes, Jackson will see if he can find the tracker while I gather supplies to remove it."

At the exam table, Rafe lifted Kristi to the flat surface. Once she was situated on her stomach, he stood near her head and closed his eyes. A second later, her small hand slid into his.

He closed his fingers around hers. Okay, he couldn't lie to himself. Holding her small, soft hand felt better than good. It was amazing. Rafe squashed the guilt rising inside of him. Callie was gone. He didn't have a reason to feel guilty, except for the fact that another man wanted to marry her and had asked for that privilege.

He reminded himself again that Kristi hadn't accepted his proposal and wouldn't. If she'd waited this long to think about marrying Ward, she wasn't as invested in the relationship as the other man wanted.

Besides, just because he enjoyed holding the woman's hand didn't mean he was ready to move on to a dating relationship or that she'd give him a chance if he asked for one. Although Callie hadn't cared about Rafe's rough background, Kristi might.

"Do you mind holding my hand?" she asked.

He squeezed. "Of course not."

"Good, because I'm not a fan of needles or knives."

Rafe chuckled. "Neither am I. You can take my word for it, though. Rio and Jackson are great medics. They'll take good care of you."

"I'll remind you of that the next time I stitch you up," Jackson said.

"You've had stitches, Rafe?" Kristi's hand trembled in his.

"A time or two." More times than he could count. His career was tough on the body. "Privacy screen is up, Jackson?"

"Yep. Kristi, I found the tracker. It's embedded under the first layer of skin so it should be easy to remove. I'm going to apply a topical medicine to numb your skin. Once the medicine takes effect, I'll make a small incision and remove the tracker."

"Will I need stitches?"

"I don't think so. The tracker is the size of a grain of rice, and the incision will be small. The cut should heal on its own. I'll put a bandage over it to keep the cut clean. Ready?"

"Do it." A moment later, she hissed. "That's cold."

A chuckle. "Wolf Pack says the same thing when I use it on them."

Rafe snorted. "We're usually in the middle of the jungle or the desert, where the temperature is hot enough to melt your bones."

"You're such a whiner, Torres."

"Bite me, Conner."

"Ha. No, thanks, buddy. You're not my type. Kristi, can you feel this?"

She yelped.

Rafe scowled. "Did you use enough?" he asked Jackson.

"This isn't a heart transplant, Torres. You keep the pretty lady calm. Rio and I will handle the medical stuff." Amusement filled the medic's voice.

His cheeks burned. "She's already uncomfortable enough. I don't want her to hurt more."

"I'm all right, Rafe," she said.

"We'll give it another minute," Rio said, his tone mild. "The tracker won't take long to remove, Kristi."

"Good. I want it out of my back as soon as possible."

Rafe squeezed her hand again. "A few more minutes. Tell Rio and Jackson the story about your father and the bridal show."

"Sounds like a good story," Rio said.

Kristi laughed, the sound of her laughter doing odd things to Rafe's heart again. "I loved the outing. My father didn't." She relayed the story of the bridal show to the men. The medics chuckled.

"What inspired you to ask to attend the show for your birthday?" Jackson asked.

"I was interested in wedding dresses as a teenager. Not the normal dreaming of marrying a dark, handsome prince someday. I dreamed of designing and making the dresses. I studied the designs, figured out what I liked and didn't like, then tried to come up with designs of my own. My first attempts were so embarrassing. I made the dresses for myself and three of my friends. My dresses were horrendous. I was all about the design, not the body wearing the dress. The women in the fabric shop didn't know what to make of me buying yards and yards of fabric meant for wedding dresses or bridesmaids' dresses. Don't even ask how much money I spent on the fabric, lace, accents, and notions. I'd be embarrassed to admit the truth."

She sighed. "It was a glorious time of learning. By the end of my first year, I was doing a better job of matching body type with dress style. I also began designing my own clothes during that year. By the second year, my friends were asking me to make clothes for them. When I graduated from high school, I already knew I wanted to own a bridal shop. I never wavered from that goal."

"Your father must be proud of you," Rio said.

"He is although he's baffled about why I chose to specialize in wedding dresses when I could have designed all kinds of clothes. That's where my heart is, though."

"Do you still design your own clothes?"

"I don't have much time to do that these days. Kristi's Bridal is growing so fast I haven't had time for a vacation in four years."

Rafe frowned. "You need a break once in a while."

Jackson snorted. "Pot calling the kettle black, buddy."

"Zip it," he snapped.

"Just saying."

So what if Rafe hadn't taken a break since leaving the military? He'd been searching for Callie's killers. The two-week break from Fortress was long overdue. If he hadn't requested time off, Brent would have insisted he take a vacation soon. Capturing Callie's killers had gutted him all over again. Perhaps he'd heal after he ensured Kristi was safe.

A moment later, Rio said, "The tracker's out. Give us a minute, then you can sit up."

Rafe squeezed Kristi's hand again. "Doing okay?"

"I'm fine." She sounded breathless.

"Doesn't sound like it. What's wrong?"

"Lying on my stomach is painful with bruised ribs."

"All set," Jackson said. "Rafe, you can open your eyes now."

He saw Kristi struggling to get up. "Wait." Rafe released her hand. "Roll toward me. I'll scoop you up and set you on your feet. Should be easier on your ribs."

After Kristi rolled into Rafe's arms, he eased her to the floor. "Better?"

"Much. Thanks."

"If the incision bothers you, let me know," Jackson said.

"Thanks, Jackson. You, too, Rio."

"No problem, sugar," Rio said. "What's next on your agenda?"

Kristi looked at Rafe.

"A session with Marcus if I can arrange it," he said.

"Use one of the interrogation rooms. Interrogation instruction isn't until tomorrow."

Perfect. "Would you like a tour of PSI?" he asked Kristi.

She brightened. "I'd love one. This is where you trained, right?"

He smiled. "One of the places." Without second-guessing himself, Rafe reclaimed her hand. "Come on."

When they walked from the infirmary, Cal's lips curved. Rafe ignored him. He wanted Kristi to be comfortable with him and trust him. This wasn't about how good her hand felt in his.

As they headed toward the back door, he slid his phone from his pocket and called Marcus Lang. The pastor answered on the second ring.

"Marcus Lang."

"It's Rafe Torres."

"Good to hear from you, Rafe. How are you?"

"Okay for now."

A slight pause. "Need to talk?"

"Yes, but I can wait. I have a friend who can't."

"Talk to me."

He summarized what had happened. "Can you speak to my friend today?"

"I'll rearrange my schedule. Where and when?"

"PSI in an hour?"

"That works. See you soon." Marcus ended the call.

Rafe slid his phone into a pocket and opened the door for Kristi.

"Who is Marcus Lang?"

"One of our counselors. He's a good man and a great friend. You'll like him."

"Do I have to talk to him?"

"You've been through a trauma that will reawaken memories of your first kidnapping."

She sighed. "I want to forget all of it."

"Talking to Marcus will help you process what happened and lessen the nightmares."

"How do you know I have nightmares?"

"You forget what I do for a living. I have nightmares of my own."

"And talking to Marcus will really help?" She sounded skeptical.

He shrugged. "Helps me. I'll be talking to him soon for myself."

Kristi tugged on his hand to get him to stop walking. "Did my rescue resurrect bad memories?"

Rafe shook his head. "The mission before your rescue was rough." In more ways than one. "I'll need to purge some of that."

"Want to talk?"

His heart squeezed at her selfless offer. She had enough to handle without adding his issues. "Maybe later."

"You told Marcus we're friends. Are we, or were you just saying that to encourage Marcus to talk to me on short notice?"

He stilled. "Do you want to be friends?"

Kristi edged closer, her face tilting up toward his. "I do."

"I'd like that," he murmured. More than he should.

"I'm a good listener. I'd like to be your sounding board when you're ready to talk."

"Fair enough." He tugged her into motion again. "Do you want to see Crime Town?"

"As long as I don't end up a hostage in a fake bank robbery or something."

Rafe chuckled. "Don't worry. I'll protect you." From a fake crime or the real thing. No one was going to hurt Kristi again on his watch.

CHAPTER NINE

An hour later, Rafe escorted Kristi to the main building. Butterflies took flight in her stomach when she realized Rafe had held her hand for the whole tour of the PSI facility.

She cautioned herself not to make anything out of the innocent touch. She'd been around the SEAL long enough to know that he took her protection seriously.

She liked Rafe's protective streak. Although she and Hugh were friends, he never worried about Kristi's safety, not that he had reason to be concerned about protecting her before now. When they ate dinner together, he didn't mind if she drove herself to the restaurant. If they walked from one place to another, he didn't insist on walking closest to the street. He didn't even walk Kristi to her SUV after dinner was over if they arrived separately. Without asking, she knew Rafe would have insisted on escorting her to her vehicle and following her home to ensure she arrived safely. Hugh Ward was no Rafe Torres.

She understood what Callie had seen in Rafe. Oh, he was handsome and polite every time she'd talked to him when he was home on leave from the Navy. But now that she'd seen him in action, he was everything she dreamed about in a perfect date. Callie had been blessed to have Rafe in her life.

After Rafe opened the door and ushered her inside the building, he stopped. "Do you need anything before you talk to Marcus? Water, tea, a snack?"

Her stomach lurched at the idea of food. Kristi swallowed hard. "No food."

He cupped her cheek lightly, concern in his eyes. "Is your headache worse?"

She shook her head. The invisible bear was still pounding on her head with that mallet, but the pain meds from the medics helped. No, her problem was the upcoming session with the counselor. She so did not want to talk to him about her kidnapping.

"What's wrong?"

"I dread talking to Marcus." She sounded so lame. Kristi wrinkled her nose. "Ignore me. I'm being ridiculous. Talking to him won't hurt me."

"Come here," he murmured. When Kristi moved into his embrace, he closed his arms around her and held her against him.

Rafe didn't speak or ask questions. He just held her. By degrees, the tension inside Kristi uncoiled until she could take a full breath. Although reluctant to move, she said, "We should go."

"Take the time you need. Marcus will wait."

Kristi indulged her need for comfort for a few more minutes, soaking up his warmth and strength. Finally, she glanced up at the dark-eyed operative. "I'm ready now. Thank you for the hug. I needed it."

A smile curved his mouth. "No thanks needed. I think the hug did me as much good as it did you. Do you want me to stay in the room with you while you talk to Marcus or wait in the hall?"

"You would stay?"

"I'd like to be there for you, but the choice is yours."

She hated to be a coward, but she had bad memories of talking to a counselor after the first kidnapping when she was younger. "Stay with me."

"If you change your mind during the session, tell me and I'll wait in the hall."

Overwhelmed with gratitude for his kindness, she rose on her tiptoes and kissed his cheek.

Rafe's arms tightened around her as his gaze dropped from her eyes to her mouth. "I shouldn't do this," he whispered, but slowly lowered his head until his mouth settled on hers. He gave her plenty of time to stop him. She didn't.

At the touch of his mouth on hers, fire streaked along her nerve endings, bringing every inch of her body to life. When his tongue brushed against her bottom lip, asking silent permission to deepen the kiss, she didn't hesitate to give him what they both wanted. Why should she deny him or herself when Kristi wanted this kiss more than she wanted her next breath?

Heat poured into her bloodstream as the kiss went on and on, the SEAL changing the angle of the kiss until the touch was perfect. Good grief. Rafe Torres had serious kissing skills. Those butterflies in her stomach now turned into dive bombers, flying this way and that as his kiss deepened further, ramping up her desire and his.

When he broke the kiss, Rafe looked into her eyes. "Should I apologize?"

"Don't you dare. I've never been kissed like that in my life, and I enjoyed every second."

Rafe's gaze darkened. "Did you enjoy the kiss enough for a repeat performance later?"

She smiled. "I'm looking forward to it."

His gaze locked with hers, Rafe raised her hand and kissed the center of her palm. "We need to go."

Right. More kisses could wait. The Fortress counselor, however, had a schedule to keep.

Soon, Rafe led her into a small room where a dark-haired man waited for them. He stood and held out his hand to Rafe. "Good to see you again, Rafe. It's been a while."

"How is your wife?"

"Staying busy with the community center. She'll want to see you if you have time to stop by."

"I'll try. Marcus, this is Kristi Stewart. Kristi, my friend, Marcus Lang, the pastor of Cornerstone Church and one of the Fortress counselors."

She shook his outstretched hand. "It's nice to meet you, Pastor Lang."

"Marcus, please. Have a seat." He indicated one of the chairs on the opposite side of the table. "May I call you Kristi?"

"I'd prefer that."

"Do you want Rafe to remain in the room or wait in the hall while we talk?"

"I asked him to stay."

Marcus sat across from Kristi. "Before we start, do you need water or a soft drink?"

She glanced at Rafe. "Do you mind getting me a drink?"

"Of course not. I'll be back in a minute." Rafe looked at Marcus.

The pastor chuckled. "I'll watch over her."

"Coffee, Marcus?"

"I'd appreciate it. I was on call overnight as chaplain at the hospital."

When Rafe left the room, Marcus said to Kristi, "Tell me about yourself while we wait for Rafe's return."

Relieved that she wouldn't have to dig into the past 48 hours without Rafe for moral support, she told Marcus about Kristi's Bridal and the story of how she became interested in designing wedding dresses.

Just as she finished, Rafe tapped on the door and walked inside with a tray. He set a to-go cup in front of

Kristi along with a bottle of water, then handed Marcus a cup and claimed the last one on the tray for himself.

After he sat, Rafe tapped Kristi's cup. "Chamomile and mint tea from Nate. He said if that didn't help to let him know. He has a few other things he can try."

She smiled. "It's one of my favorite teas." One she often used when memories pressed too close and prevented her from sleeping at night, a common occurrence.

Marcus sipped his coffee and sighed. "Nate still has the magic touch. Only Sasha's coffee is better."

"Not surprising. She owns a coffee shop," Rafe said.

The pastor shifted his attention to Kristi. "Are you ready to talk about your experiences the past few days?"

Immediately, her stomach knotted. She set down her tea, afraid she wouldn't be able to swallow more of the soothing liquid. Under the table, Rafe's hand wrapped around her own.

She turned her hand over and threaded their fingers together. Kristi drew in a breath and nodded at the counselor. "I'm ready."

"There's no rush. Remember that everything you tell me is confidential. No one will hear any of this from me, and Rafe is a vault when it comes to secrets. You can trust him. With that in mind, take as much time as you need to tell me what happened."

Kristi's fingers clenched around Rafe's. His thumb stroked the inside of her wrist, the touch grounding her in reality instead of allowing her mind to be sucked back into her nightmares. How did he do that with one simple touch?

"I drove to the Sandoval Hotel in Gatlinburg to deliver a wedding dress to one of my best friends." She stopped, her eyes widening as dismay filled her. "Abby's getting married right now. I promised her I would attend the wedding."

"She'll understand," Rafe murmured. "Abby won't care that you missed the wedding as long as you're safe."

"You delivered Abby's dress?" Marcus asked.

Kristi dragged her attention back on task. She'd make amends somehow to Abby. Knowing her friend, the ceremony would be recorded. Kristi could watch the ceremony after Abby returned from her honeymoon in a month. "I caught up with her outside the room where her rehearsal dinner was in full swing. She was very relieved to see me." A smile curved her lips. "Abby was afraid her dress wouldn't arrive in time even though I never miss a deadline or delivery time."

"Did you join them for dinner?"

"The hotel staff had dinner waiting for me in the suite. It's one of the perks of being the owner's daughter. Anyway, I've been working 18-hour days for weeks to finish Abby's dress and several others. I was too tired to change into formal evening attire and make the social rounds. Abby's mother took the dress to her suite, and I went to my room to eat dinner. When I finished, I moved the serving cart to the hallway for the wait staff and planned to go to bed. Didn't quite work out that way."

"What happened?"

"When I turned to go back inside the suite, I heard a snapping noise behind me. Before I could see what made the noise, pain shot through my body. I blacked out."

"Stun gun," Rafe told Marcus.

"Ouch," he said, his expression filled with sympathy. "What happened when you regained consciousness, Kristi?"

"I woke up when we arrived at the cabin where Rafe found me. The kidnappers dragged me from the van. I fought them, but my coordination was off, and I made them angry." Her voice broke as fear swamped her anew.

"They expected you to be terrified, cowering at their feet," Marcus said. "But you didn't do that. You stood up to them."

Her lips curved. "A lot of good that did me. I have bruises to show for my efforts."

"They hurt you."

The smile faded. "They punched me, kicked me in the ribs, yanked me off the ground, and slammed me against the side of the van. The meanest kidnapper in the bunch told me if I continued to fight, I'd pay with a lot more than bruises."

Rafe's grip tightened.

"He threatened to rape you?" Marcus asked.

"An implied threat. I was terrified."

"Understandably so. What happened next?"

"The men forced me to go inside the cabin to the bedroom where Rafe found me. They tied me to the bed." Again, she stopped. Why was this so much worse than when she had relayed the story to Rafe the first time around?

She swallowed hard and forced herself to continue. "Once I was restrained, one of the men drugged me. I lost consciousness again seconds later, and woke up when Rafe climbed through the window to rescue me."

Kristi relayed the flight to safety, including the incident where Bull found her hiding behind the bushes. "I thought he would hurt me and take me away before Rafe returned. Fortunately, Rafe has impeccable timing and knocked Bull out without trouble. Not long after that, Josh and the others arrived to help."

She continued to tell him about the harrowing ride down the mountainside. "I couldn't see much," she admitted. "Rafe wanted me on the floor of the SUV for protection. All I can tell you is I heard gunshots and explosions, and then it was over. Josh drove us to Memorial Hospital where Dr. Anderson examined me." She grinned. "I fell madly in love with that man. He's the sweetest guy I've ever met."

Marcus chuckled. "All the women say that. My wife says if she hadn't fallen for me first, she would have fallen hard for Doc Anderson. I don't know how he does it." He sobered and shifted his gaze to Rafe. "Any problems in the hospital?"

"Another thug showed up dressed as an orderly to take Kristi for a CT scan. He wasn't happy when I refused to let him near her. Josh hauled him to the station for questioning. I haven't heard the results of that yet. After that incident, Anderson released Kristi, and Wolf Pack brought her here until we come up with a plan to keep her safe."

Marcus frowned. "How did this guy find her at Memorial? You and Durango wouldn't miss a tail."

"Our best guess is someone discovered her father had a tracker embedded under her skin, learned the frequency, and followed the signal to Otter Creek. That problem has been resolved. Rio and Jackson removed the tracker."

"How do you feel about all this, Kristi?"

"Ticked off and afraid at the same time. I'm ticked off that my father tagged me like an endangered animal without my permission or knowledge. I'm also afraid the kidnappers will keep coming at me until they succeed in capturing or killing me."

"Not happening on my watch," Rafe said.

She squeezed his fingers. "I'm also afraid that Rafe or one of his teammates will be hurt the next time the kidnappers come at me again. I don't want them hurt because of me."

Marcus's expression softened. "Protecting you is their mission. They are among the best in the business, Kristi. Trust them to do their jobs."

"They're not invincible. They can be hurt. I can't live with that."

"Any injuries they might have are on the kidnappers, not you. You aren't responsible for their actions." He sipped his coffee. "Wolf Pack is highly trained. The military spent millions of dollars training them, and Fortress honed and sharpened the skills Wolf Pack learned throughout their military careers. You saw Rafe and the others in action. They must have made the kidnappers appear to be amateurs."

Durango and Rafe made the kidnappers look like bumbling idiots.

"Kristi, why were you so reluctant to talk to me?" Marcus's tone conveyed kindness and gentleness. His eyes, however, seemed to pierce her soul. Did he know about her previous kidnapping?

She glanced at Rafe to find his gaze on her. He gave a slight nod, silently encouraging her to tell Marcus the truth. "I don't want to do this," she whispered.

"Talking about the kidnapping reduces its power over you. Fight back."

Kristi squared her shoulders. She wasn't a traumatized ten-year-old kid. She was a grown woman capable of talking about her nightmarish past.

Rafe was right. She couldn't allow the kidnappers to win. If she cowered and hid from her past, she gave the memories power over her present. Kristi had fought too hard to rebuild her strength to let these kidnappers tear her down again.

She faced Marcus. "I was kidnapped when I was ten years old. Three men broke into the house while my father was away on business. They murdered my mother when she tried to stop them, and snatched me from my bed. My father received a ransom demand of $2 million which he paid. The kidnappers drove me to a park and turned me loose." Kristi began to tremble.

"What aren't you telling me?" Marcus asked. "What's making you so afraid even now?"

Telling the counselor the truth took three tries. "They locked me in a closet for three days. I still have trouble with darkness to this day."

Rafe wrapped his arm around her shoulders.

Tears streaked down her face as memories she tried to suppress resurfaced. "One of the kidnappers was a child molester."

From somewhere, Marcus produced a box of tissues and slid them across the table to her. "Did your father take you to a counselor?"

She nodded as she dabbed her eyes and face with a tissue. The tears wouldn't stop. "According to Dad, the child psychologist was the best in Nashville with many credentials and high praise from clients. I didn't like him, and he wasn't fond of me. He did, however, see me as a subject for his clinical research."

"What happened?" Marcus asked.

"He insisted on completing a few minutes of each session in total darkness. He justified it as therapy for my new darkness phobia."

"Oh, baby," Rafe whispered and kissed her temple.

"I'm guessing the therapy didn't work," Marcus said mildly although his eyes showed anger on her behalf.

Kristi gave a choked laugh. "Not a bit. I still can't stand the darkness, and I avoid counselors like the plague. No offense intended, Marcus."

Rafe groaned. "The cave. I'm sorry I put you through that, Kristi."

"You didn't know the root cause of my problem. We didn't have a choice, Rafe."

"You have more courage than most of the men I served with in the military. They wouldn't have been able to face their worst nightmare like you did."

Marcus set down his coffee cup. "How did you sleep last night in the hospital?"

"Rafe was there, and I had a light on in the room." She smiled. "I would have slept better without the nurses coming in to check on me every hour."

A chuckle. "I understand. They're great at doing that. Take a minute, and close your eyes, Kristi. Breathe deep and relax."

"Come here." Rafe turned her toward him. He wrapped his other arm around her waist and held her against him.

Safety. Security. Warmth. She could get used to this. Minutes passed as the men spoke of people and events around Otter Creek while she slowly went limp against Rafe.

Minutes or hours later, Marcus said, "Kristi, how do you feel?"

"Like I need a long nap."

Rafe palmed the back of her head, his touch surrounding her with care and comfort. "If you want to lie down, I'll find a place for you to rest."

She shook her head. "I'm not a good napper. If I sleep in the day, I can't sleep at night." When she could sleep at all, that is. Nights were never restful.

"Stay with me and Paige," Marcus said. "We have plenty of room for you and Wolf Pack."

"Thanks for the offer, Marcus, but we can't impose on you," the operative said. "The kidnappers already know we're in Otter Creek. I don't want to bring danger to your doorstep."

Kristi's heart sank. The last thing she wanted to do was endanger these good men. The truth was, though, everyone around her was at risk until the culprit behind the kidnapping had been caught and unmasked.

CHAPTER TEN

After Marcus left for another appointment, Rafe wanted to help Kristi take her mind off the trauma of her past. Even now, he'd love to learn the name of the kidnapper who abused her so long ago, track him down, and teach the abuser a lesson he'd never forget. Since that wasn't possible for the moment, he turned his focus to distracting the woman with the courage of a lion.

He stood and held out a hand. "Walk with me."

Kristi wiped the last of her tears away with a tissue and grasped his hand. "Where are we going?"

"Someplace I think you'll like." Rafe didn't know of a better place to offer a distraction in the PSI compound. He'd spent many hours there in his downtime when his own demons raged at him.

Rafe led her to the back door and headed for the S & R training facility. Although the chance of the kidnappers gaining entry into the PSI compound was low, Rafe wouldn't risk Kristi's safety by keeping her outside for an extended period of time in one place. The mastermind behind the kidnapping might have hired a sniper.

After sliding his card through the reader and entering a code, Rafe ushered Kristi inside the building. Immediately, the sound of dogs barking brought a smile to his face and unraveled the knots in his gut. During the weeks he'd trained at PSI, Rafe had discovered the S & R dogs had the ability to soothe his raw emotions, and longed for a pet of his own.

"Dogs?" Kristi turned to him with a puzzled expression.

"PSI has a Search-and-Rescue training arm. This is the indoor training facility. Do you like dogs?"

"I love them, but I've never had a pet. I loved playing with my friends' dogs, though."

"Why didn't you adopt one when you moved away from home?"

"I spent too much time building up Kristi's Bridal. Do you have a dog?"

"I'm deployed on missions frequently, and I never know how long I'll be gone. Wouldn't be fair to board a pet for weeks at a time."

Kristi opened her mouth to say something, then changed her mind.

Curious, he squeezed her hand. "What?"

She refused to meet his gaze. "You don't have anyone to watch a dog or cat for you?"

His lips twitched when he realized what she was asking in a roundabout fashion. "I don't have a girlfriend, Kristi. If I did, I wouldn't have kissed you." His name was called from the other side of the training arena.

Rafe led Kristi in the direction of Deke Creed, one of the PSI K-9 trainers. He shook the former US Marshal's hand. "How are you, Deke?"

"Can't complain. Who's your friend?"

"Deke Creed, meet Kristi Stewart. She's a friend who's also a principal. Kidnapping vic."

Deke shook her hand. "I'm glad you're safe. You have a good man protecting you."

Kristi smiled. "I think so, too."

He turned back to Rafe. "What brings you to dog central?"

"Kristi and I need a stress break. I could go a few rounds on the mat with the trainees, but this was the best place to get a break without adding to my bruises."

She gasped. "You're hurt? You didn't say anything to Dr. Anderson."

"Just a few bruises, Kristi. Nothing worth bothering the doc over." He'd suffered worse injuries on missions and kept going without missing a beat. "Tell me you have a good distraction for us, Deke."

"The trainees are out with their K-9 partners, searching for one of the trainers pretending to be a lost hiker. I do have a foster dog here that we were testing for the program."

Rafe's eyebrows rose. "The dog's not working out?"

Deke shook his head. "He's too easily distracted. He'll make a great family pet for someone, but Oliver isn't S & R material."

"What kind of dog is he?" Kristi asked.

"All American Mutt and all heart. Want to meet him?"

"I'd love to."

Deke led them to the other end of the indoor arena where a dog played with one of the other trainers. The dog's medium-length fur was a mixture of brown, white, and black. The corners of Rafe's mouth lifted. Cute dog. When the trainer tossed a frisbee, the 40-pound dynamo raced after the toy, caught it in mid-air, then raced back, dropping the toy at his feet.

"Oliver, come. Sit." When the dog plopped down on his butt, Deke knelt and rubbed the dog. "Want to pet him, Kristi? He's a sweet boy."

She knelt beside the trainer and ruffled Oliver's fur, laughing when the dog nuzzled her neck and licked her face. Her eyes twinkled.

Deke chuckled. "Want to play fetch? He loves the game."

"Sure."

He grabbed the frisbee and handed it to her. "Just toss it. Oliver is great at fetching." He grinned. "Not so great at finding hidden people or objects, though."

While she and Oliver played, Deke drew Rafe aside. "What's her story?"

Rafe summarized the events of the past two days, mentioning the first kidnapping in passing. The other man didn't need the details. If Kristi wanted to share them, that was up to her.

Deke uttered a soft whistle. "Tough few days. Any idea what the kidnappers wanted aside from money?"

"That's enough for most."

The Marshal slid him a pointed glance. "Is this kidnapping tied to her first one?"

"I don't know, but I'll find out." Digging into that crime would give him a great excuse for discovering the child abuser's name.

They watched the woman and dog play together for several minutes. "She's good with him, and it's obvious Oliver loves her," Deke murmured. "Think she's interested in a pet?"

"Maybe. Why?"

"Since Oliver is an S & R fail, he'll have to go back to the animal shelter if I don't find him a home. He'd already been there for six months without being adopted. You didn't see him when I brought him out of the shelter, Rafe. Oliver hated that place."

"How do you know?"

"I went back in the next day to sign paperwork and took Oliver with me. He didn't want to go into the building. Oliver must have thought I was going to leave him there. I don't want to take him back."

His heart went out to the dog. "Didn't they take good care of him at the shelter?"

"They do the best they can, but Oliver wants a family of his own. I think he's chosen Kristi."

"She doesn't know anything about dogs."

"How long will you be in Otter Creek?"

Rafe grimaced. "Not long enough for my peace of mind. She needs to be back in Bakerhill tomorrow for a bridal consult, and Kristi won't want to take Oliver into a potentially dangerous situation."

"I'll teach her the basics of dog care if she's interested. As far as the timing goes, I can keep him here and do more training with him until you resolve her situation."

His hand fisted. "Could be a while. At the moment, we have a male friend who wants to be her husband to advance his career, her father wants Kristi to marry the friend, and who knows how many business rivals of Stewart Group and possibly Kristi's Bridal who might resort to desperate tactics to get ahead. At the moment, they're all on my list of suspects."

Deke chuckled. "Buddy, you need to narrow the possibilities. Otherwise, you'll be on this mission for a long time."

Rafe snorted. "Tell me something I don't know."

"Okay. You have a thing for the lady."

His eyes narrowed. "A thing?"

"Yeah, a thing." Deke looked at him. "Does that mean you're finally letting go of Callie?"

Rafe's gaze shifted to Kristi. "That's what my two weeks of leave was about, to find closure. Maddox owes me twelve days. I was hiking on the same mountain where Kristi was being held, so he sent me to rescue her."

"No coincidences in our business."

"I don't see how my past could be connected to her kidnapping."

"Did you know her before this op?"

"She was a friend of Callie's. Although I talked to her while I dated Callie, no one with a brain in his head would assume Kristi and I had a relationship. We didn't."

"And now?"

He watched the beautiful woman playing with Oliver, eyes sparkling, enjoying this moment of respite from fear and stress. Her strength and courage tugged at him. So did her beauty. He was a guy, after all. He'd have to be dead not to appreciate her picturesque features. "I kissed her," he admitted. "I haven't kissed a woman since I lost Callie."

Deke squeezed Rafe's shoulder. "Don't pass up the opportunity to see if you two have something special together."

Maybe. Although he still felt tied to Callie, she was gone. Did he have the courage to risk his heart again? Provided, of course, that Kristi was interested in something beyond a kiss or two and an offer of friendship. Just because Callie overlooked his upbringing didn't mean Kristi would be willing to do the same. Society princesses didn't normally form relationships with street rats from the wrong side of town.

When Oliver dropped the frisbee at Kristi's feet and sat, panting heavily, Deke led the dog to the watering station.

As Oliver drank his fill, Deke turned to Kristi. "What do you think of him?"

"He's wonderful."

"Would you be interested in giving him a home?"

Kristi's eyes widened. "Me? I've never owned a dog. I don't know the first thing about caring for one."

"I'll be glad to give you dog whispering lessons." He smiled. "Really, all you need to do is give him food, water, exercise, and a ton of love. He's house broken. Oliver will do the rest of the work in your relationship."

She sat on the arena floor and hugged Oliver. The dog leaned against her and gazed up at her with adoration in his brown eyes, occasionally licking and nuzzling her face while he rested. "I love him," she said, running her hand over his head and down his back. "But if I take him now, he might be hurt. The kidnappers weren't gentle with me. I'd never forgive myself if anything happened to Oliver."

"I'll keep him here and do more training with him until Wolf Pack resolves your problem. After you're safe, you and Rafe can return to Otter Creek and pick up Oliver. When you do, I'll teach you how to care for this sweet boy."

She looked at Rafe, hope in her eyes. "What do you think?"

"I think you and Oliver are already a matched pair. If you want him, go for it. I'll give you a hand with him when I'm in town. I'd enjoy playing with Oliver when I'm not on a mission." And spending time with this beautiful woman.

A gorgeous smile curved her lips, tugging at his heart. "I'd like that."

"Great." Deke rubbed his hands together. "Oliver will need a good veterinarian to keep his shots up to date. You won't have to deal with that for nine months or so. I'll give you the names of vets we trust in and around the Nashville area. I'll see if I can find one in Bakerhill before you come for him."

"What do I owe you?"

"Nothing, Kristi. I'm just happy Oliver will be with someone who loves him."

"What would have happened to him if I didn't agree to take him?"

"I would have returned him to the animal shelter."

Horror filled her eyes. "Dog jail?" She hugged Oliver close as though protecting him from that fate. "No way. I'm not sending him back to jail."

Deke laughed. "It's not quite that bad, but Oliver wasn't a fan of the shelter."

She rested her cheek on top of Oliver's head. "Where will he stay until Rafe and I return?"

"With me and my family." He winked. "No dog jail."

"I can't thank you enough for introducing me to Oliver. I promise that I'll take good care of him."

"I wouldn't have offered you the opportunity to adopt Oliver if I believed otherwise."

"We need to find the rest of Wolf Pack," Rafe said. The operative bringing Kristi's tracker jewelry should be arriving soon.

Kristi sighed and hugged Oliver close for a moment before getting to her feet. "Would it be okay if I stopped to see him before I leave town, Deke?"

"If you have time, sure. Don't worry, Kristi. He'll be waiting for you when you return to Otter Creek."

"What if he forgets me?"

"Won't take him long to fall for you all over again. Go take care of business, then come get your furry boy. I'll keep him safe and happy for you. He might even know a trick or two when you return."

Rafe walked with Kristi from the training arena to the main building. He stopped by the office.

Gloria, one of the office workers, brightened when she saw Rafe. "Back for a refresher course, Rafe?"

He shuddered. "I have a few months before I have to return for Josh and Trent's brand of torture."

The lady laughed. "I hear the same thing from all the trainees. They're convinced the trainers stay awake all night coming up with ways to make them suffer untold agonies in the training rooms and on the fields."

"I wouldn't be surprised to learn the rumors were true. Brent promised to send me a package."

"It arrived five minutes ago." She tugged open a drawer and pulled out a sealed manila envelope which she handed to Rafe. "Can I do anything else for you?"

He smiled. "No, but thanks, Gloria." Wrapping his hand around Kristi's, Rafe led her to the interrogation room where she'd talked to Marcus. After closing the door, he ripped open the envelope and poured the contents onto the table.

Kristi gasped and said, "Lilies of the valley. That's my favorite flower. The jewelry is beautiful, Rafe."

Satisfaction filled him. Her expression of delight meant she would be likely to wear the jewelry. No, it wasn't the same quality of the jewelry she wore to her glitzy fundraisers. Still, Fortress made sure the tracking jewelry was as attractive as possible. The fact that Zane always seemed to know which of the five design types to send was a bit of a mystery, especially since he hadn't met Kristi yet. The communications and tech guru was sharp, though. He'd completed enough research into Kristi's background to guess the type of design she would appreciate the most.

Lilies of the valley were elegant, deceptively delicate, and reminded him of Kristi. The lady had a hidden well of strength that Rafe admired. "I know this isn't the type of jewelry you're used to, but will you wear it, even inside your home?"

Her brows knitted. "How do you know I don't wear jewelry like this?"

"I attended fundraisers and dinners with Callie, remember? You and the rest of your friend group always wore museum-quality gems set in gold and platinum designs. This isn't in the same league."

She waved his concern aside and picked up the bracelet. "Dad insisted I wear them for the sake of his image. I don't wear jewels like that on a daily basis. I'm more comfortable with simple, elegant jewelry like this. How did you know what to choose for me?"

"I wish I could claim credit for the choice, but Zane Murphy, our communications and tech wizard is responsible. He has a knack for choosing the right design for the women in our lives." He deliberately chose that phrase and waited to see how she would react.

Kristi's gaze flew to his face. "Does that include your clients?"

"Principals," he corrected. "This jewelry isn't issued to our principals."

"You made an exception for me."

"Do you want it to be an exception?"

She watched him a moment before laying the bracelet on the table and stepping closer to him. "If I told you I didn't, would I scare you off?"

Rafe wasn't one for dancing around the truth. "I don't scare off easily, Kristi." He raised his hand to cup her cheek. "Do you?"

Kristi nuzzled his palm. "No. Can I tell you a secret?"

"Sure."

"I've always admired and respected you."

Pleasant surprise whirled inside Rafe. Would it be enough to build a relationship on? "Enough to take a leap into the unknown with me?"

She froze. "You said we're friends."

A slow smile curved his mouth. "I don't kiss my friends like I kissed you. We have explosive chemistry." He brushed his thumb over her bottom lip, longing to feel her mouth under his again. "There's something between us, something that I'd like to explore if you're willing to take a chance on me."

"Yes."

He blinked. "You don't want to think about it?"

She shook her head.

Rafe slid his hand around her nape and drew her against him. "We should seal the deal with a kiss," he murmured.

"Excellent suggestion." She lifted her face to his.

He captured her mouth in a series of gentle, teasing kisses before the taste of her drew him like a moth to the flame, and he deepened the kiss. His blood heated to the temperature of molten lava as it flowed through his veins. Knowing she was safe for the moment, Rafe relaxed his guard enough to focus solely on the woman in his arms.

The longer the kiss spun out, the more Kristi melted against him. He began to wonder if he would ever get enough of her taste and the touch of her skin under his calloused palms.

The sensation jolted him back to awareness. Sometime during the past few minutes, his hands slid under her shirt to settle at her waist. His lack of control startled him. Time to dial it back before he moved them too far too fast.

Rafe broke the kiss and discovered he wasn't ready to step back. He blew out a breath and rested his forehead against hers. "Give me a minute."

"Fair warning. If you turn me loose, I'll drop to the floor." She smiled. "My legs are weak. You have serious kissing skills."

He chuckled, her humor giving him a chance to wrench himself back under control. "I'm not steady myself, lady."

At that moment, Rafe's phone signaled an incoming text. He slid the phone from his pocket and glanced at the screen. "Duty calls." He dropped a quick kiss on Kristi's lips and eased away from her. "After you put on the jewelry, we'll join the rest of Wolf Pack in the conference room."

"Did Jon and Eli learn something?"

"They did. Let's find out what they discovered." Hopefully, the information was substantial enough to give them a suspect to pursue. Rafe wanted Kristi safe. He didn't intend to lose another woman he cared about to murder.

CHAPTER ELEVEN

With Kristi's hand clasped in his, Rafe entered the conference room where his teammates waited. He ignored Wolf Pack's questioning glances when they noticed him holding Kristi's hand. He seated her, then joined Kristi at the table. "Tell me you have something good, Jon."

"Josh will arrive soon. Zane hacked the Gatlinburg police's computer system and found information on some of the kidnappers. Eli and I uncovered preliminary information about Ward."

Jon's information about Ward must warrant diving deeper into the man's background. Although Ward being a suspect didn't hurt Rafe's feelings, he didn't want Kristi hurt by a friend's betrayal.

The door opened, and Josh strode inside. Fatigue lined the Delta soldier's face.

Rafe had been there. That kind of fatigue wasn't simply physical. The mental strain of dealing with the dregs of society weighed you down. Josh needed downtime with his wife and daughters.

"Coffee?" Cal asked.

"I need a tanker truck full of coffee," Josh said as he dropped into a chair across from Rafe and Kristi.

"I'll bring the largest cup Nate has," he promised and left.

"How are you, Kristi?" Josh asked.

"Sore," she admitted. "Lingering headache along with a reminder of bruised ribs every time I breathe, and grateful to be alive."

A grim expression settled on Jon's face. "You have reason to be grateful. The identified kidnappers had records. Their arrests run the gamut from breaking and entering all the way to rape and murder."

Josh slanted him a hard look. "Do I want to know where you got your information?"

"A smart man wouldn't ask."

"That's what I thought."

"Who is the fake orderly?" Rafe asked Josh.

"Victor Harmon, and he has a rap sheet a mile long. He's been in and out of jail since he was eighteen years old."

"Juvie record?"

A nod. "Sealed."

"Want to look at it?" Jon asked.

Josh glared. "I didn't hear that."

"Hear what?"

Cal returned and set a large to-go cup in front of Josh. "What did I miss?"

"The fake orderly's name is Victor Harmon. Long acquaintance with the law in your neck of the woods."

The former homicide cop frowned. "I recognize the name. Assaults, drunk-and-disorderly, armed robbery, attempted rape?"

"That's the one."

"Last I heard, Harmon was in jail."

"Paroled. Kristi's kidnapping was his first foray into that area."

"Lucky me," she muttered.

"Do you have enough to hold him?" Rafe asked.

"Yeah. Multiple parole violations. Two of Cal's buddies from the Metro Nashville PD will escort Harmon back to Nashville tomorrow. He won't bother Kristi again for a long time."

"I want to talk to him."

"Forget it, Torres."

"Why?"

Josh leveled a pointed look at him. "Circumstances have changed."

While Rafe couldn't deny that truth, he didn't like having access to Harmon denied. "Would you back off if you were in my shoes?"

A snort. "Ethan wouldn't let me anywhere near Harmon if that criminal threatened my wife or daughters. He knows I'd kill him at the first opportunity."

Rafe's lips curved. Ethan Blackhawk, Josh's brother-in-law, was also Otter Creek's police chief and an Army Ranger with serious tracking skills. Rafe would have to set aside his plan to talk to the kidnapper. He doubted Harmon knew much anyway.

Josh sipped his coffee and turned to Jon. "I assume your hacking has been lucrative."

"Would I do that?"

He snorted. "You live to thwart law and order, frog boy."

The sniper chuckled. "I looked into Hugh Ward's background. If you're commenting on my computer skills as a Fortress operative, you know me well. If you're commenting as a cop, I'll tell you what anyone could find, then tell my teammates more interesting things."

Josh rolled his eyes and sipped more coffee. "Talk. I'm off duty."

"I can't imagine what you found," Kristi said. "Hugh's a good man."

"What do you know about him?"

"We've been friends since elementary school. He's a hedge fund manager for Starbridge. His parents and mine met in college and became fast friends. Hugh is well-liked and is a patron of many charities. He asked me to marry him. I haven't turned him down yet, but I will as soon as I have a chance to talk to him."

Josh's eyebrows rose. "Isn't Starbridge owned by Ward Industries?"

"That's right."

"Ward Industries is a rival of Stewart Group. Your father knows about Ward's marriage proposal?"

"He's pressuring me to accept. If I do, Dad will bring Hugh on board Stewart Group as a vice president."

"Sounds like he's offering a dowry to the man who marries his daughter."

Her cheeks colored. "Dad likes Hugh and views this as an encouragement to do what he thinks is best for me."

"Is it?"

"No."

The lack of hesitation or a detailed, defensive explanation settled the last of Rafe's doubts about his own relationship with Kristi. Did Ward see her as a means to a career advancement or was he truly in love with her? "What did you learn about Ward, Jon?"

"He's broke."

Kristi gasped. "That can't be true. Hugh has a large trust fund left to him by his grandfather."

"That was true at one time, but not now. At his current spending rate, he's six months away from insolvency."

"This doesn't make sense." She looked puzzled. "He's always had a good head for business. Did he make some bad investments?"

"More like bad bets."

"Gambling? I don't understand. I've never seen him gamble or heard him talk about it."

"Want to see a copy of his casino markers?"

"How could I not know this?"

"How much does he owe?" Rafe asked.

"I'm still digging, but the current total is $200,000."

Rafe whistled softly.

Kristi stared at the sniper with wide eyes.

"Oh, man." Eli shook his head. "Ward's toast if he doesn't pay that off in a hurry."

"That's just one casino," Jon murmured. "I think he has markers at other casinos, too."

"But casinos don't have leg breakers," Kristi said. "Won't they wait until he can pay them?"

"That's not how the process works." Rafe laid his hand over hers. "If he doesn't pay them by the agreed upon date, they'll take him to court and force him into bankruptcy. He'd recover from that eventually, but no one will trust money to a hedge fund manager who can't handle his personal finances."

"I don't understand why Hugh didn't use what's left in his trust fund to pay off the debt."

"He's draining the trust fund at a rapid rate," Jon said. "My guess is he's making large payments to several casinos to keep them off his back and maintain his lifestyle."

"What about his investments? Can he liquidate those?"

"He's been selling his stock for the past year, a little at a time. He sold the last of it two weeks ago."

Kristi jerked. "But that's when..." She groaned. "Oh, no."

"What is it?" Rafe asked.

"That's when Hugh began pressuring me to accept his proposal."

Had Ward assumed that Kristi would bail him out of debt once they were married or was something else going on? "Financially speaking, what would happen if you and Ward married?"

"Not much change. I'm not giving up Kristi's Bridal, and Hugh planned to work for Dad. He mentioned life insurance policies, but I think a husband and wife should have life insurance with the spouse as the beneficiary."

Ice water flowed through Rafe's veins. "Did he mention a specific amount?"

She shook her head.

He glanced at Jon. "Find out."

"On it."

Rafe turned back to Kristi. "You have a trust fund."

She nodded. "A legacy from my grandmother. I used part of the money to start Kristi's Bridal, but I repaid what I took out. I'm holding the fund for any children I might have."

"Would you have given Ward money from the fund once you were married?"

"If he needed it, yes."

"How much is in the fund?"

"Enough to bail Hugh out of trouble."

"How much?"

"About $10 million."

Holy cow. He stared. "Are you serious?"

"That would solve Ward's problem," Jackson muttered.

"Not in the long run," Josh said. "Ward's hooked."

"Hugh wouldn't arrange for my kidnapping," Kristi said. "He's not like that."

"No offense, sugar, but you didn't know Ward was addicted to gambling," Eli said.

"How do you know it's an addiction? Maybe he had a run of bad luck one night in a casino."

"When a man tries to gamble his way out of a gambling debt, he has a problem," Jon said.

"You know for a fact that's what he's doing?"

"I'm sorry, Kristi. There's no mistake. The amount of money he owes takes a while to accumulate. This wasn't an overnight binge."

"Keep digging," Rafe said.

"Look at the hedge fund," Josh said. "If Ward was over his head in debt and desperate for money, he might have looked for short-term cash flow until he could make other arrangements." He looked at Kristi.

Rafe frowned. Was Kristi part of Ward's solution to his problems? Talk about cold-blooded calculation. He hated the distress and hurt on Kristi's face. He threaded his fingers through hers. "We'll find out what's going on. If he's behind the kidnapping, he'll pay." In more ways than one. No matter what happened between him and Kristi, Rafe would see to that personally.

"Have you connected the kidnappers to Ward?" Cal asked.

"Not yet. I'm juggling several searches," Jon said.

"Can Zane help?"

"He's buried with other priorities at the moment. I'll get it done."

"We'll help when we're not on watch."

"If you have more information, talk fast," Josh said. "I'm due in a training class soon." He sent a wicked grin Rafe's direction. "Close quarters combat."

Rafe groaned, remembering multiple deep bruises he'd suffered sparring with Durango's leader in after-class sessions with the Delta soldier. "Better them than me."

"Your time for a refresher course is coming soon, Torres. I have several new techniques to teach to you."

He scowled. "Where are you finding these techniques? I'm as well trained as you are."

Josh chuckled. "I'll tell you when you come in for class."

"Can't wait," he lied. Even though he learned a lot from Cahill and his partner, Alex Morgan, Rafe hated the sessions that reminded him of the worst days in BUDS.

Josh shifted his attention to the sniper. "Anything else before I head to class?"

"I looked into Alan Stewart's background and his company."

Oh, man. Rafe didn't know how many more blows Kristi could take.

"Stewart Group has cash-flow issues."

"This situation keeps getting worse," Kristi whispered.

"More revelations will come. By the time we finish, no one will have secrets."

"Including me?"

"Do you have something to hide?" Jon countered.

She frowned. "No, but I don't want my life under a microscope."

"It's necessary," Rafe said. "Someone you know is probably responsible for your kidnapping. We have to look into your life to find the connection."

"How would you like it if your life was on display?"

"I'd hate it," he admitted. "But I was a federal cop long enough to understand why it's necessary."

"You and your team looking into my life is bad enough, but I feel terrible that you have to tear apart the lives of my friends and family, too." Kristi sighed. "By the time this investigation is complete, I may not have any friends left."

Eli stretched, pushed away from the conference table, and stood. "Rio extended an invitation to stay with him and Darcy tonight."

Rafe breathed a sigh of relief. Rio's Victorian home was large enough to accommodate all of them and was a fortress. Although a medic, Rio was as deadly as his fellow Delta soldiers and just as safety conscious. He was fiercely protective of his wife. "When do we leave?"

"Another hour. You're with Kristi until then. The rest of Wolf Pack promised to lend a hand in Crime Town."

His eyebrows rose. "You're offering to play victims?"

Jon snorted. "Not a chance. We're stalking the rescue team while they attempt to rescue a hostage."

Rafe turned to stare at Josh. "A new training technique?"

A shrug. "We have to deal with that on the field."

"Yeah, but most of these recruits are bodyguard trainees, not operatives."

"We have a few possible operatives in the mix. The training is good for all of them, though. Criminals don't play fair."

"True. Kristi and I will be at the indoor S & R training arena, playing with the dogs." After the latest revelations, Kristi needed more time with Oliver.

"I'd rather play with dogs than stalk trainees," Jackson said.

"Tough." Josh rose. "You can play next time. For the next hour, you're stalking trainees."

"You never let me have any fun," he complained.

"Keep it up, Conner, and I'll be adding to the list of fun things you and Wolf Pack do when you return for training."

Cal clamped a hand over Jackson's mouth and maneuvered the medic toward the door while the rest of the men followed, chuckling.

Rafe waited with Kristi until Wolf Pack and Josh filed from the conference room. When they were alone, he drew Kristi into his arms. "Are you okay?" he murmured against her ear.

She relaxed against him, her head nestled against his shoulder. "I will be. I dislike having my privacy invaded, and I hate to be the reason my friends and father will be under the microscope."

"It's necessary. We don't do it lightly."

She burrowed deeper into his arms. "May I ask a question?"

"Shoot. I'll answer if I can." Some things he'd never tell her because of confidentiality. Others, he wouldn't talk about to prevent worse nightmares for her.

"Did the size of my trust fund cause you to rethink a relationship with me?"

"Does my lack of a trust fund bother you?" He wasn't hurting financially. His years as a SEAL and now in black ops work had enabled him to set aside quite a bit of money. His stash, however, wasn't anywhere close to the level of Kristi's trust fund.

"Of course not. I don't care about the size of your bank account. I care about you."

Another ball of ice in his stomach melted. "Same goes for me. I wouldn't care if you had a billion dollars in that trust fund. The money isn't important to me. You are."

She studied him a moment. "You really don't care about the money, do you?"

"Why would I?"

"Do you have any idea how refreshing that is?"

He smiled. "Not a clue."

"You can take my word for it. The people in my social circle are obsessed with their investments, trust funds, and charity work."

"I didn't spend much time with them." As a SEAL, he'd been gone for weeks, sometimes months, at a time. "I remember a few conversations that almost bored me to sleep." When Kristi laughed, he mentally patted himself on the back for lightening her mood.

"Come on. Let's play with Oliver."

An hour later, his phone signaled an incoming text. Rafe scanned the message. "Wolf Pack's ready to go."

Kristi sighed and tossed the frisbee one more time for Oliver. When he returned with the toy in his mouth and dropped it at her feet, she leaned down and kissed the top of his head. "I'll see you soon, Oliver." She looked at Deke. "Take care of my dog."

The trainer gave a nod. "You have my word."

He and Kristi met the rest of Wolf Pack in the parking lot. "Looks like you survived unscathed."

"Next time, you're playing with the trainees," Cal said. "We'll take the dogs."

"Problem?"

"The wannabe bodyguards weren't happy when we picked them off one at a time. One of them took a swing at Jackson."

"Are you okay?" Kristi asked the medic.

A shrug. "He missed. I didn't. He'll be doing extra laps around the track tonight as punishment."

Rafe whistled. "That won't be the only thing he has to do when Josh finds out what happened."

"He knows. According to him, the laps are only the beginning. The trainee will be going one-on-one on the mat with Josh or Alex for the next several days. By the time they're finished with this guy, he won't be thinking about sucker punching an instructor or trainer again."

"Let's go," Eli said. "Darcy's waiting for us."

CHAPTER TWELVE

Kristi studied the three-story Victorian house. While the home and landscaping were gorgeous, her favorite feature was the porch with its hanging baskets of flowers and ferns along with several cushioned chairs that invited you to sit and enjoy the breeze.

She sighed. A refuge, Kristi thought. This was a place to let the cares of the world drop from her shoulders. She longed to sit on one of those comfy chairs with a good book and a mug of herbal tea. No time, though, and she doubted Rafe would want her sitting in full view of people on the street.

Rafe nudged her toward the amazing porch. "What do you think of the house?"

"I love it." Looking at the house and grounds gave her ideas for ways to improve the curb appeal of her own business and home.

"You wouldn't believe the shape the house was in when Darcy bought it. Ask her. It's quite a story." As they neared the porch, the front door opened.

Eli loped ahead of them and swept the woman standing in the doorway into a hug. "Good to see you again, Darcy. You look beautiful, sugar."

"You're a sweet talker, Eli. Good thing I'm madly in love with my husband, or you might tempt me." She stepped away from Eli and into Jon's embrace. "Welcome back, Jon."

"Rio is treating you right?"

She smiled. "What if I said no?"

"He'd disappear without a trace. After that, I'd go after your brother for letting Rio mistreat you."

That brought a laugh and a pat on Jon's arm. "Rio treats me like a princess."

Jackson, then Cal kissed Darcy on the cheek in greeting.

Rafe escorted Kristi up the stairs. "Hello, beautiful."

"Rafe!" Darcy hugged him. "I've missed you. Who's your friend?"

"Kristi Stewart. Kristi, this is Darcy Kincaid, Rio's better half."

"Welcome, Kristi," Darcy said. "Come inside while Wolf Pack brings in your bags."

Her cheeks burned, feeling more frumpy and wrinkled by the minute. "I don't have anything with me."

"I should have realized. Kidnappers are so inconsiderate, aren't they?" Darcy smiled as she motioned for Kristi to follow her inside the house.

The first thing she noticed was the large black piano in the living room. "The piano's gorgeous. Do you play?"

"I do. Come into the kitchen while Wolf Pack grabs their gear. Would you like something to drink?"

"Water is fine."

"Rio should be home soon. He stopped by the diner to pick up dinner. He didn't want me to cook after being on my feet at the deli today."

Kristi sat at the table. "You work at a deli?"

"I own the deli. If you visit That's A Wrap, I'll show you around."

"I'd like that. Cute name. What do you serve?"

"Breakfast and lunch wraps. We leave the dinner crowd to Delaney's Diner." Darcy set a glass of water in front of Kristi. "Rio installed a reverse osmosis system under the kitchen sink." She nudged the glass closer. "See what you think."

Kristi sampled the water, surprised at the fresh taste. "I can't taste chemicals in the water. What's so special about the reverse osmosis system?"

"Eleven stages of filtration make it easy for your body to absorb and use the water."

"I need a reverse osmosis system for my own home. This is great." The system would be well worth the cost because of the amount of water she drank daily.

"Ask Rio about it when he arrives. He can tell you what kind we use." Darcy drained her own glass of water and set it to the side. "We look like we're about the same size. I'll lay two changes of clothes on the bed in your room. Would you like a t-shirt to sleep in?"

Rafe walked into the kitchen as Darcy finished her question. "I'll give her one of mine."

Speculation lit the other woman's eyes as she studied Rafe's face, then Kristi's flaming one. "Are female hearts breaking all over town, Rafe?"

"I don't know about that, but I'm off the market."

"Oh, man. Weeping and wailing will commence as soon as word gets around. Who's the lucky woman?" Darcy's gaze returned to Kristi, her eyes twinkling.

Kristi smiled. "I am."

"Congratulations to you both. How long have you been dating?"

"A few hours," Rafe answered.

Darcy stared a moment, then burst into laughter. "You don't let grass grow under your feet when you decide you want something."

"Rio snatched you up within hours of meeting you despite your brother's threats to take him down. I've known Kristi for a few years."

"I'm glad you wised up, then."

Kristi's gaze shifted to Rafe. His interest in her had more to do with availability than wisdom. Rafe wasn't in a committed relationship with Callie now. She sighed. Kristi still missed her friend.

The rest of Wolf Pack entered the room, drawing Kristi's thoughts away from the past.

Darcy smiled at the black ops team. "The kitchen's open, guys. Rio will be here soon with dinner. I have soft drinks, water, and iced green tea." At their groans, she laughed. "I also have coffee in the cabinet. You can make a pot. If you want regular iced tea, I can make some for you."

"Don't go to any trouble, Darcy." Jackson gave her a one-armed hug. "We can fend for ourselves. You should get off your feet, though."

She patted his arm. "I'm fine, but thanks for the concern. I'll return after I find clothes for Kristi."

When Darcy left the kitchen, Kristi turned to the medic. "Is Darcy sick?"

"She has an autoimmune disease. Rio keeps close tabs on her to make sure Darcy doesn't overdo it. When his team is deployed, the other operatives in town watch out for her as do the wives of his teammates."

"How can I help?" She might be tired after her ordeal, but that was nothing compared to fighting your own immune system all the time.

Rafe cupped her shoulders. "We'll all help Darcy."

The front door opened. Rafe drew his weapon and three members of Wolf Pack formed a wall in front of

Kristi while Cal stepped to the doorway Darcy had walked through as though positioning himself to protect her, too.

Had more kidnappers had found her already? Her stomach knotted. Kristi didn't want to endanger Darcy. Maybe she should insist that Rafe and the others take her home tonight.

But Rafe hadn't slept at all overnight. Every time she woke in the hospital, he was alert at her bedside. She suspected that he'd insist on driving to Bakerhill to watch for trouble and take evasive action if necessary.

"It's Rio. I'm coming in soft." Seconds later, Rio walked in with two large bags filled with takeout containers. He set the bags on the kitchen counter. "Delaney's special for everyone except Darcy. Plastic utensils along with napkins are in the bags, too." He looked around. "Where's Darcy?"

"She's getting clothes for me," Kristi said, then turned to Rafe. "I need my bags from the Sandoval as well as my SUV."

"We'll take care of it. How to do that safely will be part of our discussion after dinner."

"I'll check on Darcy," Rio said. "The takeout box marked with a D is hers. The rest of the boxes contain the special of the day."

Except for Rafe, Wolf Pack surged toward the bags on the counter. When Kristi started to rise, Rafe held her in place with a hand to her shoulder. "I'll get yours. What do you want to drink?"

She handed him her empty glass. "Iced herbal tea."

He kissed the top of her head and headed to the counter. When he returned with a takeout container and utensils for her, Darcy and Rio walked into the kitchen, holding hands.

Kristi smiled. That's the kind of relationship she wanted, a true partnership with a man she adored. Her gaze shifted to Rafe. Would he be that kind of partner?

She cautioned herself to slow down. Their relationship was so new they hadn't been on one date. Unless, of course, she counted running for their lives through a disgusting dank cave and racing down a mountainside with stone-cold killers hunting her.

How he'd handled the kidnappers and the way he treated her proved Rafe Torres was a man of honor, one any woman would be proud to call her own. Butterflies took flight in her stomach. Rafe gave her the right to call him hers.

"This is my favorite meal at Delaney's," Cal said to Rio.

Kristi tore her gaze from her dark-haired operative and eyed the meatloaf, mashed potatoes, and green beans in the takeout container. The food looked and smelled wonderful. Rafe set a glass of iced green tea on the table for her. "Thanks."

He trailed a hand over her hair and returned for his own meal as Rio seated Darcy across the table from Kristi.

"I'll bring your dinner," Rio murmured. "Sit and relax."

"You don't have to do that, sweetheart. I had a good day."

"I like to spoil you. Let me." He winked. "You can return the favor later."

When Darcy's cheeks flushed a pretty pink and her eyes sparkled with unspoken secrets, Kristi felt as though she watched a private moment between the husband and wife, and longed for a similar strong relationship of her own.

She turned her attention to the takeout container and dug into her meal. Kristi sighed. Oh, man. The meatloaf was fabulous. "Now I know why this is your favorite meal, Cal. I can't remember when I've tasted better." And she'd eaten plenty of five-star meals in her lifetime. None of them compared to this simple, comforting meal.

"The cook at Delaney's is a genius. The meatloaf recipe was passed down from his grandmother, and he won't share the recipe."

"He won't even tell me the secret," Darcy said. "Believe me, I've tried to bribe him with one of my recipes. He's not cooperating."

"Would Nate have better luck?" Jackson asked. "His cooking is legendary around Otter Creek. Some of his recipes might tempt Ralph to share."

"I don't think so." She smiled. "Pitting Nate's determination against Ralph's stubbornness would be fun to watch, though."

"Don't alienate Ralph," Cal said. "He might refuse to serve meatloaf to PSI and Fortress operatives. That would be a tragedy. I wouldn't survive my next rotation at PSI without Ralph's meatloaf."

Rio snorted. "Nate's one of the best interrogator's in the business. If he can't get the information, no one can."

Cal turned to Jon, one eyebrow raised.

"No way. I'm not getting into the middle of this battle of wills." He forked up a bite of meatloaf. "I'll just enjoy the food. Besides, some things are better off left alone. Wouldn't want to upset the economic food balance in Otter Creek."

Darcy opened her takeout container, grabbed a fork, and dug into her grilled chicken and salad.

After Darcy finished her meal, Kristi said, "Your house is so beautiful, Darcy. You must love it."

"I love it now."

"You didn't always?"

"Oh, the house appealed to me the minute I saw it. The structure had good bones, like a classy lady. However, the inside was an unpleasant surprise. The woman who owned the house was a hoarder, and her family insisted on selling the house as it was. You literally took your life in your hands when you walked inside this place. I lost count of how many large dumpsters I filled up clearing out this place."

Kristi's eyes widened. "I can't imagine all the work you had to do." How did she finish the job with an autoimmune disease plaguing her?

"Oh, it wasn't so bad." Darcy leaned her head against Rio's shoulder. "Rio and his teammates plus an army of PSI trainees helped clear the house. All I had to do was sit back and direct traffic."

"Don't let her fool you," the medic said with a tender smile at his wife. "She worked harder than she should have."

"My house and my mess to clear. Everything worked out, though. Now, we have a beautiful home to share with friends and family when they need a refuge or a place to recover." She turned to Kristi. "I have pictures of the interior of the house before we cleaned it out if you want to look at them. They're shocking."

"I'd love to see them."

Darcy pulled out her phone and scrolled until she found the pictures she had mentioned. She handed her phone to Kristi.

She stared at the screen, eyes wide. Good grief! Stacks and stacks of stuff piled nearly to the ceiling. "It's a wonder you were able to navigate through the house at all."

"We caused more than one avalanche."

"How long did it take you?"

"A week. I had a lot of help from the trainees. Josh allowed them to use helping me in place of physical training for a few days."

Rafe scowled at Eli. "Why didn't we have the option to ditch PT for a community service project? I'd have taken that option in a heartbeat."

"We aren't bodyguard trainees, buddy."

"Some of them weren't either," Rio pointed out, his lips curving.

"No whining," Eli said to Rafe. "Josh will never give us an easy out. He trains us as hard as he does his own team because we're assigned tough missions."

Rio grinned. "I can attest to that. Although we were in the military together for years, our workout and training regimen is more rigorous now than when we were active duty soldiers."

Kristi watched the continuing byplay, amused despite a headache growing worse by the minute. By the time she finished eating, Kristi wished she had skipped food altogether. She prayed she didn't embarrass herself by getting sick, and desperately tried to think of a way to excuse herself without worrying Rafe or the others. She needed to lie down.

"Kristi."

She blinked and looked at Rafe.

He cupped her cheek. "What's wrong?"

The other people around the table fell silent, just what she didn't want to happen. "I'm fine."

"No, you're not. Your skin is pale and clammy. Tell me what's wrong so I can help, baby."

No use lying to him or the others. If something didn't change fast, she wouldn't be able to hide it anyway. "A bad headache growing worse by the second and nausea."

Jackson was on his feet in an instant. "Rafe, help Kristi to her room. I'll follow you up in a minute. Darcy, do you have chamomile or mint tea?"

"Take care of Kristi," Rio said. "I'll bring the tea and cold packs."

Rafe helped Kristi to her feet and slid his arm around her waist as he escorted her from the kitchen with Jackson following behind.

Dismay filled Kristi when she realized she didn't know which room she'd been assigned. "I don't know where to go," she murmured.

Rafe tucked her closer to his side. "Your room is across the hall from mine."

"How many bedrooms does this house have?"

"Plenty." He assisted her upstairs to the third floor and down the hall to the last room on the right at back of the house.

Instead of turning on the overhead light, Rafe turned on the lamp on its lowest setting, then mounded pillows against the headboard. "Stay upright long enough to drink the tea Rio's preparing." He crossed the room to the closet and pulled a blanket from the shelf, then draped the blanket over her.

"I'm not cold."

"You will be by the time I remove the cold packs." He turned as Jackson came into the room with his bag.

The medic pulled out a packet of capsules and handed two to Kristi. "Take these when Rio brings your tea." Reaching into the bag again, he grabbed a white packet and ripped open the package. Jackson held up a small square patch. "This is an anti-nausea patch. My teammates swear by these things. Want to try it?"

When she nodded, the medic peeled off the paper backing and pressed the patch to the skin behind her right ear. "The medicine could take up to an hour to kick in. Hopefully, the tea will help until then. If it doesn't, you might have to sip a carbonated drink to settle your stomach. When was the last time you took pain meds?"

She frowned, trying to remember. "I'm not sure."

"Did you take anything for pain after Rio gave you the pain pills earlier today?" Rafe asked.

"No."

Jackson grimaced. "No wonder you feel lousy. The meds wore off."

Rio walked into the room holding a to-go cup in one hand and two cold packs in the other. "Chamomile-mint tea and life-saving cold packs." He handed the cup to Kristi.

"This room has an attached bathroom, and all the trashcans in every room are lined. Makes it easier to take care of sick operatives and trainees." Rio smiled. "You can ask Rafe about that when you feel better."

"Shut up, Kincaid," Rafe muttered.

The medic chuckled. "Need anything else, Jackson?"

"Nope. She's wearing a patch now. Once she takes the pain pills, we'll arrange the cold packs."

A nod. "Kristi, if you need something, send Rafe to find me."

"Thank you, Rio."

After he left, Kristi took the pain medicine with a swallow of tea. Thankfully, the steeped tea was the perfect temperature to consume easily. She sighed. The mint and chamomile combination was exactly right.

"Relax against the pillows." Jackson closed his bag. "Rafe, one cold pack behind her neck and one to her forehead. Twenty minutes on. I'll be back in a few minutes to check on you, Kristi." With a pointed glance at Rafe, Jackson hefted his bag over his shoulder and left the room.

"What was the look about?" Kristi murmured.

"He ordered me to keep a close watch on you."

She grimaced. "I didn't mean to scare anyone."

"We watch over each other when we're injured." He adjusted the pillows at her back. "Better?"

Kristi nodded. "You make a good nurse."

He chuckled as he slid a cold pack behind her neck. "You wouldn't say that if I had to stitch you up on the field."

She eyed him. "Have you done that?"

"Unfortunately, yes."

"Who?"

"Me and a few teammates over the years."

"Are you serious?"

"Oh, yeah. Drink your tea. Do you mind if I sit beside you? Holding the cold pack on your forehead will be easier."

She patted the mattress beside her and obediently sipped her drink. "Were you injured badly on the field?"

Rafe settled beside Kristi with his back resting against the headboard and pressed a cold pack against her forehead. "It was touch and go a time or two." He shrugged. "Goes with the job, Kristi. What we do isn't a walk in the park."

"Were you injured while you were training at PSI?"

He growled. "Rio and his big mouth. Yeah, I was injured there."

"What happened?"

"Another trainee became frustrated during an exercise in Crime Town. He shoved me down a flight of stairs. I ended up with a concussion, and Rio brought me here for two nights to keep an eye on me."

Fury burned inside Kristi. "Was the concussion bad?"

He grimaced. "Oh, yeah."

"I'm glad you're all right now."

"Me, too. I hate concussions."

"You've had more than one?"

Another shrug. "Goes with the territory."

Kristi shivered. "I'm freezing."

"A few more minutes." Rafe inched closer to share his body heat.

"Oh, man. You're like a furnace."

He chuckled. "That's good?"

"Wonderful." She finished her tea and set the mug on the nightstand. "I'll be fine if you need to leave."

"Close your eyes and let me hold you."

He wouldn't get an argument from her. Rafe holding her was a miracle. "Will you get in trouble with the others?"

"Nope. I'm not on duty tonight."

"Because you were on duty last night?"

"That's right. Relax and let the medicine and cold packs do their job," he murmured.

Kristi kissed his jaw and closed her eyes.

CHAPTER THIRTEEN

Rafe returned to the kitchen where his teammates and Rio were gathered around the table. After tossing the cold packs into the freezer, he joined them.

"How is Kristi now?" Jackson asked.

"Asleep. I'll check on her in a few minutes. I don't want to be gone long in case she needs anything."

Eli studied him. "Have something to share with the class, Torres?"

He frowned. Did he have a neon sign on his forehead? "My business, not yours."

"If you're emotionally compromised, we need to know."

"Doesn't matter if I am or not. Neither you nor anyone else is tossing me off her protection detail."

"No one said a word about replacing you," Jon said. "If she's more than an assignment to you, assigning someone for backup protects you and Kristi."

Rafe glared at his teammate, then sighed. "Yeah, okay. I'm involved with Kristi. Happy now?"

"That was quick," Jackson muttered. "Did you smooth-talk her into dating while you ran for your lives on that mountainside?"

He knew how it looked. His jaw clenched. Too bad. Life wasn't guaranteed. He wasn't passing up a chance to know Kristi better.

Whether this relationship deepened beyond explosive chemistry and into love was anyone's guess. Rafe wanted a chance to see where this went. "She was Callie's friend. I've known her for a few years." Truthfully, Rafe knew her through Callie. Perhaps that explained why he felt comfortable with her. Even thinking in terms of a relationship after the past three years of mourning Callie felt strange but right.

"Your judgment is compromised," Jackson accused.

"Like Cal's judgment was compromised with Rachelle, or Eli's with Brenna and Jon's with Dana? They handled the distraction. Do you think I'm incapable of staying focused when the situation demands it?"

His friend's cheeks reddened. Along with anger, though, pain and hurt roiled in the depths of his eyes. What caused those emotions in the medic?

"Rafe, if you reach a point where you can't focus, I need to know." Eli folded his arms across his chest.

He gritted his teeth, hating that his teammates questioned his judgment. Rafe understood, but he didn't like it. "Yes, sir." He vowed to make sure that particular talk with his team leader wasn't necessary.

"Now that you've joined us, we need to work out a plan for tomorrow. When do you want to leave for Bakerhill?"

"Earlier is better. I'd rather arrive in Bakerhill under cover of night."

"She can sleep on the way to her home," Jon said. He turned to Eli. "Rafe's right. Darkness is safer for her and for us."

"I agree." Wolf Pack's leader checked his watch. "You didn't sleep last night, Rafe. Will four hours be enough to recharge?"

He scowled. Seriously? He'd operated for days at a time without sleep on missions. Just because a beautiful woman had captured his interest didn't mean he couldn't function as an operative while short on sleep. "As long as I have coffee, I'll be good to go."

"I'll make sure it's ready for you," Rio said, amusement twinkling in his eyes.

With a nod of thanks, Rafe turned back to Eli. "Kristi's luggage and vehicle are at the Sandoval."

"Jackson, you and Cal ride together and stop by the hotel. Rafe, we'll need Kristi to call the Sandoval and alert security that Cal and Jackson are coming. We don't want trouble with hotel security or the local cops."

He snorted. "They weren't much good when she was kidnapped. Security won't be able to stop Cal and Jackson."

"While that's true, we don't want the local cops brought in. The less they suspect you and Durango were involved with the trouble on Hart Mountain, the better. Could get complicated if they haul you in for questioning."

Rafe could justify every action he'd taken on the mountain as protecting his principal. However, if he was arrested or questioned, he wouldn't be at Kristi's side, leaving her vulnerable. That was unacceptable. "Understood."

Eli inclined his head toward the stairs. "Sleep while you can. The rest of us will split the watch." He grinned. "You're on duty tomorrow night."

"Yes, sir." Rafe pushed away from the table and headed for the stairs. The voices of his teammates discussing possible avenues of investigation followed him to the third floor. His first stop was Kristi's room. She hadn't moved since he left her.

He breathed easier. Hopefully, she would stay asleep until he had to wake her after midnight. Rafe went to his own room across the hall. After washing his face and brushing his teeth, he opened the door again, removed his tactical boots, and stretched out on the bed. He fell asleep between one breath and the next.

His internal alarm woke him at 1:30. After a two-minute shower, he dressed in the standard Fortress uniform of black t-shirt and cargo pants, pulled on his boots, and went across the hall to Kristi's room.

He paused in the doorway, his heart turning over at the sight of the beautiful woman sleeping peacefully. Rafe hated to wake her, but the early start gave them the best chance of arriving in town unnoticed.

Rafe walked to her bedside and trailed his fingers over Kristi's cheek. Her skin felt like velvet against his own rough skin. He'd never felt anything that soft in his life. "Kristi."

She sat up. "What's wrong?"

He sat beside Kristi and wrapped his arms around her. "Nothing's wrong," he murmured against her ear. "I'm sorry. I didn't mean to scare you."

Kristi relaxed against him. "It's still dark out. Why are we awake so early?"

"You said you wanted to go home today. The best time to do that is under cover of darkness." He cupped her cheeks, leaned in and kissed her. "I'll make you tea while you change clothes."

"When do we leave?"

"As soon as you're ready."

"Give me a few minutes."

Rafe left the room, closing the door behind him. Already in the kitchen, Rio turned when Rafe walked in. The rest of Wolf Pack was gathered around the table with breakfast wraps and mugs of coffee.

"Your coffee and breakfast are ready," the medic said.

He accepted the plate and mug of coffee Rio offered him with a nod of thanks.

"I can prepare a wrap for Kristi as well, but I wasn't sure if she'd be ready to eat this early."

"I doubt it, but you can ask." Unlike the operatives, she wasn't used to waking at all hours of the night. He nuked a large mug of water with two chamomile-mint tea bags, then ate quickly and drank the excellent coffee while her tea steeped. "Thanks, man. I appreciate this."

"No problem."

"Thanks for your hospitality, Rio." Eli rose with his empty plate and coffee mug in hand.

"Our door is always open, my friend."

"Yeah, you say that now. I'm betting the offer doesn't stand the next time we're at PSI for training."

A quick grin from the medic. "Only if you're injured and need TLC."

Light footsteps sounded on the stairs. Rafe turned as Kristi walked into the kitchen. As he studied her face, tension melted from Rafe's muscles. Kristi's color was better. He met her in the center of the kitchen. "How do you feel?" he asked as he drew her into his arms again. Yeah, he was becoming addicted to hugging this woman.

"Better. No wonder you and the others swear by that anti-nausea patch."

The men around the room chuckled.

"How's the headache?" Jackson asked.

"Manageable."

He handed her a packet from his pocket. "Take two capsules in an hour. Don't try to tough it out or you'll be in the same shape as last night."

She wrinkled her nose. "No, I won't wait again. That wasn't fun."

"Are you hungry?" Rio asked.

"It's too early for me to even think about food, but thanks for the offer." She glanced at the empty plates around the table. "I'm guessing the same isn't true for the rest of you."

"We learned to eat when we could. During missions, we don't always have time."

"More chamomile-mint tea?" Rafe asked her.

She brightened. "That's perfect."

"Here." Rio handed Rafe a large to-go cup. "This should hold her tea. To-go coffee all around?" he asked Wolf Pack.

"You are a true friend," Cal said.

The medic smiled. "I'll remind you of that when you return for a refresher course."

A scowl. "That wasn't an invitation to ramp up the difficulty of our training."

"I thought you wanted to prove that SEALs are tougher than Delta Force soldiers." He leaned back against the kitchen counter. "In case you wondered, they aren't."

Rafe poured Kristi's tea into the travel mug while his teammates teased Rio about the perils of being an Army grunt. When Kristi joined him at the kitchen counter, they prepared travel cups of coffee for all of the operatives.

When they finished, Rafe dropped a light kiss on Kristi's mouth. He turned to his teammates. "We need to go. Clock's ticking."

"Load up," Eli said. "We leave in five minutes."

As Wolf Pack left to retrieve their gear, Rafe looked at Rio. When the medic gave a short nod, Rafe turned to Kristi. "I'll be back in a minute. Stay with Rio."

He took the stairs two at a time, checked the bathroom to be sure he hadn't left anything, then scooped up his Go bag, and returned to the kitchen and Kristi.

"You don't have to do that," Rio was saying to her. "Darcy wouldn't expect you to do anything in return. We're happy to help."

"I want to design and make a dress for her. Will you help me?"

His expression softened. "All right. I'll email the information you need to Rafe."

"That works. Thanks."

"No pressure, though, all right? I won't tell Darcy what you plan to do. If you don't have time, it's fine. Your first priority is to heal." He sobered. "Will you talk to a trauma counselor?"

"I talked to Marcus Lang for two hours yesterday. He said I could call him when I need him."

"Good. Take him up on it. Talking to him will help you process what happened."

The rest of Wolf Pack came down the stairs and began loading the SUVs. Rafe laid his hand on Kristi's back. "Ready to go?"

She nodded. "I have a busy day ahead. The sooner I'm back in Bakerhill, the better."

"Anything beyond work?"

"I need to see Dad and talk to Hugh."

"Cal and Jackson will stop by the hotel to pick up your luggage and SUV. They need your key fob."

Relief flooded her face. "I'll call the front desk and have them tell security to let Cal and Jackson have my belongings. My key fob is in my purse." She turned to Rio. "Thank you for sharing your home with me, Rio. Please pass my thanks on to Darcy. I'll return the clothes she let me borrow."

"No problem, sugar. Take care of yourself." Rio clapped Rafe on the shoulder. "Watch your back, frog boy."

"Yes, sir." He led Kristi to his SUV, tucked her inside his vehicle, then rounded the hood and slid into the driver's seat. Rafe cranked the engine and pulled out of Rio's driveway to take the lead in their caravan.

When they were on Highway 18, Rafe unlocked his phone and handed it to Kristi. "Call the Sandoval. We're about an hour from the hotel."

Her call was answered a moment later, a man's voice streaming into the cabin through Rafe's Bluetooth connection. "Carlos, it's Kristi Stewart."

"Ms. Stewart, we heard about the kidnapping. Are you all right?"

"I'm fine. I need a favor."

"Name it."

"Two friends will stop by the hotel in an hour to retrieve my SUV and my belongings. Will you have one of the security officers let them into the suite?"

"Let me transfer your call to the security team. They'll need to hear the request directly from you."

Elevator music filled the SUV's cabin until a deep voice said, "Charles Russell."

"Charles, this is Kristi Stewart. I need a favor."

"Ms. Stewart! You're free. Thank God. First, though, I want you to know how deeply we regret the incident."

Rafe's hands tightened around the steering wheel. Incident? She'd been kidnapped on this man's watch.

"I want to reassure you that we've been working hard to revamp security, and nothing like that will ever happen again. I personally guarantee that you'll be safe in our hotel. If you're concerned about your safety the next time you stay with us, I will sit outside your suite myself to ensure you have a restful, safe stay."

"I appreciate the offer."

"Now, what do you need?"

"Two friends of mine will stop by the hotel in an hour to retrieve my luggage and my SUV."

"Are you talking about Hugh Ward?"

Rafe frowned.

"The names of my friends are Cal and Jackson. Why did you mention Hugh?"

"He's been driving us crazy, demanding updates on the investigation into your kidnapping. I'm surprised you haven't talked to him already."

"Why? He's only a friend."

A pause, then, "That's not what he says. Mr. Ward informed us that you're engaged to him."

"You've been misinformed, Charles. I'm not marrying Hugh. Will you assist my friends when they arrive?"

"Of course. Have them ask for me at the front desk. I'll escort them personally to the suite."

After Kristi asked the security chief about the wellbeing of his family, she ended the call and handed Rafe his phone.

He contacted Cal and passed along the security chief's instructions, then slid his phone into his pocket. When Rafe glanced at Kristi, he wrapped his hand around hers. "Are you okay?"

"I don't understand why Hugh told Charles we were engaged. He promised to let me think about his proposal."

"Yeah, and you know now he's growing desperate. This might be a way of getting more information where otherwise the security team would have refused to tell him anything."

"Apparently, they didn't know my condition, either."

"Sounds like that, doesn't it?"

She twisted in her seat. "You think Charles faked being surprised?"

"At this point, I don't trust anyone."

"What would Charles have to gain by planning or participating in my kidnapping?"

"Five million dollars is more motivation than a lot of people need."

Kristi's head thumped against her headrest. "Oh, man. I'll view everyone with suspicion now."

"You should."

"I hate this, Rafe."

His lips tugged upward. "Welcome to my world, babe."

"That's a sad outlook on life."

A shrug. "People hide behind masks. I'd rather be suspicious and stay alive than be caught by surprise and end up injured or dead."

"When you put it that way, I have to agree with you."

Rafe squeezed her hand. "Try to sleep. I'll wake you if anything comes up."

"Are you sure? I can help you stay awake."

His heart turned over in his chest at her offer. "I'll be fine."

"If you become sleepy, wake me. I'll share some funny stories about my fashion disasters through the years."

Another squeeze. "Deal."

Rafe kept a close eye on the mirrors and the asphalt ribbon in front of him as he drove toward Bakerhill. At the Gatlinburg exit on Interstate 40, Cal and Jackson drove toward the Sandoval Hotel while Eli and Jon stayed behind Rafe and Kristi.

An hour from her home, Kristi moaned. Her hand clenched around Rafe's.

Concerned, he glanced at her. "Kristi."

Another moan.

She must be dreaming. "You're safe, baby. I've got you."

Kristi quieted. "Rafe," she whispered.

"You're safe," he repeated. "I'm here."

She sighed and went back under.

He breathed easier, glad she trusted him to protect her. Kristi might not realize it, but he would protect her with his life as would his teammates.

Fifteen minutes from their destination, Rafe woke her. "We're close to Bakerhill."

She stretched and winced. "Ouch."

"Sore?"

"Understatement. I forgot to take the pain pills Jackson gave me."

"Take them now."

Kristi did as he suggested, swallowing the pills with some of her tea. "We made good time. No problems?"

"None. When will your clients arrive?"

She smiled. "Unlike you, my workday doesn't begin before sunrise. My first appointment is mid-morning. However, I have work to complete before my first client arrives."

"When do you want to see your father?"

Kristi glanced at the time on the dashboard readout. "Dad should already be in the office. I'd like to see him before the day's craziness kicks into full gear. Is that possible?"

"I'll make it happen." Rafe called Eli. "Kristi wants to see her father before she starts work."

"Need backup?"

"No, sir."

"Kristi, Cal and Jackson will be at your home in a few minutes. Do we have your permission to enter the premises and check the building?"

"Of course." She told Eli the alarm code. "Kristi's Bridal is on the first floor. That key is blue. My home is on the second floor."

"Rafe, watch your back."

"Copy that." He ended the call.

"Why did he say that?"

"Someone wants you bad enough to try kidnapping you a second time in the middle of a busy hospital. He won't be happy when he realizes you have a security team watching over you along with a new man in your life who is determined to keep you safe. If he's smart, he'll do his best to take me out so that you're more vulnerable."

CHAPTER FOURTEEN

Kristi's breath caught at Rafe's words. Oh, no. She didn't want Rafe or his teammates in danger because of her. Rafe would protect her no matter the cost to himself, his protectiveness central to his character. If she built a relationship with him, Kristi would have to accept that part of his job and his nature.

No, not just a job, she realized. A calling. Black ops work wasn't a job to Rafe. He and his teammates were adrenaline junkies. Rafe lived and breathed danger. She either accepted him and his career, or walked away now.

Her grip tightened around Rafe's hand. Walking away would gut her. "Do you like your job?"

"Do you like yours?" he countered.

"I love mine, but the greatest danger I face is poking my fingers with pins or handling a client who hates the dress I designed to her specifications. Your job is more dangerous than mine."

"I love my job, too. I started training at age eighteen. The job gives me purpose and a reason for getting up in the mornings."

"What happens when you're retirement age?"

"I'll transition to another role in Fortress long before I hit retirement. Once my reflexes slow, Brent will use me in a different capacity. He doesn't waste his resources."

"Would you be assigned a training role, perhaps at PSI?"

"Possibly. I can also assist in investigations."

She stared. "You can?"

"Sure. I was an FBI agent before I came on board with Fortress."

Her mouth dropped. "I had no idea you were a federal agent."

"Didn't sit well," he admitted. "I'm not a fan of the feds."

"Then why did you join the FBI?"

He sent her a solemn look. "To find Callie's killer."

Tears stung her eyes. Of course. He'd loved her enough to give up his career as a SEAL and join the agency best suited to finding murderers. "Did you succeed?"

"He and his partner are behind bars, awaiting trial."

Kristi squeezed his hand, empathy rising inside her. "Good."

Rafe was silent a moment, then said, "No questions?"

"I wasn't sure you could divulge details. It's enough to know that her killers won't be able to hurt anyone else."

He looked thoughtful. "Callie didn't understand why I couldn't talk about my work, especially where I was going or when I would return."

"I know," Kristi said, voice soft. "She complained when you deployed and worried about you."

"Ironic, isn't it? She worried about me doing a dangerous job but she's the one who died while I was deployed." He sighed. "Callie was murdered by two members of the Hunt Club."

She'd heard the news about that group of men who hunted people instead of big game. The media had been talking about the club and its members for two weeks. "The news media mentioned federal and local law enforcement, but not Fortress."

He shrugged. "We don't need the publicity. The Hunt Club targeted the wife of a Fortress operative. I was tasked with bringing in two of the members. The men my team and I handed over to the authorities were responsible for Callie's death."

Her heart ached for him. "That must have been difficult."

"Hardest thing I've ever done."

They remained silent for the rest of the drive to Stewart Group headquarters. After Rafe parked next to her father's car, Kristi led him to the front door and knocked on the glass. The building was still locked because of the early hour.

The night guard glanced up, eyes widening in surprise, and hurried to unlock the door. "Ms. Stewart, I'm so glad your father paid the ransom and that you're safe. I didn't have a good feeling about that whole situation. I'm thankful you're back safe."

"Thanks, Frank. I'm going up to see Dad. Rafe is with me."

The security guard's expression hardened. "I'll need permission from your father to allow him upstairs."

She patted the older man's arm. "Call him. He knows Rafe."

Frank cast Rafe a skeptical look as he backed away and grabbed his cell phone to make the call, suspicious gaze locked on Rafe, one hand on his gun, the other gripping his cell phone.

Kristi frowned. Frank had always been friendly and relaxed with her. Why was he fingering his gun as though he itched to yank it from his holster and face off with Rafe in a showdown? Maybe the kidnapping had easy-going Frank on edge.

On the heels of that thought came another. This one stole her breath. Was her father in danger? The kidnappers might come after him in retaliation for her escape.

The security guard ended the call and motioned for Rafe and Kristi to proceed to the elevators.

"Interesting," Rafe said as the silver doors enclosed them inside the car. "The security guard assumed your father had paid the ransom."

"Frank isn't involved in this. He's been on staff here for 30 years. He's known me since I was born." He was a pseudo grandfather to her. No, Frank wouldn't be involved in anything nefarious.

"I'm suspicious of everyone, remember?"

Right. "It's not Frank."

The elevator arrived on her father's floor a moment later. Kristi stepped out of the car and turned right toward the CEO's suite. Since Alice, her father's administrative assistant, wasn't due to arrive for another two hours, Kristi walked to her father's door and knocked.

"Come."

As she entered the office, her father stood and came around his massive desk. "Kristi." He wrapped her in a tight hug, the scent of his cologne a reminder that she was home and safe for the moment. "I'm glad to see you."

Alan released her and held out his hand to Rafe. "I can't thank you enough for the risk you took to free my daughter. I'll never be able to repay you, Rafe."

"I'm glad I was there, sir." Rafe glanced at her, the slight curve of his lips and the heat in his eyes an assurance that this was no longer just a job to him.

Kristi smiled. Her rescue might have been a mission to him in the beginning. Now, however, her safety was a more personal mission.

Alan turned back to Kristi. After his gaze dropped to her jaw, he flinched. "Are you sure you're all right, sweetheart? Your jaw looks painful."

That was nothing compared to the deep bruises on her ribs. "I'm all right."

"I'll have the doctor slot you in first thing this morning to be sure." He reached for the phone's handset. "He'll be happy to come to the house to examine you."

Kristi stopped him with a hand to his arm. "Dad, I've been checked by a doctor and two medics. They all agree I have minor injuries. I'll be fine in a few days."

"I'd feel better if our personal physician said as much. I don't trust anyone but Dr. Flannery."

"No. Seriously, Dad, I'd know if I was worse. No more poking and prodding by a doctor."

"All right." He laid his hands on her shoulders. "The code to the alarm system at the house is still the same. The housekeeper has prepared your suite of rooms, and I've doubled the security team on duty. You'll be safe." Her father looked at Rafe. "I hope you won't mind escorting Kristi to my home before you move on to your next mission."

"Dad, I'm not moving back home."

"Of course you will. Don't be childish, Kristi. We're talking about your life."

"I won't live in fear." Even though she was scared to death the kidnappers would try again. "I have a business to run. I can't hide at your home. Like you, I have immovable deadlines, and my business and equipment are at my home. I can't pack up and move to your house."

Alan sighed. "I'll send a security team to your place, then. No arguments, Kristi. I insist on that safety measure at least."

Her earlier concern for his safety resurfaced in her mind. "I already have a security team. Keep the extra security for yourself. I want you to be safe, too."

A frown. "What security team? Did you hire someone without me vetting them?"

"Rafe and his team are protecting me."

"Don't be ridiculous. They can't unmask the kidnappers and babysit you."

"I told you yesterday that I wouldn't stop until we discovered who was the behind the kidnapping and why," Rafe said. "I meant every word."

"You don't have to multitask. My security teams will protect Kristi. They're very good. I only hire the best."

"You hired Fortress because we're the best in the business. We don't walk away from an op without finishing the job. I won't walk away from Kristi."

Did her father understand what Rafe meant? "Dad, enough." Kristi folded her arms across her chest. "I don't want one of your security teams. I'm comfortable with Wolf Pack, especially Rafe. I'm safe with them."

"Hugh won't like that arrangement."

She didn't want to broach the subject with her father this early, but now seemed as good a time as any to reveal her decision. "Hugh's opinion doesn't matter. This arrangement is best for me."

Alan stared. "What are you saying? Of course Hugh's opinion matters. You're engaged."

"No, Dad. We're not. I'm not marrying Hugh."

Her father scowled. "The announcement is scheduled to be released to the press at the end of the week."

"I'm not marrying him."

"But he's signing employment papers soon."

"You can hire Hugh without him being your son-in-law."

"What's gotten into you? Four days ago, the wedding plans were going well. Now, you don't want anything to do with Hugh. What changed in four days?"

Shock rolled through her body. "What wedding plans?"

"The destination wedding in Orange Beach and a month-long cruise around the world. Hugh told me the plans last week."

Her cheeks burned. "I haven't planned a wedding and won't if the groom is Hugh."

"How could you do this to him? He'll be devastated." His cold gaze bored through Kristi. "I'm disappointed in you, Kristi. I never would have believed you'd do something so cruel to a good man."

She stared at her father, feeling as though she looked at a stranger. "I'm doing him a favor. He deserves a woman who adores him. That woman will never be me."

"Have you told him of your decision?"

She shook her head. "I planned to talk to him today. I came to see you first thing. I thought that would make you happy." Guess she'd been wrong. Turned out that starting her day by seeing her father was a huge mistake.

"Think about the marriage proposal a few more days. Let the shock of the kidnapping wear off before you make a decision you'll regret."

"I know my own mind and heart. My decision stands." She rose on her tiptoes to kiss him on the cheek. Her heart sank when he remained utterly still instead of dragging her into his arms for a hug as he normally did when they parted company. "I'll call you later."

"Be careful, Kristi. I can't lose you. I wouldn't survive."

"Wolf Pack is taking good care of me. The kidnappers will be behind bars soon."

Alan turned away from her and stared at Rafe. "Take care of my daughter, Rafe. I'm trusting you with her life."

"No one is more important to me than Kristi." He held out his hand to her. "We should go. We want your return to town as low key as possible."

"Hold it," Alan snapped. His gazed dropped to their entwined hands. "What's going on here?"

"My personal life is my business." Kristi stepped closer to Rafe.

"You're not dating this man. I won't allow it."

Kristi's eyebrows rose. "You don't have a say over my private life. You haven't had a right to do that since I graduated from college and moved out on my own."

"Where is your integrity? You're still involved with Hugh."

"That's enough, Mr. Stewart." Rafe's voice held an edge of steel.

"Stay out of this. I'll be lodging a complaint with your boss."

"Dad." Kristi waited until his attention shifted to her. "Stop. I won't change my mind."

"You've known this mercenary for two days." His scathing look at Rafe was at total odds with the hearty handshake when they entered the office a few minutes earlier.

"I've known Rafe for a few years." She started for the door. "See you later, Dad."

"You're going to regret this. Mark my words, Kristi. Rafe Torres isn't the man for you."

Kristi stopped and glanced over her shoulder. "Why not?"

"You deserve better than an assassin. He's not good enough to wipe your shoes on."

"He risked his life to save mine." She opened the door. "I love you, Dad. Keep the extra security team for yourself. I don't want to lose you."

CHAPTER FIFTEEN

As soon as the elevator doors slid closed, Kristi turned into Rafe's arms. The knots in his stomach loosened. At least she had turned to him instead of writing him off as a bad risk. Unfortunately, her father's words were the absolute truth, and soon Kristi would realize that for herself. When she did, would she walk away? What had he been thinking? Rafe didn't belong in her world or her life. A society princess shouldn't be with a man who lived in the shadows.

"I'm sorry," she murmured.

Rafe's arms tightened around her, afraid letting her go would be impossible now. He was crazy about her. When had that happened? "For what?"

"My father. I've never seen him like that. Alan Stewart might be a shark in the business arena, but he's always a gentleman."

The elevator stopped on the ground floor, and Rafe brushed a soft kiss on her lips before releasing Kristi and escorting her across the lobby and outside Stewart Group headquarters.

On the way to his SUV, Rafe scanned the area, his skin prickling. Not good. Someone was watching them. Frank the security guard, or someone else? Perhaps Alan Stewart watched them from the top floor of his empire's headquarters. Whoever it was set Rafe's teeth on edge.

"Is something wrong?" Kristi asked.

"Wait." He unlocked the SUV and assisted Kristi into the vehicle, anxious for her to be inside the safety of his ride. The security upgrades cost a staggering amount of money but had been worth the dent in the company's bank account for the peace of mind they provided him.

He closed Kristi's door and removed an electronic signal detector from his pocket. Rafe turned on the device, slowly circling the vehicle and watching the chaser lights. Near the back of his SUV, the lights turned from green to red.

Rafe blew out a breath and crouched by the wheel well. Seconds later, he removed a small black object and tossed it into nearby bushes before continuing his scan. Finding no other GPS trackers attached to his SUV, he turned off the gadget and climbed into the driver's seat.

"Something wrong?" Kristi asked.

"Plenty. Let's get out of here before we talk. Do you have a favorite coffee shop, preferably one that serves breakfast sandwiches?"

She gave him directions to Claire's Coffeehouse. After he parked in the lot outside the coffee shop, Kristi laid her hand on his arm. "Rafe, what's wrong?"

"Someone planted a GPS tracker on my vehicle when we were with your father."

Kristi twisted in her seat to look out the back window. "Did they follow us here?"

"I removed the tracker before we left, and I'm sure no one followed us, not that it matters."

"What do you mean?"

"We're going to your home and business. Whoever planted the tracker won't have to look hard to find you." His hand tightened on the steering wheel. "The person who planted the tracker also knows that I'm with you now."

"That wouldn't have been a secret for long."

True. They still didn't know about the rest of Wolf Pack. That gave Rafe an advantage if the kidnappers planned to attack him to clear a path to Kristi.

"We have another point in our favor," Kristi continued. "They don't know your background."

"Won't take long for word to circulate that I work for Fortress. Your father won't be shy about sharing that information now."

"Mercenaries aren't viewed as scary smart, and you are."

He smiled. "Scary smart, huh?"

"Oh, come on. You're a Navy SEAL, a reformed FBI agent, and now work for an elite black ops security firm. You're intelligent." She grinned. "And you're seriously ripped."

Rafe couldn't help it. He cupped her nape and kissed her. With those few words, Kristi reconfirmed that she wanted to be with him. She might change her mind, but for now she was his.

When he broke the kiss, her cheeks were pink and her breath short. "Thank you," he murmured.

"I should be thanking you." She laid her hand against his cheek. "I apologize for my father's insensitive remarks. On a better day, he wouldn't have said those things about you."

"He's right."

"About what?"

"I've lost count of the number of people who called me an assassin." Callie had been one of those accusers. That was one reason why she had been pushing him to leave the Teams before she was killed.

Kristi scowled. "You're not an assassin. You're a protector, Rafe. You tangle with the worst of humanity. You kill to protect innocents."

He stared. Was it possible he'd finally found a woman, a society princess at that, who understood him and his job, and could accept both?

Rafe skimmed his thumb over Kristi's kiss-swollen bottom lip. "We should go inside. Wolf Pack will be waiting for an update."

"Why did we come here instead of going to my home?"

"You've seen how much we eat. I doubt you have that much food on hand."

She grimaced. "Not unless they can make do with blueberry muffins. That's about all I have in the kitchen."

His eyebrow rose. "Do you cook?"

"Do you?"

"I get by." His cheeks burned as he divulged a secret that his Wolf Pack teammates didn't know. "I like to watch cooking shows in my downtime."

Kristi's mouth gaped. "Really?"

Rafe stiffened. "Hey, many famous chefs are men, and you didn't complain about Nate's cooking. He's a professional chef. Cooking shows are relaxing."

"I wasn't making fun of you, Rafe. I'm glad you can cook. I can, too. I also love to watch cooking shows. I enjoy trying out recipes I see on those shows. Some have turned out to be winners. Others have been fodder for the garbage disposal. I don't have much food in the kitchen because I've been working long hours for several weeks. Going to the grocery store was on top of the list of things to do when I returned to Bakerhill."

He relaxed. Something else they had in common. "Once the kidnappers are behind bars, we'll plan a cookout with Wolf Pack and their families." He grinned. "And Oliver. We'll use our successful recipes."

"Sounds like fun." She sighed. "I miss Oliver already."

"I know. He'll be with you soon. Come on. Let's grab food and coffee for everyone, and tea for you."

Ten minutes later, they were back in the SUV and on the way to her home. Rafe followed her directions to the outskirts of Bakerhill where her shop and home were located.

"Nice area," he said as he parked behind her SUV. His teammates were parked in front of her home, leaving the main driveway and parking spaces in the lot at the side of her home and business for her clients. "I'm surprised the town council allowed you to operate a business out of your home."

"Normally, they wouldn't consider an exception like that. This time, though, I happily used my father's name and influence with the town council to sway their opinions. The fact that Kristi's Bridal is a bridal shop also helped. My clients don't block the street when they park, and they have to make an appointment. They can't just show up and bring twenty of their friends with them. I also don't make a habit of using Dad's influence, but this house and neighborhood are the perfect atmosphere for the shop."

"Definitely has curb appeal." He came around to open her door, then handed her the bags of food and grabbed the carriers loaded with hot drinks.

Kristi headed for the porch. Eli came out of the house to take the bags from her.

"Perfect timing," Wolf Pack's leader said. "We were just talking about breakfast." He sent a pointed look Kristi's direction. "Your food supply wouldn't keep a mouse alive much less a security team."

"I know. I'm sorry. I'll take care of the stingy supplies after work today."

Eli patted her shoulder. "We have it covered, sugar. Don't worry. One of us will go to the grocery store while you work with your clients."

She looked at Rafe. "We can make a list before my first appointment arrives."

"We'll keep it simple and plan for two days at a time. Although you want to remain here, we don't know how things will go. We might have to relocate to a hotel if things get dicey."

She scowled. "I wasn't kidding when I told Dad I can't pack up and move my stuff anywhere else. All my supplies are here. I can't cart sewing machines, bolts of fabric, and bins of notions along with thread, pearls, sequins, and a truckload of lace to a hotel."

"One problem at a time, Kristi," Rafe said.

"He's right," Eli said. "Let's take care of our immediate needs first. Food and coffee, then we'll plan the security shifts." He glanced at Rafe with his eyebrow raised. "You holding out on us, Torres?"

"About what?" Rafe looked around as they traipsed through the elegant living room and inwardly winced. He hoped Kristi's living area wasn't so formal. He'd never feel comfortable in this space. This reminded him of Callie's home, so elegant he was afraid to sit down.

"I didn't know you cooked."

"You didn't ask."

His team leader scowled. "Are you telling me the pasta salad and potato salad you brought to the team cookout was homemade?"

Rafe shrugged.

"Does Nate know?" Eli asked as they climbed the stairs to the second floor of the large house.

"I dabble in the kitchen because I like to eat, but I'm not in Nate's league."

"Could have fooled me," Eli muttered. "Your salads were great."

They entered a full kitchen drenched with natural light, granite countertops, and glass-fronted cabinets along with top-of-the-line appliances. A bookcase crammed full of cookbooks stood against the outside wall beside a picture window showcasing a beautiful garden with a meandering path and a couple of benches to sit and enjoy the flowers and plants.

Rafe whistled. "This kitchen is a chef's dream." He set the drink carriers on the breakfast bar, removed her cup of tea, and handed it to her.

"I enjoy it."

Eli pulled breakfast sandwiches from the bags and set them on the counter beside the coffee. "I bet your boyfriend will, too."

Cal paused in the process of reaching for a sandwich. "What does that mean?"

"Torres has been keeping a secret."

"Besides his developing romance with Kristi?" Jackson asked.

"Yep." Eli grinned. "We have a budding chef in our midst."

Jon's lips curved. "You're slow on the uptake, buddy."

"You knew?"

"Sorry."

"How did you figure it out?" Eli demanded. "He hasn't said a word."

"You know many men who have cookbooks stashed in their bookcase and a professional chef's block on their kitchen counter?"

He scowled. "You've been to his apartment?" Eli glared at Rafe. "Why has Jon been to your apartment but the rest of us haven't?"

The heat in Rafe's cheeks spread to his ears. "He gave me a ride to the auto parts store when my battery died last month. I bribed him with coffee to keep my secret."

"I won't forget this." A slow smile curved his lips. "Especially when it comes time to do the cooking on our ops."

Rafe pointed at Eli. "I'm not getting stuck on kitchen duty for every mission, Wolfe."

Jackson reached for coffee and a sandwich. "We don't know if he's any good."

Eli snorted. "You already sampled his cooking. He made the pasta salad and potato salad he brought to the cookout last month."

Silence followed that announcement until Cal burst into laughter. "You're in trouble, Rafe. You shouldn't have volunteered that information. Now, you're stuck."

"Each of you is going to help out, including on this op. Kristi and I aren't feeding the lot of you the whole time we're on her protection detail."

"Enough for now," Jon said. "We need an update from Rafe and Kristi, then while she works with her clients, the rest of us will deal with upgrades to her security system and dig deeper into research."

Kristi frowned. "Why do you need to upgrade my system? The company who takes care of my father's security needs installed the best system they had."

"It's adequate."

"What do you suggest?"

"Fortress Security's top-of-the-line model. Because you're a client, Brent will cut you a deal."

"It's necessary?"

"I wouldn't recommend a new system if I didn't think you needed it to keep you safe."

"I thought keeping me safe was your job."

His lips curved. "We will. Doesn't hurt to have an excellent system to keep you safe when we're gone."

Rafe wrapped his arm around Kristi's waist. "If Jon says your system needs upgrading, you can take that to the bank. We're not into sales. We just want you safe." He kissed her temple. "I need to know you're safe when I'm deployed," he murmured.

Kristi's expression softened as she leaned into his side. "Evaluate my security needs and give me an estimate. Hopefully, Mr. Maddox will give me an excellent discount."

He hugged her. "Thanks."

"Relationships are two-way streets. We give each other what we need. I need a new security system, and you need peace of mind."

Unable to help himself despite their avid audience, Rafe kissed her. "You need to eat," he said as his teammates grabbed sandwiches and coffee, and sat at the large kitchen table.

"I'm not hungry. The tea is enough for now."

"Your body needs fuel to heal even if you don't feel hungry. Stress does funny things to our appetites. Some people don't want to eat at all. Others can't stop eating."

Kristi wrinkled her nose. "I guess we know which category I fall into."

"Do the best you can. Otherwise, Jackson will tear a strip off my hide for not taking care of you."

"Can't have that."

He chuckled at her unenthusiastic response and handed her a sandwich. Rafe sat beside her at the table with his sandwiches and cup of coffee. By unspoken consent, the conversation stayed light while they polished off their meal.

When they finished, Rafe helped Kristi to her feet. "What about giving me a tour of Kristi's Bridal?"

"Are you sure? Most men aren't comfortable here."

He wouldn't be comfortable, either, but walking around the first floor would help him learn the layout of her house. "I'll survive."

"Don't blame me if you break out in hives from all the lace and satin."

They returned to the first floor, and Kristi led him to the kitchen. "I know it's overkill to have two kitchens in one house, but I use this one for Kristi's Bridal. I keep water, coffee, soft drinks, and tea, iced and herbal, stocked. Depending on whether I have a morning or afternoon session, I serve muffins or cookies, sometimes a cheese platter with crackers if I know the bride-to-be prefers that. I also have other baking supplies here if the mood strikes me to make something more elaborate."

"I prefer the kitchen upstairs."

Kristi smiled. "So do I." She led him from room to room, each one containing elegant furniture until she opened the door to her workroom.

She turned on the light and stepped inside. "This is the heart of Kristi's Bridal."

Rafe followed, looking at the sewing machines, large table, a long rack with dresses in a rainbow of colors. The dresses were in various phases of completion. On the opposite wall was an even longer rack of wedding dresses.

He whistled and fought the growing urge to back out of the room before he knocked over something. He was definitely out of his element here. "Nice."

Kristi grinned. "You earned serious brownie points for not running from the room."

"I'm afraid to move. I might break something."

"Do you want to see the designs I put together for Maggie, the Marine's bride?"

Not really. "Sure."

She laughed and clasped his hand. "Come on. It won't hurt, I promise."

As Kristi started toward the computer and design table on the far side of the room, Rafe caught movement outside the window from the corner of his eye. He tackled Kristi as a bullet shattered the glass pane.

CHAPTER SIXTEEN

Rafe covered Kristi with his body and drew his weapon. When she groaned and shifted, he held her still. "Don't move." Had he hurt Kristi when he tackled her?

"Rafe!" Eli called.

"West side, last room on the left. Shooter fired one shot through the window."

"Injuries?"

"I'm okay. Not sure about Kristi." He watched the window, weapon aimed and ready, although he figured the shooter was gone since he didn't continue to fire into the room.

"Stay down until Cal and Jon clear the area."

"Copy that." Without taking his focus from the window, Rafe said, "You okay, Kristi?"

"I don't know. Everything hurts."

"I'm sorry." Although Rafe didn't regret shoving her from harm's way, hurting Kristi wasn't his intention. He might not be the tallest man on Wolf Pack, but he carried plenty of muscle from the constant workouts and brutal training regimen Eli and Jon devised to keep them all in shape. He wasn't a lightweight.

"How did you know about the shooter?"

"I saw movement outside the window and reacted." Thank God he had. Otherwise, Kristi might have been shot.

He frowned. Why would the kidnappers risk her life? Maybe they were angry that Stewart sent Fortress instead of paying the ransom, but they couldn't cash in on another kidnapping if the vic was dead.

Kristi's fast and shallow breathing caught his attention. "Slow, steady breaths, Kristi."

"Easy for you to say. You're heavy, Rafe," she said faintly. "Do you carry bricks in your pockets?"

He smiled as he shifted to place his body between her and the window. "Just packing a lot of muscle. Is that better?"

"At least I can draw a full breath, painful though it is."

"Stay still. As soon as Cal and Jon are sure the shooter is gone, Jackson will check you."

She growled. "I'm tired of medical people poking and prodding me. If Dad finds out about this, he'll push even harder for me to move back home."

"Might be best." She would be out of her normal environment and in a place harder for the kidnappers to reach her.

"Best for who? Not me. Dad would take every opportunity to promote Hugh's good qualities."

"We'll find the answers to your questions and ours."

Five minutes later, Eli walked into the workroom with Jon on his heels. "Clear."

Rafe slid his weapon into his holster and crouched beside Kristi. His heart sank at the sight of her pale face. "Get Jackson," he said to Eli.

"I'm here." The medic hurried into the room with his mike bag. His eyes widened as he scanned the room. "Holy cow," he muttered. "There's enough lace in here to give me nightmares." Jackson knelt beside Kristi. "What hurts?"

"Ha. What doesn't?"

He snorted. "Narrow it down for me."

"Ribs and head."

"Any bullet holes I should worry about?"

"No." Kristi's hand shot out to grip Rafe's wrist. "Are you okay?" Panic lent a sharp edge to her voice.

"Not a scratch." Why was she more concerned about his safety than her own?

Kristi's grip loosened. "Thank God. I want to sit up."

"Let me check you before you move." Jackson ran his hands over Kristi's limbs quickly, then moved to her ribs. "So far, so good. Rafe and Jon will give me a hand as we roll you to your back. Let us do the work."

"I'm fine," she protested. "I have work to do."

"You'll get to it faster if you cooperate."

"Hop to it, buddy. Otherwise, I'm drafting you to help with lace, silk, and pearls today."

The medic flinched. "Your woman has a mean streak, Rafe."

"That's why she's perfect for me." He squeezed Kristi's hand. "Ready to roll?"

She smiled at his pun. "Sure."

Jackson glanced at Jon. "You and Rafe roll Kristi over while I hold her head steady." When Jon and Rafe were ready, the medic placed his hands on either side of Kristi's head. "Slow and easy, boys." In less than a minute, Kristi lay on her back. Minutes later, Jackson straightened. "Congratulations, Kristi. You're the proud owner of a bruise on your forehead and more bruises on your ribs."

"Great. Do I get a sucker, Doctor?"

The medic chuckled. "I'm fresh out. Your boyfriend got the last one. I'll have to restock my supply."

"We'll add them to the grocery list. I deserve a treat after someone shot at me." Despite her attempt at levity, her voice wasn't quite steady.

A quick grin. "I agree. Ready to sit up?"

She nodded.

Jackson moved aside and motioned to Rafe. "Slow. This will hurt."

Rafe got into position and eased Kristi to a sitting position.

She groaned. "You would have a made a great professional football player. That's some tackle you have."

"I'm sorry," he said again.

"I'm not. Bruises are better than a bullet."

Jackson patted her hand. "Stay still until we're sure you won't pass out when you stand."

With Kristi resting against him, Rafe looked at Jon. "Sit rep."

"Shooter's in the wind. A male, at least six feet tall, 225 pounds, wearing tactical boots."

Not an amateur. "Weapon?"

"A 9mm handgun."

"Not a sniper, then."

"Not this time. Which of you was in the lead?"

Rafe's jaw tightened. "Kristi."

"She wasn't the target."

"Figured that."

"How do you know?" Kristi asked Jon. "Both of us were walking to the other side of the room when the shooter fired."

He indicated the bullet hole in her wall. "Angle of the shot. The shooter aimed at Rafe. The security company set up cameras outside your home. I need your password to access the system and see what, if anything, the cameras picked up on your visitor."

Kristi gave him the information he needed. "Will we see the shooter's face?"

"Maybe. I'd be happy with a look at his vehicle and license plate."

"What are the chances that will happen?"

"Not good."

Eli headed to the door as Jackson zipped his mike bag and stood. "Jon and I will check the security feed. Cal and Jackson are on duty for the next few hours." The three operatives left the room.

"I'm sorry, Rafe," Kristi murmured.

He frowned. "For what?"

"Dragging you into this mess."

Rafe kissed the side of her neck. "I wouldn't want to be anywhere else. Ready to stand now?" When she nodded, Rafe got to his feet and lifted her, holding her steady.

She looked at the broken window. "I need to clean up the broken glass. Do you have mad carpentry skills as well as awesome kissing skills?"

He chuckled. "I get by in home repairs. I'll ask Brent to send someone to take care of the window."

"He'd do that?"

"We have an army of system installers. Some of them worked in home construction, and Brent has contacts everywhere. Trust me, it won't be a problem to fix your window."

"One less thing for me to worry about today."

Rafe wrapped his arms around Kristi, his hold gentle. "Focus on your work. We'll take care of the rest. What can I do to help?"

"I need to sweep up the glass. I don't want to track shards through the house, especially to the fitting room. Sometimes, my brides-to-be are barefooted when they try on dresses."

"I'll take care of the glass before I call Brent. Where is the broom or vacuum?"

"The closet off the kitchen on this floor."

"You promised me a look at Maggie's dress options. Why don't you get those together while I take care of the glass?"

Rafe retrieved the vacuum cleaner, droppped the large pieces of glass in a nearby trashcan, then vacuumed the remaining slivers and shards. He put away the appliance and returned to Kristi. "Show me what you have."

"You don't have to look at the designs. You won't hurt my feelings."

He was curious about Kristi's work. Callie had mentioned Kristi's amazing designs, hinting more than once that she planned to ask her friend to design a wedding dress when she married Rafe.

For the first time since Callie's death, pain didn't lance Rafe's heart as he thought about the wedding that never happened. Perhaps he was healing. He studied Kristi's face. Maybe solving Callie's murder and connecting with this beautiful, courageous woman helped. Rafe had been in encased in ice for three years, but the ice melted when he rescued Kristi.

She led Rafe to the table in the center of the room and nudged a three-ring binder toward him. "Based on what she described as her dream dress, I created four designs. Then I designed one that I think is perfect for her."

Inside the binder, each dress was shown from several angles with a computer generated model who looked remarkably real. Rafe wasn't an expert on dresses, but Kristi's designs were beautiful. Some designs were classic, others contemporary. The last dress, though, was stunning. The top part was fitted, decorated with lace and pearls in an intricate design. The bottom part hugged the hips, then flared out in a waterfall of fabric. The whole thing reminded him of a vintage dress. The design was a work of art.

He tapped the last dress. "If Maggie doesn't fall in love with this dress, I'll be surprised. They're all beautiful, but this one is breathtaking."

Kristi beamed. "Thanks. I think her groom will be speechless no matter which dress she chooses. I feel good about that particular dress, though."

"The design looks complicated and time-consuming. You said Maggie and the Marine are on a short time clock. Will you have time to finish the work?"

"I'll have to work late several nights if Jill, my assistant, can't give me extra time, but I'll get the work done no matter what. This is important to me. He'll deploy to a hotspot while she waits for him to come home to her. Creating a dress Maggie will remember for the rest of her life is the least I can do to support them both."

"I can't imagine another dress designer going to this much trouble for a rushed wedding."

"They're both sacrificing for our country. What's losing a little sleep compared to that?"

A little sleep and a lot of money since she intended to sell the dress to Maggie at cost. He trailed his hand down her back. "Need anything else before I call Brent? Perhaps another ice pack?"

She shook her head. "Do what you need to do. I'm going to the kitchen to put together trays and start coffee. My first client loves iced coffee with chocolate chip cookies."

"I wouldn't be opposed to chocolate chip cookies with regular coffee. I'm not a fan of the iced variety."

"You don't know what you're missing. I make terrific iced coffee. However, I'll save a few cookies for you." She waited a beat. "For a price."

His lips curved. "What are you charging me?"

"Five kisses."

"Deal. How soon should I pay up?"

Kristi laughed. "Not right now. I'll never get anything done if you do."

"I'll be good." He winked at her. "For now."

More laughter as Kristi walked to the kitchen. Rafe stayed in the workroom and called Brent.

"Yeah, Maddox."

"It's Rafe. Someone fired a bullet into the window of Kristi's workroom."

"Anybody hurt?"

"More bruises on Kristi. Someone's going to pay for that."

A slight pause, then, "Something you need to tell me?"

"She's mine." End of discussion.

"I seem to be running a matchmaking service," came the wry reply. "Guess that's why Alan Stewart called and left a message about your lack of professionalism. Since that isn't your normal operating procedure, I figured something like this might be at the root of his anger. Are you sure, Rafe?"

"I want to give this a shot. This is the first time I've been interested in a woman since I lost Callie."

"If you need a replacement, I'll send one."

His hand clenched around his phone. "Don't go there. I won't leave her."

"Not asking you to. I was talking about sending a bodyguard replacement, not pulling you off the assignment. Recent PSI graduates are ready for supervised field work."

"I don't need a replacement."

"Tell me if the situation changes. I'm not questioning your ethics or integrity. However, your focus will be split. You also have the traumatic loss of a woman you loved in your recent past. Losing Callie left scars. Don't underestimate the impact that will have on you while you safeguard Kristi. The loss will mess with your head if you're not careful."

Galled him to admit that his boss was right. Might be time to set up a session with Marcus Lang for himself. "Yes, sir."

"Anything on the shooter?"

"Not much. Tactical boots, handgun, one shot aimed at me."

A snort. "You failed to mention that last bit of news, Torres."

"Better me than her."

"Element of surprise is gone."

"Yeah, and that's an interesting development along with the fact that someone placed a tracker on my vehicle when we were inside Stewart Group headquarters earlier this morning. I got rid of the tracker before we left the parking lot, but we're not hard to find. Kristi needs her equipment to work."

Brent blew out a breath. "You're making someone nervous. Any other surprises you haven't told me about?"

"Kristi's alarm system is worthless. She needs our top-of-the-line system with all the bells and whistles. I need her safe while I'm deployed, Brent."

"I understand."

"If she balks at the price, give her a huge discount, and bill me the difference."

"Not necessary. We take care of our own. If Kristi is yours, that makes her one of us. Anything else I can do?"

"If she agrees to the Fortress security system, I want an install team as soon as possible. One of her windows has to be replaced."

"I'll take care of it. What else?"

"I want to know where Hugh Ward and Alan Stewart were twenty minutes ago."

"I'll see what I can find out. Keep me updated."

Rafe found Jon and Eli in the first-floor kitchen with Kristi. While Jon worked on his laptop, Eli helped Kristi fill trays with cookies and other finger foods. The scent of coffee filled the room as a large coffeemaker brewed the hot liquid.

Eli caught Rafe's eye and tipped his head toward Jon. The sniper must have already uncovered useful information.

When Eli launched into the story of how he met his wife, Brenna, Rafe took a seat beside Jon. "What did you find?" he asked quietly.

"The installation team who set up Kristi's cameras didn't know what they were doing."

"You didn't get anything?"

"Not as much as I should have, but enough."

"Show me."

Jon tapped a few keys and brought up the footage of the past hour on a split screen. He played the footage on high speed until two minutes before the shooting.

Rafe frowned when a shadow appeared at the edge of the camera on the left side of the computer screen. A moment later, the camera went dark. "He cut the feed?"

"Black spray paint."

He tapped the left side of the screen. "Run the last two minutes again in slow motion." When Jon complied, Rafe kept his gaze glued to the bottom left corner. He'd seen something, but at normal speed, Rafe couldn't figure out what.

He waited until he saw the booted foot in the camera shot. "Freeze that." When the sniper complied, Rafe said, "Back up the feed by fifteen seconds." When the flash appeared, Rafe said, "Back it up again by two seconds. I want to know what that flash is."

A few keystrokes later, Jon isolated the screen shot Rafe wanted. "Can you clean that up?" When he did, Rafe frowned. "It's a specialized design. I know I've seen that before, but can't remember where."

"May I see?" Kristi walked to the table with two mugs of coffee, handing one to Rafe and one to Jon.

The sniper angled the screen for Kristi to see the design.

She gasped. "Oh, no."

Rafe captured her hand. "You recognize the design?"

"It's the marketing logo for the company that provides security for my father, Stewart Group, and my home and business."

CHAPTER SEVENTEEN

Rafe stared at the intertwined W and S. "What company provides the security?" They wouldn't be providing security for Kristi much longer if he had anything to say about it.

"Ward Security." She turned to Rafe. "They're part of Ward Industries."

"Your father recommended them?"

"Dad has used Ward Security for years without an issue. I didn't look into the company myself." She grimaced. "I guess I should have."

"Did your father check Ward Security's track record?"

"I doubt it. My father and Hugh's are best friends."

"He should have investigated the company. Ward Security isn't as good as their advertisements claim." Rafe had heard many things about Ward Security, all of them bad. "Brent's working on a bid for you."

"Good. I need a new system and monitoring company. Jon complained about the camera angles while Eli and I prepared snack trays and coffee."

"Jon's right. Too many blind spots and too little coverage."

"Where would you place the cameras?"

"Do you have paper and a pen?"

Kristi hurried in the direction of the workroom. She returned with a notepad and pen, and passed them to Rafe.

He sketched a quick diagram of her house and marked the places he would set cameras along with the viewing range of each one. Rafe showed the diagram to Jon. Who better to evaluate security coverage than a world-class sniper? "What do you think?"

Jon studied the drawing before taking the pen and sketching trees at the front and back of the house. "She needs cameras here and here."

Kristi frowned. "I'm not comfortable with any security company monitoring me or my clients through the windows."

"The cameras would show the house at an angle. No way to see inside the house. The point is to view the front of the house with one camera and the back of the house with another."

"Aren't the sides of the house vulnerable to someone breaking in unobserved?"

Rafe shook his head. "We have that covered." He tapped the cameras that would do the job. "The small blind spots don't include wall space with a window on either floor."

"I understand now why my security system should be replaced. I have two cameras at the moment, one at the front door and one at the back. Why didn't Ward Security recommend all this?"

"An interesting question. You're wealthy, and your father's net worth is greater than yours. Both of you are prime targets for crime. A single woman should have all the bells and whistles on her security system. You don't. Your security company should have called or sent a guard to check on you when the window shattered and the camera went dark. They didn't."

Blood drained from her face. "I'm lucky the kidnappers didn't take me here. If they had, I shudder to think what might have happened if the GPS tracker had failed. When will Brent call?"

Rafe's phone signaled an incoming call. He glanced at the screen. "Now." Rafe swiped the screen. "You're on speaker with Kristi, Eli, and Jon. What do you have for me, Brent?"

"A quote for Kristi. Zane pulled up schematics on her home and business plus an aerial shot of the land. I sent the proposal to your email. This is the same security system I installed at my home."

Jon's eyebrows rose.

"It includes everything I need?" Kristi asked.

"That system protects the most important people in my life, my wife and daughter."

"I'll review the quote and get back to you."

"Rafe, look at the proposal with her. I included a diagram. If you think of something else you want, we'll include it."

"Yes, sir. Any information on my other request?" The information might not be enough to point a finger at Stewart or Ward. Both men used Ward Security. Did one of them persuade a WS employee to fire a shot through Kristi's window? Would Stewart risk Kristi's life? The gunman might have hit Kristi by accident. Firing through glass was dicey.

"Waiting on confirmation. Zane will contact you soon." Brent ended the call.

Jon slid the computer toward Rafe. "Pull up your email. Let's see what he and Zane have in mind for Kristi."

Rafe logged into his Fortress email account and opened the proposal. He scanned the document, then opened the diagram.

He whistled. Rafe glanced at Jon. "Did you know Brent had all this in his system?"

"He added more security measures when he married Rowan. We have enemies, and Brent's a target. He won't take chances with his family." He looked at Kristi. "This is an excellent system. You'll be safe, and Fortress monitors the system 24 hours a day. If anything happens, they'll know and send a response team and contact the local police."

"What do you think, Rafe?"

"Take it. Your safety is paramount. If price is an issue, Brent will work something out." When Kristi sat beside him, Rafe scooted the computer toward her. "I'll be glad to explain anything you don't understand."

While she read the proposal, Eli and Jon stepped outside to talk to their wives. Rafe sipped his coffee, hoping that Kristi would agree to the new system.

When she finished reading, Kristi said, "Call Brent. Tell him I want the system installed today if possible."

He stilled. "All of it?"

"Every bit and anything else that you think should be added."

Relief swept over him in a tidal wave. "You won't be sorry, Kristi. You'll be safe."

"And you will have peace of mind. Two-way street, remember? I saw a small glimpse of what you do on missions when we were on Hart Mountain. I don't want you distracted while you're deployed. It's my way of helping you return home safe."

An invisible band tightened around his chest. His own family didn't understand his driving need to protect those he loved and cared about. This woman, however, understood and went out of her way to assuage his fears.

Rafe cupped her cheek and kissed her, slow and sweet. "Thank you."

"I need to change clothes. Jill will arrive soon." After brushing her lips over his, Kristi walked upstairs.

Rafe called Brent. "Kristi accepted the proposal. How soon can the install team start?"

"Two hours. I asked the install team to gather equipment after we spoke."

"You knew she would take the system."

"I knew she needed the system, and you needed her to have it, even if Fortress had to absorb the cost of the equipment."

"Thanks, boss."

"The install team will pick up a window to replace the one shattered by the bullet and bring it with them."

"You worked miracles. I owe you."

"Yes, you do. I will collect, Torres."

Rafe chuckled.

"Zane just came in. Hold." A short, muffled conversation later, Brent returned. "You're on speaker, Rafe. Zane, go ahead."

"Heard you had a close call," the former SEAL said.

"No damage except that I added to Kristi's bruises when I tackled her."

"Bruises heal faster than bullet wounds. I looked into Stewart's and Ward's locations when the shot was fired. Stewart hasn't left his office since he arrived at 5:00 a.m., and Ward is in a breakfast meeting at Bakerhill Bistro with four men. The bistro is across town from Kristi's Bridal. Ward is pitching his hedge fund. These men are serious investors with big bucks in their bank accounts and impressive portfolios."

Rafe rubbed his jaw, disappointed that the information didn't resolve some of his questions. "If Stewart or Ward is behind the attack, he doesn't have to do his own dirty work."

"Learn something new?" Brent asked.

"The shooter wore tactical boots with a Ward Security logo stitched on the side. WS is Kristi's former security provider. The same company handles security for Stewart

Group as well as Alan Stewart and is a division of Ward Industries."

The Fortress CEO grunted. "Third-rate company with a lousy reputation in the business. If either Stewart or Ward hired someone from Ward Security to execute the op, he wouldn't have to break into her home to get to her. He'd have all the information needed to walk in."

"Check inside her home for cameras or listening devices," Zane said.

Ice water flowed through Rafe's veins. He should have thought of that sooner. Maybe his focus was too centered on Kristi. "I'll take care of it."

"If the kidnappers are associated with Ward Security, why wait until Kristi was in Gatlinburg to grab her?"

"To prove to Stewart that they could reach his daughter any time they wanted. If Stewart's hotel staff and security couldn't keep Kristi safe, she was vulnerable anywhere."

"Maybe," Brent said. "They also had a better chance to escape without detection in the mountains surrounding Gatlinburg. Bakerhill has cameras everywhere The kidnappers were smart enough to use one of the empty rental cabins to hold her captive. Bad luck on their part that Kristi's father had a tracker implanted and knew where she'd been taken."

"Why would Stewart have his daughter kidnapped?" Zane asked. "Doesn't make sense since he hired us to rescue her."

"I'm still mulling that over," Rafe admitted. "It's possible he didn't kidnap her, but knew who took her or hired the kidnappers. I don't like the man, but I can't see him subjecting Kristi to a kidnapping sure to resurrect nightmares of her first one. I need the case file of her first kidnapping."

"You believe the cases are connected?" Brent asked.

"No clue, but it's worth a look."

"I love to hack fed databases," Zane said. "I'll send a copy of the file to your email."

"Thanks, Z."

"No problem, my friend. How does Kristi like the GPS jewelry?"

"She loves the design and is wearing every piece. I don't know how you decided which design to send Kristi, but your choice was perfect."

"No magic involved. I looked at the dresses on her website. Although the dress styles are different, the designs are all elegant. The lilies of the valley design seemed to be a perfect match for Kristi."

"Is it possible for the installation team to bring a satellite phone for her?"

"I'll have the lead installer stop by my office before they leave. You have a suggestion on the choice of cover?"

Rafe glanced around to be sure Kristi wasn't nearby. "Contact Deke at PSI and ask him to send a picture of the dog Kristi plans to adopt as soon as we run the kidnappers to ground."

"Oliver?" Brent asked.

His eyebrows rose. "Yeah. How did you know?"

"Deke mentioned that Oliver wasn't a good fit for the S & R program, but he hated to send him back to the animal shelter."

"He's a sweet boy. Oliver and Kristi have fallen for each other. Deke offered to do more training with him until we resolve her problem. We need to make that happen soon, Brent. She's mentioned Oliver several times since we left Otter Creek."

"I'm glad Oliver is going to a good home. You should get a dog, Rafe."

"I'm helping Kristi with Oliver. Zane, I owe you a favor."

"Bring Kristi to dinner at our house one night, and we'll call it even. I'd love to meet her in person, and I have a feeling that she and my wife will hit it off."

"Deal. Can we bring Oliver? Once he's living with her, she won't want to leave him behind for a while."

"Not a problem."

"Need anything else, Rafe?" Brent asked.

"No, sir."

"Keep me updated."

Rafe grabbed his Go bag from his SUV, then carried the bag upstairs to the guest room across from Kristi's bedroom before returning to the first floor.

Grabbing the electronic signal detector, Rafe started scanning in the kitchen. He found a bug in the light fixture over the dining table.

Jaw tight, he filled a glass with water and dropped the bug in the liquid. He resumed the search, wondering how many devices he would find and where.

CHAPTER EIGHTEEN

Kristi walked into the kitchen to see Jill staring at Rafe, Eli, and Jon with wide eyes. "Good morning, Jill."

"Do you need help setting up?" Jill's voice came out higher pitched than normal.

Amused, Kristi shook her head. "Have you met my security team?"

"Not yet. I just arrived."

"This is Eli, Jon, and Rafe. Jackson and Cal are somewhere close."

Jill's gaze shifted to Kristi. "Although I appreciate buff guys as much as the next woman, why do you need a team of them protecting you?"

"I was kidnapped over the weekend."

"What?" Her assistant dropped onto the chair behind her. "You're kidding, right?"

"Afraid not."

"Holy cow, Kristi. Your dad didn't mention a kidnapping. He told me you took a couple of days off because you've been working so hard."

"A group of men kidnapped me at the hotel after I delivered Abigail's dress. Rafe rescued me." She glanced at Rafe whose lips edged up at the corners.

"Are you okay, Kristi?"

She dragged her attention from the muscular operative. "Thanks to Rafe, I'm fine."

Jill stood and cupped Kristi's chin. She scowled. "No, you're not. Even the best makeup job in the world can't hide that bruise on your jaw or the one forming on your forehead." Kristi's assistant glared at Rafe. "How did she get those bruises?"

"The kidnappers hurt her. Most of the bruises are from the night she was taken."

Her jaw dropped. "There are more?"

"Jill, I'm fine," Kristi said. "Rafe saved my life more than once over the past two days. Don't blame him for the bruises. We need to start on our to-do list. Maggie will arrive with her mother soon. We have continuous appointments today." After that, Kristi would have another late night as she worked on Maggie's dress.

Her friend blew out a breath. "Right. Did you finalize Maggie's designs?"

"They're in the white binder on the cutting table. Go look at them. I'll be right there." When Jill left, Kristi walked to Rafe and brushed her mouth over his. "Everything okay?"

He shook his head.

"What's wrong?"

"I checked the first floor for listening devices and cameras."

Her blood ran cold. Based on his expression, the news wasn't good. "How many did you find?"

"Six bugs so far, and two cameras. I still need to scan the bathroom and the rooms on the right side of the hall. One of the cameras was in your workroom. The other was in the living room. Once I complete the first-floor search, I'll go upstairs."

Cold chills surged up Kristi's spine. "Can you tell how long they've been in place?"

He hugged her. "No, but I'm getting rid of everything. By the time I'm finished, you won't have to worry about someone listening to your conversations or spying on you with a camera."

"Who is doing this?" she whispered, sick at heart.

He tightened his hold. "I don't know, baby, but I'll find out."

"Kristi, those designs are amazing. I love what you did with them." Jill stopped abruptly in the kitchen doorway. "Oops. Sorry." She backpedaled. "I'll go back to the workroom." A second later, she was gone.

Jon and Eli chuckled as Kristi rested her head against Rafe's shoulder, laughing softly. "Jill will have questions. I better answer them before Maggie and her mother arrive." She kissed Rafe and headed for the workroom.

Jill's cheeks were red. "What's going on between you and the bodyguard? I thought you were marrying Hugh."

"I shouldn't have considered his proposal. I don't love Hugh and never will."

"He's rich, good looking, and fun. You're crazy for letting him get away."

He was almost tapped out and had a gambling problem, but Kristi didn't feel comfortable divulging that information yet. "Do you want to go out with him?"

Jill grimaced. "I doubt Hugh notices me. I don't run in your circles. Anyway, what's going on between you and the bodyguard? He looks familiar, but I can't place him."

"He used to date Callie. Rafe is a good man. He risked his life to save mine."

"Is that all you feel? Grateful?"

"That's the tip of the iceberg. He's kind, loves dogs, treats me like a princess and a strong woman, and he's a genuine hero with a heart of gold. I'm honored to have him in my life. I know that I'm his first priority. I won't have to worry about him paying more attention to his own reflection in the mirror than to me. Rafe won't notice other women except to assess whether they pose a threat to my safety. Rafe Torres is honorable to the core."

Jill studied her a moment. "I haven't heard you say anything like that about Hugh."

"If I did, I'd be lying. I don't see myself spending a lifetime with him." Not like she could with Rafe.

"Hugh called several times while you were gone. He was worried and didn't understand why you refused to answer his phone calls or texts."

Kristi blinked. She'd forgotten to look in her purse for her phone. "We returned to town early this morning and drove to Dad's office. I haven't checked my phone."

"Hugh knows we have several clients scheduled for today. Don't be surprised if he checks on you."

"I don't have time to talk to him. We're booked solid and will be lucky to squeeze in lunch."

"Make time," Jill said flatly. "I'll cover for you while you talk to him. You owe Hugh common courtesy no matter how you feel about him."

Although she was right, Kristi dreaded talking to Hugh. He wouldn't be happy when he realized the easy fix to his financial woes was slipping through his fingers. "You're right."

She couldn't delay the inevitable. Kristi frowned. Would her father have told him the news already? Man, she hoped not. Kristi could imagine how that conversation would have gone.

Refocusing on her primary priorities, she tapped the binder with Maggie's design choices. "What do you think about the dresses?"

"They're fabulous, especially the last one. I think Maggie will love all of them." Jill smiled. "I know her Marine will enjoy seeing his bride in them."

"Let's get to work. I've been thinking about the dress for Genevieve." Kristi explained the new concept as she went to the computer to show Jill what she'd designed before leaving for Gatlinburg.

Fabric rubbing against the wall drew Kristi's attention as Jill studied the dress design on the computer screen. Rafe walked past the workroom and into the room across the hall, his attention focused on the black device in his hand.

"This design is incredible," Jill said. "Genevieve will love the dress. When did you finish the design?"

"Before I left town."

"I'm glad you did. Otherwise, you'd be scrambling to prepare for her appointment." Jill straightened. "I should finish the Gomez dress. Juanita's fitting is this afternoon."

"I'll work on the Boswell alterations." Kristi sighed. "We need another employee."

"Yep, we do. Have anyone in mind?"

"Deidre at the fabric shop. She makes her own clothes, and they're impressive."

"She'd be an excellent choice. She's always cheerful and has great ideas when we talk about designs. Deidre not only makes her clothes, she designs some of them, too."

"Call her this afternoon and ask her to stop by tomorrow or Wednesday after lunch. The sooner I hire someone else, the better. Our workload is exploding."

When the doorbell rang, Kristi glanced at her watch. "That might be Maggie." She rose and walked toward the door, surprised to hear footsteps behind her. Glancing over her shoulder, she raised her eyebrow in silent question. "Going somewhere, Eli?"

"I'm on guard duty until Rafe finishes the search for unwanted electronic surveillance."

"I'll be answering the door all day."

"One of us will answer the door. We promise not to scare off your clients. Safety precaution, Kristi."

Wolf Pack had a protective streak a mile wide. Fighting against it was unwise and fruitless. "It's good you and the others are buff bodyguards. My clients will appreciate the view."

Eli scowled. "Now you're just messing with me."

Kristi laughed as he stalked to the door and checked the peephole.

Wolf Pack's leader sighed and glanced over his shoulder. "Heads up, sugar," he murmured. "Trouble's at the door." With that cryptic comment, he opened the door, blocking entrance to the men standing on the doorstep.

"Who are you?" a male voice demanded. "Where's Kristi?"

CHAPTER NINETEEN

Kristi's heart sank. She didn't need a confrontation with the man hanging his hopes on her trust fund on top of everything else this morning. Maggie was due any minute, and Hugh stood on the doorstep with Ward Security men, demanding to see her. Although the timing was terrible, putting him off would cause more belligerence and aggression.

"Let him in, Eli." Kristi suspected Hugh would cause a scene when she turned down his proposal. She would have to talk to him outside or upstairs, and Wolf Pack would be near if Hugh stepped out of line.

The operative allowed the man dressed in an Italian suit and loafers to push past him, but refused to admit the WS guys.

"Kristi, why didn't you return my calls?" Hugh demanded. His brown eyes glittered with fury as he stalked toward her. "I was afraid the kidnappers hurt you, and Alan refused to talk about the whole sordid business." He gripped her arms and shook her. "How heartless and insensitive can you be? You scared me."

"Let go," Eli snapped, his tone edged with frost, a hand clamped on the expanse between Hugh's neck and shoulder. He pointed a finger at the WS guard who charged into the room. "Out, or you'll regret it."

The man backed up, glaring at Eli.

Hugh's grip loosened as shock filled his eyes and blood drained from his face. He gasped and, a second later, released Kristi.

She moved out of reach, stunned at his violent reaction and Eli's quick response. Had she been totally wrong about Hugh? Before today, she refused to believe him capable of harming her. Now, she wasn't so sure.

"You okay?" Wolf Pack's leader asked her, expression grim.

She nodded. "Thanks."

Eli shifted his hold slightly, and Hugh paled even further. "If you touch Kristi again without permission, I'll take you down. Am I clear?"

After his slight nod, Eli released Hugh abruptly. The operative moved to stand by Kristi's side.

"Who is this Neanderthal?" Hugh asked in a raspy voice, rubbing his shoulder.

"Part of my security detail."

A scowl. "That's impossible. I personally chose all the men assigned to keep you safe."

Kristi stared. "You chose a security detail for me?"

"Of course. You're the most important person in my life, sweetheart."

Revulsion twisted her stomach into a knot at the term of endearment. If Rafe called her sweetheart, she would have appreciated it. The term sounded wrong coming from Hugh.

Eli folded his arms across his chest. "Some security team. They're invisible."

"Hey," one of the WS guards at the door protested.

"No one invited you into this conversation," Wolf Pack's leader said. "Zip it."

"The team I hired for you are highly qualified security specialists," Hugh said. "They're not supposed to be seen. A true professional would know that." He glared at Eli.

"Would have been helpful if they'd been around when Kristi was kidnapped."

Hugh shifted his gaze from Eli to Kristi. "You wouldn't have been kidnapped if I was with you in Gatlinburg, but you refused to allow me to go with you."

Rafe's hard hand settled at the small of Kristi's back. "Let's take this upstairs. One of your clients just arrived. Can Jill handle things for a few minutes?"

She nodded and turned to Eli. "Tell Jill that Maggie's here. I'll be down in a few minutes." Kristi had a feeling Rafe was holding onto his control with a tight leash. Had he heard the confrontation between Eli and Hugh?

"No problem, sugar." Eli looked at the WS guards crowding the door. "You boys go back to your vehicles and stay there, or you'll be having a nice chat with the local police about trespassing on private property."

Rafe motioned for Hugh to walk ahead of them. His hand wrapped around Kristi's as he climbed the stairs with her.

Hugh shoved open the door to Kristi's living space and stalked inside. When she and Rafe walked in holding hands, Hugh's face turned red. "Get your hands off her. Are you responsible for the bruises on her face?"

Oh, man. Kristi winced. Wrong thing to say.

Rafe pinned Hugh against the wall with a forearm pressed against his throat. "Unlike you, I'd never lay a hand on her in anger. If you ever touch Kristi again, I'll tear you apart." His low voice carried an edge of steel.

"I didn't hurt her," Hugh protested.

"You shook her. No man worthy of the name treats any woman with disrespect, much less one he professes to care about."

"She's going to be my wife. I'll treat her any way I want. You have no right to interfere."

Her jaw dropped. Good grief. Enough. If she delayed delivering the bad news any longer, this confrontation would devolve into bloodshed. "I'm not marrying you."

Hugh's eyes widened. "What?" he croaked. "Of course you are."

"Rafe," she murmured. "Please."

The operative released Hugh and stepped back to stand beside her. His hand rested against her lower back again in silent support.

"Kristi, you can't mean that." Hugh straightened from the wall. "We belong together."

"I don't love you." If she hadn't been sure already, Hugh's ridiculous statements and posturing would have convinced her.

He waved that aside. "We have fun together. Your father approves and plans to bring me into Stewart Group. We look good together, Kristi, and we operate in the same social circles."

"I want more in a mate, and so should you. I want a husband who puts me first instead of himself, one who adores me, and supports my goals and decisions. That man isn't you."

"You can't call off the wedding. The plans are already in place." His voice rose.

"Ward." Rafe's tone held a warning.

"You had no right to make wedding plans without my consent or input."

"You're cheating on me." He turned his scathing gaze to Rafe. "He's the one, isn't he? I saw the way he looked at you. He's constantly touching you."

"I like him touching me."

In response, Rafe slid his arm around her waist and tucked her against his side.

"Are you crazy?" Hugh snapped. "He's a security guard and doesn't belong in our social circle. Have you investigated his background? He's after your bank account."

"Unlike you, I don't need Kristi's money," Rafe said.

"I'm employed and have family money, not that it's any of your business."

"Anything that threatens her safety is my business, including you."

"I'm no threat."

"Your behavior indicates otherwise. So does your bank account."

"You hacked my account records? That's it. I'm calling the police. Hacking financial records is illegal."

"Go ahead and call law enforcement. When they arrive, I'll tell them about the irregularities in your hedge fund. I'm sure they'll find that information much more interesting."

Hugh paled. "You're bluffing."

"I never bluff. If you want to test me, go ahead and make that phone call. We'll wait for the police together while Kristi goes back to work."

"I haven't done anything wrong."

"Stealing from a hedge fund to bankroll your gambling addiction is against the law, Ward."

"I'm not an addict."

"The amount of money you owe to casinos all over Las Vegas says otherwise. You're a lousy gambler, and you planned to use Kristi's trust fund to settle your debts."

Hugh turned to her. "Don't listen to him, sweetheart. He's trying to make me look bad. We belong together. You know that."

"How much money do you owe?" Kristi asked.

"Who is this man? Do you know anything about him?"

"This is Rafe Torres. Answer my question, Hugh."

He frowned. "I know that name. Where have I heard it before?"

"He and Callie dated for a while. How much money do you owe?"

"Almost $1 million."

Kristi stared at him, and Rafe whistled. "Are you serious?"

"It's temporary. I'll pay off the debt and be back on track. I swear. One winning streak, and I'll wipe the debt clean."

"The odds are stacked in favor of the house," Rafe said. "Otherwise, casinos would go out of business."

"I have a good system. I'll win back the money."

"Is this the same system you've been using?"

Hugh's cheeks flushed. "It needs a little adjustment."

"Ditch your gambling system and get help for the addiction, Ward."

"I'm not addicted."

"Right. That's why you're in debt over your head, stole money from a hedge fund, drained your trust fund, and looked to Kristi for a quick fix to your problems. Tell me this, Ward. What happens when you pay off the debt? You planning to permanently lay down your cards and walk away from the blackjack table?"

"I can quit anytime I want."

"Really? The time to do that was long before you owed $1 million. How much did you lose overall, Ward?"

"None of your business."

Rafe shrugged. "I'll find out anyway."

"You've almost drained your trust fund," Kristi said, frowning. "Didn't you tell me that you had $20 million in the fund at one point?"

Hugh glared at her. "I planned to pay it back. You still didn't answer my question. Are you with Torres now?"

"Yes."

He snorted. "You're as much of a fool as Callie was. Can't you see that he's using you like he did her? If he marries you, Torres won't have to work another day in his life."

Kristi stiffened, expecting Rafe to go after Hugh again. Instead, he surprised her. Her operative laughed.

"Told you, Ward. I don't need Kristi's money. Better than that, I love my job." His smile faded. "What do you know about Kristi's kidnapping?"

"Nothing except what Alan told me."

"When did you learn that she'd been kidnapped?"

"Alan called me early the next morning and told me that two men grabbed Kristi at the hotel and shoved her into a van. He received a ransom demand and wanted me to be aware of what was going on in case Kristi was allowed to call me."

Even if she'd been allowed to make one call, Kristi wouldn't have called Hugh. Her first instinct would have been to contact her father and now Rafe. She sighed. Her heart had never been involved with Hugh. He wasn't and never would be the person she turned to in a crisis. Rafe, however, was a different story. She couldn't imagine anyone more capable of handling a crisis.

"Where were you the night Kristi was kidnapped?"

Hugh's jaw dropped. "Are you kidding me? I didn't kidnap Kristi. I would never hurt her." When Rafe's eyebrow rose, Hugh's cheeks darkened. "All right. Fine. I would never seriously hurt her. If you're implying that I would kidnap her to force Alan to cough up $5 million, you're nuts. I didn't have to do that. I was planning to marry her."

"Not soon enough to cover your debt," Rafe said, voice soft. "The casinos are threatening to take you to court, aren't they? Once word gets out that you're basically insolvent, your career as a hedge fund manager is toast. Who trusts a hedge fund manager with personal money when he can't keep his personal finances under control? What does your girlfriend say about the debt? Does she know?"

Girlfriend? Kristi frowned. Who was Rafe talking about?

Hugh glanced at her, a guilty expression on his face.

"You were seeing someone else?" Kristi demanded.

"I was lonely, and you're always busy, working long hours. Besides, she doesn't mean anything to me. I just wanted some companionship."

Rafe snorted. "Is that what you call spending weekends at hotels and resorts holed up in your room, ordering room service? Companionship? That's called having an affair where I come from."

Kristi sighed. "If you enjoy her companionship so much, why don't you marry her?"

"I can't," Hugh muttered.

"Why not?"

"She's married."

Kristi groaned. "Unbelievable."

He scowled. "It's your fault, you know."

"How do you figure that?"

"You never had time for me. A man has needs. I guess you made time for Torres's needs."

"That's enough," Rafe snapped. "Insult her again, and I'll do more than shove you against a wall. Call off the security team who was supposed to keep an eye on Kristi."

"She needs protection."

"My team and I have that covered. She's severing her contract with Ward Security this morning."

"That's insane. Kristi, you need protection."

"I've made other arrangements. I need to go. I have a client waiting."

"Can't we talk about our wedding alone? Please, reconsider. We'd be good together."

"Hugh, I wouldn't marry you if you were the last man on the planet."

His expression hardened. "You'll regret this."

"Not a chance. Rafe will see you to the door."

"I know my way out." Hugh headed for the stairway.

"Ward." Rafe waited until Hugh turned to look at him. "If I find out you had anything to do with Kristi's kidnapping, you'll wish you had never been born."

CHAPTER TWENTY

Rafe stood in the doorway, watching a furious Hugh Ward drive away from Kristi's home. That guy was a powder keg. One spark, and he'd explode.

"That is an angry man," Eli murmured. "Kristi broke the bad news?"

"Had to be done. Kristi didn't know about the other woman in his life."

"Other woman?"

"The lady is married which is why he can't marry her. Ward blamed Kristi for his cheating. She wasn't catering to his needs."

"Unbelievable. How did you hear about the other woman?"

"Zane."

"I'm glad you swept Kristi off her feet. Otherwise, she might have married that jerk."

"I don't think so. She's too smart for that." Rafe was glad she chose him over Ward. Now, he had to figure out how to keep her.

When Ward skidded around the corner, barely missing an oncoming car, Rafe closed the door. "Ward said he chose Kristi's former security team. I want names and bios for them."

"Jon will find the information." They walked to the kitchen where the sniper was working on his laptop. "Have another search for you."

"What do you need?"

"Ward chose Kristi's former security team." Rafe folded his arms across his chest. "I want their names and backgrounds."

"More hacking." Jon's lips curved. "Makes my day brighter."

Eli chuckled. "Did Zane send the file from Kristi's first kidnapping yet, Rafe?"

He shook his head. "Phantom's in a hotspot. I should have the file soon."

Jon grabbed his phone. "I'll find out if he needs help."

While the sniper spoke to the Fortress tech wizard, Eli turned to Rafe. "Is upstairs clear of bugs and cameras?"

"I bagged a bug and camera in every room except the bathroom."

Eli scowled. "Including the bedroom?"

He nodded. "I haven't told Kristi yet. She'll be upset." Who had been watching her and for how long? If Ward Security was responsible the cameras, including the one in the bedroom, what purpose did the violation of Kristi's privacy serve? Rafe's gut said someone on her security team was responsible for the electronic surveillance.

Did Stewart or Ward instigate the unethical spying? Rafe frowned. He wouldn't be surprised if Ward authorized the spying. Although Stewart was protective of his daughter, Rafe didn't believe he would sanction a camera and bug in Kristi's bedroom.

"Do yourself a favor, and don't wait long to tell her. She won't thank you for holding back the truth to protect her."

Rafe wanted to ignore his team leader's advice, but that would be a colossal mistake.

Jon ended his call. "Zane accessed the FBI database. You'll have a copy of the file in a few minutes."

"Things settled down for Phantom?"

"Yep. They were in Costa Rica, rescuing an American hostage from a drug cartel. The jet just went wheels up with the vic. No injuries."

"Excellent." He'd been in that area several times as a SEAL and in his short stint as an FBI agent. Cartels were a serious problem.

He glanced at the coffee pot. The carafe was empty. Rafe rinsed out the container and prepped the coffeemaker. After starting the appliance, he scanned the food trays. His lips curved. Kristi's cookies and muffins were popular. He refreshed the tray, filling in the gaps with more sweet treats.

Rafe glanced in the refrigerator and snagged bottles of water for Jill and Kristi. He'd coax Kristi to eat as soon as Maggie and her mother left. He walked to the workroom and found Jill at a sewing machine.

She glanced up. "Hi, Rafe. Looking for Kristi?"

"I brought water for you both." He set one bottle of water on the nearby table.

"She's in the next room, showing designs to Maggie. Go on in. Kristi will be happy to see you."

He studied her neutral expression. "Problem, Jill?"

"You tell me. You're the one who popped into her life unexpectedly, rescued the damsel in distress, and claimed the damsel for a girlfriend, all in the space of two days."

"She's lucky to have you as a friend."

"Why do you say that?"

"You care enough about Kristi to suspect my motives."

"Your appearance in her life at this particular time is suspicious in my book."

"Understandable. I have Kristi's best interests at heart. I would take a bullet for her in a heartbeat."

"That's handy, especially considering what's happened. But what about her heart?"

"I'll protect her heart as fiercely as I will her body. She matters to me, Jill." More than he'd thought possible in their short time together. Perhaps the stories he heard about her from Callie or Rafe and Kristi's intense hours together on the run from the kidnappers paved the way for their deep connection.

Kristi fascinated him on every level. For the first time since losing Callie, Rafe could envision a future with a different woman. "Kristi is safe with me."

"I guess we'll see." Jill folded her arms. "If you hurt her, you'll answer to me. I don't care if you're capable of killing me in a thousand different ways. Kristi is a good friend, and I'll make you pay."

"The warning isn't necessary, but I'm glad you care enough to watch over her." He walked to the next room and tapped on the door.

Inside the room was a woman in her fifties, a dark-haired woman in her mid-twenties, and the woman who was becoming more necessary to him than his next breath.

Kristi came to him, concern in her eyes. "Hey. Is everything all right?"

"I brought you water," he murmured. "How are you holding up?"

"I'm fine."

His eyebrow rose.

"If you're too nice to me right now, I'll cry," she whispered. "I don't want to upset Maggie or her mother."

"I'll offer you a shoulder later." He winked. "And a few skillful kisses."

That made her laugh. "Deal." She threaded her fingers through his. "Come meet Maggie and her mother."

After the introductions, Rafe turned to Maggie. "Kristi showed me the dresses she designed for you. Have you chosen one?"

"They're all beautiful, but I fell in love with this one." She tapped the fifth design, the one Kristi said was perfect for her.

"Excellent choice. Your Marine is a lucky man."

The bride blushed. "Thank you."

"Do you ladies want more tea or snacks?" When they declined, Rafe brushed a light kiss on Kristi's mouth and left the room. As he walked away, Rafe heard Maggie's next words.

"Rafe is very handsome, Kristi. If he's the man who rescued you over the weekend, I hope you hang on to him. He looks like a keeper."

"He is."

Rafe retrieved his laptop from his room and returned to the kitchen. He grabbed two bottles of water from the refrigerator and tossed one to Jon, keeping the second for himself.

"Thanks."

Rafe booted up his laptop. The FBI file on Kristi's first kidnapping was in his email.

Opening the file, he started to read. By the time Rafe finished, he wanted to gather Kristi into his arms and hold her close for a long time. He learned the basics of the kidnapping from Kristi. The FBI file contained forensic evidence from the scene of her mother's murder and the place where Kristi was held for those harrowing days, locked in a closet and abused by a child molester.

He slammed down the laptop lid, shoved back from the table, and walked out the back door. Sick at heart and emotionally gutted, Rafe headed for a bench in Kristi's flower garden.

He'd handled hard things as a SEAL and an FBI agent, but knowing Kristi had endured a nightmare at a young and impressionable age tore him to shreds. How had she emerged from that experience whole and healthy? Yeah, she was afraid of the dark. People who weren't traumatized as a kid had the same fear. Kristi was strong, but was she strong enough to go the distance with him?

He dragged a hand down his face. The fact that he was considering a permanent relationship with Kristi told him how deep she'd burrowed into his heart.

A whisper of sound alerted him to one of his teammates approaching. Jon sat on the other end of the bench. He remained silent for a few minutes. Finally, he glanced at Rafe. "Want to talk or should I mind my own business and enjoy the sunshine?"

Rafe gripped the edge of the bench. "I read her FBI file."

"Ah." Jon kept his gaze on the colorful vista in front of them. "How bad?"

"The worst." He tore his gaze from the flowers and looked at his teammate. "One of the kidnappers was a child molester. Repeat offender."

Jon's jaw hardened. "Did they catch him?"

Throat tight, he nodded. "I want to follow up on every man involved in her first kidnapping. While one of them being involved in this kidnapping isn't likely, it's another line to tug."

"Want help?"

"Not yet. Your searches on Ward and Stewart take precedence along with the information on her former security detail. If I run into a roadblock, I'll let you know."

"That kind of trauma never goes away," Jon murmured. "Time helps but the memories leave scars."

"How do I help her?"

"Be a sounding board when she needs it. Hold her when memories and nightmares crowd reality. Understand that her darkness phobia will likely stay with her for life."

"Doesn't seem to be enough. After what she went through, I'm amazed Kristi allows me to touch her. She's a walking miracle and the strongest person I know."

"High praise."

"Absolute truth."

Jon looked at him. "She'll have to be strong to survive the danger circling around her, and to handle a relationship with you."

He flinched. "I won't hurt her."

"I was referring to our career. Being involved with an operative isn't for the faint of heart."

"She can handle it." But would she want to?

Jon stood. "I have the names of the men assigned to your woman's protection detail." His lip curled. "Most of them aren't worth their pay."

"I'm not surprised." Rafe rose. "Show me."

They returned to the kitchen, and Rafe sat beside Jon as his teammate called up the first file.

"Roderick Hale." Jon clicked on the picture of the unsmiling man. "This guy's a real prince. Dishonorably discharged from the Army for assaulting fellow soldiers and civilians. Some of the injuries were severe enough to land people in a hospital for weeks. Hale hired on with Ward Security four years ago. Same track record. Run-ins with the law and some complaints by principals."

Rafe stared. "I'm surprised he still has a job. Why did Ward assign him to Kristi?"

"He's built like a Mack truck and is trained to fight. He was on duty the night Kristi was kidnapped in Gatlinburg."

His hand fisted. "Are you serious?"

"Hale and his partner, Fleming, were in the bar, tying one on."

"They should be fired," Rafe muttered.

"They shouldn't have been hired to begin with. If nothing else, Ward should have insisted on better men to protect Kristi."

"Next one."

"Mike Fleming. At one time, he worked for Silver Star Security."

Rafe rolled his eyes. "Another third-rate outfit. What happened?"

"They booted Fleming out the door after one of his principals accused him of driving her vehicle while drunk. That wasn't the only time he was accused of being drunk on duty."

And Ward trusted this man with Kristi's safety? Rafe shook his head. "Next."

Another click of the keyboard. "Meet Sean Howell, a rent-a-cop at a series of malls before Ward Security hired him. No military or law enforcement experience in his background."

"Why did WS hire him?"

"His father was in the same fraternity as Hugh's father. They were close friends."

"Any skeletons in Sean's closet?"

"He was fired from the malls because he lifted merchandise."

"Terrific. Who's the last winner?"

"Dan Adams. This one is interesting. He used to be Special Forces. Dishonorably discharged when he punched a superior officer and decked a civilian in a bar fight."

"Reason?"

"The officer suspected an ambush on an operation, but sent Adams' unit in anyway. Adams lost his best friend in the firefight."

"I want their files."

"Already sent to your email." Jon inclined his head toward the picture of Adams. "This one has the training to pull off the kidnapping and the shot through the window. So does Hale."

"We'll look at all of them." Feminine laughter drew Rafe's attention to the hallway. He rose and followed the sound to the living room where Kristi stood with Maggie and her mother.

"Are you sure you can finish the dress in time for the wedding?" Maggie asked. "It's beautiful, but intricate."

"I won't let you down. Let me worry about the dress. You concentrate on the rest of the details for your wedding and honeymoon."

Maggie hugged her. "I'll never be able to thank you enough for this."

"Spread the word to your friends and family about your dress designer. That's thanks enough."

"Oh, I will." The bride smiled at Rafe. "I'm glad Kristi has someone special in her life. You'll look out for her?"

"You have my word."

As soon as the women left, Kristi turned to Rafe. "Did you finish the search for electronics upstairs?"

Oh, man. He didn't want to have this conversation with Kristi right now. "I did. Your living quarters is clear now."

"Did you find anything up there?"

"Quite a bit. We'll talk about it when your workday is finished."

She sighed. "That bad, huh?"

Rafe hugged her and glanced up as another vehicle pulled into her small parking lot. "Looks like your next client has arrived."

"Right on time." She smiled up at Rafe. "Too bad. I was hoping to score one of those kisses you promised me."

"You'll have something to look forward to. I'll send Eli to the grocery store for dinner ingredients. Is there anything you can't eat or don't like?"

"I'm not fond of fish. Other than that, I'll try anything."

"Perfect. What I want to make is simple, fast, and so good you'll be tempted to keep me around for a long time."

"I can't wait to taste the food." She kissed him lightly. "Or you," she whispered before turning away to greet her client.

After Kristi introduced him to the bride-to-be and escorted her down the hall, the Fortress installation team pulled up in two vans and a pickup.

Rafe went out to meet them, pleased to see a friend had been assigned to the installation team. He held out his hand to Santos Massey. "Good to see you, Santos. How's your family?"

"Fantastic, my friend. Rosita has been after me to ask you to dinner."

"I'd love to come and bring my girlfriend to meet your wife."

Santos stared. "Girlfriend?" He clapped Rafe on the shoulder. "It's about time. Rosita will be pleased to hear about the new woman in your life. Who is she?"

"Kristi Stewart."

An eyebrow rose. "The woman who lives here?"

"The same. She's in trouble, Santos. Kidnapping victim plus a gunman fired a bullet through her window this morning."

His friend sobered. "Connected?"

"No question. Complicated situation."

"I'll personally make sure everything is in perfect working order before I sign off on the job."

"Thanks, man. I owe you."

"Happy to do it. If you'll give Mathis a hand with the window, I'll organize the rest of the crew, and we'll get to work."

"Sure. Start your crew upstairs or at the back of the house. Kristi runs her business out of the first floor. She'll have clients coming and going most of the day. I'll introduce you to Kristi, then help Mathis."

After introducing Santos to Kristi, Rafe found Mathis. Together, they unloaded the window and went to the workroom.

The day passed quickly with Rafe assisting the installation team. He should have been researching or taking a nap since he had the watch overnight. His driving need to ensure Kristi was protected by a security system was his first priority.

CHAPTER TWENTY-ONE

Rafe glanced over his shoulder when Kristi wrapped her arms around his waist. He set aside the forks he used to shred the cooked chicken, wiped his hands on a towel, and turned to hold her against his chest. "Finished?" he murmured.

"For the moment. I have to work after dinner."

He wanted to insist she give herself a break and delay the work until tomorrow, but that wouldn't be wise. Rafe suspected she'd be working late on Maggie's wedding dress. The deadline was approaching fast. "If I'm not on duty, I'll keep you company."

"You aren't going to lecture me about working too hard?"

He tightened his grip. "Would it do any good?"

She laughed. "No. I have a lot of work to do on Maggie's dress and few days to finish."

"I'll pick my battles and save my wise advice for another time."

"Hugh wouldn't be so understanding."

Rafe grunted. "You're comparing me to Ward?"

"There is no comparison," she assured him. "You leave Hugh in the dust."

"Good to know."

"Since I'm taking a break, do you need help with dinner?" When Kristi turned her head to see what he was doing, she winced.

He frowned. "Is your headache back?"

"The pain never left. My neck and shoulders are tight."

Rafe led her to a chair at the breakfast bar. "Sit here." When she complied, Rafe massaged her shoulders and neck.

She moaned. "You're hired as my massage therapist for life."

He chuckled. "Glad I have career options."

Jackson, who sat at the other end of the breakfast bar with his laptop, snorted.

"You heard the lady." Rafe smiled at his teammate. "Magic hands."

"The lady is biased. You should have better taste in men, Kristi. When you tire of Torres, come see me. We'll ride off into the sunset together, and you won't remember his name."

"Hey." Rafe lightly punched the other man on the shoulder before resuming the massage. "Find your own girl."

"All the good ones are taken." Jackson closed his laptop and stood. "What time is dinner?"

"Thirty minutes."

"I'll be outside until then." Seconds later, he was gone.

Rafe frowned. What was eating at Jackson?

"Is he all right?" Kristi asked.

"I'll find out later."

"How? Wolf Pack doesn't share feelings with each other."

Rafe chuckled. "I'll hassle him, of course. What else would a good friend do?"

"Is he upset because we're together?" She twisted to face him. "I don't want to cause a rift between you and your teammates."

He kissed her, aware they could be interrupted by his teammates or the installation team. "Something's been bothering Jackson for a while. I'll find out what's going on. Do you feel better or should I continue the massage?"

"I'm better. How can I help?"

"How are you at assembling a salad?"

"I'm the salad prep queen. When I'm pressed for time and need a quick meal, grilled chicken on top of a salad is my first choice."

"You're hired. Salad stuff is in the refrigerator."

"What's dinner?"

"Chicken fettuccine and salad."

She stared. "You made fettuccine from scratch?"

"Not this time. When we have time, I'd like to try it together. I used pre-made pasta and alfredo sauce."

When they finished the meal preparation, he called in his teammates and went to look for Santos.

Rafe found his friend on the second floor, wiring the outside access door for the alarm system. "How's it going?"

"We have at least three more hours of work. Sorry, buddy. We're moving as fast as we can."

"No problem. Dinner's ready if you and your team want to eat."

Santos stared. "Are you serious? You made dinner for us?"

He shrugged, cheeks burning. "It's nothing fancy. Just a good, hearty meal. I made enough to feed an army."

The other man grinned. "We'll take it. Thanks, Rafe. Do you want us to come down in shifts?"

"Not necessary if your guys don't mind sitting on the floor."

"We'll meet you downstairs."

As Rafe retraced his steps, Santos gave an ear-splitting whistle and told his team to head to the first-floor kitchen.

An hour later, everyone had eaten, and Jackson and Cal volunteered for kitchen cleanup. "You and Kristi did the hard work," Cal said. "Eli and Jon are sleeping. You have night watch and should rest yourself."

"Kristi has to work. I'll keep her company for a while." Even with the security system in place, he'd feel better if he was with her.

Kristi threaded her fingers through Rafe's. "The workroom has a comfortable couch. I use it when I'm working late and need a power nap." She smiled as she tugged him toward the hallway. "I'll give you a pillow and blanket."

"Sounds good." He squeezed her fingers as he followed her to the end of the hall.

Inside the workroom, Kristi frowned as the installation work resumed. "Will you be able to sleep with that racket?"

"I'll be fine."

She grabbed a pillow and blanket from the closet and handed them to Rafe. "The pillowcase is fresh." After giving him a quick kiss, Kristi went to her desk and sat in front of her computer. Minutes later, a large printer began to print pattern pieces.

Fascinated, Rafe watched the printing process as Kristi left the room and returned with bolts of fabric.

She unrolled the material. "I thought you needed to sleep."

"Soon. This process is interesting."

"You've never seen a garment made from scratch?"

He chuckled, thinking of the mess his mother had made of pajamas bottoms for him and his brothers for Christmas one year. She never attempted to make clothes from scratch again. "My mother made matching pajama bottoms for me and my brothers one year. She never tried to sew again."

"Didn't turn out well, huh?"

"We wore them anyway, but Mom wouldn't let us use them when we had sleepovers with friends. She said if anyone saw the pajamas, she wouldn't be able to face our friends' parents."

"How old were you boys when she made them?"

"Elementary school. We were growing so fast back then that she was able to cut them up to use for cleaning rags within six months." He grinned. "Best rags ever. They were covered with pictures of race cars."

"How many brothers do you have?"

"Two, both older." He set aside the blanket and stretched out on the couch with the pillow beneath his head. "Keep the curtains closed, and stay away from the windows."

"All right. Rest now. I'll wake you if there's a problem."

Not necessary. He'd know if she needed him. Rafe fell into a light sleep with Kristi's movements around the room and the installation team's work as background noise.

Three hours later, he woke when someone headed down the hall in their direction. Rafe stood up as Santos strode into the room. "Finished?" he asked his friend.

A nod. He turned to Kristi. "You're all set, Ms. Stewart. If you'll take a break, I'll show you how your new security system works."

She set her scissors aside and straightened with a wince. "Please, call me Kristi."

Rafe followed her and Santos to the living room where his friend helped Kristi choose a code for her system and showed her how to arm and disarm the alarm. Following a quick tour of the security room set up in an unused closet on the first floor and a demo on how to access the security footage, Santos showed Kristi the screen mounted in her bedroom that allowed her to see the property.

"If anything happens or makes you feel uneasy, check the screen. Fortress monitors the system twenty-four hours a day. If anything happens, they'll notify the police, Wolf Pack, Rafe, and you."

"Who will be notified if Wolf Pack is deployed?"

"Maddox and one of the black ops teams in town will respond immediately," Rafe said. "We have you covered."

"Maddox and black ops teams respond to alerts under normal circumstances?"

He shook his head. "Because we're dating, Fortress will take extra precautions." He'd have to talk to Kristi about what to tell her father and friends about his work, and the safety precautions she had to take from now on. Twenty minutes later, Santos and his team packed up their equipment and left.

"I can't believe how fast Santos and his crew installed everything."

"He and his team are the best installers we have." Rafe drew her into his arms. "Need another shoulder and neck massage?"

She gave a soft laugh. "In the worst way. However, if you work out the knots, I'm afraid I'll fall asleep, and I still have work to finish."

"How soon can you stop?"

"Perhaps another hour. I need to cut the material so Jill and I can sew the dress tomorrow. We'll have Maggie come in the day after to check the fit and make alterations before we apply the pearls and lace. The detail work will take the longest to finish."

"I'm amazed at how fast this part of the work is going." He brushed a kiss over her mouth and walked downstairs with her. "Do you need a snack or drink?"

"No food for me while I work with the dress. I can't risk staining the material."

"What about water?"

"As long as I drink somewhere besides at the cutting table."

Rafe nudged Kristi toward the workroom. "I'll bring water and my laptop so I can work while you finish."

He walked to the kitchen where Cal stood at the back door, peering into the yard. "Problem?"

"Nope. Regular security check. I'll do a perimeter sweep soon." He turned and refilled his mug with coffee. "Kristi asleep?"

"I wish. She's working on the Marine bride's wedding dress and needs at least another hour." He grabbed two bottles of water and his laptop. Although Rafe wanted to give Kristi the treat he'd asked Eli to pick up at the store, he'd wait until she stopped work for the night.

He returned to the workroom and opened one of the bottles of water for Kristi. After she drained the bottle, she returned to cutting fabric pieces while Rafe booted up his laptop.

He clicked on his email and started to read. Rafe should have a chat with Kristi's former security team, especially Adams. The Special Forces soldier had the skills necessary to pull off the kidnapping and shooting. He hated to think an operator would use his skills to harm an innocent.

Roderick Hale was another matter entirely. Military trained, he could have pulled this off. If so, what motive would he and the others have? Money was one answer. Jon was working night watch with him. Perhaps his teammate would have time to follow unusual money trails.

Two hours later, Kristi straightened with a groan. "I'm finished for now. I'll start assembling the dress tomorrow morning before my clients begin to arrive."

He glanced at his watch. Not too late for a couple of chocolate-covered strawberries. Closing the lid of his laptop, Rafe stood and held out his hand to Kristi. "I have a treat for you."

Her eyes twinkled. "Kisses?"

He chuckled. "Those, too. A sweet treat first." In the kitchen, Rafe set his laptop on the breakfast bar.

Cal turned. "Finished for the night?" he asked Kristi.

"I have to be. My vision is blurry. I can't afford to make a mistake with the wedding this close."

Rafe retrieved the small box containing the strawberries from the refrigerator. "Make your favorite tea, and we'll go outside for a few minutes."

She smiled. "Sounds romantic."

"That's the idea." When her tea finished steeping, they walked outside.

Kristi went to the outdoor couch on the deck. "Want to sit here?"

"That's perfect." Kristi would be comfortable, and the couch was in a place not easily seen from the street.

Rafe sat beside her, lifted the lid on the box, and placed the container on her outstretched hands.

She peered inside. "Chocolate-covered strawberries are my favorite treat. How did you know?"

"I have my sources." He rested his arm along the back of the couch, enjoying the balmy night. When Kristi finished the strawberries, Rafe took the empty box from her hands.

"Thank you." She leaned her head against his shoulder. "I'm sorry I don't have anything to offer you."

"Being with you today, knowing you're mine, is more than enough." He kissed her temple and drew her closer. The news he needed to share would be difficult for her to hear. "I mentioned earlier today that I found cameras and bugs upstairs."

She stiffened and started to shift away from him.

Rafe held her in place. "Stay," he murmured.

"Tell me. I'd rather know the truth than live in ignorance."

"Cameras and bugs were set up in every room upstairs except the bathroom."

She slowly lifted her head to look into his eyes. "My bedroom, too?"

He nodded. "I'm sorry."

"How could anyone do that to me?" Her voice broke. "What if the footage leaks to the Internet?"

Rafe cupped her cheek with his palm. "I won't let that happen. Don't give them the satisfaction of seeing you shaken by this. Demonstrate your strength by holding your head high. They believe you're weak. They're dead wrong, baby."

He held her close for several minutes, then reached into his pocket and grabbed the Fortress phone. "I have something else for you."

"Rafe, you're spoiling me," she protested.

"Let me." He passed her the phone.

Kristi looked at him with a puzzled expression. "I have a phone."

"This is an encrypted satellite phone so we can communicate safely when I'm deployed." He tapped the phone. "No one will be able to intercept our messages. We're frequently deployed to places without cell coverage. A satellite phone works around that problem. Turn it over."

With a bemused expression, Kristi did as he requested. She gasped. "Oliver. Did you take the picture when we were in Otter Creek?"

"Deke took one and sent it to Zane. Santos brought the phone."

"Oliver's picture was your idea, wasn't it?" She kissed him. "Thank you, Rafe. I love the picture. I'm glad I'll be able to communicate with you while you're gone. How often are you deployed?"

"One month on deployment, one month off. When we're off rotation, we train."

"Are you ever called in during a training month?"

"If there's a pressing need, yes. Fortress is short-handed, and Maddox is constantly recruiting new teams. He just hired a team of brothers not too long ago, but they haven't joined the rotation yet. It won't be like when I was a SEAL and deployed for months at a time or whenever they needed my team."

When she studied his face in silence, Rafe's heart sank. Had Kristi decided he wasn't worth the risk after all? "Have a question?"

"I'm not Callie," she murmured.

He froze. Of all the comments he'd expected, that wasn't on his radar. "Where are you going with this?"

"Callie enjoyed being a society princess and wanted a permanent escort to all the functions and fundraisers she attended. She worked hard for charity, but didn't have an interest in pursuing a career. That's not me, Rafe."

His eyebrow rose. "You attend functions and raise money for charity yourself. What makes you different?"

"I have a business to run whether you're home or deployed."

"Does that mean you won't miss me?"

She poked him gently in the chest. "You know better than that. I'll miss you like crazy, but I won't curl up in a ball and go into a deep depression. I'll keep myself busy and look forward to text messages or phone calls from you each day. My point is that I can and will handle your absences. When you're home, I'll enjoy spending every minute I can with you."

The longer she spoke, the faster the ball of ice in his stomach melted. Kristi wasn't going to walk away. Thank God. "So, you're not kicking me to the curb, huh?"

"No." Another kiss from the beautiful woman in his arms, this one longer and deeper. "I'm keeping you."

He tightened his grip. "I don't want to escape."

She smiled against his mouth. "Good to know. Kiss me."

Rafe captured her mouth for a series of long, intense, and deep kisses. He craved her touch and taste, and feared he'd never get enough of Kristi Stewart.

He broke the kiss as the realization that he was in love with this woman hit him with the force of a hurricane. Telling her the truth of how he felt wasn't an option. Definitely too soon to share the news. He needed time to win her heart before he bared his soul and begged her to spend the rest of her life with him.

"Is something wrong?" Kristi asked.

"Everything is exactly right." All he had to do was convince Kristi that he was worth the risk to her heart.

CHAPTER TWENTY-TWO

An hour later, Rafe walked with Kristi inside the house and upstairs to her bedroom. He paused at the doorway, wrapping his arms around her, reluctant to let her go.

She glanced over her shoulder into the bedroom. "Are you sure you found all the cameras?"

"Positive."

"I don't know if I'll ever feel comfortable sleeping in my own bedroom again."

"Don't let them win, Kristi."

"I can't sleep if the room is dark. That means someone watched me sleep." She shuddered.

"That will never happen again." When he found out who gave the order to place a camera in Kristi's bedroom, Rafe's conversation with him might involve his fists.

He longed to tell Kristi that he loved her, but this wasn't the time or place. He also needed time to show the lady how much she meant to him. "I'll be on watch from midnight to four. If you need me or if something spooks you, even a nightmare, come to me."

Concern filled her eyes. "Three hours of catnapping on the couch doesn't seem like enough."

"I had less sleep than that each day for weeks at a time during BUDS." He kissed her lightly. If he indulged in a deeper kiss, he might not be able to stop. Kissing Kristi was addictive.

"If something happens, come get me."

"I will." Rafe nudged her inside her bedroom. "Leave the door unlocked." He stepped back.

"No good night kiss from my favorite Navy SEAL?"

Rafe tapped her nose. "Not wise, beautiful. My legendary control is like mist around you."

Kristi smiled. "I'll take that as a compliment. See you in the morning." She closed the door.

Rafe headed to the kitchen to get his laptop and continue reading the files before he began his shift. He wanted to reread the FBI file as well. Hopefully, he'd be able to view the file without strong emotion blindsiding him.

He sighed. Fat chance of that happening. Studying that file without wanting to kill the men responsible for hurting Kristi wasn't possible with his emotions tied in a knot.

Jackson was alone in the kitchen, standing watch at the back door. The medic seemed to be a million miles away. "Jackson."

His teammate glanced over his shoulder before resuming his perusal of the yard. "How's Kristi?"

"Exhausted."

"Understandable."

Rafe waited, hoping his friend would talk to him. Nothing. Should have known. "What's up, Jackson?"

"Nothing."

He snorted. "That's the same answer Mom gives me when I ask what's bugging her. Try again."

"Are we going to be BFFs now, Torres?"

"You've been out of sorts for weeks. I want to help. Wolf Pack had my back when dismantling the Hunt Club renewed the pain of losing Callie. I'm returning the favor."

"Appreciate the offer."

"But mind my own business?"

The medic lifted one shoulder. "You said it, not me."

Rafe rolled his eyes. Stubborn man. All of his teammates were mule stubborn. "If you want to brood, I'll let you. For now. Kristi's worried that our dating relationship upset you. Dial it down around her. She has enough to worry over without adding your resistance to our dating into the mix."

Jackson spun, frowning. "This has nothing to do with Kristi. In fact, I'm happy that you've healed enough to let go of Callie. Her loss was eating you alive, and I hated that I couldn't help."

"You didn't sound supportive a few hours ago."

The other man growled. "Look, I want a wife and a family. I thought I met the right woman. Turned out that she was nothing like I thought. Jon and Eli are married to women they adore. Cal is engaged to Rachelle, and now you're with Kristi. It's not easy to be the only one alone."

Rafe picked through all the peripheral stuff and focused on the bottom line. "The dating relationship was that bad?"

"She's toxic, and I'm better off without her," Jackson said flatly. "I'm disappointed. I'll survive. I have the right to keep my own counsel, Torres. The last thing I want to do is talk about my disastrous relationship with a bunch of SEALs who are in committed relationships. Might take time, but I'll pull out of my funk. And don't even think about having Eli or the boss pull me from duty. I can handle the job while I brood."

"I'm sorry. Don't give up hope."

"My business." He folded his arms over his chest, lips curled in a half-hearted sneer. "Are we going to sit around discussing our feelings and braiding each other's hair or get back to work?"

He snorted. Smart aleck. "I'll say one more thing, then shut up on the subject. I thought I'd never be happy again after I lost Callie. I was wrong."

Jackson studied him a moment. "You're in love with Kristi."

Rafe gave a slight nod.

The other man whistled. "Does she know?"

"Do I look stupid?"

A quick, genuine grin. "You don't want me to answer that."

"Watch it." His lips curved. "I plan to romance her before I spring that on her. Lots of romancing."

"Cupid's arrow moved at the speed of light."

"I'm aware."

"Most people will say it's too fast. With our jobs, though, we see the value of life and how quickly time could run out."

"I've known Kristi for a few years because she was friends with Callie. I knew a lot about her before the rescue on Hart Mountain. I learned a lot about her during those hours on the run from her kidnappers. I believe those factors moved this relationship to a higher level faster than normal."

"I'm betting her father won't approve."

"The only person whose approval matters is Kristi."

"While that's true, Stewart is an important part of his daughter's life. Unless you can win him over, his disapproval will be a roadblock in the long run."

"I hear you." Kristi was his priority, not Alan Stewart. After she was safe, Rafe would romance the woman who captured his heart and earn her father's respect if not his approval.

Rafe clapped the medic on the shoulder and grabbed his laptop. "I'll be on the second floor until my shift starts."

"Want me to stay on her couch while you're on watch?"

A nod. "Thanks."

"Go. You're distracting me from watching the grass grow."

With a chuckle, Rafe retraced his steps to the second floor and settled on Kristi's couch to reread the file from her first kidnapping. From what he could see, the feds had nabbed the right men, and the forensics team hadn't missed anything.

Going back to the beginning, he focused on the men involved in the kidnapping. Three men had broken into the house, killed Kristi's mother, and taken Kristi to hold for ransom. Those men were captured by the FBI and sentenced to prison. Jeff Adkins died in federal custody. The second kidnapper, Raymond Clark, had been sentenced to 20 years in prison. The judge sentenced Trevor Cain, the child molester, to 30 years in prison.

Rafe glanced at his watch. Time for his shift. He'd have to follow up on Clark and Cain later. After shutting down his computer, he stored the laptop in his Go bag and went to relieve Jackson.

He walked into the kitchen and filled a mug with coffee. "I have the watch," he told the medic. "Get some rest."

"Jon's in the security room. No one will slip past me, Rafe. I'll keep her safe for you." Jackson left.

Security room. Rafe snorted. The room was a closet. He'd relieve Jon later to give the sniper a chance to stretch his legs.

Once Rafe had downed half the coffee in his mug, he disabled the alarm and checked the perimeter. So far, nothing had changed. No signs of incursion or trespass.

A few houses down, a dog barked. Rafe frowned. He moved to the shadowed corner of the house and waited, alert for trouble. The neighbor's dog went silent.

When the silence continued, he resumed his circuit around the property. Although Rafe didn't spot anything out of the ordinary, his skin crawled. Returning to the house, he reset the alarm and walked to the security room.

"Anything?" Jon asked.

"Heard a barking dog. Nothing's changed, but something isn't right out there."

"I'll keep an eye out."

"Want coffee?"

A nod. "Thanks."

Rafe retraced his steps to the kitchen, poured coffee into a mug, and took it to Jon.

"Want to join me in this luxurious security suite?"

"Where? It's barely large enough to accommodate you."

Jon inclined his head to the folded chair in the corner. "Courtesy of Santos. You can watch one of the screens between perimeter checks."

Rafe set the chair next to Jon's. "Jackson is sleeping on Kristi's couch."

"You figure out his problem?"

"Woman trouble."

The sniper glanced at Rafe. "Kristi?"

"Nope. A woman he'd been dating turned out to be a nightmare. Jackson didn't share details."

"Huh. Explains a few things."

They lapsed into silence as they watched the monitors. When it was time for Rafe to make another circuit around the property, the only movement the operatives had seen was a cat prowling through the front yard along with tree limbs and bushes rustling in the night breeze.

Rafe stood. "Need a break before I check the perimeter?"

"Not right now." He tapped the screen, focusing Rafe's attention on sector ten. "While you're in the backyard, check this corner."

"Did you notice something?" The motion detector hadn't alerted them to movement.

"Too many places to hide in the yard."

Yeah, Rafe had noticed. Asking Kristi to rip out the flowers and bushes causing the shadows in that part of the yard wasn't an option. "Yes, sir."

While Eli was Wolf Pack's leader, no one questioned Jon's orders. Both SEALs had leadership roles in the Teams. Eli, however, was better suited to deal with the public. More often than not, Jon came off as surly and impatient.

Rafe disabled the alarm and headed out the back door. Pausing in the shadows, Rafe scanned the yard, focusing on the dark corner. Easing his Sig from the holster, he waited several minutes for movement.

Nothing.

Rafe made his way to the front of the house. No changes. Vehicles parked around the neighborhood were in the same place. No furtive movements in the unlit places in the yards.

His hand tightened around the grip of his Sig. His skin still crawled. What was he missing? Looking at one of the cameras, Rafe used a hand signal to tell Jon that he'd circle behind the property.

After holstering his weapon, Rafe set off down the street, scanning for what set off his internal alarm. At the end of the block, he changed direction and headed for the street behind Kristi's.

Two minutes later, he made his way between two houses and approached Kristi's back fence. In the bright moonlight, Rafe studied the wooden slats. A black streak marred the surface of one of the slats.

He grabbed his phone and shot Jon a text, warning the sniper that he was coming over the fence at the corner. Rafe slid the phone away and scaled the fence, landing in a crouch on the other side. The black mark on the wooden slat was in the exact spot that Rafe's boot had scraped. Someone else had hopped this fence.

Retrieving a penlight from his cargo pocket, Rafe aimed the light toward the shadowed section in the corner. He searched the area slowly, unsure what he was looking for. From what he could tell, nothing had changed, but his gut said something was off. He just had to find it.

Rafe walked deeper into the shadows, zeroing in on the tree in the corner, and aimed the beam on the trunk. He scowled when he noticed another black streak on the light-colored bark at the back of the tree. The person who hopped the fence shimmied up the trunk.

He traced the trunk with the beam until he reached one of the branches about twenty feet off the ground. Nestled between the branch and trunk was a camera aimed at Kristi's bedroom window.

Fury heated Rafe's veins. From the camera's angle, the view would be minimally obstructed with leaves. Someone had scoped the view and chosen the one place the camera was likely to go without detection.

He hadn't considered the possibility that WS placed a camera outside the house, aimed at Kristi's bedroom. He should have. Her security team had gone to a lot of trouble to keep tabs on her. Either the security detail had done that of their own accord, or they'd been asked to do it by Stewart or Ward.

Scouring the yard for other cameras wasn't an option until daylight. One of the neighbors might call the police and report a prowler in Kristi's yard. As soon as the sun rose, he and his teammates would search the property for more WS cameras. At the moment, he'd have to settle for disabling this one.

Rafe leaped up, caught the bottom branch, and scaled the tree until he sat on a branch below his target. Grabbing thin rubber gloves from a pocket, he plucked the camera out of its resting place and removed the battery pack. The red light faded to black.

He'd see what Jon could get from the camera. If he struck out, Rafe would ask Brent to send the equipment to one of the private labs Fortress used to process evidence.

After his feet were on the ground again, Rafe headed for the back door. Whoever was spying on Kristi would be angry that the camera was offline. Would the culprit check on the camera or count it as a loss and move on?

He walked into the kitchen and laid the camera on the breakfast bar as Jon entered the room.

"Where did you find that?"

"The tree in the corner that you wanted me to check." Rafe flicked the plastic casing with his gloved finger before retrieving the battery pack from his pocket. "The camera was aimed at Kristi's bedroom."

Jon scowled. "How did we miss this?"

"That's on me. I was so concerned with removing the surveillance inside the house that I didn't think to check for it outside. I assumed the cameras we knew WS mounted were the only ones out there. I'll remedy that as soon as the sun rises."

"It's on all of us for not thinking of it. Did the camera get a close-up of your face?"

He shook his head.

"What made you check the tree?"

"Scuff marks on the back of Kristi's fence and a matching one on the back of the tree trunk."

"Good work." Jon dragged a pair of gloves from his own pocket and picked up the camera. "Cheap construction. Serial number is filed off. I might be able to get more if I insert the battery."

Rafe grunted. "I'd rather have Brent send it to the lab. I don't want you or your family at risk. Far better for an observer to see a blank white wall with a masked lab worker than take the chance on you being recognized."

"Agreed. I'll contact Brent in a few hours."

"One of Kristi's former security detail is responsible for this."

Jon gave a slight nod. "Take over in the security room. I want to clear my head and walk the perimeter myself." He left by the back door as Rafe headed for the security room after refilling his coffee mug.

He settled in front of the monitors and watched Jon's progress around the outside of the house and the perimeter of the property. His teammate was thorough, checking and rechecking dark places while wearing a face covering to keep another camera from getting a shot of his face.

Rafe grimaced. He'd ask Zane to redouble the efforts to scan for his facial image or mentions of his name for a while. Other cameras in the yard would have been recording his movements throughout his perimeter sweeps tonight and his short date with Kristi on the deck. Some security expert he was turning out to be. Although he hated to consider it, Rafe might need to step back from the security detail and allow Maddox to send in a temporary replacement while he focused on safeguarding Kristi.

Jon returned to the security room. "We'll need to do a more thorough search in daylight, but at least two more cameras are in the backyard and one more in the front." He pointed out the areas with the additional cameras on the monitors.

"We're sure Fortress didn't mount any of these cameras?"

"Positive. Santos knows I'm twitchy about electronics. He showed me where he mounted each of our cameras. These three don't have tactical value. Their placement indicates personal interest."

Rafe dragged a hand down his face. How long had someone been stalking Kristi?

CHAPTER TWENTY-THREE

Throughout the remainder of his shift, Rafe and Jon switched out checking the perimeter twice an hour, varying the time between circuits. Thirty minutes before their shift ended, one of the quadrants on Rafe's monitor flashed red. "Jon."

With one click of the mouse, Jon expanded the view of the quadrant. A figure dressed in black walked into Kristi's backyard and toward the tree where Rafe had confiscated the camera. "Go. You'll have backup in less than a minute."

Rafe ran to the front door, disabled the alarm, and raced toward the side of the house. The stranger's movements indicated he was trained, probably by the military. The man acted as though he had prior authorization to be on the premises.

Rafe eased up behind him. "Don't move," he said softly.

The man froze. "This isn't what you think," a deep voice muttered.

Was this man a member of Kristi's former security team? "You armed?"

"I have permission to be here, and I'm with Ward Security. Of course I'm armed."

Nice to know Rafe's instincts were still on target. "Place your weapon on the ground slowly and kick it away from you."

"I'm reaching for my weapon." The man moved in slow motion, sliding the Sig from his holster and placing it on the ground by his feet. He kicked the weapon into the flowerbed nearby.

"Now your backup."

A muffled curse, but the intruder bent and removed his backup piece, tossing it toward his Sig.

"Knife, too."

His knife joined the other weapons. "Okay for me to turn around now?"

Rafe took two steps back, his weapon trained on the man. "Go ahead." He had a pretty good idea who the WS employee was. Seeing the man's face seconds later confirmed the intruder was Dan Adams, the Special Forces soldier assigned to protect Kristi. "Why are you prowling around Kristi's yard at 3:30 in the morning, Adams?"

Eyes narrowed, Adams said, "How do you know my name?"

"Answer my question."

"Ms. Stewart is under my protection. I'm a member of her security detail." Adams' glance shifted to someone over Rafe's shoulder.

"Guess he didn't read the memo," Eli said as he stopped beside Rafe.

Adams frowned. "What memo?"

"You and your team are no longer Kristi's security detail. She terminated her contract with WS yesterday."

Concern filled Adams' eyes. "She needs protection," he insisted. "Ms. Stewart was kidnapped a few days ago, and as far as I know the threat hasn't been neutralized."

"She has a team protecting her," Rafe said.

A snort. "The men who grabbed Ms. Stewart are dangerous and desperate. She needs a real security team, not a bunch of country bumpkins with peashooters and zero training."

"Oh, that hurts my southern heart," Eli drawled. "Let's take this inside, Adams. We'll have a nice chat before we decide whether or not to call the local cops and turn you over to them for trespassing."

"I have a legitimate reason for being here," he insisted.

"Yeah, yeah. Get moving toward the back door. No fast moves or your face will be in the dirt. Personally, I wouldn't mind if my friend trussed you up like a Thanksgiving turkey and hauled you inside. But we'd prefer not to traumatize the lady."

Rafe scooped up Adams' weapons and followed Eli. As Adams stepped on the deck, Jon opened the door.

In the kitchen, Eli pointed to a chair at the table. "Sit."

Adams glanced at the operatives, then scanned the room for threats before he took a seat. "What now?"

"Let's talk." Eli flicked a glance at Rafe.

He sat across from the soldier as Wolf Pack spread out around the room, blocking exits. "Why are you here, Adams?"

"Who are you?"

"Rafe." He pointed at each of his teammates in turn as he introduced them. "Eli, Jon, and Cal. Your turn to answer my question. Why are you here?"

"Checking malfunctioning equipment. I was on duty when one of our cameras went black. You took it down, didn't you?"

"You make a practice of pointing cameras at the bedrooms of your principals?"

He flinched. "Wasn't my decision," Adams muttered. "I argued against it. Orders came down through the chain of command to install the camera anyway."

"Who issued the orders?"

A shrug.

"Can't or won't say?"

Silence.

"We'll check for prints on the camera. Whose prints will we find?"

Adams' jaw hardened. "Mine. Run them. You won't find much on me aside from a military record."

"Ranger or Delta?"

Brown eyes stared hard at Rafe. "Ranger. How did you know?"

"Hugh Ward hired your team to protect Kristi. Did he also authorize you to set up fifteen cameras inside the house along with listening devices?"

More silence.

"I'll take that as a yes. Did Ward tell you to put a camera in Kristi's bedroom?"

A scowl. "No. I didn't know a camera was in there. The rest, sure. I wouldn't have let an invasion of privacy on that scale slide without going up the chain of command to protest. No one should do that to a woman."

"Yet you didn't fight to protect her privacy when you installed that camera pointed at her bedroom window."

"I didn't like it, but kept my mouth shut when I realized she always keeps that curtain closed. It's a blackout curtain."

"Rafe?" Kristi's soft voice came from the kitchen doorway. "What's going on?"

He went to Kristi, drawing her into his arms. "I'm sorry we woke you." Rafe glared at Jackson who shrugged. He'd deal with the medic later for allowing Kristi to walk into a potentially dangerous situation. "Go back to bed. You still have a few hours to rest." Rest that she desperately needed.

"Who is this man?"

"Meet Dan Adams, a member of your former security detail."

The other man straightened. "I'm glad to meet you in person, Ms. Stewart. It's been an honor to be on your security detail."

She studied his face. "Haven't I seen you somewhere before?"

"Possibly. I watched over you several nights a week." A small smile curved his mouth. "No offense, ma'am, but you have predictable routines. Keeping you safe wasn't a hard job."

"Except that you and your team allowed Kristi to be kidnapped," Rafe said.

"I wasn't on duty that night. Hale and Fleming were."

"What about Howell?"

Adams grimaced. "Off for the weekend."

"Have an alibi for your whereabouts Saturday night and Sunday morning?"

"My mother."

Everyone stared at Adams.

"She had surgery Saturday morning. I'm an only child, and Dad passed away a few years ago. The nurses at St. Thomas Mid-Town will vouch for me. I stayed at Mom's bedside until Sunday around noon. I went home, showered and changed clothes, then returned to the hospital. I've been off duty until last night at 6:00."

"And no one told you that your team had been replaced."

"That's right." He frowned. "Why didn't anyone let us know or tell us to remove the electronics?"

"Where's your partner?"

He rolled his eyes. "Probably sleeping in our vehicle down the street."

Eli folded his arms across his chest. "Why are you working for a third-rate company like Ward Security?"

"Finding a job isn't easy. I applied to hundreds of companies after I separated from the military. WS was the only company willing to give me a chance."

"You were dishonorably discharged," Jon said.

"How did you know about that? Who do you work for?"

"Fortress Security."

Adams froze. "Brent Maddox's company?"

A nod from the sniper.

"How did you get hired on with Fortress? I heard Maddox doesn't accept applications." He sighed. "Not that it would do me any good to apply with my record. Maddox would never consider me for a position."

"Depends on the reason for the discharge." Eli sat in the chair Rafe had vacated. "What's your story?"

The Ranger's expression darkened. "Major Kline sent my team into an ambush. He suspected the Taliban were waiting for us and sent us in anyway. I lost good men that day, including my best friend, and was shot twice myself protecting my team. When I was strong enough to stand up, I tracked Kline down at a bar off base and decked him."

"What about the civilian you assaulted?"

Adams scowled. "If you've seen my record, you already know what happened."

"Records don't tell the whole story."

"What difference will it make?"

Rafe seated Kristi at the table. "The reason for the assault matters." Since Kristi wasn't going back to sleep, Rafe grabbed a mug from the cabinet, dropped a bag of peppermint tea into water, and heated it.

"Yeah, all right." Adams rubbed his jaw. "I was in another bar fight. A male civilian was hitting on a female staff sergeant. The jerk came on strong, refused to take no for an answer, and scared her. When I moved between them and told the guy to back off, he threw a punch at me."

"Land it?"

Another snort. "Nope. I decked him with one punch. His buddies swore I was the aggressor. Cops got involved and reported the incident to the military."

"No one else saw how the incident unfolded and spoke up?"

"The place was packed and noisy." He shrugged. "Wasn't really a fight."

"What about the staff sergeant?" Eli asked. "Did she speak up for you?"

A nod. "Didn't matter. The major had labeled me a violent troublemaker, and this incident was the last nail in my coffin. The major pushed the brass for a discharge."

Rafe set the tea in front of Kristi and sat beside her. "Why do that instead of reducing your rank?"

A wry smile curved Adams' mouth. "I threatened to tell the media about the debacle with my team. Major Kline was angling for a promotion. Bad publicity could have made the top brass look into my team's mission and the man who ordered us into an ambush. He wanted me gone before I threw a spanner into his promotion. He accomplished his goal."

"Did you follow through on your threat to go to the media?"

"What was the point? Most of my team was dead, and my career was over. All I wanted to do was leave the whole mess behind me."

"Did you?"

"Sure." Bitterness filled his voice. "The only things I have left from my military career are PTSD and the knowledge that my team died on my watch."

Rafe glanced at Eli and gave a slight nod. Wolf Pack's leader handed Adams a business card.

The Ranger frowned. "What's this?"

"My contact information. Do you want to continue working for Ward Security?"

He straightened. "No, sir."

"If you want a shot with Fortress, send your contact information to my email. I can't guarantee Maddox will hire you, but I'll get you in the door for an interview. You interested?"

"Yes, sir. What happens if Maddox hires me?"

"You'll spend some quality time with two Special Forces teams at our training facility in Otter Creek. You need it. You've lost your edge."

Adams glanced at Rafe. "Yeah, I have. You shouldn't have gotten the drop on me."

"Your skills are rusty. They better not stay rusty at PSI. Otherwise, you'll be out on your ear. Our trainers don't mess around." He ought to know. They sharpened Rafe's skills when he was there and gave him a few new ones to carry into his black ops career.

"Wait." The Ranger frowned. "PSI. Personal Security International. Isn't that where a Delta Force team trains bodyguards?"

"That's right. It's a tough training regimen." And because Rafe knew how he felt being trained in a bodyguard school after being a SEAL, he added, "The training is a gateway into being an operative." Adams might have the skills to be an operative, but with his track record, he'd have to prove himself during training and a probationary period. Maddox might let Adams run a few missions with an established team as a test if Cahill and St. Claire believed he was qualified to be an operative. "You'll have to prove yourself to the trainers, and that won't be easy. Are you up for the challenge, or do you want to continue wasting your time and military training with Ward Security?"

Adams looked at Eli. "You're serious, sir?"

"I'll ask Brent to bring you in for an interview. The rest is up to you. Are you in?"

"I'm in."

"Good. As soon as you send the contact information, I'll call Maddox."

"I don't know how to thank you, sir. I won't let you down."

"Tell us about your security team."

"What do you want to know?"

"Everything."

"Fleming is a lush. He can't stay away from bars. He even drinks when he's at home. That man drinks on the job and off."

Eli frowned. "How did he get a job at Ward Security?"

"No clue."

"Why would Hugh choose Fleming for my security team?" Kristi asked as she pushed her empty mug aside.

"An excellent question." One Rafe wanted answered.

Adams' eyes widened. "Mr. Ward requested him?"

"Ward says he chose the team himself."

"I wouldn't hire Fleming to watch my dog much less the woman I planned to marry."

Kristi flinched. "I'm not marrying Hugh."

The Ranger stared. "Does he know that?"

"I told him yesterday. He wasn't happy."

"I'll bet. He's talked about you nonstop for the past few weeks, ma'am."

"I can imagine. Look, Hugh and I were friends, but that's all. I'm interested in someone else."

Adams' gaze shifted to Rafe. "I can see that."

"What about Hale and Howell?" Eli asked, dragging the conversation back on track.

"Hale is a loose cannon. Doesn't take much to set him off. He was dishonorably discharged, too, but he's a company favorite as a bodyguard since he's big and strong." He grimaced. "The ladies seem to love him."

Kristi frowned. "He followed me around for a couple of days when I complained to Dad that I thought someone was watching me. Hale said I was imagining things."

Rafe kissed her palm. "Always trust your instincts, Kristi. You were right."

"What about Howell?" Eli asked.

"Loser with a weakness for stealing stuff. He was mall security before Ward hired him. Can't figure out how he keeps his job. The dude sleeps on shift all the time."

"Is he your partner?"

Adams grimaced. "Yeah. He asked for the night shift on this detail. I had already been assigned to night watch. I have trouble sleeping at night. Makes the most sense for me to work the graveyard shift. Besides, I don't have a family except for Mom, and she doesn't live with me. No one complains when I'm gone all night on watch."

All of that matched up with the information Rafe had read on Adams' team. "Who fired a bullet through Kristi's window yesterday?"

CHAPTER TWENTY-FOUR

Kristi's breath caught at Rafe's blunt question. Guess he should have told Kristi that he suspected one of her security team members had fired into her workroom.

Adams stared at Rafe. "I didn't know about the window. How do you know one of the security team fired the shot?"

"Educated guess. We saw the company's logo on the side of a tactical boot."

"Doesn't mean one of us is the culprit. Ward Security employs hundreds of people."

"We'll tear apart the lives of every person in your company if necessary to find the culprit."

"Including Hugh Ward?"

"Already in progress. I won't let him slide." Especially since Ward had a motive for having Kristi kidnapped for ransom. If he'd engineered the kidnapping, Ward either did a poor job of planning the snatch-and-grab, or hired inept kidnappers. They had botched the job by hurting Kristi and allowing her to escape.

Adams looked at Eli. "Need more information? I have to check in soon."

"We'll find you if we have more questions."

"What about the equipment? WS will want it returned."

"Tell your supervisor that Kristi's new security team confiscated the cameras and flushed the bugs. If WS wants the cameras, your supervisor will have to contact Maddox. Can you access the security footage recorded before we removed the cameras?"

A nod.

"Will you duplicate the footage and send it to Eli?" Rafe appreciated Adams analyzing the situation before answering. The man had honor and integrity, and wouldn't cross those boundaries.

"Depends."

"On?"

"What you plan to do with the footage." He flicked a glance at Kristi, then returned his gaze to Rafe. "I may not be on Ms. Stewart's security detail any longer, but she was my responsibility and I don't want the footage to wind up all over the Internet."

Rafe held Adams' gaze. "I won't allow that to happen. Kristi means too much to me. I'll always have her best interests at heart."

"Strong words, but you still didn't answer my question."

"I'll review the footage to look for anyone nosing around Kristi's property and inside the house while she was gone."

"I'm on the footage."

"Then I'll see what you were doing and when, won't I?"

"I could tamper with the footage before I send it to Eli."

"Will you?"

Adams shook his head. "I don't have anything to hide."

"Neither do we. Our goal is to protect Kristi. The footage will help us do that more effectively. By the way, our tech wizard would know if you tampered with the footage."

A frown. "He's that good?"

"Z is a genius with technology of any kind. You could try to fool him, but you'd fail and destroy any hope of landing a job with Fortress in the process."

"I realize you don't have much reason to trust me, but I want to help. I don't like the way this is shaking out. I'm concerned about Ms. Stewart."

He wasn't the only one. Rafe needed to unmask the culprit soon. "Getting the security footage will be a start." Rafe wouldn't assign Adams another task until he ruled the soldier out as a participant in Kristi's kidnapping.

"I'll send you the footage after I'm off shift. Why aren't you asking me to lie to my supervisor about the cameras and bugs?"

"Letting the people above you deal with Maddox is more fun. The boss will make mincemeat of them."

"They deserve it," Adams muttered. "Somebody up the food chain thinks spying on women is acceptable. It's not."

"What do you know about Hugh Ward?" Eli asked.

"Enough to be glad I don't deal with him one-on-one very often. He's an arrogant jerk who throws around money and influence to suit his own ends." He glanced at Kristi. "Sorry, ma'am, but that's the truth."

"Don't apologize, Mr. Adams. You're right. I'm sorry I didn't see him for what he was before now."

"Know anything about his financial situation?" Jon asked Adams.

His brows furrowed. "No. Should I?"

"Are you aware he's drowning in gambling debt?"

The Ranger's jaw tightened. "No, sir, but I can't say I'm surprised."

"Why?"

"He shows up once or twice a week during the day shift to talk to Hale. I thought the discussions concerned Ms. Stewart's security. Now, I'm not so sure."

"Does Fleming know Ward met with Hale so often?"

"He said he didn't."

"They're partners. Why didn't Fleming push for more information?"

A snort. "Have you seen Hale in person? Fleming is eight inches shorter and one hundred pounds lighter. When Hale tells him to back off, Fleming buries his head in a bottle instead of risking Hale beating him to a pulp. So, Ward's in debt, huh?"

"He's $1 million in the hole."

Adams whistled softly. "Plenty of motive for a kidnap-for-ransom scheme. You think Hale is involved in the kidnapping?"

"Your team had the best access to Kristi. You know her routine. Wouldn't be hard to plan a grab-and-go, keep her drugged for a day or two, then turn her loose when her father forked over the money."

"They wouldn't have released me," Kristi said. "The kidnappers didn't cover their faces."

Adams scowled. "They're either idiots or they planned to kill Ms. Stewart once they had the money. Check my alibi and rule me out so I can help."

"We will. If you have anything to hide, we'll uncover it."

"I don't. The worst thing on my record is the dishonorable discharge."

Rafe inclined his head toward the back door. "Better go so you can check in on time. We'll be in touch."

"Yes, sir." Adams stood. "Ms. Stewart, I wish I'd been on duty the night you were kidnapped. I would have done my best to stop the men from taking you."

"Call me Kristi. The kidnapping wasn't your fault. You were taking care of your mother."

"I'm Dan. I feel like the fault is mine. I was supposed to work that shift, but I called out when my mother's surgery was rescheduled for Saturday. If I'd been on duty, I would have protected you."

Rafe's eyes narrowed. Perhaps Adams' absence was the reason the kidnappers grabbed Kristi in Gatlinburg instead of a different time and place. "Why wasn't your partner on duty?"

"He refuses to work when I'm off."

Cal snorted. "No one else would put up with him."

"Send me your contact information," Eli reminded Adams and opened the door for him. After the Ranger left, he turned to the others. "Impressions?"

"I believe him," Cal said. "He got a raw deal with Kline and will pay the price for the rest of his life unless someone cuts him a break."

"Jon?"

"Same."

"Jackson?"

"Ditto."

"Kristi?"

She jerked. "You want my opinion?"

"Why wouldn't I?"

"In that case, I agree with the others. Dan deserves a chance to prove himself."

Rafe looked at Jon. "We need to look closer at Hale."

"Adams didn't throw any of his teammates under the bus," Eli pointed out. "While I agree with you, what makes you more suspicious of him than the others?"

"Ward is singling him out."

Jackson's lip curled. "Fleming can't stay sober long enough to plan and execute the kidnapping."

"He also doesn't inspire confidence as a leader." Cal leaned against the counter. "No one would risk their necks to follow his leadership on this scheme. No payday is that enticing."

Jon grunted. "Men have followed leaders for much less than $5 million. I'm already digging deeper into all of their backgrounds. I'll let you know what I find, Rafe."

With a nod, Rafe turned to Kristi. "Do you want to lie down for an hour?"

"I'm wide awake. I'll get ready for the day, then start on Maggie's dress."

Rafe tugged Kristi to her feet. "I'll walk you up." He threaded his fingers through hers and escorted Kristi to her room. "Take your time. When you're dressed, come to the first-floor kitchen. I'll have breakfast ready." He held up a hand when she wrinkled her nose. "I know you don't feel like eating, but your body needs fuel. You have a long day ahead of you."

"You don't have to make breakfast. A piece of toast will be fine."

"Not for me or my teammates. You've seen the amount of food we eat." He studied the expression on her face. Uneasiness and worry. "Do you want me to stay in your living room while you shower and dress?"

"Would you mind?"

"Of course not." Didn't she know he'd do anything for her?

She brushed her mouth over Rafe's. "Thank you."

"Any time, baby." After another light kiss, Rafe walked to the living room and pulled out his phone. Despite the early hour, he figured Zane was already awake. On the chance that he was wrong, Rafe sent a text.

A minute later, his phone signaled an incoming call. "You're up early, Z."

"Yep. What do you need?"

"Two things. I need your bots to do a continuous, deep Internet search on my name and Kristi's."

"Problem?"

"Hugh Ward wasn't happy when Kristi turned down his proposal yesterday and informed him that she'd fired his hand-picked security team."

"I'll take care of it. What's the second thing?"

Rafe explained about the camera in Kristi's bedroom. "I don't know how long the camera had been recording her. One of her original security team members promised to send us a copy of the security footage. Once we have it, hack into Ward Security's server, find that footage, and delete every bit of it."

"I'll be glad to do that for you. How is she?"

His hand clenched around the phone. "Afraid to go into her own bedroom."

"The fear will pass." In the background, a baby cried. "Oops. I have to go. Claire is in the shower. Talk to you soon." Zane ended the call.

Twenty minutes later, Rafe and Kristi were back on the first floor in the kitchen. Between the two of them, they prepared pancakes and coffee for Wolf Pack and peppermint tea for Kristi.

When the group finished eating, Eli said, "I'll clean the kitchen. Kristi, what's on the menu for your clients?"

She grimaced. "More chocolate chip cookies that I need to bake, and cheese and crackers."

Rafe and his teammates exchanged glances. The members of Wolf Pack could handle a grill, but baking cookies might be beyond their skill set. "Chocolate chip cookies from scratch?" he asked.

"They're slice and bake."

He relaxed. "I can handle the cookies. Does the cheese need to be sliced?"

"It's pre-sliced. You just need to arrange the slices on the platter with the crackers."

"We'll take care of it. Go work on Maggie's dress."

"Thanks, Rafe. You're a lifesaver."

"I'll remind you of that when I need to get myself out of the doghouse."

She started for the hallway, then stopped and glanced over her shoulder. "I can help in here so you can go to bed sooner."

"You already helped prepare breakfast. This is a team effort. Besides, baking cookies won't take that long since the dough is already prepared. Go work on that beautiful dress."

After blowing him a kiss, eliciting a series of catcalls from Rafe's teammates, Kristi laughed and hurried from the room.

After a couple of beats, Cal murmured, "If you don't marry that woman, you're an idiot, Torres."

He flashed a grin at his friend. "My mother didn't raise a fool."

While Eli cleared the breakfast dishes, Rafe started a fresh pot of coffee and sliced cookie dough, arranging the slices on sprayed baking sheets. Two hours later, the kitchen was clean, cookies were arranged on trays, and the house was filled with the scent of freshly baked cookies. He might have sampled one or two. He considered it the baker's privilege since he had to be sure the cookies tasted good.

After washing his hands, Rafe walked to the workroom to check on Kristi. "How's it going?"

She stopped sewing and smiled at him. "Coming along. I've been smelling those cookies. Did they turn out?"

"They're delicious." He grinned.

Kristi laughed. "Did you leave any for me?"

"Of course. I saved a couple for you. They're in a plastic bag, hidden in your tea cabinet."

"Perfect spot. None of your teammates will bother looking in there." She rose and came to him. "Going to bed now?"

"For a few hours. Eli and Cal are on duty. Jon's asleep and Jackson will be close. If you need me, come get me."

"I'll be fine. Sleep well."

Rafe decided not to push. If something happened, he'd know. One of his teammates would wake him. He'd as good as declared his intention to marry Kristi a couple of hours ago. That news would make his teammates all the more protective of the woman who held his heart.

He climbed the stairs to the second floor, stretched out on the bed, and dropped into a light sleep.

CHAPTER TWENTY-FIVE

Kristi concentrated on assembling Maggie's dress until Jill arrived. She glanced at her assistant who held a large to-go cup in her hand as she shuffled through the doorway with dark circles beneath her eyes. "Late night?"

Jill shrugged off her sweater and dropped her purse in the closet. "Mom was having a crisis. She and her fifth husband are fighting, and she's worried that her latest marriage is imploding."

"I'm sorry. That must be difficult for all of you."

"Understatement. Is that Maggie's dress?"

She nodded. "Want to see?" When her assistant nodded, Kristi held up the partially completed dress for Jill's perusal.

Jill gasped. "This dress was a concept yesterday morning, and now it's coming together right before our eyes. You've worked like a demon on that masterpiece. So, exactly how early did you get up this morning?"

"You don't want to know."

"I thought so." She frowned. "You should have waited for me. I planned to help you assemble the dress."

"I couldn't sleep. We'll be slammed again today. Since you're here now, I'll let you take over. I need a break."

"Take your time." She sipped of her drink, set the cup on the desk, and sat in front of the sewing machine Kristi used. "Show me where you stopped."

Two minutes later, Kristi walked into the kitchen where Jackson perched on a stool at the breakfast bar with his laptop.

He looked up. "Taking a break?"

She nodded. "Is Rafe still asleep?"

"Yeah." The medic glanced at his watch. "He should wake soon. Need anything?"

"A good night's sleep." She stretched, wincing. "And fewer bruises on my ribs. Sore ribs, leaning over a cutting table, and feeding material along the arm of a sewing machine don't mix. I feel every sore spot today."

"Do you still have the pain meds I gave you?"

Another nod.

"Take two. If the pain medicine doesn't help, I can use athletic tape on your ribs to give them support while they heal. You have a choice of black or blue tape." He frowned. "I think I have gray, too."

Kristi opened a bottle of water. "You don't have pink tape?"

"Not if I want to avoid being the punch line for jokes for months to come. My teammates are merciless. Sorry, kiddo, you're stuck with boring masculine colors." Jackson slid from the stool and placed a cookie on a small paper plate. "Eat this, then take the meds. I'm on watch for a few hours if you decide you want your ribs taped."

She consumed the cookie and drank half the water before asking, "Does the tape hurt?" She popped two pain pills into her mouth and swallowed them with water.

"Only if you pull off the strips without taking a long shower first. You'll remove a layer of skin with the tape."

"Ouch. Definitely don't want to do that. I'm already in enough pain." She patted Jackson's shoulder. "Thanks for the cookie and advice."

"No problem." He looked as though he wanted to say something else, then stopped.

She waited. When he remained silent, she said, "Go ahead. If I can survive kidnappers, I can handle what you want to say." Probably. What if the medic warned her away from Rafe? Didn't matter. She'd made her choice.

"I'm sorry for sounding surly earlier. My grouchiness doesn't have anything to do with you dating Rafe. I'm happy he's smart enough to recognize how special you are."

Kristi relaxed. "Thanks, Jackson."

"Look, our career is dangerous. Forming a relationship with an operative is challenging on good days and harrowing on bad ones. We're careful, but sometimes our work follows us home."

"Why are you telling me this?"

"Rafe lost a woman he loved to violence. He'll be overprotective. Work with him. He's not an overbearing, controlling jerk. He wants to keep you safe." He shrugged. "That's all I wanted to say. I'll keep my opinions to myself now."

She hugged Jackson. "Thanks."

He patted her back. "Go back to work. You're making me blush."

Laughing, Kristi made her way to the workroom and dived into the next project. She perused various designs for a bride coming in this afternoon and narrowed down the list of possible dresses to six. This wedding, however, wasn't for another six months. She had time to fine-tune the design for Faith.

An hour later, she exited the lounge with a client and saw Rafe standing at the end of the hall, looking at his phone. He glanced up and smiled.

Kristi's heart went into overdrive. The Fortress operative was drop-dead gorgeous. She was in so much trouble. Rafe was winding invisible tendrils around her heart, and she was more than half in love with him. Of the men she'd dated, Rafe was the only one with the power to break her heart into a million pieces.

"Who's the hottie?" whispered Aurora.

"Rafe, the man I'm dating."

"Lucky you."

Kristi laughed. "Why are you noticing his hot looks? You're getting married in a few months."

"Very true. I'm also not dead. I appreciate fine workmanship, and Rafe qualifies."

Yes, he did. More important to Kristi than the attractive body and face was the heart of gold beating inside his chest. "Want to meet him?"

"Is the grass green?"

More laughter, this time from both of them. She and Aurora walked to Rafe. "Aurora Matthews, this is Rafe."

He shook Aurora's hand. "You're here for a wedding dress consultation?"

"I am. Kristi and I have been friends forever, and she promised in high school to make my wedding dress when the time came. I'm happy to say I need her services."

"Congratulations. When's the big day?"

"December 31. We're counting down the days." Aurora turned to Kristi. "I have to go. I have an appointment with the florist in thirty minutes to talk about the flower arrangements. Rafe, I'm glad Kristi finally came up for air long enough to fall for you. Take good care of her."

"You have my word."

After Aurora left, Rafe folded his arms. "What was all the laughter about?"

"You."

His eyebrow rose. "What's so funny?"

"Aurora wanted to know who the hottie was. She was impressed that you and I were dating."

Rafe's cheeks darkened. "Hottie, huh?"

Kristi brushed her lips over his. "Oh, yes. Perfect description, too."

"Is that right?" His lips curved.

"I've been thinking you're drop-dead gorgeous, but hottie works."

"I heard that," Jackson called with, laughter in his voice. "You need your eyes checked, Kristi."

Rafe groaned. "I'm toast," he murmured, then raised his voice. "A good friend would forget that private conversation."

"Ha. You're out of luck. That's too good to pass up."

Rafe flinched. "Can't wait until he's dating someone to return the favor," he muttered.

Kristi grinned. "Sorry."

"No, you're not." He scowled, but his eyes twinkled with amusement. "You will be, though. You're in for razzing by the rest of Wolf Pack, too. I won't be suffering alone."

"Incoming," Eli said from the living room. "Four ladies to meet the hottie."

Rafe groaned. "Shut up, sir."

Wolf Pack's leader chuckled.

Kristi stole another quick kiss. "That should be Natalie Harmon and her entourage."

"She always arrives with a pack?" Eli teased.

"Every decision she makes is vetted by her group."

Rafe shook his head. "Slows down the decision-making process."

"Every choice takes at least thirty minutes, sometimes longer. That's why I block out 90 minutes for each of her appointments." She hurried toward the living room as Eli opened the front door and greeted the women.

Kristi beamed at one of her favorite clients. "Natalie, it's great to see you." She held out her hand to the bride-to-be.

"Oh, Kristi, look at your face." Natalie looked horrified. "What happened?"

"Long story. I'm fine."

"Did your boyfriend hit you?"

Beside her, Rafe stiffened. Kristi reached back and wrapped her hand around his. "No, nothing like that. In fact, this is my boyfriend, Rafe. Rafe, meet Natalie, Ginger, Maryanne, and Lola."

He shook hands with each woman, then asked their snack and drink preferences. Once they were seated in the consultation room with one tray of cookies and a carafe of coffee, Rafe pressed a kiss to Kristi's palm and retreated to the kitchen.

The women watched him until he left the room, then Natalie said, "Lady, you have fine taste in men. Your Rafe is a keeper." Her friends chimed in with their agreement.

"You're right." Kristi squeezed Natalie's hand, then retrieved the three-ring binder with the latest round of wedding dress designs. "I used what you told me from our previous discussion and came up with six new designs for you. See what you think."

An hour later, Natalie and her friends decided on the dress Kristi would have chosen for the bride. As the women paused at front door, Natalie said, "I don't know how to thank you. I can't wait for Jerome to see me in that dress."

"He'll be stunned speechless," Lola said.

"He better not be speechless for long." Maryanne smiled. "Otherwise, he won't be able to say 'I do' when the time comes." That sent the women into another round of laughter.

When they finally left, Kristi turned into Rafe's arms with a soft groan.

"Hey, are you all right?"

"I need another massage."

"When does your next client arrive?"

"Thirty minutes. It's a fitting, though. Jill can handle it without me for a few minutes."

"Good. Come with me." He led her out the back door to one of the benches in the garden. When they sat, Rafe turned Kristi so her back was to him and began to massage her shoulders and back.

Ten minutes later, Kristi felt boneless. "Mr. Torres, you're hired for life."

"I don't know, Ms. Stewart. My price is steep. You might not be able to afford me."

"Whatever you charge, I'll gladly pay."

He chuckled. "You don't know the price yet."

"With talented hands like yours, I don't care."

More masculine laughter behind her as he eased her back to rest against his chest. "What about dinner at least once a week for the foreseeable future and play dates with Oliver?"

"No kisses? I'm disappointed. I thought for sure kisses would be the price for shoulder and neck massages for life."

"I'll steal as many of those as possible." Rafe urged her to lean her head against his shoulder. "Let yourself rest for a few minutes. I'll keep track of the time."

With the soft breeze, warm sun, and Rafe's body heat lulling her into a light doze, Kristi let her responsibilities and worry drift away, secure in the knowledge the Rafe would handle anything that cropped up.

Sometime later, her phone signaled an incoming message, stirring Kristi out of her light slumber. She checked the screen and groaned. Not something she wanted to deal with today.

Rafe's arm tightened around her waist. "What is it?"

"Dad wants to see me in two hours. I don't have time. We're booked solid through six o'clock tonight, and then I have to finish assembling Maggie's dress so it's ready for her fitting tomorrow."

"Did Stewart say what he wanted?"

She frowned. "No, and that's odd. He usually does."

"Can he call you instead?"

"I'll find out." Kristi sent a text, asking her father to call. She frowned at his reply. "He says he can't discuss this over the phone, that he needs to break the news in person. What if he's sick, Rafe?"

He kissed her temple. "Let's not anticipate the worst. What do you want to do?"

"Hire five more people in the next hour to help me with all the work. I have a woman coming for an interview in the next couple of days. We can use Deidre as much as she's willing to work."

"See if she can help part-time while she decides if she's wants to come on board full time."

"That's a good idea."

"What do you want to do about your father's request?"

"I need to meet him. Otherwise, I won't be able to concentrate on anything. He'll have to wait until after our appointments are finished, though. Jill can't handle everything alone."

"Find out where he wants to meet. We'll go after dinner."

She grimaced. "I doubt my father will be more civil now than he was yesterday."

"I can handle Stewart's bad attitude. Don't tell him I'll be with you."

Kristi told her father she could meet him at 8:00. The response had her eyebrows rising. Huh. She hadn't expected him to make that request.

"Something else wrong?"

"Not really. Just an odd meeting place."

"Where is it?"

"One of the Stewart Group warehouses." She shrugged. "Dad must have a meeting with the warehouse manager. He's probably making time to talk to me between meetings."

"Does he always work that late?"

"Most of the time. He started the habit after I entered high school."

Behind her, Rafe stiffened. "You were in the house alone?"

"We had a live-in housekeeper who was like a second mother to me. Mrs. Wolcott still works for Dad. Believe me, I couldn't have gotten into trouble if I'd wanted to. I think she has eyes in the back of her head."

He chuckled. "All kids believe that of their mothers." Rafe stood. "It's time to go back. Your next client arrives soon."

Kristi took his extended hand. "Thanks for the back rub and the company."

Inside the kitchen, Rafe gave her a light kiss. "I'll take care of dinner." He slid a pointed look to Cal. "I'll be drafting help."

His friend winced. "Might not be wise, Rafe. I'm all thumbs in the kitchen."

"You're a SEAL. You can handle a knife."

"So?"

"You can chop and slice vegetables. You're hired as the sous chef." Rafe turned to Kristi. "I'll be close if you need me."

"What's for dinner?"

"A surprise. You'll find out as soon as you finish your client appointments."

"Now you have my curiosity stoked."

"Good. That means you'll work fast."

With a laugh, she traipsed down the hall to the workroom. Her breath caught when she saw Maggie's dress on the dressmaker's dummy. "You finished the dress. Good work, Jill." Even without the embellishments, the dress was beautiful.

"You did the hard part. I worked on the rest of it between other projects."

Kristi would be able to meet her father without facing with another late night. "After Maggie's fitting, we'll make the adjustments, then start on the lace and pearls. Have you talked to Deidre yet?"

"I was going to call her in a few minutes. Why?"

"When you ask her to come in for an interview for a full-time position, find out if she's willing to work part-time until she decides if she wants to work for us. We've been working too many late hours, and our schedule will be worse over the next few months."

"I can already tell you Deidre will accept the offer of a part-time job. She's saving for a week-long cruise next summer."

"Good. We need her. If we're satisfied with what we hear during the interview, we'll offer Deidre the full-time job. I hope the fabric shop won't make Deidre work her full two weeks after she gives her notice."

Jon appeared in the workroom doorway. "Another client arrived."

"Thanks, Jon." Kristi looked at Jill. "Call Deidre. I want to interview her as soon as possible."

"I'll take care of it."

Kristi walked to the living room to greet the client and usher her to the consultation room.

Ten minutes before the work day ended, Deidre arrived. Although Kristi was glad to see her, meeting her father on time would be difficult because of the interview. Alan Stewart was a businessman, though. He'd understand she was late because of work. He'd been late often enough coming home to her when she was in high school.

She mustered up a smile for the seamstress. "Deidre, thank you for coming to talk to us on short notice."

"Are you kidding? I'm thrilled with the possibility of working for Kristi's Bridal." She handed Kristi a portfolio. "I stopped by my house to pick up a portfolio of my designs. I realize you need a seamstress, but I thought you might want to see this side of my work, too."

"That's great," she said, curious about Deidre's designs. "Come to the consultation room, and show me your portfolio." An hour later, she held out her hand to Deidre. "If you want the job, it's yours."

"Really?" Deidre grinned. "Thank you, Kristi. I'll do a good job for you. You won't be sorry you hired me. I can't wait to get started."

"That's great to hear because we need you as fast as possible. When can you start?"

"Will Monday be soon enough?"

Relief flooded Kristi. "That's perfect. Welcome to Kristi's Bridal."

After walking Deidre to the door and seeing Jill off, Kristi shut the door and pressed her back against the flat surface.

"Kristi."

She opened her eyes and smiled at Rafe.

"You okay?"

"Tired, but good. Deidre starts work on Monday."

"Excellent news." He held out his hand. "Ready for dinner?"

"I'm starving."

"Good. I have your plate ready." He escorted her to the kitchen and seated her at the breakfast bar.

"Where is everyone?"

"Eli and Cal are napping. They have the watch overnight. Jackson went to the grocery store under protest and should return soon. Jon is on watch in the security room."

"What about you?"

"I've been conducting perimeter checks. As soon as Jackson returns, he'll take my place while I accompany you to see your father."

Rafe set a plate in front of her. On it were two rolled tortillas along with chicken strips, onions, and green peppers. He set two small bowls beside her plate, one with shredded cheese and one with sour cream along with a spoon for each.

"You made fajitas."

"It sounded good to me. Wolf Pack didn't complain about the taste."

"The food looks and smells amazing."

He nudged the plate closer. "Eat. I'll get your drink." A moment later, Rafe set a glass of water by her hand.

When she finished the meal, Kristi sat back. "I don't think I'll order this in a restaurant again. I've never tasted better fajitas than yours."

"Good to know." Rafe cleared her dishes and utensils before pulling two bottles of water from the refrigerator. "We should go."

She slid from the stool. "I'll grab my identification in case we're stopped by a guard."

Soon, Rafe escorted Kristi to his SUV. Once they were buckled in, he drove away from her home. Although exhausted, she was anxious to discover what was going on with her father.

"Where are we going?" Rafe asked.

She gave him directions to the warehouse district where Stewart Group owned several buildings. Twenty minutes later, he turned into the industrial complex and drove toward the back of the property.

"Which warehouse?"

"Building 244. It's in the corner."

Rafe turned off the SUV's lights and drove toward the designated meeting place. He scanned the area. "Doesn't appear to be anyone around," he murmured.

"The building has three offices inside. Dad's probably in one of them."

Rafe stopped three warehouses away from Building 244. He backed into the alley between two warehouses and turned off the engine.

"Why did we park here?"

"In case of trouble. The SUV is black and will be hard to see in the alley."

"You're worried?"

"Aren't you? I don't want our ride compromised."

Kristi's stomach knotted. "I should have refused to meet. What if I put us in danger, Rafe?" Even considering that was bizarre. Her father was angry, but he'd never hurt her.

Rafe squeezed her hand. "We'll be fine."

"We should leave. I'll text Dad and tell him I can't make it tonight, that I'm too tired." Not a lie, either. If not for the adrenaline pouring into her veins, she could fall asleep right now.

"We're already here." Another hand squeeze. "I can check the warehouse without you."

"Not a chance. Let's go. I want to hear what Dad has to say and leave."

"Wait for me to open your door."

As he circled the SUV's hood and helped her to the asphalt, Kristi prayed she didn't regret her decision.

CHAPTER TWENTY-SIX

Rafe tucked Kristi against his left side, keeping his right hand free. He scanned the area for potential threats. Too many places for people to hide in the shadows. Although security cameras dotted the area, the lighting was too dim to suit him. "I don't see a vehicle." In fact, the target warehouse appeared deserted.

"Dad might have parked at one of the other of the warehouses and walked from there. Stewart Group owns ten warehouses in this industrial complex. They're on this row and the next two rows."

"We're thirty minutes late. Is it possible your father left already?"

"Not without ranting at me over the phone for wasting his valuable time." Kristi glanced around. "I've never been in the industrial complex at night. This is creepy."

When they reached the door to the warehouse, Rafe twisted the knob. It turned easily under his hand.

"Dad must be inside. He's careful to lock up when he leaves one of the warehouses at night. So are the warehouse managers."

That might be true, but Rafe didn't like this set up. Bakerhill wasn't exactly a den of criminal activity, but leaving a warehouse door unlocked at night wasn't safe. Although he wanted to check the warehouse alone, Rafe couldn't leave Kristi in the dark without protection.

Standing to the side of the threshold, Rafe pushed open the door and listened. Silence. If someone waited inside to ambush them, he didn't want to turn on the lights, and make himself and Kristi easy targets. With a dim light coming from the left side of the building, Rafe stepped into the warehouse and led Kristi away from the doorway.

In silence, he nudged Kristi toward the wall. Large boxes and wooden crates were stacked in an orderly fashion throughout the warehouse, creating aisles as far as he could see which wasn't far enough to satisfy him. Rafe's gut urged him to take Kristi away from this building. Although Alan Stewart had sent his daughter a text to meet him here, the building felt deserted. "Where are the offices?" he whispered.

"To the left. If we follow the perimeter of the building, we'll reach the hall where the offices are located."

Rafe hugged the wall as he led Kristi around the perimeter of the cavernous warehouse. Near the corner, he peered around the row of boxes toward the area where the offices were located. Dim light streamed from the hall.

He glanced at Kristi. "Don't call out to your father. This doesn't feel right." When she nodded, Rafe started toward the hallway.

At the entrance to the hall, he peered around the corner. The deserted hallway should have reassured him that all was well. It didn't. Rafe stepped into the hall and tugged Kristi after him. Three closed doors.

When they reached the first office, Rafe tried the knob. Locked. With a hand signal for Kristi to remain in place, Rafe grabbed his lockpicks, crouched in front of the knob, and went to work. In less than 30 seconds, he stepped to the side of the doorway, twisted, and shoved the door open. Nothing. After peering into the empty office, he glanced at Kristi and shook his head.

The second door's knob turned easily under his hand. Nudging Kristi's back to the wall to make sure she wasn't in the line of fire, Rafe pushed open the door. No shots, but also no greeting from Stewart. He peeked into the office. Empty except for a desk, two chairs, and a table with a small coffee maker and cups.

After another head shake, Rafe led Kristi toward the last office. He twisted the knob and pushed open the door. The office light was on, but Stewart didn't call out. Not good. Rafe didn't want Kristi to walk in on her father injured or dead. He signaled for her to wait, then looked into the office.

No Stewart. Standard office furniture. Sitting on top of the desk was a brick of C-4 with multiple wires, a detonator, a cell phone, and a digital clock counting down to detonation.

Adrenaline flooded Rafe's veins. He didn't have time to deactivate the bomb. He grabbed Kristi's hand. "Run!" She sprinted down the hall with him without asking questions.

In his head, the clocked ticked down. They wouldn't be able to escape before the bomb exploded. Rafe's goal was to put as much space between them and the office as possible.

When the time clock in his head hit two seconds, he shoved Kristi to the floor in the corner and covered her body with his. He wrapped his arms around her head.

The bomb exploded, blowing out windows and tossing boxes everywhere with several of them catching fire. Something hard slammed against Rafe's back. He grunted and shook off the weight.

As soon as the larger debris settled, Rafe tugged Kristi to her feet. Using the wall as a guide, Rafe resumed the journey to the door, coughing every few steps. Smoke billowed and filled the warehouse.

Kristi stumbled. Rafe caught her before she hit the floor and tucked her tight against his side. "Not much farther," he shouted over the roar of the fire, and prayed he'd spoken the truth. He didn't know what was in the crates, but they were going up in flames quickly.

"We have to go back for Dad."

"Didn't see him."

By the time Rafe grabbed the knob and shoved open the door, he and Kristi coughed continuously. After they stumbled from the warehouse, Rafe hurried Kristi toward his SUV.

When they reached the vehicle, he opened the passenger door, scooped Kristi into his arms, and set her on the seat. Rafe rounded the hood, climbed behind the steering wheel, and drove farther from the warehouse.

"Are we leaving?" Kristi asked between bouts of coughing.

"I wish. Security cameras caught my license plate, and we were recorded entering the warehouse before the fire. The police will have questions." He grabbed his phone and called 911, called Eli for backup, then Maddox.

"Yeah, Maddox."

"It's Rafe. I may need one of our lawyers soon."

"Talk to me."

Rafe summarized events quickly as the sirens from emergency vehicles grew louder. "My backup will arrive in five minutes." He went through a round of coughing.

"I'll alert one of the lawyers. Let the EMTs check you and Kristi. If they offer a trip to the hospital, take it."

He grimaced. He hated hospitals with a white-hot passion. "Yes, sir." Rafe ended the call and turned to Kristi as a police car followed the fire truck heading for the burning warehouse.

Abruptly, the police car skidded to a stop. Knowing what was coming next, Rafe leaned over and brushed his lips over Kristi's. "Wolf Pack will be here soon. The police will have questions for us, and they might put us in handcuffs," he said as he slid his weapons into a lockbox built into the floor of his SUV. Being unarmed made him uncomfortable, but he preferred to keep his weapons if possible. The police would be more suspicious if he was armed. "When the police ask questions, they might separate us. Tell them the truth. We don't have anything to worry about."

An officer shined his flashlight into the SUV. "Get out of the vehicle with your hands in plain sight," he ordered.

Rafe glanced at Kristi. "Ready?"

She nodded and broke into a round of coughing.

They both needed medical attention. "We'll open our doors at the same time. Move slow and make sure your hands are in sight."

Knowing further delay would heighten the tension and suspicions of the officers, Rafe opened his door and stepped out of the vehicle with his hands raised. He followed their orders to lay on the ground with his arms and legs spread.

He didn't protest the weapons search, but Rafe kept close watch on Kristi and the officer searching her for weapons.

When he was allowed to stand, Rafe said, "The EMTs need to check my girlfriend." He broke into a coughing fit.

"Looks like you got a lungful of smoke yourself. I need to see your license."

"My identification is in my right side pocket."

"Move slow."

Rafe handed the officer his license plus his Fortress identification while Kristi handed hers to the second officer.

"How long have you been with Fortress Security, Mr. Torres?"

"Just over a year."

"It's obvious you and your girlfriend were in a warehouse that's burning to the ground. What were you doing in that building at this time of night?"

"I'll be happy to answer questions, but Kristi needs medical attention."

"Yeah, all right." The officer pointed at Rafe. "Don't move." He flagged down the approaching ambulance. Soon, Kristi and Rafe were seated side by side at the back of the ambulance. They answered questions from the police while being checked for injuries by the EMTs.

Fifteen minutes later, one of the EMTs told the officers, "They both need treatment for smoke inhalation."

The senior officer waved them on. "Ms. Stewart, Mr. Torres, you can expect detectives to track you down at the hospital to ask more questions."

"Can't wait," Rafe muttered.

When the officers moved their squad car, Eli approached Rafe. "Jackson will drive your SUV to the hospital," he murmured.

"Thanks." Rafe tossed Eli the key fob, then helped Kristi into the back of the ambulance and climbed in behind her.

The next hours passed in a blur with medical personnel coming in and out of Rafe's exam room. To the aggravation of the nurses, he pushed hard to be moved into Kristi's exam room. They ignored him. He opted not to relocate himself because Jackson used his paramedic license to gain access to Kristi's room and stay with her, and the room was across the hall from Rafe's. If he sat at the end of the exam table, he could see who came and went from her room.

Finally, two detectives arrived to question him and Kristi about their presence in the warehouse after hours.

When he explained that Kristi's father was Alan Stewart and had asked his daughter to meet him in the warehouse, the detectives exchanged glances.

"You entered the warehouse and went to the offices. All of them were empty, and the bomb was in the last office."

"That's right."

"Know anything about bombs, Mr. Torres?"

"Enough."

A frown from one of the detectives. "What does that mean?"

"I'm in black ops, Andrews. We're trained to handle explosives. Some of the Fortress operatives are experts in that field."

"Are you?"

"No."

Narrowed eyes glared at Rafe. "I ran a background check on you."

"I'd have been disappointed if you hadn't."

"You're holding out on me."

"I'm not required to give you a detailed history of all my training. I can't discuss much from my background."

"You used to be FBI."

Rafe inclined his head in silent agreement.

"Why did you resign so soon after starting a career with them?"

"I don't play well with other feds. No patience for bureaucracy."

Andrews' partner, Detective Willis, snorted. "I hear that," he muttered.

"You were in the Navy," Andrews continued.

"Ten years."

"I couldn't see anything in your record aside from the basics. You weren't a regular sailor."

Willis straightened. "A SEAL?"

Rafe didn't reply.

"That's enough confirmation for me." Andrews folded his arms over his chest. "So, Torres, you've had more than Fortress Security's basic training in explosives. Could you have disarmed the bomb in that office?"

"I don't know. I didn't have time to examine the device. EOD isn't my specialty, but I can hold my own in a pinch."

"More than that if my information about SEALs is correct. You have a reason to blow up that warehouse? Maybe to get back at Alan Stewart?"

"No to both questions. I don't have a problem with Stewart."

"That's not what I hear."

"I wouldn't put Kristi's life in danger or wantonly destroy property."

"We attempted to contact Stewart to inform him of the destruction of his warehouse without success. Where is he, Torres?"

"I don't know. Kristi is my priority, not her father." Not entirely true, but close enough.

"Why did he want to meet his daughter late at night in that particular location?"

"I don't know. He said he needed to tell her something in person."

"Why did you go to the warehouse with Ms. Stewart?"

"Would you let your wife or girlfriend go to an industrial complex at night by herself?"

Andrews' cheeks flushed red. "This isn't about me. It's about your motivation for being at that warehouse tonight."

"Protecting Kristi."

"How long have you been together?"

"Not long."

Willis shifted his weight. "How did you meet?"

"I've known her for a few years. She was friends with my former girlfriend." That led to a discussion of Callie's death.

Andrews rubbed his jaw. "The Hunt Club was a bad business. I'm sorry for your loss."

"Thanks. Any more questions, Detectives? I want to check on my girlfriend."

"Stay available."

Rafe stood. "I'm on deployment rotation this month with Fortress. My team could be sent out of the country at a moment's notice." Unlikely, especially since Rafe would refuse to go if Kristi's life was still in danger.

A scowl from both detectives. "How long would you be gone?"

"Unknown. Our missions last anywhere from a few days to a few weeks. If you have more questions while I'm deployed, contact Fortress headquarters. They'll send me a message, and I'll call you as soon as possible."

"We'll hold you to that, Torres," Willis said. "If you don't cooperate with our investigation, we'll meet your company plane with an arrest warrant."

"Not necessary. I want answers more than you do."

"I doubt that."

"You'd be wrong. Someone set that bomb to blow with us in the warehouse."

"How do you know?"

"The bomber was either in the area to make the call to the cell phone attached to the timer or watched the security feeds from the cameras to know when we were inside the building. We were more than 30 minutes late arriving at the warehouse."

Andrews sent his partner a pointed glance before turning back to Rafe. "We'll be in touch."

Rafe waited for the men to walk toward the waiting room, then went to the hallway to stand beside his team leader.

"Those boys don't believe your story." Eli's arms were folded over his chest.

"Don't know what gave you that impression."

"Maybe because the detectives looked like they were mentally measuring you for an orange jumpsuit, courtesy of the Bakerhill PD. One of the Fortress lawyers is on standby."

"Here's hoping I don't need the legal service. Any word on Stewart?"

"Not yet."

Rafe frowned. That didn't make sense. The text to Kristi had come from his phone. "Didn't one of the Fortress techs track his cell phone?"

"Phone's turned off."

Huh. Not what he'd expected. "All right. I want to check on Kristi and see if I can convince the doc to spring both of us."

"Your girl will want to find her father."

"I know. The first thing I want to do is change clothes. They smell like I've been standing in the middle of a bonfire."

Eli chuckled. "Good luck convincing Kristi to go along with your plan."

Rafe crossed the hall and knocked on the door to Kristi's room before going inside. Like him, she was sitting on the end of the bed.

The doctor stood with his arms folded. "Ms. Stewart, I strongly recommend you stay overnight for observation."

She shook her head. "I'm coughing a little now and then, but you said yourself that I'm doing well. I need to check on my father. He's not answering his phone, and a message from him is the reason I was in that warehouse to begin with."

"I'll keep an eye on her, Doc," Jackson said. "If she gets worse, I'll make sure she returns to the ER."

The physician frowned at Rafe. "I assume you want to leave as well?"

"Yes, sir."

The other man sighed. "I suppose I can't force you to stay, and we're expecting patients from a traffic accident any moment. I'll release both of you as long as you listen to Jackson's medical advice. If he says you need to come back, don't argue." The physician headed for the hall. "The nurse will bring your discharge papers."

As soon as he left, Kristi reached for Rafe's hand. "Have you heard anything about my father?"

"Not yet. The Fortress tech says his phone has been turned off."

"Something is wrong, Rafe. We have a standing arrangement that we don't turn off our phones without first notifying the other one. I'm afraid something terrible has happened to him."

He cupped her cheek. "As soon as we're released, we'll return to your home and change clothes. After that, we'll check your father's home. Do you have the phone number for your father's administrative assistant?"

She nodded. "Shirley has been with Dad since I was a freshman in high school."

"Excellent. While we drive to your place, call Shirley and ask what appointments your father had tonight."

"We could just go straight to his home instead of detouring to mine."

"We could," he agreed. "Although you're beautiful, we look rough at the moment."

Kristi looked down at herself and wrinkled her nose. "We also smell like chimneys," she muttered.

"That, too." He wrapped his arms around Kristi, grateful she was alive and unhurt. "We'll find him."

"I can't lose Dad. Who wants to hurt us?"

"I don't know, but I'm working on it." He needed to work faster. The trap was closing around them.

CHAPTER TWENTY-SEVEN

When Rafe cranked the engine of his SUV, Kristi called Shirley Waters, her father's administrative assistant, placing the call on speaker. The woman answered two rings later. "Shirley, it's Kristi. I'm sorry to bother you so late."

"No problem, Kristi. What can I do for you?"

"I'm looking for my father, and he's not answering his home or cell phone."

"That's not like him. I tease him all the time about his phone being attached to his hand. Perhaps he doesn't realize his cell battery is dead."

"Maybe." She doubted it, though. Her father was obsessive about keeping the battery charged. "Do you know if he had appointments tonight? I want to catch up with him."

"I'm logging into my computer now to check his schedule." The sound of keys clicking came through the speaker. "He had a dinner meeting with Hugh Ward at 7:00 and a conference call at 9:00. He was going back to the office for the call. I imagine he's still on the phone. This deal is complicated, and he's been working on it all day. Do you want me to call him at the office?"

"No, that's not necessary. I'll go there. I'm not far from the office now."

"All right." Shirley paused. "Is everything okay, Kristi? You sound upset."

Not nearly as upset as her father would be when he learned of the warehouse's destruction. "I just need to talk to Dad about something."

"Does it have anything to do with your kidnapping, sweetheart?"

"It's possible."

"Well, let me know if I can do anything to help."

"Thanks, Shirley. Good night." She ended the call and turned to Rafe. "Dad wouldn't have set up that meeting with me at the warehouse if he was having dinner with Hugh followed by a contract negotiation. He wouldn't have had time."

"Probably not."

A ball of ice formed in her stomach. "Unless he aim was to give himself an alibi," she whispered, and immediately felt guilty. "No, I don't believe that. Dad might be angry with me for refusing to marry Hugh when he thinks that will make me happy, but he wouldn't hurt me or burn his own warehouse."

Rafe glanced at her. "According to Jon's research, Stewart Group is losing money."

"I don't know why that's happening, but Dad wouldn't take the easy way out and use the insurance money to pay down debt. Is it possible someone told Dad about the warehouse fire, and he drove to the industrial complex to see the damage for himself?"

"Let's start our search at his office since that's where he should have been at 9:00." He parked in her driveway ten minutes later and escorted Kristi inside with Jackson and Eli on their heels.

Cal and Jon met them in the living room. "What happened?" Cal asked.

Rafe waved Kristi toward the stairs. "Go change while I update them and get water to take with us." As she hurried upstairs, Rafe began to tell his teammates about the night's events.

Kristi grabbed fresh clothes and dashed into the bathroom. She looked like she'd cleaned out a chimney. Black smudges streaked her face and clothes.

Minutes later, she exited the bathroom, dressed in clean clothes. After brushing the tangles from her damp hair, Kristi tossed her brush onto her dresser, grabbed her phone, identification cards, and keys, then returned to the first floor kitchen.

Rafe turned. "Ready?"

She stared at his clean face. "You've already showered and changed."

He smiled. "The military trained me to shower fast."

Jackson slid his medic bag over his shoulder, and scooped up the three bottles of water on the breakfast bar.

"You're going, too?" Kristi asked.

"I promised the doctor I'd keep an eye on you. I can't do that from here."

They walked to Rafe's SUV. Rafe said, "Office first since that's the last place on his schedule for tonight. If we don't find your father, we'll go to his home."

Fifteen minutes later, he parked in front of Stewart Group's headquarters. "Wait for me to come around," he murmured as Jackson exited the SUV.

While he circled the hood, Rafe scanned the area. "Will the night guard let you inside the building?" he asked when he opened Kristi's door.

"I have everything I need, including a VIP Stewart Group identification card and keys to the building. Even if the guard is new, I'll be able to get inside."

"Let's go," Jackson said. "I don't like being out in the open."

"Same," Rafe murmured.

Kristi walked to the glass doors at the front of the building and knocked to get the night guard's attention.

When the man glanced up, he scowled. Kristi sighed. A new guard. Great. How long of a delay could she expect?

The guard stood and approached the door with his hand resting on the butt of his gun. When he stopped on the other side of the door, he said, "Stewart Group is closed. We open for business tomorrow at 8:00 a.m."

"I'm Kristi Stewart. Alan Stewart is my father." She held up her VIP card and her driver's license. "Open the door, please."

He unlocked the door and held it open. "Who are they?" he asked, indicating Rafe and Jackson.

"My boyfriend, Rafe, and his friend, Jackson. Is my father here?"

"I don't know. I came on duty a few minutes ago."

"Check," Rafe said. "You must have a log of who's in the building."

Another scowl. "Wait here." The guard went to the front desk. After checking to be sure the three of them remained in place, he tapped a few keys on the computer's keyboard. "According to the records, he left the building at 7:00 p.m. and hasn't returned."

Kristi sucked in a breath. "He had a conference call scheduled at 9:00."

"I can only tell you what I see in the computer."

"I want to check for myself."

"I can't let you go up by yourselves at night. Company policy."

"Come with us." She glanced at his name tag. Without giving Richard an opportunity to argue, Kristi headed for the elevator.

"Is it possible to alter the log?" Jackson asked.

Richard stiffened. "Are you accusing me of tampering with the system?"

"I'm asking a question. You work with this security system. That makes you the expert. Is it possible to alter the log?"

"Yes, but that requires authorization higher than mine." The guard punched the button for the executive floor. The elevator doors slid shut with a soft whoosh, and the car rose to the top floor.

When they stepped into the reception area, Kristi headed for her father's office. When she reached for the knob, Rafe caught her hand with his.

"Let one of us go in first, just in case there's a problem."

"I'll go in," Richard said. He knocked on the door. "Mr. Stewart? It's Richard with security. Your daughter's here, sir."

No response.

He knocked again. "Mr. Stewart, I'm opening the door, sir." Richard twisted the knob and shoved open the door. He froze, then cursed.

"What's wrong?" Kristi asked. She started to push past the guard, but Rafe held her in place with an arm around her waist.

"Someone trashed the office. I gotta call my supervisor." Richard pivoted on his heel. "Don't touch anything," he ordered as he strode into the hall outside the office suite.

Heart pounding against her rib cage, Kristi hurried into her father's office and stopped just inside the doorway. Her father's ruthlessly organized office was a shambles. Two short filing cabinets were overturned, the drawers upended with files tossed everywhere. The desk chair lay on its side. The phone was on the floor with the cord ripped from the wall.

Rafe and Jackson eased past Kristi. The medic whistled as he moved further into the office. His attention was captured by something on the floor. "Rafe," he murmured, indicating a spot on the other side of the desk.

Kristi followed Rafe and gasped at the sight of the pool of blood on the floor. "We have to find my father. He's hurt."

Rafe wrapped his arm around her as he studied the office. "Jackson, check his computer screen. Let's see if he was working on something when he was interrupted."

The medic tugged a pair of thin rubber gloves onto his hands and wiggled the mouse. He studied the screen. "The East Coast Shipping file is open. Looks like a proposed contract." Jackson straightened and circled to the front of the desk. "Mean anything to you, Kristi?"

"East Coast Shipping is one of Stewart Group's largest customers. Dad doesn't leave his computer folders open when he leaves the office. He must have been working on it when someone attacked him. If he left at 7:00, the guard on duty would have noticed if Dad looked as though he'd been in a fight."

Rafe glanced around the office again. "Is is possible to leave this office without going through the lobby?"

She pointed to the paneled door behind her father's desk. "Dad has a private elevator."

"Where does it go?"

"To an underground garage. Dad usually parks in front of the building. He says the workers appreciate knowing that he works longer hours than they do. If he's here late, though, he parks in the garage."

"Can you access the elevator?"

She nodded. Kristi waved her VIP card in front of the scanner. The door slid open. More blood stained the elevator floor.

"Looks like Stewart left the building by this elevator." He frowned. "Wouldn't the system log him accessing the elevator?"

"I don't know how the system works. Richard might know."

Jackson grunted as the elevator door closed again. "Have a feeling he's new to the job."

"Only one way to find out." Kristi walked to the office door. "Richard."

The guard strode back into the office. "You haven't touched anything, right? My supervisor is coming from the security office on the first floor. If he thinks it's necessary, he'll call the police."

"You need to call law enforcement," Rafe said. He motioned for Richard to go around the side of the desk. "Take a look."

Richard swallowed hard. "As soon as my supervisor authorizes it, I'll call the cops."

"There's more blood in Stewart's private elevator. Does your system log when the boss leaves the building from this elevator?"

"I can answer that question," came a deep voice from the doorway. A salt-and-pepper haired man with a barrel chest wearing the standard Ward Security uniform walked into the office. He scowled at Richard and the rest of them. "I'm Hank Hardy, chief of security. You're contaminating a potential crime scene. Get out."

"Answer my question," Rafe snapped.

"The answer is no. Mr. Stewart didn't want to be tracked that closely. It's usually not an issue since he uses the front door like everyone else most of the time."

Rafe scowled. "A serious flaw in your system. The security system should log in every card use for each worker, including Stewart."

"That's not what he wanted."

"It's your job to advise him on the safest policy. Based on what I'm seeing here, someone attacked Stewart and took him out of the building through the executive elevator."

A frown. "That's impossible. No unauthorized person can access this floor, especially after hours."

"Look for yourself. There's blood on the floor here and inside Stewart's private elevator. How do you explain that?"

The man's jaw tightened. "I can't."

"Call the cops. Your boss's life is on the line."

"Who are you?"

"Rafe, Kristi's boyfriend."

"What makes you an expert?"

"I work for Fortress Security, and I'm a former FBI agent. You're wasting time. Call the cops."

"As soon as you leave the office. You better not have touched anything."

"Do your job, Mr. Hardy," Kristi said. "We'll get out of your way."

"The police will want to talk to you."

"We came up with Richard and discovered this mess together. He can provide the same information to the police." Rafe pulled a card from his pocket with the name of one of the detectives who talked to him and Kristi at the hospital. "Call the detective and report this. He and his partner are investigating a bombing at one of the company warehouses."

A scowl. "What do you know about that?"

"Not much. Make the call. If the detectives want to talk to us, they have our numbers." He threaded his fingers through Kristi's.

"Ms. Stewart, you need to stay," Hardy insisted.

"I need to find my father." She, Rafe, and Jackson left the office with Richard trailing behind them.

"I don't understand what's going on around here," the guard said as they rode the elevator to the lobby.

"How long have you worked here, Richard?" Rafe asked.

"Two weeks."

"Noticed anything odd?"

"I don't know. Maybe."

"Explain."

"I worked with another security company before WS. I've never known of other security employees showing up on my shift when they're not scheduled to work at this location."

"Did you catch their names?"

He grimaced. "No."

Jackson's eyebrows rose. "What night did they show up?"

"Every night since I started work." He frowned. "What good will knowing that do you?"

"You'd be surprised what we learn by asking the right questions."

Kristi smiled. A great answer that told Richard nothing. When they exited the elevator and the guard walked them to the door, Kristi said, "Thanks for your assistance, Richard. I'll be sure to mention your help to my father." If they found him.

Once they were inside Rafe's SUV, she asked, "How will we find my father, Rafe? You said his phone was turned off. What's left?"

"Call Ward. See if your father showed up for his dinner meeting. If he can leave the headquarters building without security knowing, he can get inside undetected, too. Once you talk to Ward, we'll access the security cameras at your father's office building."

Kristi grabbed her phone and called Hugh. When he answered, she said, "Did Dad meet you for dinner tonight?"

A snort from the man. "No. He didn't even call to cancel the appointment."

"Dad's missing."

"What?"

"His office is a mess, and there's blood on the floor in there as well as his private elevator."

"I'm sorry. How can I help?"

"Call me if you hear from him or from someone who's seen him tonight."

"Of course. Call me when you find him."

"Sure." She ended the call. "Dad never showed up," Kristi told the operatives.

"I'll contact Fortress," Jackson said.

Rafe glanced at his teammate in the rearview mirror. "Call Jon. He's faster than anyone on staff except Zane. We'll go back to Kristi's until we have a place to start tracking Stewart."

"The police won't be able to do anything, will they?" Kristi turned to look at Rafe.

"They'll do what they can. Since we don't worry about red tape or mind computer hacking, we can follow the trail faster."

From what she'd seen, Jon was skilled on the computer. But would he be able to locate her father or give Wolf Pack a starting point in time to save her father?

CHAPTER TWENTY-EIGHT

Rafe escorted Kristi up the walkway to her home where Eli met them in the living room. "Anything?" he asked his team leader.

"Jon hacked into Stewart Group's computer system and is hunting for the right camera feeds."

"Where is he?"

"Kitchen. Update me while Jon works his magic."

Rafe walked with Kristi and Jackson to the kitchen while he summarized what they'd seen at Stewart's office.

Eli dropped onto a chair across from his partner. "Whoever took Stewart is probably the one who planted the bomb to kill Kristi."

"Why?" Kristi demanded. "Are they angry because they didn't get the ransom money for me?"

"It's possible. More likely, they did it to torture your father."

Rafe frowned. "What if this isn't about money?"

Cal and Jackson exchanged glances, and Jon snorted.

He held up his hand. "Okay. Point taken. What if this isn't only about money?" Something was bugging him, something he'd seen in the files. But what? "I need to check something."

Rafe took the stairs two at a time and retrieved his laptop. Back in the kitchen, he sat at the table and booted up his computer. Kristi set another bottle of water by his hand. "Thanks," he murmured, breaking the seal and sipping while he scanned the first file.

She sat beside him. "What are you reading?"

"The file from your first kidnapping."

"That was twenty years ago, Rafe. What does that kidnapping have to do with what's happening now?"

"I'm not sure it does, but if this kidnapping wasn't only about money, another possible motive is revenge."

"Dad's competitive in the business world. Any number of business competitors who lost a contract to him should be added to the list of possible suspects with motive to harm Dad."

"While that's true, I can't see a business competitor using you as a means to twist the knife in your father," Cal said. "They'd be more likely to outbid him or plant a spy at Stewart Group."

"I thought you suspected Hugh."

"His alibi checked out," Rafe said. "While he's not off the suspect list, I've dropped him from the top spot." Much as it pained him to do so. Rafe would have taken great satisfaction in laying Ward out with one punch if he'd been guilty of setting up Kristi's kidnapping.

Eli pulled out his phone. "I need to update Brent. Although I hate to wake him, he'll want to know about Stewart."

"Need help scanning security feeds, Jon?" Cal asked.

"Soon."

Jackson brought a bottle of water to Kristi. "Drink."

"I'm all right."

He merely raised his eyebrow.

Sighing, Kristi broke and seal and drank half the water before setting down the bottle.

Rafe scanned the document he'd pulled up. A word caught his eye. He stopped, reread that line, and frowned. Switching to the files of Kristi's former security team, he clicked on Dan Adams' file first. Not this one. Good. He wanted Adams to have a chance with Fortress. The soldier would be a good asset for the company, and Brent desperately needed skilled help. The requests for Fortress assistance were growing exponentially.

He checked Sean Howell's background. Adams' partner was a lazy bum with a couple of connections to Ward Security that helped him secure a job, but nothing that raised a red flag.

Rafe shifted his attention to Mike Fleming's background. Although he had a record of DUIs and some time in the county lockup for drunk driving and public intoxication, his personal behavior wasn't a problem. His father, however, had been in prison for kidnapping and assault. George Fleming had died while behind bars. No obvious connection to Kristi's first kidnapping.

Rafe clicked on Roderick Hale's file. Halfway down the second page, he stopped. While no birth father was listed, Hale was born to an unwed mother.

Rafe clicked on his preferred search engine and typed in Angie Hale's name with her date of birth and social security number. When a link popped up, he clicked and read the document. His brow furrowed. Angie Hale had passed away from cancer last month. Roderick was her only child and heir. Angie had worked dead-end jobs, often two or three at a time to keep food on the table. No history of drug or alcohol abuse.

He scanned further and discovered that the woman never finished high school. A quick calculation told Rafe that Angie became pregnant in high school and dropped out to give birth to Roderick and raise him. Tough decision.

Rafe had nothing but respect for the scared teen who made a hard choice and did her best to put a roof over their heads and food on their table. According to the file, Angie hadn't been the recipient of much support from her family and received nothing from the baby's father.

He clicked on another file, this one a summary of the estate she left to her son. The house and her old clunker of a car. According to the records, Roderick had sold the clunker, but kept the house and used it as his primary residence now.

Rafe sat back, frowning at the screen. Knowing Hale's birth father might be important. Getting that information was the problem.

He shifted back to the search engine and hunted for Angie's high school. If he could figure out the names of some of her friends, he might be able to find one or two willing to talk about her background. Checking her social media posts might be of some help there, too.

"Need help?" Cal asked Rafe.

"Grab your laptop."

His teammate returned with his computer and sat beside Rafe. "What am I looking for?"

"Angie Hale's social media posts. She passed away last month. I'm looking for a friend or two willing to talk to us."

"Why?"

"I may be on the wrong track, but I want to know the name of Roderick Hale's father. The name's not listed on Hale's birth certificate."

"I'll see what I can find."

"I found the camera feeds," Jon said. "Eli, Jackson, since Cal's occupied, I'll split up the footage we need to review and send it to your work email."

Both men left the kitchen and returned with their laptops and got to work.

Rafe toggled back to the files of the original kidnappers. All three men had been inmates in the same Tennessee federal prison. Raymond Clark was due to be released sometime in the next year. Trevor Cain, the child molester, still had ten years left on his sentence.

On a hunch, he went to West Gate High School's website, the school Angie attended before she dropped out to have her baby. He clicked on the yearbook link for the years Angie attended West Gate. He typed Angie Hale's name in the search box and digitized annuals from two years popped up.

Rafe stared. Angie would have been around 16 when she had Roderick.

"What do you see?" Kristi asked.

"Roderick Hale's mother only attended two years of high school. She never graduated."

Jackson glanced up from his computer. "She was only 15 or 16 when she had Roderick?"

"Looks that way." Rafe picked up his phone and called Fortress tech support. He asked for a copy of Angie's medical records. Assured that the information would be in his email within fifteen minutes, Rafe ended the call.

"Do you think the information matters?" Kristi asked.

"My gut says yes."

"We need to find my father," she whispered, tears sheening her eyes. "He's hurt, maybe worse, and we don't know who has him or why."

"We're working as fast as we can plus the local police are searching for him. If we tug the right thread, this whole tangled knot will unravel."

At that moment, Cal whistled and sat back, his gaze glued to the computer screen in front of him.

"What do you have?" Rafe asked.

"The names of Angie Hale's two best friends."

"Great. Get their contact information, and we'll try to persuade them to answer a few questions."

SEAL'S RESOLVE

"You're in luck there." Cal grabbed his phone. "I know one of them. I investigated her husband's murder and arrested his killer. I don't think we'll have a problem getting the answers we need."

"I know it's late, but please call her," Kristi said. "It could mean my father's life. We'll send her a bouquet of flowers to thank her for her time."

"Laura loves daisies."

"Then she'll have a big basket of them tomorrow."

Cal made the call and placed it on speaker. Three rings later, a woman answered. "Laura, it's Cal Taylor."

"It's so good to hear from you again, Cal. How is Rachelle?"

"As wonderful and beautiful as ever. I apologize for calling so late."

"Oh, you know I'm a night owl. Used to drive my husband crazy. What can I do for you, Detective?"

"Just Cal now. I left MNPD and now work for a private security company. I need information about your friend, Angie Hale."

Silence, then, "Angie passed away from cancer last month." Her voice came out choked.

"I know. I'm sorry for your loss, but the information is important."

"What do you need to know?"

"The name of her son's father."

A soft gasp. "Why? That's ancient history, Cal. No good will be served if the information came out. Angie made me promise not to tell the secret."

"A man is missing, Laura. The crime scene indicates he was kidnapped, and his daughter is worried sick. If the information you share doesn't relate to the kidnapping, I won't mention the name to anyone. You know I'll keep my word."

Laura sighed. "All right. I certainly don't want this victim's daughter to lose her father like my children did theirs. I also trust your judgment."

"Thank you for helping. Who is Roderick Hale's father?"

"A no-good loser named Trevor Cain. I don't see how that knowledge can help, Cal. Cain is in prison and isn't due to be released for several more years. He never had anything to do with Angie after she got pregnant."

Kristi clamped a hand over her mouth and dashed from the kitchen. Rafe followed behind her seconds later as she raced for the bathroom attached to the workroom.

By the time Rafe walked into the workroom, Kristi was throwing up. He found a washcloth in one of the vanity drawers and wet the cloth with cold water. Wringing it out, he pressed the cloth to the back of her neck with one hand while he supported Kristi with an arm around her waist.

When her stomach was empty, Rafe helped her sit on the side of the tub, then retrieved a bottle of water from the small fridge in the workroom and handed it to her. "Sip this. I'll be right back."

Returning to the kitchen, he nuked a mug of Kristi's favorite peppermint tea while Cal pumped Laura for information about Cain and Angie's relationship, added a dash of sugar, and took the brew with him to the bathroom.

Rafe sat on the edge of the bathtub beside Kristi and wrapped her hands around the warm mug. "This will help," he murmured.

Since her hands shook, he kept his hands over hers and helped her hold the mug while she sipped the tea. When she finished the drink, he set the mug on the floor and wrapped his arms around Kristi, holding her until the shaking stopped. She melted against him.

"I'm sorry," she murmured, nuzzling his throat. "I didn't mean to fall apart like that."

"Don't. You have nothing for which to apologize. Your reaction is understandable."

"I thought I was stronger than this, but hearing his name sent me back into that closet like a scared ten-year-old."

"Baby, you're so strong, you amaze me. Hearing the name of Hale's birth father caught you off guard. Anyone who survived what you did would have a strong reaction."

She sighed. "Roderick Hale kidnapped my father, didn't he?"

"We'll see what the security camera footage shows. This may be a coincidence. We don't know if Angie told her son who his father was."

"You don't believe that."

No, he didn't. However, he'd learned over the years as a SEAL and an FBI agent not to leap to conclusions. "No matter what I believe, we need evidence. If Hale is involved, we still don't know where he might have taken your father since we can't track his phone." Adams might be able to give them a hand with that, though. "Do feel up to returning to the kitchen? No one will think less of you if you're not ready."

"I'm not giving in to my fear and hiding in a bathroom." She stood. "Let's go."

Rafe's teammates were still around the table, working on their computers. As soon as Jackson saw them, he stood and came to Kristi. "You okay?"

"I'm better. Sorry for the disruption."

"No problem. Come sit down. Rafe, the boss wants you to call him."

Rafe seated Kristi and brushed his mouth over hers. "I'll be back in a few minutes." After a light brush of his fingers over her cheek, he walked out the back door to the deck railing and called Brent. "It's Rafe."

"Someone's been attempting to access Stewart's personal financial accounts," his boss said in lieu of a greeting.

"How do you know?"

"I instructed the techs to keep an eye on his bank accounts when I learned about the warehouse fire."

"Good call." One he should have thought of himself. In all fairness, though, Rafe had been more concerned about Kristi's wellbeing rather than her father's money. "I'm assuming they haven't been successful."

"Nope," Brent said, amusement in his voice. "The techs watching the accounts said the attempted hacker kept entering the wrong the password. The hacker is locked out."

"That will make someone angry."

"Oh, yeah."

"Either Stewart gave the kidnappers the wrong information or he deliberately keyed in the wrong password."

"Probably the latter. You know what's coming next."

"Yes."

"What will you do?"

"Whatever I have to do to protect Kristi." No matter the cost to himself.

CHAPTER TWENTY-NINE

Rafe scanned Angie Hale's medical file. When Angie had given birth to Rodcrick at 16 years of age, Travis Cain had been 25. Only one reason why Angie had kept Cain's identity a secret when she was in high school. Angie thought she was in love with him and had protected him from prosecution for statutory rape.

Sick at heart over the whole situation, he returned to the kitchen. Kristi sat at the table with tears trickling down her face. Jackson had his arm from her shoulders, offering silent comfort. "Kristi?" Rafe started to go to her, but Eli waved him toward Jon. Oh, man. The security feed. What had Kristi seen?

"Show me," he murmured to his teammate. On Jon's computer, Rafe watched as Alan Stewart stumbled from an elevator. Blood streamed from a wound on his scalp, streaking down one side of his face. At his side walked a man in a Ward Security uniform with a baseball cap pulled low on his forehead. The guard's arm was around Stewart's shoulders as though assisting him to his car. The position of his other hand, though, indicated the guard had a pistol shoved against the executive's side.

Rafe watched until the two men moved out of camera range. The guard's baseball cap prevented a positive identification. "Do other cameras show the guard's face?" He suspected the kidnapper was Hale, but Rafe wanted proof.

"Elevator camera gave me this." Jon's fingers danced across the keys and brought up more camera footage.

On screen, Stewart practically fell into the elevator. He spun and tried to shove the guard from the car as the doors started to close. The guard punched Stewart in the face. The executive hit the elevator wall and slid to the floor as his attacker turned with a smirk and jabbed a button on the wall panel.

Rafe scowled. "Run it again in slow motion."

"This is what you're looking for," Jon murmured. He clicked the mouse, and a still shot of the guard's face filled the screen.

The picture was fuzzy. Why was the picture out of focus? "Can you clean that up?"

A minute later, the man's image was clear. "Hello, Roderick Hale," Rafe said. "Is he the only one involved?"

"Nope. Look at this." Jon opened another file.

The screen shifted to show the lobby of Stewart Group headquarters. Mike Fleming stood at the front desk with Richard. Behind the guard, a light flashed on one of the screens Richard should have been watching. When Richard grabbed his cell phone to answer a call, Fleming slipped behind the desk and did something at the keyboard to stop the flashing and typed a few more commands. Fleming was involved with the kidnapping. He must have tinkered with the security system so it showed that Stewart left the building at 7:00. The time stamp on the footage indicated that Hale kidnapped Stewart shortly after the workday ended.

Jon glanced at him. "Fleming has computer skills."

"How do you know?"

"I had to piece together the footage we needed. Someone did a good job of corrupting the footage, then deleting it from the server."

"Fleming. You found the footage and cleaned it up," Rafe said, indicating the frozen screen shot on Jon's computer.

"Fleming's good. I'm better."

Eli placed a box of tissues in front of Kristi and patted her shoulder.

"Thanks," she said, her voice thick.

Time was running out before Hale or Fleming called her with a ransom demand. Both men wanted easy money at the very least. With Stewart's financial accounts locked, the men would turn to Kristi. Didn't take a genius to know she'd pay any amount of money to free her father.

Trevor Cain was Hale's biological father. Did the security guard also want revenge for a perceived injustice? Rafe frowned. If Hale had contacted his father, Cain likely gave his son a different version of events than was in the record. Hale might feel that the abuse charges were trumped up and the 30-year prison sentence unfair.

He looked at Eli. "Call Adams. Tell him what's going on. If he can call Hale or Fleming and keep him on the phone long enough, we can track the signal. Ask if Adams is willing to talk to me."

"While I do that, you need to talk to Kristi."

Her eyes widened. "Why? What's wrong?" She grimaced. "Besides the obvious."

Eli was right. Rafe couldn't delay the conversation any longer. "Come outside with me for a few minutes." Rafe led her to the outdoor couch on the deck.

Sitting beside Kristi, he gathered her against his side. "You saw the footage."

She nodded.

"Hale and Fleming are in this together, and others may be involved who weren't at your father's office."

"What aren't you telling me, Rafe?"

"I talked to Brent a few minutes ago. The computer techs at Fortress have been watching your father's financial accounts. Someone tried to access his accounts several times and messed up the password."

She looked at him. "The accounts are locked?"

He nodded. "Hale and Fleming want money. They're out of luck unless they find another source of cash."

"Me."

"You're the easiest target to reach."

"But wouldn't they force my father to access Stewart Group accounts?"

"I imagine they tried. However, when the techs told Brent about your father's personal accounts, he had them lock down the company's accounts as well. He also called Stewart Group's chief financial officer. Walters knows what's going on. Hale and Fleming will call you with a ransom demand."

"What do I say?"

"Depends on what they want." And how they wanted the money delivered. He didn't have a problem with Kristi transferring money into their account. Jon could track and reroute the cash to Kristi's account. Cash delivery was a different problem altogether. Unfortunately, Rafe suspected the greedy security men would want traveling cash and a money transfer to an offshore account.

"I don't care how much they want. I need my father, Rafe. I don't want to lose him."

"We'll get him back, hopefully without any money exchanging hands or bank accounts."

"We should go inside now," she murmured although she didn't move.

"I need to hold you a minute." Rafe's gut twisted into a knot as he contemplated the likely scenarios that could occur over the next few hours. None of the outcomes were acceptable.

"They want money, not me."

"You don't know that. So many things could go wrong."

"You'll protect me." She kissed his jaw. "I know you have my back."

Fair enough, he supposed. She had his heart. Rafe wanted to tell her how he felt, but he didn't want that revelation tainted by uncertainty and fear. "When this is over, I have something to tell you."

"Tell me now."

He chuckled at her impatience. "No way, Ms. Stewart. My secret gives you something good to wonder about and anticipate."

"All right. I have something to tell you when Dad's been rescued."

Rafe stilled, heart leaping into his throat. Was Kristi in love with him? "Something good, I hope."

"Yes." She smiled. "Now you have something to think about other than worrying over my safety."

He cupped her nape and drew Kristi closer for a long, deep kiss that conveyed the depth of his feelings. Rafe reluctantly broke the kiss. He wanted a lifetime with her. "We need to go inside." They had plans to make.

Inside the kitchen, Rafe sat beside Kristi at the table. "What did Adams say, Eli?"

"Call him. He's willing to tell you what he knows."

"Did he talk to Hale or Fleming?"

Eli shook his head. "Calls to both men went straight to voice mail. The phones have been turned off."

"How will we find my father?" Kristi asked.

"Adams may have some ideas." They would locate Stewart. The problem was protecting Kristi and rescuing her father before Hale or Fleming killed him. No matter how much money Kristi paid, Hale's end game was Stewart's death and probably Kristi's as well. Rafe's hands fisted. That wouldn't happen on his watch.

Eli called Adams. "It's Eli. You're on speaker with Wolf Pack and Kristi. Rafe has questions."

"How can I help?" the Ranger asked.

"Do you know where Hale and Fleming might take Stewart? They'll want an isolated place without nosy neighbors. Can't be a property in their names. Maybe property under a relative or friend's name. They used a rental cabin on Hart Mountain to hold Kristi, but they won't take Stewart back there with us in the picture. They know we're hunting for him."

"Hale doesn't have a place like that. His circle of friends is small, and he told me his mother's family disowned her when she became pregnant with him. He never knew his father's name."

"We think he knows who his father is now. Did you notice a change in his behavior in the past two months?"

"Hale's been more aggressive and sullen."

"Did the change start before or after his mother's death?"

"A few weeks before. That was also when Ward started showing up to talk to Hale."

Rafe frowned. Had Ward told Hale about his birth father? If so, what purpose would that serve except to stir up Hale against Stewart? Perhaps he used Hale's anger to solicit the guard's help. "What about Fleming? Does he have family or friends who would let him stay in an isolated place for a few days without asking questions?"

"He comes from a family of low-income workers who don't have extra cash to buy a vacation place."

That left Ward as a source for a hiding place. Rafe wrapped his arm around Kristi's shoulders. Stewart was a dead man if Wolf Pack didn't find him soon. If Ward was the mastermind behind this scheme, he couldn't afford to let Stewart live. "All right. Thanks."

"I want to help, Rafe. I'm trained and available. Use me."

He glanced at Eli who nodded. "As soon as we make a plan, we'll be in touch." He ended the call, then grabbed his own phone to text the Fortress tech who sent Angie Hale's medical file.

Kristi turned to Rafe. "Hugh is involved in this?"

"Still no proof."

Kristi's phone rang. She glanced at the screen. "Unknown number."

"Pre-paid phone," Jon said, and typed on his keyboard. Within seconds, he looked at Kristi. "Answer the call. Keep them talking as long as you can. Maybe we'll get lucky."

Rafe wasn't holding his breath. Hale and Fleming were savvy enough to pull off Stewart's kidnapping without a hitch. They wouldn't miss the likelihood of Fortress tracking their phone call. "Put the call on speaker."

Kristi swiped the screen and tapped the speaker button. "This is Kristi."

"How much do you love your father?" came the mechanical voice. No way to confirm if the caller was Hale, Fleming, or Ward.

"Who is this? What do you want?"

"We have Alan Stewart. His safe return will cost you $10 million transferred to an offshore account and $100,000 cash delivered in person. We'll be in touch in three hours with instructions."

Jon circled his finger, silently telling Kristi to keep them talking.

"Wait. How do I know he's still alive?"

"You don't."

"That's not good enough. You can't expect me to take your word that my father is alive and well. I'm not paying a penny until I have proof of life." She glanced at Rafe.

He gave her a nod of approval. She was handling this like a pro.

Thumps, curses, then Alan Stewart spoke. "I'm all right for the moment, sweetheart." He sounded weak, his speech a little slurred. "I love you. Tell Rafe I'm sorry."

The sound of a fist hitting flesh came over the speaker followed by a loud male groan.

"Dad! Please, don't hurt him. Tell me how to get the money to you and when. I need time to gather that much cash."

"Don't test my patience," the mechanical voice said. "Stewart has the cash in his home safe. You'll bring it to me. If you don't, your father will pay with his life."

"All right. I'll get the money. When do you want it?"

"We'll give you instructions in three hours." The call ended.

"Anything?" Rafe asked Jon.

"Not long enough," he said.

Kristi sighed. "I'm sorry. I held them on the phone as long as I could."

"Hale and Fleming work in security. They know how long establishing a lock on their location takes." Rafe kissed her temple. "You did a great job, Kristi. Thanks to you, we know your father is still alive and coherent enough to talk to you." For the moment.

"The kidnappers knew about the cash in Stewart's safe," Jackson said. "Did he tell them or did they already know?"

"I didn't tell anyone how much money Dad keeps in his safe." Kristi leaned her head against Rafe's shoulder.

"Did Ward mention your father's safe in a conversation?" Cal asked.

"Several times."

"Do you have a safe?" Rafe asked.

She wrinkled her nose. "Dad insisted. He's given me several pieces of jewelry over the years. Some of the jewelry belonged to my mother. I don't wear much jewelry unless I'm hosting a fundraiser with Dad. Other than that, it stays in the safe in my bedroom."

"Has Ward been in there?" Cal asked. He held up a hand when Rafe scowled at him. "Chill, Torres. No judgment, but we need to know."

Kristi laid her hand over Rafe's "I didn't invite Hugh to my bedroom, Cal. However, he walk into the room when he volunteered to get my purse or phone."

"In the last month?" the former cop persisted.

"The last time was two weeks ago. We were going to dinner with friends, and I was working on a wedding dress. I wanted to finish a couple of things before we left. Hugh volunteered to get my purse to save time. I don't know how long he was up there. I was distracted. However, after that incident, he talked about safes with my father. Dad mentioned his home safe and the brand because Hugh asked for recommendations."

Jon snorted. "He wanted to know what kind of safe your father had. Wouldn't surprise me if he planned to steal money to hold off the casinos."

"Have you looked inside your safe since Ward was in your bedroom?" Cal asked Kristi.

She shook her head. "I haven't opened the safe in weeks."

Rafe sighed. "Check my email, Jon. Zane sent the video footage from the cameras WS installed on the second floor."

A slight nod from his teammate.

Eli inclined his head toward the hallway. "Check the safe, Kristi."

Kristi followed Rafe upstairs to her bedroom. "Why are we checking my safe? Hugh doesn't know my combination."

"Humor me." He couldn't forget the camera that had been installed in Kristi's bedroom. From the position of the camera, anyone watching the security footage would see Kristi input the combination to open the safe.

She walked to the painting of a woman wearing a wedding dress and moved the painting aside. Kristi typed in the combination and twisted the handle to open the safe.

"See if anything is missing."

She gathered the boxes in the safe and set them on her bed. One by one, she opened the boxes, eyes widening in horror when she discovered half of them were empty. "Oh, no," she whispered. "Hugh did this?"

"We don't know yet if Ward is the culprit. One of the other security team members might be to blame." Rafe wrapped his arms around her. "Jon's checking the footage now. We'll find out who stole your jewelry and do our best to get the pieces back."

"He stole my mother's jewelry." Kristi's voice broke.

Fury burned in Rafe's gut. "Come on. Let's see what Jon discovered."

His teammates glanced up when they walked into the kitchen. "Ward knew the combination. How much did he take?" Jon asked.

"All of my mother's jewelry," Kristi said.

Cal looked at her with sympathy in his eyes. "With his desperate need for money, Ward would have sold the pieces. If we're lucky, the store that bought the jewelry will have a record we can use to track the pieces if they've been sold to someone else."

"The settings were old fashioned. If Hugh took them to a legitimate jewelry store, the store would take the jewels from the old settings and placed them in new ones."

"I'm sorry. We'll do what we can."

Rafe tipped up her chin and brushed his mouth over hers. "Come sit down. We need your help. Think about isolated properties that Ward and his family own."

"I made a list of their properties along with a picture of each," Jon said. He slid three pieces of paper down the table.

She scanned the first page and shook her head. "None of these. The neighbors are too close." She looked at the second page.

Kristi tapped a large rustic home. "This is a possibility. I've been there with my father and the Wards. It's out in the woods and isolated." Her lips curved into a wry smile. "Not too isolated for Mrs. Ward, though. Plenty of shopping nearby."

Continuing to the last page, she skimmed to the last listing. "This one also fits the parameters you laid out. It's where Hugh's father likes to go when he's in the mood for fishing."

"How often is that?"

"Once in the last five years. The cabin is by a lake and surrounded by 200 acres of forest owned by the Ward family."

Jon took the pages. "I'll see what I can found out about these two possibilities."

"Work fast, Jon," Rafe said. Stewart's hours of life were running out.

CHAPTER THIRTY

Kristi sipped water as the men discussed options for rescuing her father. Her head spun with the number of scenarios Wolf Pack and Dan Adams developed. Her former security guard had arrived soon after Wolf Pack began debating the best approaches to the likely locations of the kidnappers' hideout.

"I still don't like it," Rafe said. "Too many risks."

"Face it, Rafe," Dan said. "You won't like any of the plans because they involve an element of risk to Kristi."

"All of you are at risk, too," Kristi said.

"We're trained for this," Rafe said flatly. "You aren't."

"Nothing will happen to me. I trust you." Her gaze swept over the rest of them. "I trust all of you."

"Trust isn't the issue. Real bullets are." Pain and fear for her lurked in the depths of his eyes. "Don't ask me to do this, Kristi."

"Rafe." Eli waited until Rafe's gaze locked with his. "If you can't wall off your emotions, you'll be a liability."

Eyes narrowed, Rafe said, "If you try to lock me out of this operation, I'll resign from Fortress. No one will stop me from protecting her."

"Did I mention kicking you off this op?" Eli snapped.

Rafe straightened. "No, sir."

"I've been where you are. I won't order you to stand down. History won't repeat itself. Callie didn't have Wolf Pack at her back. Kristi does." He inclined his head toward Dan. "We also have Adams to tip the odds in our favor."

"We don't know how many men might be involved in this kidnapping. Odds are good that we'll be outnumbered again."

"We're better trained and more disciplined than anyone Fleming and Hale con into helping them and Ward pull this off. We also have backup. Brent has a team on standby."

Kristi's phone rang. She glanced at the screen. "Unknown number again."

"On speaker," Jon said.

When Rafe gave her the signal to answer the call, she swiped the screen and tapped the speaker button. "This is Kristi."

The mechanical voice rattled off an address. "You have two hours to bring the money. If you're one minute late, we'll kill your father. Come alone. No cops. No boyfriend. If anyone else but you shows up, all of you will die." The call ended.

"Too short." Jon shut the lid of his laptop.

"No surprise. Gear up," Eli said. "Adams, do you have what you need?"

"Yes, sir."

"Get your gear. You'll ride with me and Jon. We'll set you up with one of our comm devices. Rafe, help Kristi get ready. We don't have much time."

While the team scattered to carry out Eli's orders, Rafe walked with Kristi to the second floor. He led her into his bedroom and grabbed his bag from the floor. Rafe showed her a small electronic device, then slid the gadget into her ear and tapped it.

Voices of Rafe's teammates came through the device. She smiled. "I can hear your teammates." Several of them chuckled.

"Music to your ears," Jackson teased.

"They can also hear you." Rafe's gaze swept over her quickly. "You need a dark, long-sleeved shirt that buttons and isn't form-fitting. Don't put it on yet. If you have black jeans and tennis shoes, change into them while I gear up."

Kristi hurried to her room, found what she needed, and changed. She returned to Rafe. "Will this work?"

"That's perfect." He shouldered his pack and threaded his fingers through hers. "Let's go. You need one more item before you're ready."

They left the house, locking up behind them since the rest of the men were waiting in the vehicles. Rafe stopped at the back of his SUV and pulled out a black vest. "Hold still," he murmured and settled the heavy vest over Kristi's shoulders. He adjusted the straps, then helped her slip on the button-up black shirt. Rafe eyed her critically. "That's the best I can do. I should have asked Brent to send a vest your size."

"Do you have a backup vest for yourself, Rafe? You aren't going into a dangerous situation without all your gear."

Rafe lifted his shirt enough for her to see that he wore a vest, too. "You're wearing my backup."

"Time to go, Rafe," Eli said. "We'll park one block from the house. Kristi, you drive. Fleming might tap into your father's security system to see if you follow orders."

"He'll see Rafe in the SUV."

"I'll drop to the floor when we're a few blocks from your father's home." Rafe closed the hatch and climbed into the backseat while Kristi settled behind the steering wheel.

"You can talk to Rafe, but remember the rest of us can hear every word you say," Jackson warned. "Don't make me blush."

"Shut up, Conner," Rafe said as his teammates chuckled. "I'll get you back when you have your own woman to worry about."

"From the way things look at the moment, buddy, I won't have to worry about a woman for a long time."

"It's just a matter of time and the right woman."

"Watch your speed as you drive, Kristi," Jon said. "We don't need a traffic stop, especially with the equipment Rafe and the rest of us carry. No time for long explanations."

Kristi eased up on the accelerator. Twenty miles over the speed limit would draw the wrong attention from the local police.

She drove as fast as she dared to the other side of Bakerhill where her father lived in a large house on a twenty-acre estate. Thankfully, at this early hour, sparse traffic cut the commute time in half.

When she turned onto the street where her father's home was located, Rafe slid to the floor. At the security gate, Kristi entered the access code. The gate slid open, and she drove to the front of the house.

"Leave the front door unlocked when you get the money," Rafe said. "If you run into trouble, I'll be inside in less than a minute."

Run into trouble? Kristi swallowed hard. She should have thought of that possibility. Hale and Fleming worked for the company providing security for her father's home. They could have someone inside waiting to grab her.

She exited the SUV, walked to the front door, and unlocked it. She left the door open and headed for her father's home office, turning on lights as she went.

Kristi opened the safe and removed the stacks of cash, dropping them into the bag she brought to carry the money. "Leaving now," she murmured.

"You're clear outside," Rafe said.

A minute later, Kristi climbed behind the steering wheel and laid the cash bag on the passenger seat. She drove away from the house.

"I programmed the address into my phone's navigation app," Rafe said. "The drive will take 90 minutes if you drive the speed limit."

"Is that what I need to do?"

"We need a few minutes to get into position," Eli chimed in. "Drive a little faster than the speed limit, then take your time getting out of the vehicle and walking to the cabin."

"Do you have a bazooka handy? I can probably hit some of Hale and Fleming's friends with that."

More laughter in her ear and from the backseat. Rafe laid his hand on her shoulder and squeezed. "You don't need a weapon. We're prepared for just about anything."

"As long as we get Dad out of there, I don't care what happens to the rest of them." Her hands tightened around the steering wheel.

"Including Ward?" he asked.

"Especially Hugh. He lied to me, stole from me, and cheated on me. Worse, he's threatening my father's life."

"Rafe, Jon sent a file to your email," Eli said. "Pull it up, and we'll fine tune the plan now that we have the target location."

"Yes, sir."

The buzz of conversation between Wolf Pack and Dan Adams became background noise as Kristi followed the navigation directions to the address the kidnappers gave her. She contemplated the conversation she and Rafe had earlier that night. What was Rafe's secret? Was it possible he had serious feelings for her?

Butterflies took flight in her stomach. She hoped one day he might come to love her as much as she loved him. Rafe Torres was the only man for her. If he rejected her, no other man would measure up.

Ten minutes from their destination, Eli said, "Kristi, go to the rest stop ahead. Rafe needs to change vehicles."

Although she wanted Rafe to stay with her, Eli was right. Hale and Fleming weren't likely to trust her.

"Everything will work out. We have your back and your father's."

"Backup is ten minutes behind us," Jon said. "Trust us to do our job."

Two minutes later, she took the exit Eli had indicated and parked. The other vehicles pulled in on both sides of Rafe's.

After exiting the SUV with his equipment, Rafe handed the duffel to Jackson, opened Kristi's door, and kissed her, hard and fast. "I won't let anything happen to you. Listen for our instructions. Obey them to the letter. If we tell you to drop, do it." Another hard kiss. "Be safe, baby."

"Be careful, Rafe."

"Always. I have the best reason in the world to keep breathing." He flashed her a grin. "You." With that, he closed the door and climbed into Cal's SUV.

The operatives waited for Kristi to back out, then fell into line behind her. Five minutes from her destination, Wolf Pack pulled off the road and into the cover of trees near the roadway.

"Drop your speed, Kristi," Rafe said. "Give us time to move into position."

"Okay." She eased up on the accelerator.

"What do you think about attending a rodeo?"

She smiled. "Sounds like fun."

"Have you been to one?"

"I watched one on television a few months ago."

"Not as good as being there in person. The music, the clowns, and the crowd make the experience worthwhile."

"What's the best part of the rodeo?"

"The food," Jackson chimed in.

"The horses," Cal added. "I'm taking Rachelle this year. She's never been to one, either, but she asked me to take her when she saw an advertisement for one."

"What do you think about a double date with Cal and Rachelle?" Rafe asked Kristi. "Would you like that?"

"I'd love to go with them. I'm looking forward to meeting Rachelle as well as Jon and Eli's wives." She slowed and turned into a graveled driveway. "I see the cabin."

"Go as slow as you can," Rafe whispered.

For the first time since Rafe had slipped the communication device into Kristi's ear, no one spoke. She would give just about anything to hear Rafe's voice right now.

He wasn't far away, she reminded herself. Her job was to stall as long as possible and stay alive. If anything happened to her, Rafe would never forgive himself. She didn't intend to die because she had plans of her own that included a life with the Navy SEAL who had captured her heart.

As ordered, Kristi slowed her speed. She remembered being at this home several times before she left for college. This wasn't a rental cabin. The Wards had built a vacation paradise for when the family wanted to get away for a weekend and frequently invited their friends to join them.

Kristi parked under tree cover. "I parked halfway up the driveway."

"Copy," came a whisper of acknowledgment through the ear piece.

Grabbing the bag of cash, Kristi exited the SUV and walked toward the front door. Before she'd gone more than ten feet, a man dressed in black walked from the forest with a scowl.

"Why did you park here?"

Kristi lifted her chin. "I'm in an unknown situation with no idea what's going to happen. You and your buddies might have placed a bomb in front of the cabin like you did in Dad's warehouse."

The man scoffed. "Can't believe the boss wanted to marry you since you're as dumb as a rock. Why would we bomb your vehicle when you brought the money?"

Wolf Pack had been right. Hugh Ward orchestrated her kidnapping and her father's, and stole her mother's jewelry.

The lookout turned toward Rafe's SUV, a gun in his hand. "Anyone else in your vehicle?"

She shook her head.

"Don't move. I'll make sure you didn't bring your boyfriend."

"I was instructed to come alone. Do you think I'd risk my father's life? I don't care about the money. I want my father to be safe and free."

"Then you won't mind if I check." With another warning to remain in place, Lookout yanked open the door to the backseat, gun aimed into the interior. He peered inside and checked the cargo area, then closed the door again. "Lucky for you and your old man that you followed orders."

He returned, eyed the bag, and said, "I'll take that."

Conscious of the need to draw things out as much as possible, Kristi stepped back. "My instructions were to bring the money to the cabin. I'm not handing the bag to one of the flunkies hanging out in the dark when my father's life is at stake." Her own, too, she imagined.

"Careful, baby," Rafe murmured through the ear piece.

Lookout growled, grabbed Kristi's arm, and jerked her toward him. "Shut up and walk." With a painful grip, the man forced her to resume her journey to the cabin.

She fought his hold. "How much is Hugh paying you to hurt a defenseless woman?"

"Hold position, Rafe," Eli whispered.

"I bruise easy," she said to Lookout. "I'll have your finger marks on my arm in a few hours." Did Rafe understand what she was telling him?

"I have her in sight," Jon said. "She's okay."

"Kristi, give us intel without compromising your safety," Eli said.

Lookout's grip tightened as he forced her to move faster, but he remained silent. He propelled her up the stairs to the wraparound porch, opened the front door, and shoved Kristi inside the cabin.

Hale and Fleming stood with guns in their hands and smirks on their faces.

"Well, look who's here. Hale and Fleming. Some security team you are. You're responsible for my kidnapping last weekend, aren't you?"

Hale motioned with the gun. "Get the money," he told Fleming. "Ms. Stewart won't be needing that anymore."

Goosebumps surged across her skin at the ominous words. When Fleming reached her, Kristi's stomach lurched at the scent of alcohol on his breath. His eyes were bloodshot, too. The obvious signs of intoxication worried her, especially since he had a gun pointed at her chest. "You smell like a brewery, Fleming."

"Nice job," Eli murmured.

Kristi's former bodyguard scowled. He yanked the bag from her hand and tossed it toward Hale. "Check to be sure her boyfriend didn't pull a fast one on us."

A glare from Hale. "You're not in charge of this operation. Besides, you watched her pull the cash from the safe in her old man's office on the security camera."

Kristi shuddered. Thank goodness Rafe had remained in the SUV. "I followed your directions to the letter. Where is my father?"

"Not so fast." Hale tossed the bag aside and lumbered closer. "There's the matter of $10 million to deal with before you see your old man."

"Stall," Rafe whispered in her ear. "Men in the woods."

Hale motioned toward the laptop set up on the coffee table with the barrel of his big black gun. "Transfer the money or I'll put a bullet in you."

"You're not getting another penny until I see my father."

Eyes narrowed, he aimed the weapon at her. "Don't kid yourself, lady. I'll shoot you without regret and be done with you. You and your old man stole something from me that I'll never get back."

A soft growl came through her ear piece. Rafe.

"Focus," Eli hissed.

"You could shoot me," Kristi said to Hale. "You won't."

"Oh, yeah? Why not?"

"You're not the one in charge of this operation." Her former bodyguard might have the desire for revenge, but he hadn't put together this plan.

He stiffened. "What makes you say that?"

"You'll score some cash, but someone else is pulling the strings, letting you take all the risks while he'll walk away a millionaire." She turned toward the man who walked into the room, dressed in jeans, hiking boots, and a black t-shirt. "Welcome to the party, Hugh. Where is my father?"

CHAPTER THIRTY-ONE

"Point that gun somewhere else," Hugh snapped at Hale. "Kristi can't transfer the money if she's dead."

Nice to know he cared enough to keep her alive for the moment. Kristi glared at her former friend. "What have you done, Hugh?"

"What I had to do." He frowned at her. "This is all your fault. If you had followed the plan, everything would have been fine."

"For you." Kristi suspected she wouldn't have survived long as Hugh's wife. That $2 million life insurance policy might have been too tempting for Hugh to resist.

A scowl. "I would have divorced you in a year or two. No harm done, and no hard feelings. We would have simply grown apart and gone our separate ways."

"After you cleaned out my bank accounts and my trust fund. Did you plan to cash the $2 million life insurance policy you took out on me last month?"

"How did you....?" A muscle in Hugh's jaw twitched. "Never mind. It doesn't matter now."

"Actually, I think it does. You haven't canceled the insurance policy. Why stop at $10 million when you can have $12 million, minus the payments to your small army of thugs?"

Hale and Fleming exchanged glances, then turned to Hugh. "You promised us $25,000 each," Hale said, fury in his eyes. "The rest of the guys only get $10,000 a piece. We're taking all the risks, and you're walking away with enough money to retire on an island and live like a king."

Kristi laughed. "The way he spends money, he won't live like a king for long. He'd have to come up with a new source of money to feed his gambling habit."

"Shut your mouth, Kristi," Hugh snapped. He rounded on Hale, Fleming, and Lookout. "I planned to give you bonuses. I didn't know how much money Kristi had left in her accounts. I just used $10 million as a starting point."

"A bonus." Fleming scowled. "You expect us to believe that?"

"It's the truth. Look, if you want, I'll give you three the bonuses and keep the other guys at the same payout. You'll walk away with $100,000 each. Once Kristi transfers the money, I'll redirect the bonuses to your accounts. The other men will never know."

Hale gave a slow nod. "All right. You've got yourself a deal." He aimed his gun at Hugh. "If you don't transfer the money, I'll shoot various body parts until you comply. Believe me, you'll be begging to transfer that money."

Kristi smiled. "Looks like you hired someone smarter than you are, Hugh."

"I told you to keep you mouth shut." Eyes glittering with fury, Hugh slapped Kristi's face hard enough to knock her to the floor.

Stunned, she stayed where she fell, her face burning where Hugh's hand struck her.

"I'm almost there, baby," Rafe whispered. "Hang on."

"Get up." Hugh kicked her ribs with his booted foot.

Pain exploded in her side. She couldn't hold back the groan. Hugh just had to kick the ribs that were already sore from tangling with her kidnappers.

"On your feet, or I'll break your ribs next time."

She sucked in a shallow breath. "I'm pretty sure you did this time. If I can't function, you don't get a dime from me. Take me to my father."

"I'll kill you myself," he threatened.

"The account password isn't written down. If you kill me, you get nothing except a death sentence in prison."

"Get up," Hugh shouted.

"I need a minute." She hoped that would be enough time to gather her strength. Kristi had a feeling standing up would be an exercise in torture.

Muttering an ugly curse, Hugh reached down and yanked Kristi to her feet.

She moaned and pressed her arm against her injured ribs. Oh, man. Hugh's boot had done a number on her rib cage.

"Stop whining." Hugh dragged her toward the staircase. "You want to see Alan? Here's your chance. After that, you will transfer that money or I'll kill your father in front of you."

"I don't know if I can climb the stairs."

"If you want to see your father, you'll get up there any way you can." He sneered. "I'm not helping you. You can crawl, or you can make the short walk to the computer and take care of business."

"Thanks for nothing," she muttered. "Where is Dad?"

"A guest room."

"Which guest room? You have five in this cabin."

"What does it matter which room?"

She stopped halfway up the stairs and frowned at him. "I'm having trouble walking and getting my breath. Isn't that reason enough to ask how far I have to walk?"

"Suck it up and deal, Kristi. Alan's in the room across from the master bedroom."

"Oh, man. Are you serious? The corner bedroom? You might as well have put him in outer Mongolia."

"Good job, baby," Rafe whispered.

"Cal, Jackson, corner bedroom," Eli murmured.

"Copy," came the response.

Hugh shoved her into motion. "If you stop again, your father will pay the price. Move, Kristi."

Afraid to drag this out longer, she climbed the stairs to the second floor. On the landing, Kristi paused. "The master bedroom is still on the left?"

"You're stalling." Hugh backhanded her.

Kristi hit the wall. Her lip stung. When she touched the fingers of one hand to her mouth, they came away stained with blood. Great. The jerk had split her lip. "Does splitting my lip make you feel more in control, Hugh?"

"I'll kill him," Rafe whispered into the comm system.

"Your boyfriend is around here somewhere, isn't he?" Hugh stalked toward her. "I told you to come alone or you would all die."

"I wouldn't risk Dad's life."

"You're lying." He wrapped his hand around the front of her throat and squeezed. As she wheezed in a breath, Hugh leaned in close and murmured, "You just condemned your boyfriend to die. Did you think I wouldn't have help out here? He's alone and outnumbered. Hope you can live with that on your conscience."

She dragged in a wheezing breath. "Let go."

"You're lucky I don't strangle you to death." He released her throat. "Let's go." Hugh propelled her down the hall to the guest room.

Kristi stumbled into the room. Her father sat in a chair with his arms and legs restrained, his head lolling against his chest. "Dad."

She hurried to her father. With trembling hands, she cupped his chin and lifted his face toward hers. She gasped. His face was bruised, swollen, and bloody. "You beat him? What is wrong with you, Hugh?"

"Is he breathing?" Jackson whispered. "Check his pulse."

"Dad, can you hear me?" She eyed the rise and fall of his chest as she leaned close to check for a pulse. "His breathing is shallow, pulse is faint," she whispered to the medic.

"You've seen him," Hugh growled. "Let's go. I want that money."

"I need to help him."

"No need. He won't be feeling pain for much longer."

Footsteps pounded down the hallway. For a minute, Kristi's heart leaped, wondering if Rafe had arrived. The next instant, she realized he wouldn't make a sound.

Fleming appeared in the doorway. "We've got trouble. Sutton, Steele, Marsh, Chavez, and McDaniel aren't responding. Neither are Christensen, Roberts, Carter, Shaw, and Vega."

Hugh spun toward Kristi. "I warned you what would happen." He glanced at Fleming. "Shoot Stewart."

"No." Kristi lunged toward her father a split second too late. Fleming's gun bucked when he fired. The bullet slammed into her father's left shoulder. "Dad!" She wrapped her arms around him to protect him from another bullet. "He didn't do anything to you, Hugh. How could you shoot him?"

"You should have listened. I would have trained you to listen to me once we were married. It's too late now." Hugh yanked her back and dragged her toward the door. "Your boyfriend's death will be on you."

"He's already taken out ten men. Nothing will stop Rafe from coming for me. Let me go, Hugh. Maybe Rafe will let you live."

"You think Hale, Fleming, and Rostov are the only ones left? There are five more men out there, more than enough to keep your boyfriend busy until it's too late to stop me from getting what I want." He shoved her into the hall. "You'll do what I tell you, or your father will get another bullet, this time in his head."

"Why should I? You're going to kill us anyway."

A cold smile curved his mouth. "You're smarter than I gave you credit for."

"Why should I help you if you're going to kill me?"

"Easy. If you don't, I'll make your death slow and painful."

"You don't have the stomach for it."

He lifted one shoulder. "Maybe not, but Hale does, and he has an excellent reason to hate your father."

She glared at Hugh. "I have a reason to hate Trevor Cain. Did you tell Hale about his father?"

"What's the big deal, Kristi? I needed help, and he was happy to offer his skills and connections to other mercenaries to exact a little revenge and earn money. It's a win for both of us."

"You must know what his father did to me."

"I know what you claimed. Maybe you lied." His lips curved. "At least, that's what Hale believes."

"In position," Rafe murmured.

"Copy," Eli replied. "Hold. Kristi, go to the kitchen. Cal, Jackson, go."

Kristi jerked away from Hugh's punishing grip on her arm. "I need water." She scowled at him. "My throat is raw where you choked me along with the smoke from the fire at the warehouse. Your doing, I suppose?"

He stared at her. "Fire? What fire?"

She laughed. "Sounds like Hale doesn't follow orders well."

"He was supposed to grab you at the warehouse and bring you here. But you screwed that up by bringing Rafe."

He sighed. "Never mind. I'll deal with the fire details later."

"What does that mean?" Kristi descended the stairs and turned toward the kitchen.

Hugh tightened his grip on her arm, holding her in place. "Money first, then water."

"Jon?" Rafe whispered.

"Clear shot."

"Do as Ward says, baby."

"Last chance to do this the easy way, Kristi," Hugh snapped.

"All right."

Forcing her to walk in front of him, Hugh poked at her back with a gun he must have had hidden. "You have a gun, Hugh? I didn't know you knew how to handle one of those."

Another fierce jab. "You don't know a lot of things about me, including the fact that I'll be taking over Stewart Group after tonight."

"You are out of your mind. You haven't been on the job yet. Why would the board vote you in as CEO?"

"I had a contract prepared earlier today. While we were waiting for you to arrive, Alan and I had a long, persuasive chat. He signed the contract, giving me the job as CEO if anything happened to him."

"He signed under duress. That contract will never hold up in court."

Hugh laughed. "Who's going to object? Not you or your father. Hale and his friends have lots of reason to keep quiet. Finally, I'll be where I should have been all along, in the president's suite of offices at the helm of a billion-dollar company."

He shoved Kristi into the living room and toward the laptop. "No more stalling," Hugh said. "Transfer the money, and I'll let you say goodbye to your father."

Praying Wolf Pack was ready, Kristi sat on the sofa and pulled the laptop toward her. She hesitated with her hands hovering over the keyboard. "You promise to let me see my father?"

Hale strode to the sofa and pressed the barrel of his gun against her temple. "Do it or you and I will be getting more intimately acquainted before I kill you." He studied her a moment. "Might be fun."

She shuddered and brought up her bank's website. Two minutes later, her account had a zero balance. "It's done," she murmured.

"The money will return to your account in one minute," Jon murmured. "Kitchen, Kristi. Now."

Kristi lowered the laptop lid, putting the computer to sleep and buying herself a few more precious seconds. "I'm getting water, then going to my father. I hope you choke on that money, Hugh."

"Go with her, Fleming," Hugh snapped. "Don't let her out of your sight. I don't trust her."

"We should kill her and be done with it," Hale growled.

"You may be a total monster, but I'm not. I got us the money, didn't I? I'm paying you for this job. You want that money, you'll follow my orders."

"Move, Kristi," Jon murmured.

Fleming motioned for her to get going with his gun, making her stomach twist into a knot. She circled the sofa as Hugh rebooted the laptop.

Kristi pressed her arm against her ribs and walked to the kitchen. The room was dark. She forced herself to continue moving deeper into the room.

"Need to turn on a light in here," Fleming muttered.

"Drop," Rafe whispered.

Kristi hit the floor a second later, pain stealing her breath. Behind her came a choking sound, a scuff of boot, then silence.

A moment later, Rafe dropped to his knees beside Kristi. He laid his hand on her back. "Let's get you to safety."

"I can't leave Dad."

"Jackson and Cal are with him. Can you sit up?"

She nodded. Pain ricocheted through her body as she shifted position. When she was finally upright, Rafe had to steady her.

A shot rang out in the living room.

Rafe slid one arm behind Kristi's back and one under her knees. "This will hurt," he murmured, and lifted her.

Kristi couldn't stifle the moan. She'd never hurt this bad in her life.

"I'm sorry, baby." Rafe started toward the back door.

"Not so fast," Hugh snapped, and turned on the light.

CHAPTER THIRTY-TWO

Rafe froze. Resolve hardened his jaw. No matter what the cost to himself, he wouldn't allow Ward to get his hands on Kristi again. "Where's Hale?" he whispered. Did he have two men to worry about or just Ward?

"No longer a problem," the sniper replied.

"Put Kristi down and step away," Ward ordered. "Don't try anything, Rafe. I have a gun pointed at you. Since I haven't had as much practice as you, I might hit Kristi by accident. You don't want that to happen."

Rafe crouched and lowered Kristi to the floor. "Lay flat," he whispered.

She gripped his hand. "We'll face him together."

"Trust me."

"Step away," Ward repeated.

Once Kristi complied with his request, Rafe stood and turned, keeping his body between Ward and Kristi. "Put down your weapon, Ward. You can't win this."

"Kristi's my ticket to wealth. I don't need you."

Rafe inched closer to his target. "If you want the money, you deal with me."

"You have nothing I want. You're a washed-up soldier with minutes to live."

"I have her account number and password. I'll give them to you in exchange for her life."

Ward's eyes narrowed. "I don't believe you. She wouldn't trust me with that information, and I've been friends with her for years. You're wasting my time." He aimed the barrel of his weapon at Rafe's chest. "On your knees."

Kristi drew in a ragged breath. "Hugh, don't. I'll give you the money. Just don't kill him."

Rafe got on his knees, angling his body to keep his right hand hidden from Ward's view. He slowly reached for his weapon.

Ward scowled at Kristi. "He's a killer for hire and after your money."

"Your contempt for Rafe is ironic since you want my trust fund for yourself."

Rafe's hand wrapped around the grip of his Sig.

Rage filled Ward's eyes. "I've had enough of your smart mouth." He shifted the aim of his weapon to Kristi. "I've changed my mind. I'll take what I need from the company accounts. No one will question the new CEO of Stewart Group."

As Ward squeezed the trigger, Rafe threw himself in front of Kristi and fired his own weapon. The bullet from Ward's gun slammed into Rafe's vest, tossing him against the woman he loved. Ward dropped the floor, groaning as he clutched his right shoulder and cursing.

Rafe dragged in a painful breath. Getting shot in the chest hurt, even with the vest for protection. "Ward's down," he murmured. He staggered to the fallen man, stripped Ward of his weapon, and frisked him for more. Finding nothing, Rafe returned to Kristi. "Are you okay?"

She nodded. "He shot you."

"He was aiming for you." He glared at the cursing man. "Ward's lucky I didn't kill him."

"How bad are you hurt?" Jackson snapped.

"Bullet hit my vest."

"Other injuries?"

"They'll wait."

Kristi's hand clamped over Rafe's forearm. "You're injured?"

"A scratch on my arm. I'm more concerned about you. Ward beat you."

"I want to see your arm."

Rafe turned for Kristi to examine the injury making itself felt along the back of his left arm. Now that the firefight was over and Kristi was safe, the pain in Rafe's arm took precedence over the ache in his chest.

She gasped. "You need stitches. You've lost a lot of blood, too. Your left side is covered with blood."

"I'll have it checked later. Jackson, status on Stewart?"

"An ambulance will arrive soon. I've stabilized Stewart for now, but he needs surgery as soon as possible."

As the medic gave his update, sirens sounded in the distance. "Eli?" He helped Kristi sit up, wrapped his uninjured arm around her, and kissed her temple. If Rafe had been one second slower, Ward would have shot her. He shuddered. Too close.

"We're clear. Ward's men are restrained, and Adam Walker's team will be gone before the police arrive."

Good. Rafe didn't want Phantom unit to be tied down answering questions about their role in this operation.

"Jackson, is Stewart stable enough for you to check Rafe?" Eli asked.

"I'm fine," Rafe muttered with a scowl. The weakness swamping his body would pass. Probably.

"He'll hold until the EMTs take over," Jackson said.

As soon as the medic strode into the kitchen with his mike bag, Kristi asked, "How's Dad?"

"Holding his own for the moment. I used pressure bandages to control the bleeding."

"Internal injuries?" Rafe asked. He blinked hard to push back the darkness crowding the edges of his vision. Sprawling flat for a minute to catch his breath sounded like a great idea.

Jackson gripped his shoulder. "I want to see your arm."

"I'm fine," Rafe groused. He shrugged off the medic's hold and listed to the side as the world tilted.

"Rafe!"

Kristi's arms tightened around him, but she couldn't hold his weight and he didn't want to hurt her. "Somebody kick Ward in the ribs for me."

"You already put a bullet through his shoulder. That will hurt him longer than a kick to the ribs. Lay down before you face plant in front of your woman," Jackson snapped, taking Rafe's weight and easing him to the floor.

Sweet relief rolled through his body. "Check Kristi first. Ward hit her more than once."

"You're the one bleeding all over the floor. I need to see how much damage the knife did."

"Lucky swipe."

"Yeah, sure." The medic glanced over his shoulder to Eli. "Help me roll Rafe onto his side."

Rafe braced himself but the wave of pain almost did him in. He fought off the darkness with grim determination, breathing deep.

Jackson whistled. "Some swipe. Kristi's right. You need stitches, buddy."

"Just tape it. I'll be fine."

"Ha. You wish. I'll clean your arm and use butterfly bandages to hold the wound closed, but you're going to the hospital with Kristi and her father."

"Hurry up, then check Kristi." He flinched when Jackson cleaned his arm with antiseptic wipes. "Where's Adams?" he asked Eli.

"Waiting out front for the police. Jon?"

"They're three minutes out."

"Come join the party."

"Copy."

"How did Adams do out there?" Rafe asked Eli.

"He impressed the boss enough that Maddox scheduled him for an interview in two days."

Two minutes later, Jackson sat back, medical detritus littering the floor. "That's all I can do for now. Stay on your back unless you want to embarrass yourself by passing out." He looked at Kristi. "Which side did Ward kick?"

"The bruised side."

He scowled and grabbed a chemically-activated cold pack. After shaking it, he handed the pack to Kristi. "Place that against your lip."

"Cops and ambulances are here," Adams announced through the comm system.

"Copy that." Eli stood. "Do what you can for Kristi, Jackson. We'll be knee-deep in twitchy law enforcement in a minute. I'll hold them off as long as I can."

"Yes, sir." By the time several officers with weapons drawn stormed into the room, Jackson had finished checking Kristi for injuries. The medic kept his hand on her shoulder to hold her in place. "Stay down," he murmured.

"I want to see Dad."

"If you go, Rafe will drag himself upstairs with you. Do him a favor, and stay where you are." He patted her shoulder. "I'll go to the hospital with you and update you on his condition."

Eli strode into the room with another cop. "Our medic has to go with the vics to the hospital."

A frown. "Our paramedics are well trained."

"We aren't sure that our principal is safe. Her boyfriend is injured and won't accept treatment unless she's protected." Eli gave the cop an easy smile. "It's how we operate. You'd do the same for one of your witnesses, Lt. Sloan."

The lieutenant rubbed his jaw. "All right. One of my officers will follow the ambulance and help with protection until the detectives finish questioning the rest of you. After that, your principal's protection is on you. We're a small department with a limited budget."

"We'll handle the security." Eli tipped his head toward Ward. "Hugh Ward is the man behind all the trouble tonight."

Sloan's eyebrows winged up. "Huh. We've never had trouble out of the Wards. Sounds like an interesting story, Wolfe."

"Complete with multiple players with their own motives for going along with Ward's scheme." Eli looked at Jackson. "Go with Stewart. The county sent three ambulances. Someone from Fortress will meet Rafe and Kristi at the hospital."

After learning that Rafe shot Ward to protect Kristi, the lieutenant asked for his weapon and Ward's. Rafe handed over the weapons, glad that he had another Sig in his collection at home.

As four EMTs walked into the kitchen, Sloan motioned one pair to Ward and the other pair to Kristi and Rafe.

After answering a stream of questions from the paramedics and enduring their cursory examinations, Rafe leaned hard on Eli as his team leader helped him to the ambulance.

"Would have been easier to use the gurney," Eli said.

"Shut up, sir."

He chuckled as he practically lifted Rafe into the back of the ambulance, then did the same for Kristi. "Keep an eye on him," he told Kristi. "Rafe isn't a good patient."

"I have a feeling that's true for all of Wolf Pack."

"You know us well, sugar." When the paramedic climbed into the back of the ambulance with Rafe and

Kristi, Eli shut the doors. Seconds later, the vehicle began the journey to the hospital.

In less than fifteen minutes, Rafe and Kristi were in one examination room with Brent Maddox standing guard in the hallway. The Fortress CEO had assisted Phantom and Wolf Pack in the woods around the Ward cabin and volunteered to stand watch.

By the time the doctor finished treating them, Rafe was beyond ready to leave the hospital and find a comfortable bed, but they were waiting on word about Kristi's father, and the local police wanted to talk to them.

"We have questions for you and Ms. Stewart," Detective Olson said. "You can answer them here or at the station."

"My girlfriend's father, Alan Stewart, is in an operating room at the moment. Frankly, I could use a vat of coffee. I vote we go to the cafeteria."

"Coffee sounds good," Detective Lawson said. "Lead the way."

Three hours later, the detectives' questions had been asked and answered multiple times, and fatigue weighed on Rafe like a wet wool blanket. A glance at Kristi told him that she wasn't doing much better.

Rafe stood and helped Kristi to her feet. "Kristi needs to check on her father. If you have more questions, contact us tomorrow."

"We're not finished," Olson protested.

"Yeah, we are. Other questions can wait."

Brent walked up. "Go, Rafe. I'll take care of the detectives."

Rafe escorted Kristi from the cafeteria to the sound of the angry detectives protesting Brent's interference, and Brent threatening to call in the company lawyers.

After Jackson's response to his text, Rafe escorted Kristi to the elevator. "Sixth floor. Your father's in recovery."

They met Jackson in an empty waiting room. "He'll be fine," the medic said to Kristi. "He'll need rehab on the shoulder, has a concussion, and needed stitches in his forehead. The surgeon also repaired some minor internal injuries. Considering what he endured, he's doing great."

"When can I see him?"

"Go to the desk. The nurse will take you back. I know you're worried, but keep the visit short. He needs rest to heal. Your father is sleeping off the anesthesia, so he's in and out."

"Will you come with me, Rafe?"

"Sure." He threaded his fingers through hers and accompanied Kristi to the desk. When they entered the recovery room and saw her father, Kristi stopped abruptly, her wide-eyed gaze fixed on Stewart's face. Rafe squeezed her hand. "I know he looks rough, but he'll heal and be back to buying and selling companies in no time."

Kristi wrapped her hand around her father's. "Dad, can you hear me?"

Several seconds passed without a response. Finally, Stewart opened his eyes and blinked. He looked confused when he saw her, then he frowned. "You're hurt."

"A few cracked ribs. Everything else is superficial. You and Rafe have the worst damage."

Her father shifted his gaze to Rafe. "How bad?"

"Cracked ribs and a knife wound with lots of fancy stitches, courtesy of the doctor." He smiled. "I'll heal faster than you."

A faint smile. "Younger." Stewart sobered. "Sorry."

"For what?"

"What I said to you. I was wrong."

Rafe gave a slight nod.

"You saved Kristi. Thank you."

"You don't have to thank me for that. She will always be my first priority."

Stewart studied him although he fought to stay awake. "Should I ask your intentions toward my daughter?"

"We'll talk when you're better." He touched his hand to Kristi's lower back. "We'll let you rest and check on you later, Mr. Stewart."

"Take Kristi home."

"Dad, we'll stay in the waiting room."

"No need. I'll sleep anyway." Another slight smile. "Heavy pain medicine. Rest, sweetheart." Stewart roused enough to stare at Rafe. "Protect her."

"With my life."

"I love you, Dad," Kristi said, her voice thick.

"Love you, honey." Stewart's eyes closed again.

"We should go," Rafe murmured. He didn't know if Kristi would agree to leave the hospital. If not, he'd find a blanket and pillow for her.

Jackson stood as they entered the waiting room. "Was he awake?"

"For a few minutes," Kristi said. "He wants Rafe to take me home."

"Your father's in good hands, Kristi. The best thing you can do for him is take care of yourself." Jackson laid a hand on her shoulder. "I'll stay with him."

"You'll call if he asks for me or if there's a change?"

"Count on it." He glanced at Rafe. "Cal brought your SUV. He'll drive you to Kristi's and have the watch until you're ready to take over."

"Eli and Jon?"

"Still at the cabin and will be for a while. Maddox is on watch with me." He handed both of them a bottle of water. "Drink those on the way home."

With a nod of thanks, Rafe wrapped his arm around Kristi. "Stay or go?"

She leaned against his side. "I want to stay, but Dad won't know if I'm here or not." She looked into his eyes. "You need to rest, and you won't do that here."

Thank God. Although he wouldn't admit the truth aloud, Rafe wasn't sure how much longer he could remain alert. "We'll return later in the morning." He escorted her to the elevator, holding her close as the car descended to the lobby.

Cal straightened from the wall as Rafe and Kristi exited the elevator. "The SUV is parked close to the entrance."

Good thing Rafe didn't have to walk far. In less than a minute, he and Kristi were fastening their seat belts, sitting side by side in the backseat. "We need a smooth ride, my friend."

Cal glanced into the rearview mirror. "Take a nap, Torres. I'll wake you if I run into trouble."

After consuming the water as ordered by Jackson, Rafe tucked Kristi close and drifted off.

He woke when Cal parked the SUV in Kristi's driveway. Although he hated to wake her, Rafe couldn't carry her inside without ripping out stitches. "Kristi."

She stirred. "Problem?" she asked sleepily.

"We arrived at your house."

"I can't wait to stretch out on a bed. My ribs hurt."

"Mine, too."

"Come on, you two," Cal said. "Let's get you inside." He took the keys from Kristi and unlocked the door. Cal checked the house quickly and returned. "Everything is secure. Sleep, Rafe. No one will get past me."

"Thanks, Cal." Rafe escorted Kristi to her bedroom. He brushed a gentle kiss over her swollen mouth. "I'll be across the hall if you need me."

Once Kristi was in her room, Rafe took a change of clothes into the bathroom, and stripped. He cleaned up, grimacing at the deep bruise forming on his chest, then dragged on fresh clothes.

Stumbling to the bed, he stretched out and dropped into sleep.

CHAPTER THIRTY-THREE

Kristi woke to the scent of cinnamon and sugar. She made the mistake of breathing deep and wished she hadn't when a sharp pain reminded her of the night's events and her cracked ribs. She hoped Hugh felt worse than she did today.

A glance at the clock told her she needed to get up. She had to juggle her work schedule for the day to free up time to spend with her father.

She swung her feet to the floor and made her way to the bathroom. Man, she felt a million years old at the moment. Hopefully, a hot shower would loosen her muscles.

Thirty minutes later, she emerged from her bedroom and peeked into Rafe's room. Empty. Kristi suspected he was responsible for the mouth-watering scent.

She went to the kitchen where Rafe stood in front of the oven. "What smells so good?"

The drop-dead gorgeous chef in black glanced over his shoulder with a smile. "Cinnamon rolls."

"How long have you been awake?" Cinnamon rolls made from scratch took several hours.

"Long enough to send Cal to the grocery store for the ingredients. I made the quick version with crescent rolls instead of making dough from scratch." He inclined his head to the platters of mini cinnamon rolls drizzled with icing lined up across the breakfast bar.

"These look wonderful. You made a bunch, though."

"We weren't here last night to make snacks for your clients."

Kristi kissed him. "Thank you, Rafe. My clients will love this treat. You'll have to teach me how to make them."

"They're easy. Try them." He handed her a plate with four rolls and a travel mug of tea. "I talked to Jackson a few minutes ago. Your father is in a private room and doing well. He sent a message for you to take your time before coming to the hospital because he was enjoying his naps."

Relief swept through her. Thank goodness. Seeing her father fragile and wounded hours earlier had scared her. "After breakfast, I'll see what responsibilities I can shift to Jill today."

Rafe joined her at the table with coffee and his own plate of cinnamon rolls. "How do you feel?"

"Sore. What about you?"

"Same."

"Any word on Hugh and his buddies?"

"Ward wants me charged with attempted murder. If I'd wanted him dead, he'd be on a slab in the morgue. According to Eli, Ward's accusation against me was met with suspicion when the police found the contract he forced your father to sign. Your father's blood was on the document."

"Anything else?"

"The money from your trust fund has been returned to your account. The money from your father's safe is now evidence. No telling when that will be returned. Also, since

Jon discovered Fleming's computer skills, he hacked into the other man's computer. Turns out that Fleming is responsible for the money Stewart Group lost. He's been skimming the company's accounts and funneling the money into two offshore bank accounts in the Cayman Islands, one for him and one for Hale. They both have a quite a nest egg."

Kristi sighed. "Well, that explains why Hale and Fleming were willing to accept a measly $100,000 payout when Hugh was going to walk away with millions of dollars. Wolf Pack and Dan are uninjured?"

"A few minor bruises."

When they finished breakfast, Kristi stacked their dishes in the dishwasher. "We have a few minutes before Jill arrives. Come sit with me on the deck. I'd love to go to the garden, but I don't think my ribs can tolerate the hard bench."

When they sat on the outdoor sofa with Rafe's uninjured arm around her shoulders, Kristi said, "Curiosity is driving me crazy. You said you had a secret to tell me. What is it?"

He smiled. "I thought you would ask me before now."

"If I hadn't enjoyed the cinnamon rolls so much, I would have. Tell me before I have to hurt you."

A soft chuckle. "No need for that." He sobered and cupped her cheek. "I love you, Kristi." He trailed his finger over her bottom lip. "You don't have to say anything now. I know this is fast." He kissed her, his touch light. "What's your secret?"

Kristi smiled, joy overflowing inside her at his admission. "I love you, Rafe."

He stilled. "You do?"

"Oh, yeah. I definitely do, and I'm keeping you."

The operative hugged her. "You don't know how glad I am to hear that."

They sat for several minutes, holding each other and enjoying the peaceful morning. Once Jill arrived, the craziness of the day would begin in earnest.

Finally, Rafe stood and held out his hand. "We should go inside."

After he escorted her to the workroom, Kristi heard Jill's knock on the front door.

Four hours later, she was able to leave with Rafe to visit her father. When they walked into his hospital room and she saw that her father's eyes were open, Kristi smiled. "You're awake."

"Hard to sleep more than an hour around this place. Nurses are in and out all the time to take my vitals and ask me the same questions." Alan motioned to the man standing on the other side of the bed. "Have you met Jake Davenport?"

"I haven't had the pleasure." She held out her hand. "I'm Kristi. You're a friend of Rafe's?"

"Yes, ma'am. I'm the medic for Phantom unit."

"Your team helped us last night."

"Wolf Pack did most of the work. Torres took down five men in the forest. Didn't leave much for the rest of us to do."

Kristi stared. "Five men besides Hugh and Fleming?"

Rafe shrugged.

"How's the arm, Rafe?" Jake asked.

"Hurts like a bad toothache."

"Take anything for the pain today?"

Silence.

The medic rolled his eyes, then dug into his pocket for a packet of familiar capsules. "Swallow two of these, and don't whine about it."

"Yes, Dad," Rafe groused, but he popped two into his mouth and swallowed them.

Jake chuckled.

Kristi looked at her father. "How do you feel?"

"Not great, but I'm alive." He frowned. "Your face is bruised, and your lip is swollen."

"Have you looked in the mirror lately? You have more bruises than I do." She squeezed his hand. "I'm all right, Dad."

"What happened last night? I don't remember anything after Hugh forced me to sign the contract giving him the CEO job if something happened to me."

"The police know you signed the contract under duress. You signed to protect me, didn't you?"

"I would do anything for you."

For the next several minutes, Kristi and Rafe told her father everything that happened from the time he'd been kidnapped.

Alan sighed. "I'm surprised the police haven't questioned me about the warehouse fire. With Stewart Group losing money, I'm a prime suspect for torching my own warehouse to collect the insurance money."

"Fleming skimmed money from the company's accounts. The police will receive an anonymous tip about his computer activities today," Rafe said. "The police need information from you to make their case against Ward and his cronies. Kristi and I gave our statements while you were in surgery."

"I'll tell them everything I know." He looked at Kristi. "I'm sorry, sweetheart."

She squeezed his hand. "For what?"

"Pushing you to marry Hugh. He's a snake. I should have seen him for what he is."

"He fooled many people, including me. He took out a life insurance policy on me a few weeks ago. I think he planned to cash it in after he'd drained my trust fund."

Alan scowled. "He promised to let you live if I signed the contract. I don't understand why he wanted your trust fund. Hugh has one of his own."

"His fund is almost depleted. Hugh owes money to Las Vegas casinos. Marrying me was a quick fix for his problem. He also has a mistress who's married."

Her father groaned. "Now, I'm even more sorry for pushing you to marry him. In my defense, I thought he cared a great deal about you, and you seemed fond of him. What about Hale? Did he participate in the kidnapping for money?"

Kristi shook her head. "His father is Trevor Cain. Hale blamed us for his father being in prison with extra time tacked on for what he did to me."

"His father is a monster. Hugh pieced together his background and brought him in on the scheme, didn't he?"

"Yes, he did."

"Would you mind going into the corridor? I need a minute with Rafe."

"You're kicking me out?"

"Not for long."

Kristi glanced at Rafe. "Want coffee?"

"I'd appreciate it. Thanks." He brushed a soft kiss over her mouth.

Jake followed her from the room. "What was that about?"

"I think my father will ask Rafe his intentions toward me." Her lips curved. "I'm thirty years old."

"You're still his daughter, and he loves you."

She gave him a sidelong glance as they walked to the elevator. "Do you have children?"

"Not yet. My wife is a full-time student with plans to go to medical school. How serious are you and Rafe?"

"I love him."

"He's a good man."

"I'm blessed to have him in my life."

They returned with three coffees and one iced herbal tea for Kristi. After spending another hour with her father, his eyes grew heavy.

Kristi kissed him on the forehead. "We'll let you rest, Dad. We'll come back later."

"You need to rest yourself." His gaze shifted to Rafe. "Bring her tomorrow. I hope the doctor will give me an idea when I'll be released by that time."

"Yes, sir."

Although Kristi didn't want to admit the truth, she was exhausted. How did Rafe keep up this pace when he was on a mission? "I'll call you later."

"Love you, sweetheart."

"Love you, too, Dad." She walked out with Rafe after getting a promise from Jake to call if her father's condition changed.

Rafe wrapped his arm around her as they walked to the elevator. "Jackson will take over for Jake in two hours. He'll be on watch through the night."

She sighed, relieved that the Fortress medics were staying with him. "Good."

"Are you hungry?"

"No, but you must be."

"I could eat."

Kristi laughed. "Know any good restaurants around here?"

"One of the nurses recommended a family restaurant near the hospital. Want to give it a try?"

She nodded.

They sat at a table for two in the corner of McCoy's dining room. After placing their orders, Rafe captured Kristi's hand. "If you could do anything you wanted tomorrow, what would you do?"

"Drive to Otter Creek to get Oliver."

He smiled. "I noticed a pet store on the way to McCoy's. Do you want to stop to pick up his supplies on the way home?"

"I'd love to. Do you know what he needs?"

"Deke sent me a list of his recommendations early this morning."

"That's great. I'm so excited about Oliver. I've missed him. Do you think he's forgotten me?"

Rafe chuckled. "Don't worry. That boy adores you." He squeezed her hand. "So do I."

"I'm glad you came back into my life. If you could do anything that you wanted tomorrow, what would you do?"

"Find a justice of the peace and slide a wedding ring on your finger."

She stared, her heart skipping a beat. "Are you serious?"

"Oh, yeah, baby. I'm dead serious. However, I won't rush you. I know you want your father to be there, and you need time to be sure I'm really the man you want for a husband." He leaned over and kissed her. "One day soon, I'll ask you to marry me."

"When you do, I'll say yes."

"Maybe I'll rush you a little," he murmured. "I want to come home to you every night."

"We're a matched pair, Rafe. I want the same thing. I don't want a long engagement."

The waitress approached with their orders. After they finished their meals, they drove to the pet store.

Kristi had a blast shopping for Oliver. When they loaded the purchases into the SUV, Oliver's supplies filled the cargo area. "I guess we'll have to wait until next week to go to Otter Creek."

"Why? Deidre's coming Monday to start work. Between her and Jill, they'll help you catch up on tasks you delay for a day or two."

"But Dad's still in the hospital."

"He's under a doctor's care and has a Fortress paramedic with him around the clock. Oliver will be a great family dog. I bet your father will love him. We'll tell Alan about the trip to Otter Creek and see if he minds you being out of town for a day."

"You're on a first name basis with Dad?"

"When I told him I loved you and wanted to marry you, he insisted."

"That's what you talked about when he kicked me out of the room."

"He knew how you felt about me. Your father was doing his job, Kristi. Protecting his daughter." He glanced at her before refocusing on the road. "He loves you."

"Whatever you said must have impressed Dad for him to give you his blessing."

"I answered as many of his questions as I could. Some things I couldn't answer for security reasons. The same will be true with you. I'll tell you as much as I can."

An hour later, they met Eli and Brenna at Kristi's house. "How are you feeling, sugar?" Eli asked Kristi.

"My pain medicine has worn off."

"Go inside and take your meds," Rafe said. "You can show Brenna around while Eli helps me unload Oliver's gear. She'll appreciate all the lace and pearls."

"You're adopting Oliver?' Brenna asked. "He's the sweetest dog."

"Deke introduced me to him while I was in Otter Creek. I love Oliver."

"Where's your daughter?" Rafe asked Eli.

"With Jon and Dana."

For the next two hours, she and Rafe visited with Eli and his wife. When Kristi yawned, Eli said, "Get some rest. I'll be on watch tonight. Brenna will keep me company."

"Sounds like a great plan. Rafe made mini cinnamon rolls this morning. They're in the refrigerator. Help yourself to whatever you and Brenna need."

"Thanks, sugar. Sleep, Rafe. I'll keep an eye on things."

"Yes, sir." After giving Brenna a one-armed hug, Rafe walked upstairs with Kristi. He kissed her. "I love you."

"I love you, Rafe."

"I'll be close if you need me." He nudged her inside her room and went to his own.

Kristi finished her bedtime routine quickly, crawled into bed, and fell into a dreamless sleep.

CHAPTER THIRTY-FOUR

"Go to Otter Creek, sweetheart," Alan Stewart said. "I'm not going anywhere." He frowned. "The doctor won't release me for two more days. Rafe's friends are taking care of me, and they're good company. Bring Oliver home. I'm looking forward to meeting him."

Rafe relaxed. Excellent. He'd already contacted the two sets of detectives and informed them that he and Kristi would be out of town for two days. While the detectives weren't happy about it, they admitted having many loose ends to tie up regarding the case against Ward, Fleming, and Hale, as well as the other men Ward and Hale hired to kidnap Kristi and her father. For a man without much cash, Ward threw money around to get the assistance he needed to pull off his scheme.

"Are you sure?" Kristi asked. "We can ask Deke to watch Oliver for a few more days. I don't think he'd mind."

"It's obvious that you love Oliver. Bring him home. Once I'm out of the hospital, bring him to the house so I can meet him."

"All right. Do you need anything before we go, Dad?"

He shook his head. "If I think of anything, Jake or Jackson will take care of it for me."

"Happy to," Jake said. "We'll watch over him, Kristi."

"Thanks." After kissing her father, Kristi held out her hand to Rafe. "Let's go get Oliver."

Although Rafe believed all the players in Ward's scheme were behind bars or in the morgue, he remained alert until he drove onto the grounds of PSI.

He parked near the S & R training facility and walked with Kristi into the building. A joyful bark rang out, and Oliver raced toward Kristi.

"Oliver!" She dropped to her knees and greeted the dog.

"She was worried the dog would forget her," Rafe murmured to Deke.

"Not a chance. Oliver has moped around the training facility and my house since you two left town." He turned to Rafe. "Everything is settled now?"

He nodded. "The man who wanted to marry Kristi for her trust fund was behind her kidnapping and her father's."

Deke's eyebrows rise. "He wanted her money but not her?"

"He owes money to several casinos in Vegas, and had almost wiped out his own trust fund to stay afloat. He'd also dipped into the hedge fund he was managing."

A soft whistle. "Rough for Kristi."

"Ward and his cronies beat her father and shot him. He'll recover, but he has a long road ahead of him."

"What about you and Kristi?"

He scowled. "Ward cracked her ribs and hit her."

"Is he still breathing?" Deke asked wryly.

"Yeah."

"You injured?"

"Cracked ribs from a bullet to the vest and sixty stitches in my left arm. I'm fine."

The trainer laughed. "I can see that. Do you and Kristi have supplies for Oliver?"

He snorted. "We bought out the pet store, and brought enough supplies for two days."

"Excellent. He's ready to be part of a family. When will you marry Kristi?"

"If I had a choice, tomorrow. She doesn't want a long engagement."

Deke grinned. "How soon are you buying the engagement ring?"

"If you keep her busy this afternoon, I'll take care of it today."

"I'll get her started now."

"Perfect. Thanks, Deke."

"Yep. Get her something spectacular. She deserves it."

She deserved everything, but for now, he'd settle for an engagement ring as beautiful as the woman he loved. Rafe crouched beside Kristi and Oliver. He rubbed the dog's head, then said to Kristi, "I need to run an errand. Deke will start your training lessons while I'm gone. I won't be long."

Kristi smiled, her eyes filled with happiness. "We'll be fine. See you in a few minutes." She kissed him and turned to Deke. "Oliver and I are ready to work."

"Come with me. Since the day is so beautiful, we'll work outside for a while." He glanced at Rafe for his approval.

"Sounds like a good plan." Rafe cupped Kristi's cheek for a moment. "Have fun, baby." After a pointed glance at the trainer, he left PSI and drove into Otter Creek.

Two hours later, he strode into the S & R building and smiled at the sound of Kristi's and Deke's laughter and Oliver's barks.

Kristi saw Rafe and grinned. "Come see the trick Oliver learned this week."

He stopped by her side and brushed his mouth over hers. "Show me."

"Oliver, sit."

The dog plopped down, tail wagging.

"Shake."

One paw came up.

Rafe chuckled as he bent and shook Oliver's paw. "Good boy."

"He can do two more tricks, too, but we'll show you those later. Did you finish your errand?"

He nodded, glancing at Deke. "Do you need to work longer with Kristi?"

"Nope. She's a fast learner. Oliver would enjoy a walk, though. He worked hard while you were gone."

Rafe held up Oliver's new leash clutched in his hand. "Thanks, Deke."

"No problem. I'll be here for another two hours if you think of questions you want to ask."

"We'll check in with you before we go to Rio's for the night."

"Good enough."

Rafe attached the leash to Oliver's collar. "Come on, Oliver. Let's go for a walk with Kristi."

Oliver barked and trotted beside them toward the door.

"Did you enjoy yourself?" Rafe asked.

"I had the best time. Oliver is as wonderful as I remembered." She summarized the information and techniques Deke had taught her. "Oliver is smart, Rafe. Dad's going to love him."

He guided her toward a bench on the walking trail. When they sat, Oliver stretched out on the ground in a patch of sunlight. The dog heaved a big sigh.

Rafe took Kristi's hand in his. She'd already promised to tell him yes when he proposed. He was still uneasy. What if she'd changed her mind? "I love you, Kristi. You're a miracle to me. I never thought I'd fall in love again, but you captured my heart. Your generosity, kindness, and compassion amaze me. I admire your talent. You make me whole just by being in your presence, and I want to be a better man because of you."

"Rafe," she whispered, tears gathering in her eyes. "I love you so much."

He pulled the diamond solitaire from his pocket. "Enough to marry me?"

She gasped. "Oh, Rafe. The ring is gorgeous."

"Baby, the ring pales in comparison to you. Will you marry me?"

Kristi leaned in and kissed him. "Yes, I'll marry you."

"Soon?" he persisted.

She laughed. "Soon. Lucky for you, I already have my wedding dress made."

He stilled. "You do?"

"My wedding dress was the first dress I made when I opened Kristi's Bridal. I hoped to wear that dress when I married the perfect man for me. You're that man, Rafe. I can't wait to be your wife."

"You won't regret taking a chance on me. I'll do everything in my power to make you happy."

"I'll do the same for you."

Rafe wrapped his arms around Kristi and hugged her close. He needed to make arrangements for their honeymoon and request time off from Fortress. "How does Hawaii sound for a honeymoon destination?"

"I've always wanted to go there."

"I'll make the arrangements as soon as you tell me the date for the wedding."

"I want to talk to Dad and his doctors first, but I think two months from now the weather would be perfect for a small outdoor wedding in my backyard. What do you think?"

"The sooner, the better." He didn't want to wait long. Kristi would be required to testify against Hugh and the others. Rafe wanted the right to support her night and day, and didn't want to be separated from her unless he was on a mission. "You don't want a large wedding?"

She shook her head. "I want a small, intimate ceremony with our friends and family to help us celebrate a new beginning."

The perfect description. A new beginning with the woman of his dreams.

SEAL'S RESOLVE

ABOUT THE AUTHOR

Rebecca Deel is a preacher's kid with a black belt in karate. She teaches business classes at a private four-year college outside of Nashville, Tennessee. She plays the piano at church, writes freelance articles, and runs interference for the family dogs. She's been married to her amazing husband for more than 25 years and is the proud mom of two grown sons. She delivers occasional devotions to the women's group at her church and conducts seminars in personal safety, money management, and writing. Her articles have been published in *ONE Magazine*, *Contact*, and *Co-Laborer*, and she was profiled in the June 2010 Williamson edition of *Nashville_Christian Family* magazine. Rebecca completed her Doctor of Arts degree in Economics and wears her favorite Dallas Cowboys sweatshirt when life turns ugly.

For more information on Rebecca . . .

Sign up for Rebecca's newsletter: http://eepurl.com/_B6w9

Visit Rebecca's website: www.rebeccadeelbooks.com

Printed in Great Britain
by Amazon